THE PRETENDER:
A BLACKGUARD
IN DISGUISE

by

Ta`Mara Hanscom

SIOUX CITY, IOWA

Acknowledgements

To my blessed crew of faithful and loyal volunteers: Thank you!

Heidi, A.J., and Laura, for making the summer of 1996 one to remember. For bringing me food at my computer! For your great ideas and input when the Casellis became part of our family... "My people are calling me..." ☺

Julie, for giving me that ancient computer with the daisy wheel printer and for your encouragement at my window as the first draft came forth.

Peggy, for your obedient ear to our Lord and beginning the preparation of His work years before we even met, for not being afraid to exercise your spiritual gifts as you lovingly edited these pages for our Savior and His message, and for your technical knowledge!

Charles, Jordan, and Sarahi, for being the best spouses that a mother could ever hope for her children. You are answers to our prayers and gifts from God.

Laura and Sarahi, as you put up with every pose imaginable to get the photography just right and for listening to my heart and making my vision appear.

Jordan, for making the cover come together in a day. Wow.

My church family and all the women who fell in love with the Casellis and their story.

Mom, for teaching me how to cook and be a mom; and Dad, for teaching me to play the guitar and making sure that I knew the Lord Jesus. The two of you have blessed a multitude of generations with your gifts.

Most of all to my beloved Jim—my greatest earthly treasure is in you. Without your inspiration, we wouldn't be on this amazing adventure. If ever a life was absolutely perfect, this one is—this one I share with you. *My message for you: Jeremiah 31:3.*

Thank you, Jesus, for giving me life more abundantly!

"Love is patient, love is kind.
It does not envy,
it does not boast, it is not proud.
It is not rude, it is not self-seeking,
it is not easily angered,
it keeps no record of wrongs."

I Corinthians 13:4-5, niv

Foreword

"My Jean-Marc's uncle was married to an English woman, and she told us once, a very long time ago, that in this world there are men of two kinds. The one, the knight, is the man possessing only strength and quality of moral character. He will never ask a lady to compromise her honor for less than a vow, and never, *ever* will he consider another once he has captured her heart. A knight keeps his vow, even when it hurts, and the honor of a knight is a thing a country is built upon. A knight comes along only seldom these days.

"Now, a blackguard is a man who can be found quite easily, for it is an *easy* thing to be a blackguard. He attempts to trick the young ladies into taking him home and caring for him, making them believe their honor can be given away as a mere trifle, offering no vow, and making only human demands. The blackguard is to be avoided at all costs, for to settle for someone like him is to settle for something less than ideal…"

Sophia Pasquelucci
Italia, April 1945

PART I

NOAH

Chapter 1

Rapid City, South Dakota
April 1975

Beneath the chilly moonlight, Noah Hansen stole his way clumsily through the trees of the small orchard. His boot caught on a fallen branch, and in his half-drunken state, he stumbled and struck his head against the trunk of an old apple tree. *Thank you, God, for putting that tree there*, he thought as he caught hold of the trunk for balance with one hand and gingerly stroked the side of his head with the other. *Hopefully nobody heard that.* He peered at the house from behind the tree. Lights glowed from the kitchen windows...*Good grief, they're still up!* He snorted. *They're gonna ride my tail for being out again...*

He'd turned off his motorcycle about a half mile down the road and snuck the rest of the way through the orchard on foot...*or they'd be waiting on the back step instead!* He'd wanted to sleep in his own bed tonight, but he knew there would be questions from his brother about where he'd been for the last several days—questions he wasn't about to answer.

"Whatever, Josh," Noah grumbled as he sat down at the base of the tree. He pulled his heavy denim jacket around his neck and leaned his head against the trunk. "I'll sleep out here before I'll go in there and talk to you."

*****

"We're too *old* for this business!" Reverend Joshua Hansen threw his arms into the air and shook his head as he paced across the kitchen floor. "We're forty-three years old!"

"You mean *he's* too old for this," Joshua's wife, Mona, grumbled in her heavy Southern accent. She sat at their kitchen table, sipping club soda and watching Joshua's usually loving, brown eyes boil with anger.

"I'm just so tired of all the garbage. He's not like us at all," he spat. Unlike Mona, Joshua had been an only child until December of his twentieth year. Then, toward the end of his tour of duty in Korea in 1951, he received a startling letter from his parents. His mother had given birth to a baby boy, and they'd named him Noah.

"There's nothin' you can do, Joshua, but throw him out!" Mona's green eyes blazed as she tossed her red hair away from her face.

Joshua stopped in his tracks. "Throw him out? What will that solve?"

"I had this uncle," Mona began, and Joshua winced. She sighed and continued, "Yes, my darlin', I have another story. Believe it or not, you ain't heard 'em all yet. Anyway, I had this uncle. Uncle Mason. Now, Uncle Mason laid drunk from the time he was fifteen until he was well into his thirties. Everybody loved Mason. Why, he was the life of the party! But his wife and five kids were pretty much fed up with the way he behaved. Waitin' up nights for him, cleanin' up his mess, and wonderin' if he'd buy groceries or booze with his paychecks. Well, he was a dirty devil, is what he was! Anyway, he came home one night, drunker than a skunk. My Aunt Suzie, Uncle Mason's wife, had finally gone over the edge with his actin' up. Aunt Suzie had packed up all of her things and the things of the children and moved it all over to my Aunt Myrna's place. Now, Aunt Myrna was an old spinster, still is, so she had plenty of room. Anyway, Aunt Suzie set fire to that old trailer house he had 'em all livin' in, and it burned to the ground with everything in it."

"I don't get it," he grumbled, missing the point to Mona's tale.

"It's high time we do somethin' *drastic*. It's time Noah realizes there are consequences to his actions. He ain't no boy no more, Joshua; he's a man. He hasn't drawn a sober breath since his fifteenth birthday. And I think his drinkin' has gotten even worse since he came back from Vietnam. How much longer do we *allow* this to go on?" They'd taken care of Noah since shortly before his fifth birthday, when Joshua's parents were killed in a car accident. According to the Hansens' attorney, MacKenzie Dale, Joshua's parents had named him and Mona as Noah's legal guardians.

Joshua took a deep breath and sat down at the kitchen table. He looked at the clock on the old stove and then into Mona's tired eyes. It was almost two o'clock in the morning, and they hadn't seen Noah for three days. He wasn't sure if he wanted to hear the rest of Mona's story, but it was just too tempting. He *had* to ask her. She wouldn't *volunteer* the remainder of the story unless he asked. It was a game they'd played for years.

"What happened to your uncle?"

"He went to stay with his parents, my Grandpa and Grandma Spencer. I guess Grandpa whipped his butt with a stick out behind the shed 'til he was sober—" She had to stop her story there because Joshua had started to laugh. "Now listen to me, Joshua. It's the truth. Uncle Mason *never* drank again. He became a very successful man, and Aunt Suzie and the kids took him back."

"Were there any charges filed against Suzie?"

"No. People just don't do things like that to a righteous woman in the South. Why, she did the community a service."

With a sad smile, Joshua began to nod. "I think I know what you're saying, Mona. It's time to ask Noah to leave. He's got a steady job and maybe, if he has to spend his money on rent instead of drugs and booze, he'll straighten himself out."

He sighed and cast a glance through the moonlit window over the kitchen sink. From there he could see Noah's old tire swing hanging from one of the trees in the orchard, and it brought back a million memories. That was the place where Noah had accepted the Lord Jesus as his Savior shortly after he'd come to live with them.

Mona looked down at the table. "I have always loved that child."

"I know, Honey," Joshua said as he reached over and took a gentle hold of her hand. "I love him too."

*****

Rosa Caselli sat in the window seat of her Sioux Falls home and looked longingly toward the west. Her precious daughter, Tillie, had left that morning on a high school trip to the Black Hills of South Dakota, but it wasn't her daughter she was lifting up in prayer.

"*E questo che prego* (And this I pray)," she whispered in her first language as she gazed at the horizon, "that your charity may more and more abound in knowledge and all discernment, so that you may approve the better things, that you may be upright and without offense unto the day of Christ, filled with the fruit of justice, through Jesus Christ, to the glory and praise of God."

Guiseppi listened to his wife's heartfelt prayer and the Spirit came upon him. Rosa had prayed that prayer for Noah Hansen since Christmas of 1960. Though she'd never met Noah, Rosa knew plenty about him. MacKenzie Dale, the Hansens' attorney, was the brother of Frances Martin. Frances was Rosa's dearest friend and neighbor, and she shared with Rosa the trials of a young boy who'd lost his parents and was struggling with the authority of his older brother.

Guiseppi drew a soft breath and made his way to the window seat beside Rosa. She looked up at him and smiled into his lined, black eyes as he reached for her hand.

"No one prays as beautifully as you, my love," he said with a smile. "God must certainly love to hear the music of your voice."

Rosa patted his hand. "Have you heard anything of Noah lately?"

Guiseppi nodded. "I spoke with James Martin at the Mulligan's Spring Ball last month. Noah is in desperate straits, my love." He shuddered as he recalled the conversation with Frances' husband. "Dear Noah seems to visit the county jail on a regular basis. Drinking, womanizing. Gads! He is quite a handful for poor Joshua."

"Thank the dear Lord our children have not behaved with such disobedience, for I surely would not have survived."

"Nor I." Guiseppi followed Rosa's gaze out the window, and his black eyes sparkled. "Angel should be just about there by now." Even though their daughter's given name was "Tillie," her brothers had nicknamed her "Angel" when she was a baby.

"Yes," Rosa said with a pensive frown. For an instant her stomach dipped and left her dizzy, feeling as if she'd gone over a hill. She swallowed hard and took a breath, trying to disguise the uneasiness in her spirit. "Perhaps our little artist will sell some of her work this weekend."

Guiseppi sensed the change in Rosa's disposition and looked at her with curiosity. "What is the matter?"

She shook her head. "Nothing. I just miss her, I guess." After all, this was their Angel's first trip away from home…*shouldn't she be just a little nervous?*

*****

Shortly after one o'clock in the afternoon, the Greyhound bus pulled up in front of the hotel just off Interstate 90 at Rapid City, South Dakota. For the past seven hours, the senior class of Junior Artists of America from Washington Senior High School in Sioux Falls had traveled the interstate between South Dakota's two largest cities.

"Wake up, Ginger!" Tillie gently nudged her best friend. "We're here, and it's beautiful," she whispered as she looked past Ginger and out the window of the bus. Tillie Caselli had the sparkling black eyes of her father; the delicate, feminine smile of her mother; and curly black hair.

Ginger opened her eyes and saw the Black Hills of South Dakota spread out before them. Purple mountains stood against a blue-green sky, dark green masses of trees dotted the hillsides, and stark-white caps of snow covered some of the higher peaks.

"I didn't think they were gonna be *that* big," Ginger murmured. Ginger Engleson was tall and slender with strawberry-blonde hair that hung perfectly behaved upon her shoulders. Tillie had envied Ginger's soft, wonderful hair all of her life, but Ginger always wished for Tillie's curls.

Tillie shook her head. "Me neither. They said Black *Hills*, not Black *Mountains*. And they're really not *black*. They're kinda *purple*." She snickered. "Like '*purple mountains majesty*.' " Her gaze returned to the mountains…*I'd sure like to see them up close…*

Excited chatter filled the bus as they made their way down the steps and into the parking lot. Once outside the bus, they stared with renewed awe at the breathtaking scenery before them. Tillie took a deep breath of the dry, crisp air; caught the scent of pine; and smiled. She hadn't lived a day in her life without the intense humidity that consumed Sioux Falls.

Tillie and Ginger quickly found their luggage and Tillie's paintings and went into the lobby to find the chaperone, Mrs. Malone. They were assigned to a room with two drama students from their senior class—Sara and Melissa.

Their room was like any other hotel room, but to make the accommodations even more exciting, there was an indoor pool located just a few steps away.

Cards displayed on the table in the corner of their room advertised for carry-out pizza and gave instructions on how to order room service from the restaurant downstairs. Among the other advertisements were miniature golf, a nearby shopping center, and Maggie May's (a bar just a short walk away).

"This place is *great!*" Melissa said as she flopped down on the bed. "Is this as great as the hotels in Massachusetts, Tillie?"

Tillie's dark eyes shined. "Yes, except that I had to share my room with Ma`ma and Papa, and Papa snores!" The other girls laughed.

"We promise not to snore," Sara said.

"By the way," Melissa continued with a wink, "how *was* Massachusetts?"

"It was fine," Tillie answered.

"She danced with him," Ginger suddenly offered, and Tillie threw a pillow at her. Ginger caught it and laughed. "And *he* asked *her* to dance. *Twice!*"

Melissa sat straight up on the bed, eyes wide with surprise. "You danced with Alex? Why didn't you tell us?" Alex Martin had been the love of Tillie's life since anyone could remember. She had talked of no one else from the time she was five years old, but he was seven years her senior. Alex's older sister, Kate, was married to one of Tillie's older brothers, Vincenzo. Their families had been well acquainted since the Casellis immigrated to America in 1956.

Tillie rolled her eyes and looked at her friends. "It was no big deal."

"Oh, *please*," Ginger muttered and mimicked Tillie's eye roll.

"So," Sara continued as she took a seat on the edge of the bed, "he's the big Harvard grad now, and soon you'll be done with school too." All of the girls but Tillie burst into giggles again.

"He is *such* a hunk," Melissa swooned. She had gotten a few glimpses of the handsome, black-haired, six-foot-five-inch Alex Martin and was consistently impressed with his perfect body and striking good looks.

"Ah, don't you think he's a little too old for me?" Tillie said with a frown.

"Tsk!" Ginger rolled her eyes again. "*You're* the one that's had a crush on him since you were like five or something."

"Yeah," Sara giggled. "And we're all pretty much convinced that there's gonna be an Alex Martin in your future."

Tillie sighed and shook her head. *Now if I could just convince Alex.*

*****

Noah shut off his Harley about a half mile down the road and pushed it into the orchard. He crept through the trees in the warmth of the spring afternoon, picking his way along his usual path with more grace than he'd had the previous evening. It had been a cold night out under the stars, but at least he'd made it to work on time.

He made his way to the kitchen door, praying every moment Joshua and Mona wouldn't be home to confront him. He used his key to unlock the door and then removed his boots to glide his way in silence through the house. It was quiet, and he stopped to listen as he looked all around. *No lights, no radio.*

"Mona," he called out in a whisper, prepared to bolt out the back door if she answered. Silence. *Good. She's not home.* Lately Mona had started to ask him where he was going and when he was coming home. *That* wasn't any of her business.

When he realized there wasn't anyone home to stop him, he hurried upstairs for a shower and a change of clean clothing.

Noah was a handsome, young man with sandy-brown hair and dancing blue eyes. He held down a steady job at the meat packing plant, but at the age of twenty-three, he was still living with his brother.

It was Thursday. Not only did that mean he hadn't showered since Monday, but it also meant buy-one-get-one-free night at Noah's favorite hangout, Maggie May's. Good ol' Maggie never hassled anybody. They could be as loud as they wanted, and Maggie always had room for Noah and his clan.

He threw his dirty clothes on the middle of his bedroom floor, loosed the string that held his ratty ponytail, and jumped into the shower. He didn't want to take the time to shave or comb his hair. When he'd finished showering, he tied his ponytail back into place and dressed in his usual attire—his last clean pair of ripped up jeans, a t-shirt, and boots. *I'll have to see if I can get Mona to wash some clothes.* He glanced at the pile on the floor.

He was headed for the back door, thinking he'd pulled off another "scrub and run," when Mona appeared. He skidded to a stop and stared at his sister-in-law with surprise. *She's almost like a vapor these days!*

"Where are you off to tonight, Noah?" she asked in her heavy drawl.

"Maggie May's," Noah answered with a smile and wink. "Wanna come?"

Mona sighed with a frown. "Why don't you stay home tonight and visit your brother? He wants to talk to you."

Noah raised both brows and smiled. "No thanks. But you and Josh be sure to have a good time without me."

"Noah, we haven't seen you all week." Mona's frown deepened. "We didn't raise you to behave like this. When is it going to stop?"

"Mona, darlin'," he mimicked her accent, "I'm just not *ready* to stop." He gave her a loving kiss on the cheek and smiled. "You and Josh and that little church he pastors have gotten just a little too uppity for me."

"The Bible says not to let anything master you."

"Nothin's mastering me. I can stop anytime I want to. I just don't want to stop *now*."

"You need to stop before you ruin any more of your life."

Noah rolled his eyes and sighed. *This is goin' nowhere fast.* He gave Mona another kiss. "I know what I'm doin'." And he hurried out the back door.

*****

After a refreshing swim, the girls returned to their room and found a cart of prepared sandwiches, fruit, and soda waiting for them.

They'd received explicit instructions from Mrs. Malone to remain in their rooms for the rest of that evening.

They wrapped their wet hair in towels, hung their suits in the bathroom, and snuggled into the *cool* white robes the hotel had provided.

"This place is *so* awesome!" Ginger exclaimed as she took a sandwich to the bed and made herself comfortable against the pillows. "I can't believe we can eat right here in our room!"

Melissa took a sandwich and seated herself at the only table in the room. She flipped through the advertisements and picked out a few of the interesting ones. "What should we do when we're done eating?" she asked with a mouth full of food.

Tillie snuggled into the covers with her sandwich and flipped through the channels with the remote. She paused when she saw the familiar copper-colored Firebird racing across the screen. *The Rockford Files.*

"That is *so* boring," Sara moaned as she seated herself, sandwich in hand, on the end of the bed and began to watch.

"It's my favorite." Tillie took a bite of her sandwich. "He reminds me of Marq."

"He doesn't look *anything* like Marquette," Ginger disagreed.

"I know," Tillie answered with a shrug. "But I imagine Marq's life to be wild and crazy. You know, like Jim Rockford's."

"What does your brother do anyway?" Melissa asked.

Tillie swallowed her bite and answered simply, "Catches people doing really bad stuff and has 'em put in jail."

"He is *such* a babe," Melissa added.

Tillie frowned. "He's married," she scolded.

Melissa rolled her eyes and took a bite of her sandwich. "Marriage didn't make him ugly. He's still a babe."

"I love his ponytail," Ginger added with a smile.

Through her mouthful of food, Melissa asked, "By the way, how in the world did your Italian brother get such a French-sounding name?"

Tillie nodded with a smile. "My paternal grandfather, Petrice Marquette, was named after Father Jacques Marquette. Father Marquette was a Jesuit who loved to explore and had the amazing ability to learn other languages—"

"Shhh," Sara said. "It's a really good part."

"Thought it was *so* boring," Ginger giggled.

Tillie chuckled and whispered, "My brother was named after my grandfather—that's how they do it in Italy—"

"Shhh," Sara repeated, and they were quiet as they watched the rest of the program in the fading evening light.

When the show was over, Tillie got up off the bed and searched through her suitcase for some pajamas.

Ginger flipped through the channels with a sigh. "There's nothing on. What should we do now?"

"We're not supposed to leave our room. I think we should just go to bed," Tillie said as she continued to look through her suitcase.

Melissa was looking at some of the advertising cards before her. "Here's a good one," and she gave the card a toss in Sara's direction.

"Miniature golf?!" Sara gasped. "You know I hate that. Don't make me do that."

"Okay," Melissa laughed. "That was just a joke. I wouldn't make you do that."

"Good," Sara said as she opened her suitcase.

"Aren't we supposed to stay in our room?" Ginger reminded as she pulled out some pajamas and headed for the bathroom.

"Hey, did anybody bring a hair dryer?" Tillie asked from near the bathroom. She had already changed, but her thick hair hung in soaked ringlets.

Sara got her blow dryer and walked over to Tillie with it.

"Thanks," Tillie said as she turned from the rest of them, plugged in the dryer, and began to work on her wet hair. She couldn't hear anything but the drone of the blower fan.

"Okay, how about this?" Melissa tossed another card—this time at Ginger, who caught it and looked it over.

"Are you *nuts?*" Ginger frowned at Melissa. "We'll get tossed out of the competition for something like that."

"*Only* if we get caught," Melissa said with a glint of mischief sparkling in her eyes.

"You *can't* be serious," Sara muttered as she took a look at the card advertising Maggie May's. "Besides, Tillie will *never* go for it. You know how strict her family is."

"Oh, come on," Melissa encouraged. "We've never done a naughty thing in our lives. What's wrong with checkin' out a bar? Besides, Sara and I are already eighteen. We're legal to drink beer." Which was true. Even though the state's legislation had discussed raising the drinking age in South Dakota, nothing had been changed. For the time being, both girls could legally be served in a bar.

"Tillie and I are Christians," Ginger pointed out.

Tillie noticed the small gathering around the card and turned off the hair dryer. "Hey, what are you guys talking about over there?"

Melissa was the first to look up. She took the card from Sara and walked over to Tillie with a haughty expression. "We wanna do this."

Tillie looked at the card. "Are you *kidding?* You'll have to go without me." She frowned and turned on the hair dryer.

Melissa walked back to where Sara and Ginger sat. "Come on, you guys. It'll be fun."

Sara began to nod her head. "Okay. But just for a few minutes. Then we gotta come right back."

"Not me," Ginger retorted with a shake of her head and a frown. "I'm not goin' into no bar."

"Suit yourself," Melissa said as she reached for her suitcase and looked for clothes. "But we're gonna have some fun."

"What idiots," Tillie grumbled as she and Ginger watched their friends from the hotel room window. Sara and Melissa crossed the parking lot and went into the bar.

Ginger shook her head. "That's drama students for ya. What are they gonna do if Mrs. Malone checks our room?"

Tillie rolled her eyes. "Mrs. Malone *won't* check our room. Why would she? We're the *good* kids."

Ginger nodded and settled back into the bed for a movie. Tillie left the window and joined her. They were both so instantly absorbed in the story line that they were surprised when the movie ended and it was after ten o'clock.

"They've been gone for *three hours*," Ginger said. "Do you s'pose something bad happened to them?"

"Probably," Tillie grumbled as she got out of the warm bed to look for her jeans.

"They've been raped and murdered by now." Ginger reached for her own jeans and pulled them on over her pajama pants.

"We gotta go get 'em." Tillie reached for her jacket. "And don't make me go in alone."

Ginger shook her head and pulled her shoes on. "I won't. But what if our parents find out?"

"Pray they don't," Tillie answered, "because they'll kill us if they do."

*****

Joshua Hansen had given his father's old bar to Maggie May West in 1968, the summer before Noah turned seventeen. When his father owned it, it was just a place that sold sandwiches and barbecued ribs. Over the years, Joshua's father started serving beer; and when he died,

Maggie added hard liquor to the menu. So instead of selling the place, Joshua gave it to her. It had been a point of contention between his parents for years, and he didn't want the memories anymore. It had been hard enough for him to face the death of his unbelieving father.

Maggie had been at the bar since 1945. People around town said she'd been born and raised in New York's Hell's Kitchen, but no one knew for sure what had brought her to South Dakota. For a young lady of African-American descent, there wasn't much Maggie May could do in 1945. She applied for a job at the bar, and Joshua and Noah's father gave her a position as a waitress. Earl hired her sister, Estelle, too, and they'd worked there ever since.

Maggie and Estelle were both big ladies. Maggie was now nearly fifty years old and Estelle a spry forty-five. And not only were they tall, but they were bulky. They used their tough appearance to settle down unruly customers when necessary. Maggie's black hair had streaked with silver as she aged, and she kept it in the same beehive style that she'd worn since 1963. Estelle, on the other hand, had bleached her hair white for as long as anyone could remember and kept it ratted into a puffy, more-modern style.

"Set us up, Stellie!" Noah called from his regular booth. "Me and Randy are ready to go again."

"Comin' right up, boys," Estelle yelled in answer from behind the bar.

Maggie sighed and shook her head. *He's drinkin' way too much again.*

It was sad what had happened to Noah over the past few years, especially since his return from Vietnam. He reminded Maggie and Estelle so much of his father, with his dancing blue eyes, witty humor, and smile. But he'd gone from being a nice kid to a blithering alcoholic. Noah couldn't say no to a drink if he tried, and Maggie suspected drugs were involved as well. Yet Noah was always sharing a little Scripture with them and frequently gave them the Lord's message of having to be "born again." Maggie and Estelle would laugh and shake their heads because they did *not* believe in God. They believed in hard work and making it for yourself. They were sensible women, and they didn't need some anonymous God screwing up their lives the way He'd screwed up Noah's.

Maggie saw Tillie and Ginger hesitating by the glass doors and knew immediately who *they'd* come for. *This oughta get real good— the goodie-two-shoes coming to get the naughty girls.*

Tillie and Ginger peered into the bar. A long counter was straight ahead, where they saw Maggie making adjustments at a wall of bottles set against a mirror. At one end of the bar, there was a very large bulletin board with a collage of snapshots, while the wall at the other end of the bar was empty. A few people were seated at the counter, sipping drinks and visiting quietly amongst themselves. Several small tables with chairs were scattered around the old wooden floor, and quite a few black booths lined the perimeter of the bar. It was hazy with smoke, but it wasn't dark like they'd imagined it would be, and it seemed fairly clean.

"There they are," Tillie said, pointing to a corner booth. Melissa and Sara were seated with two very rough-looking men and obviously enjoying themselves. Melissa's mouth was wide open, laughing, and Sara wiped tears of laughter from her eyes.

"Oh, brother," Tillie grumbled in a whisper. "How are we gonna get 'em out of there? What I wouldn't give to have one of my brothers here with us right now."

"Let's just call the cops," Ginger whispered. "Let *them* sort things out."

"We can't do *that!* Everyone's entitled to one mistake. Let's just get 'em out of there."

"But I'm scared. What if those guys grab us and rape us?"

Tillie shook her head. "I don't think we'll get raped. The place is full of people, and look at the size of the woman at the bar." They looked through the glass and back to the bar, sizing up a very large Maggie May. She looked directly back at them. "Oh." Tillie hesitated and looked at her feet. "She saw me looking."

"We are *so* dead," Ginger whispered.

"Come on." Tillie put her hand on the handle of the door and looked at Ginger. "It's now or never." Ginger nodded, and Tillie pulled open the door.

Noah's eyes followed the two through the door and over to the table where some of his buddies entertained two ladies. He noticed Tillie right away. The darkness of her skin set her apart from the rest of the usual crowd, as did her curly, black hair. He smiled, downed a shot of whiskey, and looked at the young man seated across from him.

"Now *that's* what I'm talkin' about," he said as he leered at Tillie. "I'll take the dark one. I think I'm in *love.*"

His companion snorted and tipped back a shot. "Don'tcha think they're just a little too young for us?"

"They look plenty old enough to me."

Tillie and Ginger hurried to Sara and Melissa's booth and stood just close enough to speak with their friends. They maintained what they felt would be a safe distance from the two men sitting with them.

"I see you changed your minds," Melissa slurred, and Sara answered with a very loud giggle.

"We *haven't* changed our minds," Tillie replied. "You guys have been gone for three hours. You have to come back *right now*."

"Is this your mother or something?" one of their drunk companions asked.

"No!" Melissa burst into giggles. "These are our friends. Ginger, Tillie, this gentleman next to me is Theo, and the guy beside Sara is Arnie. They're very nice."

"I'm sure." Ginger's brow knit into a deep furrow. "How much have you two had to drink?"

"Barely a drop," Sara answered with a giggle.

Ginger shook her head. "Come on. We gotta go *right now*."

"No," Sara and Melissa whined in unison, which caused another upset of giggles.

"You're gonna be in *big* trouble," Tillie scolded as she pointed her index finger at the two of them.

"You two look like you could use some funzies." Theo smiled as he reached out with one of his long arms, grabbed ahold of Tillie, and drug her onto his lap. Tillie reacted with a slap to his face and bolted from his lap. He looked very surprised, and the rest of the bar suddenly went silent.

"There's gonna be trouble," Maggie muttered to Estelle as she reached for her Remington beneath the counter.

"Oh, brother," Noah grumbled. He got to his feet while his companion, Randy, tried to squelch his laughter. He'd just been *waiting* for someone to do that to Theo.

"Now young lady," Theo began as he staggered to his feet, "you didn't have to go and do that."

"Stay away from me," Tillie warned, "or I will have you arrested."

Theo took a step toward her, and Tillie took a step backward, away from him.

"I'm warning you, buster," she wagged her index finger once again.

Theo laughed. "Why, you're just as pretty as a picture, maybe a little too spunky, but I think I'll just take you home with me."

"I don't think so, Theo," came a voice from behind Tillie, and she jumped and turned around to see a haggard and scruffy young man behind her.

"Mind your own business, Noah," Theo replied with a frown as he took another step toward Tillie.

A loud *chuc-chuc* cleared the air. Maggie had pumped the twelve gauge, and everyone looked toward the bar where she stood with Estelle. Maggie held her shotgun in steady aim at Theo, while Estelle stood at attention with her arms crossed and a perfect "don't move or you're dead" frown on her face.

"I'm gettin' cranky, boys," Maggie barked.

Arnie left his place beside Sara and took ahold of Theo's elbow.

"Let go of me," Theo grumbled, but Randy was soon on Theo's other side.

"Come on, Theo," Randy said as he and Arnie each took an elbow. "Let's go for a ride." Theo sighed with a frown and stumbled out the door of the bar with Arnie and Randy.

Sara and Melissa squelched their giggles and staggered to their feet beside the booth, hanging on for balance.

"Guess we better go back now," Sara slurred, and Melissa giggled in response.

Tillie looked from Noah to Maggie, and then at Ginger.

"We're lucky to still be alive," Ginger whispered, and Tillie nodded.

Maggie engaged the safety but left the old Remington loaded, putting it back in its place and turning around to resume her work as if nothing had happened. Estelle sighed, shook her head, and went into the kitchen. The rest of the customers in the bar resumed their conversations, and everything was back in order.

"I'm sorry about that," Noah apologized, and Tillie gave him a soft frown.

"Don't worry about it," she said as she looked away and stepped closer to her friends.

Noah followed her. "I'm not like them."

"I'll bet," Tillie answered, not even casting him a glance. She frowned at Sara and Melissa and scolded, "I hope you two realize you almost *died* here tonight."

"Well, can I have your phone number?" Noah asked from behind her, and she looked over her shoulder, surprised he was still there.

"Are you serious?" she scowled.

Noah smiled and nodded, waiting patiently for her next reply. Tillie shook her head in disbelief.

"Come on, Baby. How 'bout a ride?" he attempted.

Tillie huffed. "My name is not 'Baby,' and no, I don't go for rides with people I don't know—especially when they've been drinking."

Noah responded with a smile, and Tillie noticed how his blue eyes seemed to dance when he looked at her. "Well, what's your name?"

"*You'll* never know," she snapped.

Noah's expression stopped its twinkling, and the corners of his eyes pulled down.

Tillie saw the change in his expression. *Woops...I didn't mean to hurt his feelings.* She afforded him a polite smile. "By the way, thanks. I really appreciated your standing up to your friend."

Noah nodded and his eyes began to dance again. "You're welcome. Can you stay a little bit longer?"

Tillie shook her head. "No. I have to get my friends out of here."

"Well, maybe you can come back tomorrow night?" Noah suggested.

Tillie shook her head again as she and her friends walked toward the door, with Noah close on their heels.

"Listen," he continued as they walked out the door, "I get off work at three o'clock tomorrow. Can we meet? Can I take you for a ride then? I promise to be *stone sober.*"

Tillie paused and looked at him. He was a very handsome man, even with the unkempt beard and ponytail. There was something kind and gentle in his dancing blue eyes, and she felt herself drawn to him. She didn't *want* to refuse him, but her upbringing made her shake her head. "I don't know you. I just can't."

"Oh, come on," Noah pleaded as he reached over and touched her hand.

For some reason Tillie couldn't jerk her hand away like she knew she should. The warmth of his skin felt familiar against hers, and the expression in his eyes made her feel something she'd never felt in her life. *Who are you, and why do I feel like I should know you?* She swallowed to find her voice and blurted out, "I'll pray about it."

"Sure, no problem. I will too," Noah said with a smile as he let go of her hand. Tillie turned and began to walk away with her friends.

"Meet me right here," he called after her happily. "Okay?"

Maggie watched Noah float in through the glass doors and up to the bar.

"I've found the love of my life, Maggie May." He reached for a bottle of whiskey and poured himself a shot.

"You'd better keep your word to that girl," Maggie growled. She reached for the bottle and put it back in its place. "You promised to be *stone sober,* and she doesn't look like the kind of gal who let's you break your word."

Noah hesitated with the shot glass paused at his lips. "You heard that?"

"You were still in the doorway when you made the deal."

Noah held the shot glass for another second, and then he sighed and set it down. "Better keep my word."

Maggie nodded, picked up the full shot, and drank it herself.

Chapter 2

Tillie filled two bags of ice at the machine down the hall and stormed back to their room. *Those two*, she thought as she flung open the door and threw one at Melissa and one at Sara. They moaned in their beds, holding their aching heads.

"Oh, gimme a break," Tillie snapped. "You were sure grown-up *last night*, but you're acting like babies this morning. These are the wages of your sin."

Ginger hid behind the bathroom door and tried to stifle her laughter, *but Tillie is just so funny!* Poor Melissa and Sara had dreadful hangovers but received no pity from Tillie.

"And you'd better get some water into your systems!" Tillie barked. "You're probably dehydrated beyond belief! You're just lucky you don't have to perform until tomorrow." She shook her head in disgust as she collected her things for the art show.

Ginger crept out of the bathroom. She picked up Tillie's paintings and dashed toward the door so no one would see her smile.

"Aren't you gonna stay with us, Ging?" Melissa cried.

"No. I'm going with Tillie."

"Who's gonna help us?" Sara croaked.

"You took care of yourselves last night," Tillie scolded. "I guess you'll just have to take care of yourselves this morning too!" And with that, Tillie and Ginger left. They allowed the door to slam loudly behind them, and Ginger laughed.

"Tillie, you are *so* funny!"

Tillie smiled. "Did I sound mad?"

"I was scared," Ginger teased.

Tillie snickered. "I can't believe they'd do something *so stupid*. How did they imagine they'd feel? They haven't had a drink in their lives. Don't they watch TV? This stuff happens every week on the tube."

Ginger shrugged. "Hey, how about that cute guy last night? Are you gonna go out with him?"

Tillie rolled her eyes. "I think he's probably too old for me. He was just too drunk to see it."

"Maybe. But wouldn't it be fun? He could show you the Black Hills." She sighed softly. "Might even be romantic."

"I don't think so, Ging."

"Tillie, you'll be eighteen in just a few months. You're old enough to make your own decisions now, and he seemed really nice."

"Imagine this, then," Tillie began with a frown. "What if I really like this character and then drag him home to meet my family. Do you honestly *think* he'd fit in?" She cleared her throat and mimicked her family's soft accent, "You dreadful blackguard. Perhaps we shall kill you now for corrupting our baby sister—" Her performance was cut short by Ginger's laughter.

"I know," Ginger agreed.

✶✶✶✶✶

Tillie had spoken of nothing but sketching and painting for the last ten years. She'd filled her parents' home with paintings and drawings that amazed her family. To their delight, Tillie had transformed several old photographs from their life in Italy into magnificent portraits. The Casellis' blessed days in their first homeland, now just dim memories, were brought back to life on Tillie's canvas through the pretty hands God had given her. Chiante was vibrant and alive again.

For the art show, Tillie had brought two large watercolors of her mother with her beloved horse, Delia. They were displayed side by side and entitled simply *Obedience*. This particular scene was inspired by an old photograph Guiseppi had taken on the day they left Italy in 1956. Rosa's hand rested beneath Delia's chin as she watched her family pack their few bags into a relative's car. Every bit of Delia was black, except for her grey muzzle. Tillie had taken special care to use the same color and texture in the horse's mane as she used for her mother's hair.

Rosa had told Tillie of that day many times and had said that, shortly after Guiseppi snapped the photo, she had to tie her Delia to the back of the D'Anennccis' buggy. The horse was left in their care as arrangements could not be made to bring the animal to America. It was a very dramatic photograph, and Guiseppi had cherished it for years. He had enlarged the photo, had it framed, and hung it in the entryway of their home. Tillie named her portrait *Obedience* because it was how she saw her mother's actions in having to leave her beloved pet behind in order to follow her husband.

Tillie had also finished several acrylics and brought them along. Most were smaller in size and were paintings of her brothers, each entitled by their first names: *Petrice, Vincenzo,* and *Marquette.*

She'd also brought along a very special portrait, and it was Ginger's favorite. Tillie had taken two different photos, one of Ginger's brother, Andy, and another photo of Tillie's brother Marquette in their military uniforms. She then placed them side by side in the painting but added Marquette's glorious ponytail and Andy's Bible. Tillie had done a duplicate and given it to Ginger and her family. Both of the brothers had returned from Vietnam, unable to speak about the experience except with each other, so Tillie entitled the paintings *Refugees.*

She'd also done several charcoal sketches. One of them came from a photo Guiseppi had enlarged after his only brother, Angelo, passed away. It was one Rosa had taken of the brothers together shortly before Angelo left for the mountains. Tillie entitled her sketch *Warriors.* Guiseppi had told her about World War II in Italy and how he and Angelo fought side by side with the Allies to drive the Nazis from their homeland.

Another sketch was a photo of Tillie's brother Vincenzo on a horse, riding up to the main house of his ranch. She called that one *Happy Life.* Vincenzo dearly loved the life he'd made on a ranch he'd named "Reata." Vincenzo inherited the ranch when Uncle Angelo passed away in 1964. Reata, Vincenzo explained to Tillie, came from the name of Rock Hudson's ranch in the 1956 movie classic *The Giant,* one of his favorite movies.

"That one's still my favorite," Ginger commented as she looked upon the image of her brother and Marquette.

"Ma`ma and Delia is mine…" Tillie spied the judges and gulped. "I'm next. Pray, Ginger, pray."

Ginger nodded as three suited men and two professional women approached Tillie's gallery. They did a lot of nodding as they visited and took notes. Soon they moved on to the next booth.

"They were really looking at your ma`ma and Delia," Ginger whispered as she watched them perform the same process at the next booth.

"It's Ma`ma's favorite too. And she always talked about Italy while I worked on it."

The girls watched the judges as they walked through the galleries, remarking and taking notes. Tillie and Ginger wondered how long it would be before they were done and when the decisions would be made. After what seemed like forever, the group of judges walked back to Tillie's gallery and smiled.

"First prize for watercolors," one of the men said as he placed a blue ribbon on *Obedience.* He surprised Tillie by placing another blue ribbon on *Refugees.* "And first prize in acrylics." The judge hesitated and smiled. "Honorable mention for your sketch of *Happy Life.* If we would have had a category for charcoal, it would have been first place." And then the judge placed a purple ribbon on the sketch of Vincenzo. "Congratulations, young lady. You're a fine artist." The judge extended his hand to a speechless Tillie.

"Thanks," Tillie managed to croak as she took the man's hand and gave it a shake.

When the judges walked away, Ginger grabbed Tillie in an excited hug. "No wonder those two were our favorites!"

Tillie was still speechless, but she managed to whisper, "I can't believe it, Ging. Ma'ma and Papa are going to be so happy for me!"

The large room began to fill with people. After the judging, Junior Artists of America always offered their work for sale to the local business owners.

"Put a 'not for sale' sign on the winners," Ginger instructed.

Tillie scrounged for some scrap paper and a pen. As she looked through her things, she heard Ginger gasp.

"What?" She looked up at Ginger to see her wide-opened eyes staring.

"*It's that woman,*" Ginger whispered.

"What woman?" Tillie searched the approaching crowd of people.

"*You know!* The one from the wild, wild west bar. *The one with the gun!*"

"Oh," Tillie gasped in a whisper when she saw Maggie heading straight for her booth.

"Wonder if she's packin' any heat this morning," Ginger giggled nervously.

Tillie laughed and whispered, "I just hope she packin' some *cash.*"

Maggie approached Tillie's booth and smiled at the two of them. "Hello, ladies." She raised one of her black brows and grinned with mischief. "How's everybody *feeling* this morning?"

Ginger gulped away her laughter, but Tillie could not.

"A little green around the gills, huh? Well, that's the way it goes I guess." Maggie shook her head and looked at Tillie's work. "Who did the paintings?"

"I did," Tillie said. She quickly put the 'not for sale' signs on the winners, adding, "But I can't sell these. My parents will want them."

Maggie nodded as she continued to look at Tillie's work. "I don't know how you can part with any of them. Who are the refugees?"

"They're our brothers," Tillie answered, pointing at herself and then at Ginger. "They were in Vietnam."

Maggie nodded again, and her eyes fell upon her favorite, the watercolor of Rosa and Delia. "Who's the pretty lady?"

"That's my Ma`ma."

Maggie smiled. "I'll take it."

Tillie's eyes opened wide with surprise as Maggie handed her the money, in cash, and took her painting off of the easel. Maggie looked at the signature in the corner of the painting and noticed that it read, "Angel, 1975."

"Thank you," Tillie breathed, overwhelmed that someone would give money for her work.

"You're welcome, Angel," Maggie replied with a smile, and then she turned and left with her new painting.

"She gave me *cash*," Tillie whispered.

Ginger giggled. "You're gonna be *rich*, Tillie Caselli!"

*****

Noah Hansen couldn't stop thinking about the girl he'd met at Maggie's. As soon as his shift ended, he headed straight for home and showered. He shaved off a week's worth of whiskers and combed out the ratty ponytail.

"You are one handsome devil," he said to himself in the mirror as he splashed on a little Old Spice. He noticed his tattooed forearm in the mirror, frowned, and headed back to his closet for a long-sleeve shirt. He stood back from the mirror and admired himself. Clean jeans, clean shirt, clean hair, clean face. *What more could a gal possibly want?*

He headed downstairs, hoping to avoid Mona this time, but it was Joshua who met him in the kitchen.

"Where are you going, Noah?" he frowned.

"Maggie May's," Noah answered with a wink. "And you can't come tonight, Josh, 'cause I think I got a date."

Joshua shook his head. "How late were you out last night?"

Noah crossed his arms over his chest. "What do you care anyway?"

"You know I care, Noah. We really need to talk."

"Listen, Josh," Noah said as he shook his head and looked away, "we don't need to talk. You're just gonna say everything you've already said a million times."

"Not this time, Noah. This time Mona and I are going to ask you to leave."

Noah's eyes grew wide with surprise, and he looked at his brother. "Leave? Like move out?"

Joshua nodded. "I think it's time for you to find your own place. You've got a good, steady job, and it's not right for you to sponge off Mona and me while you squander your money on booze and women. You're all grown up, Noah. I've done my part."

Noah couldn't hide his astonishment, and for a long moment he stared at his brother, unable to come up with a single smart remark. "Tomorrow is Saturday. I'll get my things out then."

"That'll be fine," Joshua answered, and Noah left through the back door without a word.

Joshua shook his head and felt tears in his eyes. Mona came into the kitchen and put her arms around her husband.

"It won't be like this forever," she said. "I know it's gonna get better."

*****

Ginger was in the jazz dance competition that afternoon, and she looked perfect performing in her black-and-pink leotard. Her soft, strawberry hair caught the lights above, creating a halo effect over her head. Sara and Melissa felt well enough to attend the performance, and they were sitting with Tillie in one of the back rows.

"My head still hurts," Melissa grumbled as she sipped a big glass of water.

Tillie smiled but kept her eyes on Ginger. "You should have seen yourselves last night."

"Oh," Sara moaned, "I don't even want to hear about it. I just want to forget the whole thing even happened."

"What about that nut with the gun?" Melissa remembered.

"She bought one of my paintings this morning," Tillie replied.

"Hmm," Sara mused. "She can't be all bad then."

*****

Maggie May stood on a stepladder, hanging her new painting on the far side of the bar. She was finally dressing up that old, empty wall, and she felt good about that.

Noah sauntered in, walked to where she was hanging the painting, and looked it over. "Must be livin' large, Maggie May."

"What are you talking about?" Maggie responded in her familiar bark.

"Expensive painting?"

"No," she answered as she came down the stepladder. "I bought it from your girlfriend."

"Carrie?"

Maggie laughed and handed Noah her hammer while she folded the stepladder. "No. Does Carrie paint?"

"I don't know," Noah answered as he tucked the stepladder under his free arm and followed Maggie back to the bar. "Where do you want me to put this?"

"In the kitchen by the sink," Maggie answered as she resumed her place behind the bar and studied her work from there. "The girl you made the date with last night."

Noah smiled with recollection. "Oh, yeah." He put the ladder in its place, rejoined Maggie at the bar, and looked at the painting. "She painted *that?*"

Maggie nodded. "Got it over there at the hotel. Some kind of contest or something." She gave Noah a good looking over, noticing he'd shaved and combed his ponytail. "Say, you're looking pretty good today. Where's the big date taking place?"

"I told her to meet me here." Noah looked out through the glass doors. "I thought she'd be here by now. She didn't come in before I got here, did she?"

Maggie shook her head. "I haven't seen her since this morning. She's probably still at the doin's over at the hotel."

"But I told her to meet me *here*." He gave his chin a thoughtful scratch. "You don't think she stood me up, do ya, Maggie?"

Maggie laughed and shook her head. "I don't know what to think of that deal, Noah. She's a pretty nice gal. Do you really think a gal like that would give someone like you the time of day?"

Noah's eyes couldn't hide how much Maggie had just hurt his feelings. "Thanks, Maggie. That was below the belt."

"Listen, Noah, you know what I mean. You're the one that says you're gonna make your own decisions and live your own life."

Noah sighed. "Josh kicked me out. I gotta be out of the house by tomorrow."

"Well, you're twenty-three years old. I was on my own by then."

"Aren't you just a pillar of support today," Noah grumbled. "Where's this doin's?"

"Over at the hotel, and her name is 'Angel.' "

Noah turned from Maggie without a word and headed out the door.

"Hey," Maggie yelled at Noah's back, "if you do get a date, would you stop by so I can take her picture? I want it for my bulletin board, for when she's famous."

Noah proceeded through the door without answering Maggie, and she just shook her head as she looked at Estelle.

"He'll be back, *with the girl*," Estelle assured and returned to her work.

The Washington Room was filled with people and judges watching the jazz dance competition. Noah spied Tillie and her friends in the very back row. Her pretty curls lay softly upon her slender shoulders, and her dark eyes were shining with excitement as she watched the dancer perform. Her perfect mouth smiled slightly, and he saw she held a paper of some sort in her graceful hands. He noticed there just happened to be an open seat beside her. *How convenient.*

Ginger's solo dance was nearly complete, and Tillie watched with anticipation. Ginger had never danced as well as she danced that day, and Tillie was certain of a blue ribbon for her.

She paid no attention when someone sat down in the seat beside her, assuming it was just another spectator. When she glanced his way she was pleasantly surprised to see the man from the night before. He had shaved off the scruffy whiskers of the night before, and his hair was combed. His ponytail wasn't as elegant as Marquette's, but it was twice as long, and...*he smells good*, she thought.

"So did you stand me up or what?" he whispered with a curious frown.

She gave him a half smile. She hadn't even had time to think about the "date" all day. "No, I've been too busy."

"Well, how much longer are you gonna be *busy?*" His blue eyes danced as he waited for an answer.

"Are you a stalker or something?" Tillie whispered, trying her best not to smile at this stranger who made her feel so unusual. It was almost like floating when she looked into his eyes. He laughed, and she couldn't help but notice how warm his smile was.

"No, I'm not a stalker. But I can take you to this really great place for dinner. Are you old enough to go on a date?"

It was Tillie's turn to laugh. "I'm old enough to date," she whispered in answer, trying to justify her decision. The truth was, she wouldn't be eighteen until June, and her father had forbidden her to go unchaperoned with a boy until that time. Even Vincenzo and Kate had submitted to the rule when they'd dated. They toted Mr. Martin or Guiseppi along for nearly two years before Kate and Vincenzo were both eighteen.

"Well, when can you leave?" Noah whispered.

Tillie looked back up at the stage where Ginger was still performing with all of her heart and soul. "She's just about finished. She's my best friend, and I have to make sure she gets the blue—"

"And then you can go?" Noah interrupted.

Tillie hesitated and looked into his eyes. *What'll Ginger say? What'll the other girls say? We're not allowed to leave the hotel at all, and a date with a biker probably doesn't qualify for any kind of an exception. I'll be breaking Papa's rule…I'll have to sneak out…but I want to…*

She bit her lip. "Okay. But just dinner, and then I have to be right back."

Noah nodded in agreement.

Ginger's number ended, and the room began to applaud. Before she could leave the stage, a judge presented her with a blue ribbon, and everyone applauded again and got to their feet. Ginger happily accepted her award and then raced from the stage to her friends while the judge presented the other awards.

"You were awesome," Tillie said as she embraced Ginger.

"Thanks." Ginger smiled and looked from Tillie to Noah, and then back at Tillie. "What's going on?"

Tillie leaned over and whispered, "I'm going to dinner with him. Would you cover for me if anybody asks about me?"

Ginger's eyes opened in wide surprise. "But you don't even know his name."

"I'll find out," Tillie giggled.

Ginger took a soft breath and whispered, "Do you promise not to do any drinking or anything else that we've agreed not to do until *after* we're married?"

"I promise."

Ginger nodded.

Sara and Melissa's mouths hung open as they watched the exchange between Tillie and Ginger. *Ginger gave her blessing?*

They were astounded as they watched Tillie leave with Noah. She followed him out of the Washington Room and into the lobby of the hotel. *This isn't like Tillie at all!* All of her romantic intentions were expressly reserved for Alex Martin. Normally she would have never looked at someone so irresponsible and reckless—especially knowing about the drinking part of the man's personality.

"I can't believe you let her do that!" Sara was aghast.

"Oh, please," Ginger replied with a frown. "It's not like she's gonna go out and get drunk."

"How do you know?" Melissa questioned.

Ginger rolled her eyes. "Like you care, Melissa. You thought it was just fine when you and Sara went over and got yourselves good and loaded last night."

"But this is *different*," Sara argued. "We don't know anything about this guy. We don't even know his name."

Ginger frowned. "Tillie's almost eighteen years old. She's old enough to make her own decisions."

"Have you ever been on a Harley?" Noah asked as he led Tillie to his bike.

She shook her head and wondered what in the world she was getting herself into. Noah helped her onto the back of the bike, and then he got on in front. He started and revved the engine.

"Hang on!" he said above the noise, and Tillie put her arms around his waist.

Noah eased out of the parking lot. If she'd never been on a bike before, he was certain she'd probably have a difficult time keeping her balance.

The weather was unusually warm for April, and the breeze felt good as they drove along.

It's fun to ride a motorcycle, Tillie thought, *and it's fun to be out and away from everyone, including my family*. She felt a little guilty when she thought of them, as she knew they wouldn't have approved of her choice in activities, especially in the company of a possible blackguard.

Soon they pulled into a sparsely filled parking lot, and Noah hopped off the bike.

"This place is great," Noah said with a lopsided grin. "And it's early enough. We'll be able to get a good table." He helped her from the bike and escorted her inside.

Tillie smiled as they paused by the door, wondering what Noah's response would be. Surprisingly, he opened the door for her and allowed her to enter *first*.

Okay. I'm impressed. She took one point away from the blackguard's column and put it into the knight's.

The steak house was filled with windows lighting the otherwise dark decor. The walls and booths were brown, and western-style oil paintings hung everywhere. The hostess seated them near a window, handed them two menus, and walked away. They opened their menus, and Tillie noticed they served alcohol. She decided if he ordered anything to drink, she'd be calling herself a taxi.

A waitress appeared. "Anything to drink?"

"Just a couple of Cokes, please," Noah answered.

Tillie's stomach jumped with excitement, but she kept her eyes on her menu. At least he would be sober for *this* date, and he got another point in the knight's column.

The waitress returned with two icy glasses of the soft drink and asked for their orders.

After they'd given their requests, the waitress instructed, "And you can help yourselves to the salad bar."

Noah stood and offered his hand to Tillie. She was impressed again. *He must have learned manners from someone.* Hesitantly, she put her hand into his and rose from her seat.

Noah looked from her hand into her eyes. "You have very pretty hands."

Tillie smiled back, surprised at his comment. "Thank you."

"You're welcome," and he escorted her to the salad bar.

"It's all you can eat," he whispered as he handed her a plate. "I love their pickled okra. You gotta try some."

Tillie took the plate and proceeded through the salad bar behind Noah. When they returned to their seats, he waited for her to sit down first and then seated himself.

"So, where do you come from?" he asked as he put his napkin on his lap and rolled up his sleeves, forgetting that he'd intended to hide the tattoo.

Tillie had already taken a big bite of salad and was thankful she couldn't answer right away. She didn't want to tell him *too* much about herself, not yet anyway. She swallowed and answered, "The eastern part of the state. By the way, what's your name?"

"My name's Noah." He smiled and gave her a mischievous wink. "And you're Angel?"

Tillie was surprised. *Where did he hear that name? Only my family calls me "Angel."*

Noah saw the surprise in her eyes. "I saw your painting at Maggie's this afternoon. She told me. You're a fine painter."

Tillie regained her composure. "Thank you."

"So who's the mysterious lady in the painting?"

"It's my Ma`ma and her horse."

Noah nodded and took a huge bite of his salad, and that's when Tillie noticed the tattoo on his forearm.

"What's that?" she asked with a frown.

Noah almost choked on his salad. He swallowed hard and rolled his eyes. "That's a sword."

"Why did you do that to yourself?"

Noah looked nervous. "Well, it was sort of a dare…there was this really mean tattoo lady in Saigon—"

"You were in Vietnam?" *He's a lot older than he looks.*

"Served my entire time near Saigon. Came home shortly after Christmas of '71."

Wow. Service to his country. She added ten additional points to the knight's column. "My brother Marq was in Vietnam."

"Marine?"

Tillie shook her head. "Army."

Noah sighed, glad to have *that* little conversation out of the way. He'd change the subject deliberately now, as he always did, unwilling to discuss Vietnam. He hated every part of that chapter in his life and wished nothing more than if it would just go away and be forgotten by the rest of the world.

Casually, he began to ask different questions, mostly about her artwork and what she was planning on doing with the rest of her life. Tillie's black eyes sparkled when she described her different paintings and sketches and when she told him she wanted to be an art teacher.

By the time their steaks arrived, they had both talked and laughed about their different dreams and plans for the future. Noah surprised Tillie when he told her he wanted to build houses, but he'd dropped out of school before graduating.

"You can always go back," Tillie suggested.

Noah raised one sandy-colored eyebrow. "Don't you think I'd look a little *weird?* You know, here comes this twenty-three-year-old guy and sits down in the classroom with little fifteen-year-old kids?"

Tillie laughed. "You don't have to go back to the traditional class-room. Haven't you heard of the GED program?"

Noah shook his head and looked into her encouraging eyes. It had been a long time since someone actually *encouraged* Noah. Usually people were trying to *discourage* his horrible behavior.

Tillie continued, "What you do is enroll first in a night-time class to study for the GED, which stands for General Equivalency Diploma. You're in a class with other people, all ages, and you don't have to feel *weird*."

Noah smiled with interest. *She's sweet. Maybe I should check it out.*

After dinner, Noah coaxed Tillie into one last ride before having to return her to the hotel. The sun had started to set, but the air was still warm enough to enjoy the ride. Noah drove the bike with care, so as not to upset his new rider on the back. He liked how her hands felt around his waist, as if they'd always been there *and should be there forever. Wow! Where did that come from? I'm not into any kind of a commitment. Never have been. Love 'em and leave 'em.* He shook off the errant emotions and focused on the road.

About fifteen minutes into the ride, they turned onto a blacktop road that wound around channels of water, and finally Tillie saw a lake. Noah stopped the bike and shut off the engine, hopped off, and offered her his hand. She gladly accepted, and he helped her from the bike.

"This is Canyon Lake Park," he said as he led her toward the lake. "And during the day there are usually a lot of geese and ducks out here, so watch your step."

"Watch my step?" She wanted to tighten her grip on his hand, but she didn't want to be *too* obvious.

Noah chuckled, "You know, they *go* everywhere."

"Oh," Tillie acknowledged with a smile.

It was quiet as they walked along the path beside the lake. They watched the sun set over Rapid City and listened to the quacks and honks of the birds around them. Crickets and frogs made soft noises, and a romantic breeze softly stirred the air.

Tillie had never been alone with another man besides her father and her brothers. It was scary and fun all at the same time to notice the different things about him and experience the unusual feelings he stirred within her. His hand was warm and strong as it gently clasped hers. His stride was slow and careful, so they could walk side by side without an effort on her part to keep up to him. Occasionally she caught the scent of his Old Spice and drew it in deeply. She would remember *that* forever.

Noah, on the other hand, had been with lots of women. They seemed to just fling themselves at him. But his experience with this particular woman was entirely different from all of the others. For one thing, she was *nice.* There would definitely be NO fooling around, and he'd known *that* the moment he'd laid eyes upon her. And she wouldn't settle for some drunk biker. He'd have to really clean up his act, possibly even have to finish that GED program she had talked about at dinner, before she'd really spend much more time with him. Her small, pretty hand felt perfect in his own, like it had always been and should always be there. *Wait a minute. Get ahold of yourself. She's just a girl!*

He deliberately drew a very deep breath in order to shake his *crazy* thoughts away. "So," he said as they walked along, "how long will you be in town?"

"We have to leave on Sunday," she answered with a glance into his wonderful expression. *I've never seen someone with such blue eyes.*

"What do you have going on tomorrow?" he asked as he came to a stop and looked intently into her eyes. *She's got the most wonderful eyes I've ever seen.* "I have Saturdays and Sundays off."

"Nothing," she answered as she got lost in his gaze and felt him take a gentle hold of her other hand.

"Can I come and pick you up tomorrow?" *Please don't say no.* "We could go for a ride through the Hills. You'd love it up there."

Tillie nodded, even though she knew better. "But maybe I should get back now. My friends might worry."

Noah smiled and led her back to his bike.

The moon was full and bright above them when he pulled into the hotel parking lot. He parked beneath the canopy at the front door and helped her off the bike.

"I had a really great time," he said as he walked her to the door and paused to look into her eyes again. *She's amazing.*

"Me too," Tillie said as she smiled back at him.

"And you'll meet me right here in the morning?"

"What time?"

"Say, seven?"

Tillie agreed without hesitation and Noah smiled. Very slowly he lowered his lips to hers and softly kissed her.

Tillie's *first* kiss, and she closed her eyes. Perhaps she would float away. She felt the softness of his lips and the stubble of his chin at the same time, and it made her heart beat in a way she'd never felt it beat before. All too soon he pulled away, and she opened her eyes to look back into the dancing blue eyes of Noah. *That was perfect...how all first kisses should be.*

"Don't forget about me tomorrow," he reminded with a smile.

"I won't." *How will I ever forget you now?*

"Do you want me to walk you to your room?"

Tillie shook her head and whispered, "You'd better not."

Noah nodded and began to back away. Tillie smiled and gave him a small wave, and then she turned and hurried into the hotel and out of his sight.

Noah sighed and began to walk back to his bike when he suddenly remembered that he'd forgotten to stop by Maggie's for the picture... *Oh well, maybe tomorrow...*

Chapter 3

Noah was awake most of the night, thinking only of Angel. He loved her soft laughter and ideas and the familiarity of her presence. Everything about her encouraged him to want to be a *different* person.

He arose before six o'clock, before Mona and Joshua, and made another secretive exit. *I know I promised to move out today, but it can wait until Sunday, after Angel leaves. After all, how long is it possibly going to take me to move my stuff out? I don't even have any furniture. They won't mind me being here one more day.*

He pushed his bike down the road before he started it. When he felt he was a safe distance away, he revved the engine and headed for town.

*****

Tillie hadn't slept either. She lay awake, remembering the sincerity in his eyes and the tender strength of his hand leading her safely along the path. He was quiet when they spoke of Vietnam, just like Marquette; the strength of his inner character was unmistakable. He hadn't tried to touch her in any inappropriate ways, nor had he suggested anything improper. *They're all there…the signs of a knight.*

She brushed her soft curls into a ponytail and dressed in sturdy jeans and a pink sweatshirt. She loaded her father's old camera with film and placed it into her backpack.

"Just tell Mrs. Malone that I'm sick," she said to Ginger as she put on her jacket.

"You mean you're not gonna watch our drama and theater?" Sara whined from the bed.

Tillie rolled her eyes. "You mean like you watched my art exhibit?"

"Come on, Tillie," Melissa said as she struggled to sit up in the bed. She narrowed her eyes and scolded, "This is *way* worse than what we pulled. You can't just go off somewhere with some man. What if he gets you up in those hills and leaves you for dead?"

Tillie smiled and shook her head. "I don't think he will—"

"Listen," Ginger interrupted, "Tillie's a good judge of character, and she's gonna be alright."

"When will you be back?" Sara questioned.

"Don't look for me until after supper," Tillie answered as she swung her pack onto her back.

"I think it'll be okay," Ginger whispered, and she gave Tillie a hug. "But don't forget what we learned in self defense, just in case."

Tillie nodded as she slipped into the hallway. She hurried through the hotel without being seen and let herself out through the lobby doors. The morning was chilly, and Tillie was thankful she'd worn her jacket. Hopefully this day would warm up like it had the day before.

Noah was just pulling his bike into the parking lot when Tillie stepped out the door. He wore a heavy jean jacket this morning and sunglasses, and he looked more handsome than any movie star she'd ever seen. Tillie's heart fluttered and she took a breath. *What is this? I've never felt like this in my life.*

Noah pulled under the canopy, and Tillie hopped on the bike, put her arms around his middle, and held on tight. As Noah pulled out, he felt her arms around his waist. Sheer contentment filled his heart. *What is it about this girl that's so different from all of the others?*

He drove his bike into Maggie's parking lot in order to pause and say good morning. "I can't believe our perfect timing," he grinned as he pulled down his sunglasses just enough to look at her. "And you look *great* this morning."

Tillie smiled into his happy, blue eyes. "So do you."

"How 'bout some breakfast?"

"I'm starved. I didn't get time to eat before I left."

"Me neither. Have you ever seen Mt. Rushmore?"

Tillie shook her head.

"Well, it's about a half hour's drive. We can eat in the dining room up there. Can you make it that long?"

"I can make it," she answered, eager to see the Hills and the memorial.

Noah was wearing gloves, but he noticed Tillie was not. "Your hands are going to get really cold. Just tuck them into my jacket pockets. We'll get you a pair when we get up to the memorial." Noah turned in his seat, revved the engine, and they headed down LaCrosse Street again. Tillie tucked her hands into his jacket pockets and clutched his middle, praying every moment that she wasn't doing something stupid.

Noah turned his bike onto East North Street, turned right when he got to Omaha Street, and then turned left at Mt. Rushmore Road.

"Will this take us all the way?" Tillie yelled from the back of the bike.

Noah nodded.

They drove by several businesses along the city street until it led them past an unusual wooden arch, opening into a pine-covered mountainous expanse before them. The smell of pine was overwhelming, and Tillie closed her eyes and inhaled deeply, enjoying the cool wind in her face. The road began to wind and climb steadily as it led them further into the wooded National Forestland.

As they drove along Highway 18, winding through the mountain landscape and Black Hills' spruce, they passed through two small towns. Rockerville was the first; it was a little town just to the left of the highway, perfectly tucked into the trees. Keystone was the bigger town, and its main street was lined with shops and restaurants, horse rides, and a helicopter service. Noah pulled into an empty space beside the old wooden sidewalk and turned off the engine.

"This is the world-famous taffy shop," he said as he got off the bike and reached for her hand. "You can't come to Keystone without getting some of their taffy. It's the best."

Tillie followed him into the old taffy shop. Enclosed in a glass room, an old-fashioned taffy machine was hard at work, pulling fresh candy. A young man smiled at them through the glass as they walked in the front door. Their senses were greeted with the wonderful smells of fresh candy. Bins filled with cut and wrapped taffy lined the small perimeter, and bushel baskets loaded with packages waited on the glass counter.

Noah smiled as he looked around and headed for the counter. "I *love* this place. I usually just get one of these variety bags. There's a few of each flavor." He purchased a bag for himself and an extra one for Tillie. " 'Cause you might want some too," he grinned.

Tillie laughed. "You mean you need a *whole bag?*"

He only grinned in reply, and she laughed again.

As they left the taffy shop, Noah pointed out the old Indian on the other side of the street. On the corner beneath the awnings of the other businesses sat this very old man. His skin was the color of mahogany, and deep lines furrowed his face. His eyes were chocolate brown, and the corners of his full lips turned up in a soft smile. He was dressed in genuine Sioux Indian regalia, with his horse tethered to an old-fashioned post nearby.

"He's been there for as long as I can remember," Noah said as he faced the old Indian and held up his palm in greeting.

The old Indian returned his greeting.

"Wow," Tillie breathed.

Noah took her by the hand, and they got back on his motorcycle. After driving a short distance down the road, Noah rolled his bike into the parking lot at the Gutzon Borglum Memorial and turned around.

"As we continue up this highway, be sure you're looking straight ahead," he said with a smile. "You'll be able to see Mt. Rushmore as we approach."

"But I thought we were still a mile or so away," Tillie said, remembering a sign she'd seen earlier.

Noah nodded. "But you can see it from the road. Be sure to watch for it."

Tillie smiled in understanding, and Noah revved the bike and took off. She kept watch for the monument. Shortly, Noah pointed above them, and Tillie looked up to see the magnificent monument. Four stern faces carved into the side of a white mountain with green pine trees flowing down beneath them. The sky was brilliantly blue above them, and Tillie gasped.

The bike slowed as it climbed further and further. They pulled into a line of other vehicles and waited their turn. Noah gave the man in the booth a dollar, and he was allowed to drive his bike inside and park. He shut off the engine and hopped off before helping Tillie from the back. It was colder here than it had been in Rapid City, and they could see their breath.

Tillie was still staring at the monument when Noah gently took her hand and began to lead her through the parking lot. "Come on," he quietly laughed. "Don'tcha wanna have some breakfast?"

"It's just so amazing! My family would *love* this place."

"Did you bring a camera?"

"I did!" Tillie swung the backpack from over her shoulders and around in front. She pulled out the old camera and let the bag drop to the ground. "And I think I'll take a picture from here," she said as she wound the camera. She looked through the lens, captured the image of Mt. Rushmore, and clicked the shutter. She smiled at Noah as she placed the camera back into her pack.

"Can I carry that for you?"

Tillie shook her head. "It belongs to my Papa. I promised to be very careful with it."

Noah smiled in answer, and they continued a romantic walk through the pines and down the path of the Avenue of Flags, where every state's flag flew above them. They went through the Visitors' Center and into a separate building that contained a gift shop and the Buffalo Dining Room. It was set up cafeteria style, and Tillie and Noah got into the line. They filled their trays with scrambled eggs, sausages, cinnamon rolls, orange juice, and coffee. Noah paid the bill without hesitation, and Tillie was impressed again. The points in the knight's column were adding up quickly now.

They took seats at a free table near the windows with a view of Mt. Rushmore. The clink of silverware and dishes was soft in the background, as was the aroma of the delicious morning food being prepared.

"This is just wonderful," Tillie said as she looked from the memorial into Noah's eyes. It was *so* strange how comfortable she felt with him.

"I really love it here, but it's been especially fun to have somebody to share it with." He looked back at the memorial and then at Tillie. "My friends really don't care about the Hills and the memorial. They're just not interested I guess."

"How can you *not* be interested? It's unbelievable."

Noah shrugged as he looked at Lincoln's face. "It took Borglum twelve years to complete the project, you know."

Tillie shook her head. "But why is it called Rushmore?"

"Charles Rushmore was this little attorney from New York that had come to visit some mining interests in the Black Hills. Anyway, or so the stories go, he asked the name of the mountain, and his guide said that it was named Rushmore."

"What year did Borglum finally get it finished?"

"His son actually finished the project after Borglum died, and I *think* that was in 1941."

Tillie frowned playfully. "Are you some sort of a history buff or something?"

Noah blushed. "Actually, *yes*. I love history."

"So does my brother. He lives in New York, and there's a ton of American history on the East Coast. He loves it there."

"What does he do in New York?" Noah asked.

"He's an attorney."

"So, how many brothers and sisters do you have?"

"No sisters. Just my three brothers. How about you?"

"I have one brother," Noah said as a frown formed on his face. "And he's pretty mad at me right now."

"Why would he get mad at *you?*"

Noah sighed. "Angel, I'm a *really* rotten person."

Tillie laughed as she shook her head. "No, you're not. You're just rebellious."

But Noah shook his head, and Tillie saw the sadness behind his eyes. "I've disappointed my brother since I was a little kid. You see, he's a preacher, and he'd like me to live my life a little more worthy of God. In fact, I'm supposed to be moving out today, but I decided to put it off until tomorrow."

"You live with your brother?" She was surprised but took note of his repentant tone.

Noah nodded. "And his wife, Mona. She's the greatest gal."

"Is it the drinking?" Tillie asked, and Noah nodded. She continued, "Well, then, why don't you *stop?*"

Noah shrugged. "I s'pose I'm an alcoholic or something."

"Bah!" Tillie quietly scolded. She rolled her eyes and gave him a sharp frown, and if Ginger would've been there, she'd have declared Tillie's resemblance to Guiseppi once again. "My Papa says that He who is in *you* is far more powerful than he who is in the *world*. Do you know what that means? You can say no to a drink if you really *want* to, *especially* if it upsets your brother and sister-in-law so much. And your friends are probably part of the problem. Are they Christians? Are you a Christian, Noah?" Her black eyes narrowed as she looked into his.

"Yes," he answered. "I'm a Christian, but my friends aren't."

Tillie sighed and shook her head as if to say, *I thought so.* "You've already told me they're not interested in the Black Hills or the memorial, which you have expressed great interest in. What on earth do you have in common with these people? What do you do together with them, Noah, that serves *your* interests? Or do you just live to please *them?* 'Cause if you're a Christian, Noah, you're supposed to live to please the Lord."

Noah shrugged and looked away. He smiled nervously, feeling the heat of embarrassment flush in his cheeks. Joshua had said all of these same things to him before, but never quite this way. Joshua's lectures were always centered around how much he and Mona were hurt by Noah's behavior.

"I'd dump those *losers* if I were you," Tillie ranted. "And I'd find myself some really nice friends who were interested in some of the things I was interested in."

Noah looked into Tillie's cross expression. When she saw his eyes dancing and sparkling, her frown instantly softened and she smiled.

"Sorry about that. Sometimes I get a little carried away."

Noah shook his head and laughed. "Don't be sorry. It's the best lecture I've had in a long time." He reached across the table and took her hand into his own. "And what else would you do if you were me?"

Tillie looked into his gentle eyes. "I'd get a GED and figure out a way to get into a building school, because *that's* what you want. You know, Noah, God puts His desires into our hearts, and I bet you'd meet some really cool friends at a building school. Do they have one in Rapid City?"

"We have a vo-tech...I mean, a vocational training school. They might have something out there. But how do you pay for something like that?"

"Well I imagine the GI Bill will help you out," Tillie suggested. "Also, lots of my friends are getting school loans. You don't have to start paying them back until after you graduate, and they let you make payments."

Noah smiled into her encouraging eyes. She was right, and he knew it. He had to do something with his life other than party it away, and now he had a reason.

After they finished their breakfast, they walked through the gift shop and found a pair of gloves for Tillie. She also picked up a pretty Native American doll in traditional dress, explaining that it was for her niece, Alyssa. She found a small war drum with drumsticks, and tapped on it as she listened carefully.

Noah laughed at her thoughtful antics. "What are you doing?"

"This is going to be for my nephew, Angelo." She raised her eyebrow. "And he makes enough noise the way it is."

Tillie got several excellent shots of the monument and Noah. She posed him on some rocks with the monument just over his shoulder in the background. With his jeans-and-boots attire and the black-and-white film, the photos would become one of her sketch projects and perhaps a painting or two.

After leaving the monument, Noah drove them through the Hills, heading north past Sheridan Lake and the crystal waters of the Pactola Reservoir. They stopped occasionally to hike and take pictures. Tillie allowed Noah to use the old camera of her father's a few times so he could take some shots of her at Pilot Knob and tiny Roubaix Lake, where two old fishermen were happy to take a photo of the young couple as they sat together on a rock by the water.

The day warmed in the Hills, and they removed their jackets, tucking them into Noah's saddlebags. Many of the hardwood trees in the national forest had buds on them, and the early spring heat began to open their green leaves. Screeching hawks soared in the blue skies above them, and the song of robins ready to begin their nests sang happily on the air.

They talked like they'd known each other for years, and the hours passed quickly as they hiked near Bridal Veil Falls in Spearfish Canyon. Tillie spied a delicate, violet flower and stooped to pick it, but before she could, Noah gently stopped her hand.

"Don't pick that. It's Pasque. It'll make you itch."

"No kidding?" Tillie looked curiously at the pretty flowers along the small pond beside the waterfall.

Noah nodded. "I found out the hard way. My sister-in-law grows them, and you hardly ever see them in the wild. It's our State flower you know."

Tillie shook her head. She had no idea the Pasque was South Dakota's state flower. *He's amazing.* She looked from the Pasque and into Noah's blue eyes and then to the waterfall above them. The filmy, foamy water flowing over the rocks gave the appearance of a long, taffeta bridal veil as it trailed gracefully down the aisle of a church. *No wonder it's called Bridal Veil Falls.* She was again awestruck with the beauty of God's creation in the Black Hills of South Dakota.

"You know," Noah said as he watched her marvel at the tumbling waters, "there's a great old story that goes along with that."

"How does it go?"

Noah took a breath and cleared his throat. "Those falls weren't always there. It all started when an Indian warrior became engaged to a girl who had a white mother and a Sioux Indian chief for her father. One day the warrior had to leave to fight a great battle. When he returned to his tribe, his betrothed had taken ill and was dying from a fever. Her parents took the only thing of value they had, which was the bridal veil worn by the chief's wife on their wedding day. They gave it to the warrior and sent him to buy medicine with it. Doing as he was told, the warrior took the veil to the nearest settlement, bought medicine, and returned as quickly as he could to his dying bride. She took the medicine and soon was well again.

"Now the bride had nothing to wear on her head because it had been sold for medicine, but they went ahead with the wedding anyway, right here, on this very spot. And when the warrior kissed his bride, God broke open the rocks above and let a veil run through for her. The old chief said it was God's affirmation of the warrior's noble and pure heart and that the waters would flow here forever."

Tillie looked at Noah and was again amazed. She was under the impression that only her brothers and her father could ever be that romantic, and Noah didn't even seem to be trying. The words had gracefully tumbled from his mouth, like they would have from a great storyteller.

"That's the most beautiful story I've ever heard."

Noah shrugged and looked embarrassed. He looked back into the waterfall and added, "That foamy stuff freezes in the winter. People climb it all the time." He sighed. "I'm hungry. My brother's got a cabin not too far from here. What do you say we go there and see if we can find something to eat?"

"You mean *steal* his food?" Tillie raised her eyebrow.

"Oh, dear," Noah sighed as he looked away. Her conscience was going to be the death of him. "There's a little store just along the way where we can buy some bread and stuff to make sandwiches."

Tillie nodded and laughed, and he smiled back at her. She was so beautiful at that moment it almost took his breath away. The way the sun was shining into the canyon lit a halo over her curls, and her black eyes sparkled. He wondered for a moment if she were actually real.

"Are you ready to go?" he asked with a smile, and she nodded. He took her hand gently into his own and gave her a very soft kiss on her lips. Tillie's *second* kiss, and it was as wonderful as the first. She felt herself begin to float again as she closed her eyes and was drawn into the moment of his kiss.

Noah thought he heard thunder and smiled. *Wow. Is it just her?* He slowly pulled away and looked into the sky above them, noticing the dark cloud approaching the sun in the canyon. *That* was definitely thunder.

"We really gotta get somewhere," he said as he began to lead her down the path. "There's a storm coming."

"Can we make it to your brother's cabin?"

"No, but I think we can make it to a little place just outside of Spearfish."

He helped her put her camera into one of the saddlebags, and then he got her on the back of the bike. He jumped on, revved the engine, and headed north through the canyon as quickly and as safely as they could make it. The sky above them began to darken, and the thunder was getting closer and louder.

Noah took a right at the exit of the canyon, and in a few minutes Tillie saw a small restaurant come into view. Giant raindrops were starting to fall, and the thunder crashed loudly around them. Noah parked beneath a canopy connected to the front of the small restaurant just as the clouds gave way and poured with all of their might. He turned off his bike, jumped off, and then helped her off.

"We just made it," he laughed. "And we even have a dry place to park the bike!"

They went inside the small, nearly empty cowboy-styled restaurant. Scattered everywhere were wooden tables and chairs Tillie had only seen in old John Wayne movies. Cattle horns hung from the walls here and there, as did Western oil paintings. Three older men sat on stools together at the front, singing together in harmony. One played a guitar, another held a harmonica, and the third waited with his mandolin.

"That's the Cowboy Band," Noah whispered as he showed her to a seat close to the dance floor. "They always practice in the afternoons." He pulled out the chair for her, and Tillie sat down. By this time, any points remaining in Noah's blackguard column were gone, and the knight's column was filled to overflowing.

They ordered burgers and fries and visited some more while they waited out the Black Hills' spring storm and listened to the Cowboy Band practice their old tunes.

"Oh, I *love* this song," Tillie said suddenly as she recognized the tune to her father's favorite folk song, *Annie Laurie*.

Noah smiled with recognition and began to sing along with the words, "Her brow is like the snowdrift, her throat is like the swan, her face it is the fairest, that e'er the sun shone on." And then they both laughed, and he said, "Well, your brow isn't exactly like a snowdrift. It's pretty dark."

Tillie smiled as she looked into his kind expression. *Who are you? Are you the one?*

"Do you want to dance?" he asked as he stood and offered her his hand. She immediately placed her own into his and went with him onto the small, empty dance floor. She nestled into his arms and followed his slow, waltzing steps while the Cowboy Band sang another delicate chorus of the precious *Annie Laurie*.

"You have such pretty hands," Noah remarked again. He gently drew her hand to his lips and placed a soft kiss upon it. "So, do you like old music?"

"I do, and Papa loves old music. So I've heard a lot of it. Dean Martin is actually his very favorite, but he's got tons of these old cowboy records like Eddie Arnold and The Sons of the Pioneers."

"I love old music." Noah smiled into her sparkling black eyes and kissed her lips.

Tillie thought perhaps the floor would give way beneath her, and it would be alright if it did because Noah's arms would be there to hold her—forever. *Is this what real love feels like? How does it happen so quickly? Alex never makes me feel this way. I've been totally wrong about him…*

Noah took a soft breath. *What's happening here? I've only known her for two days, and I don't ever want to stop holding her. She must be the one. Coffee in the mornings before I go to work, rides on Iron Mountain Road, hikes in the Hills on the weekends…babies…*

The Cowboy Band had finished their practice and sat silent as they watched the young couple slowly waltz around the empty dance floor. They finally clapped to draw Tillie and Noah's attention toward them, and Noah laughed in embarrassment.

"I guess they're done," he said, with his cheeks showing a faint blush.

Tillie giggled in agreement, and they reluctantly left the dance floor and went back to their table, where the waitress had left their order.

The weather had cooled significantly when the storm ended. As they stepped out of the restaurant, the sun was beginning to set, and they were surprised they'd spent that much time talking during their meal.

Noah got their jackets out of the saddlebags, being sure to keep her old camera safe. That's when he noticed the foreign script on the outside of the case. "Hey, where did you say you got that camera?"

"It's my papa's, and he tells this really dramatic story about it. Do you want to hear it?"

"Love to."

"Papa was in the second world war. He and my Uncle Angelo, that was his brother, fought with the Allies in Italy. Papa was with a man he calls 'The Count,' and The Count is the one who gave him the camera. Papa was part of a band of men that captured Mussolini. It was Papa's job to lie on the top of a hill and watch for Mussolini's convoy and take a photo of the truck they believed Mussolini to be inside. Papa's friends, Pietro, Lorenzo, and Sergio were with him. They ambushed the convoy and pulled the old Duce from the back of the truck. Some of the others hauled him away and executed him."

"So your dad was a soldier too?"

Tillie smiled and shook her head. "No. Papa says they were *powerful warriors,* and the people shook with fear when they saw him and Uncle Angelo coming."

"He sounds like a very brave man."

Tillie's black eyes sparkled. "He's the best. And my brothers are *exactly* like him."

The smile faded from Noah's face and he searched her eyes. "What do you think he would say if you brought a character like me home to him?"

Tillie was surprised at the question, but she answered as truthfully as she could. "I think if you were sober he'd trust my judgment and probably really warm up to you."

"Sober. I can stay sober." He took a deep breath. "Angel, I have a really great job—well, not really *great*—but it pays well; and there are some benefits, like insurance and retirement." He stopped as he continued to look into her eyes. *I want to tell her, but how can I say it? I've never said that to another person in the whole world, except for Mona and Josh.* He took another deep breath and swallowed hard. "Do you think there might be a chance you'd come to Rapid City…just to see me?"

Tillie smiled and nodded. Noah sighed with relief as he gathered her into his arms and buried his face in her curls. "I was hoping you'd say that," he whispered as he gave her a kiss on the top of her head. "Now we gotta get you back."

As Noah helped her onto the back of his bike, he remembered Maggie's request of two nights before. "Can we stop at Maggie's? She just wants to take your picture. She's got a huge bulletin board filled with snapshots of the customers. She thinks you're gonna be a famous artist someday and wants your picture."

An hour later, they pulled into Maggie's full parking lot and got off the bike. Tillie retrieved her camera, and Noah took her gently by the hand as they walked toward the glass doors.

"Do you think your little buddies will be in here tonight?" Noah joked as they walked in, surprising a very busy Maggie May.

"No," Tillie laughed. "I think their drinking days ended the other night."

"Well, if it isn't my ol' buddy, Noah," Maggie's gruff voice rang out as they stepped up to the bar. "Where ya been?"

"I've been busy, Maggie," Noah answered as a touch of blush came to his cheeks. He glanced at Tillie. "And this is Angel. She's come to have her picture taken. Angel, this is my dearest friend, Maggie May."

"Well I'll be darned," Maggie said with a grin. "The famous little artist." She pointed at Tillie's painting on the other side of the bar and asked, "How do you like where I put it?"

Tillie smiled. "It looks just perfect there."

"So what are you doing with a scruffy, old biker like this?" Maggie asked, pointing her thumb at Noah.

"Touring the northern Hills," Tillie answered, noticing Estelle getting her camera ready at the end of the bar.

"And the monument?" Maggie asked.

Tillie acknowledged Maggie with a smile and a nod.

"And she promised her friends she'd be back by about now," Noah said, "so let's get this picture over with so she can leave."

Maggie looked at Estelle. "Get a couple of good ones, Stellie."

Estelle came around to the front of the bar. "Turn your back to the bar." Tillie and Noah turned to face the camera, and Noah put his arm around Tillie, holding her close to his side.

"And could you take one with my camera?" Tillie asked.

Estelle set down her own camera, reached for Tillie's, and backed up to take the first picture. She clicked the shutter and returned the camera to Tillie. Then she picked up her own, clicked the shutter, and rewound it. Before she could click off another photo, Noah gave Tillie a delicate kiss on the cheek, and Estelle captured the scene as she clicked the lens again.

"There," she said with quiet satisfaction, "I got two good ones Maggie. Want any more?"

Maggie shook her head. "No, that'll be good…oh…" Maggie turned her head in the direction of a voice that was calling to her, and she looked back at Tillie and Noah. "I gotta run. We're really busy. It was nice to meet ya." And she was off.

Noah grabbed one of the cocktail napkins off of the bar and began to scribble some numbers on it. "This is my phone number," he began to explain with a smile. "And I want you to call me when you come back. I'd really like to ask you for yours, but I'm afraid you might say no."

Tillie swallowed hard as she took the napkin from Noah and tucked it into her jean pocket. "Noah…" She hesitated and looked into his blue eyes. "I should have told you this earlier. I'm not eighteen yet."

Noah let out a quiet, little gasp and stared at her with wide-open eyes. He whispered with astonishment, "You mean I've been running around the Black Hills with a *minor* all day?"

"But I promise to come back. I'll turn eighteen in June, but I think I can be back before then. I'm not allowed to date until I'm eighteen, and if some man started calling the house, he'd be in *big* trouble."

"It's okay." Noah gave her a smile and took her by the hand to lead her out the door. "I'm not gonna worry about it. You just call me when you come back."

They left Maggie's and walked across the street to the hotel, holding hands and wishing the night would never end. When they got to the door at the lobby, Noah looked into her pretty, black eyes. "You leave tomorrow."

"But not until noon. Can you come by and say good-bye before I have to go?"

"Sure. When do you think you'll be back?"

Tillie shrugged and tried to think…*I have no idea how to even plan this, let alone give him a certain time. Papa's gonna be really upset when he finally finds out.* "The very latest will be June," she finally answered.

Noah took a very deep breath and blurted out, "I love you."

Tillie looked into his dancing blue eyes and smiled. There was no other possible response. "I love you too."

Noah smiled and took another deep breath. "And I want to be married. I want to be with you forever," he whispered as he took her into his arms and held her close.

Tillie could only nod her head. Her heart felt as if it was about ready to explode from the pounding. She *loved* Noah. She couldn't explain it and she didn't care, but she *loved* him.

"When you turn eighteen," Noah whispered, "you call me. We'll get together and plan a nice wedding."

"And we'll honeymoon in the Hills."

"And we can live over by Canyon Lake. They've got cheap cabins over there for rent," Noah added.

Tillie laughed. She really *would* marry this man, and she decided at that moment to give him all of the information he'd need to contact her. Before she could get the words out, she saw Mrs. Malone coming down the hall toward the lobby.

"I gotta go," she whispered as she started to back out of his arms and toward the door. "But please, come tomorrow. I have to tell you something very important."

"I will," Noah whispered as he saw a woman approaching.

"Get out of here!" Tillie whispered with a smile.

Noah turned and jogged across the parking lot to hide himself in the shadows.

"Tillie Caselli?" Mrs. Malone said when Tillie came into the lobby. Tillie tried her best to look nauseated.

"Oh, hi, Mrs. Malone. I thought I'd try to get a little air."

Mrs. Malone's eyes were filled with pity, and it left a guilty pang in Tillie's chest. Mrs. Malone put her arm over Tillie's shoulders and gave her a gentle hug. "Are you feeling any better, Tillie?"

"Oh, yes, much," Tillie answered, feeling more guilt at the continuation of her lie but also praying that Mrs. Malone didn't smell the cigarette smoke from Maggie's on her clothing.

"That's good. I was getting really worried about you."

Tillie felt horrible about her successful lie as the two of them walked back to her room together, and she silently prayed for forgiveness from God.

*****

"I'm gonna tell him everything," Tillie announced as she and her roommates packed their things that evening. Tillie had relayed the entire romantic day's events to her friends, who were still a little nervous about her taking off with a stranger. Ginger even had to admit she was worried when it got dark outside and Tillie hadn't come back yet.

"Oh, don't do it," Ginger pleaded. "Your family will kill you if he starts coming around. And what if he shows up drunk?"

"I don't think he will," Tillie said as she tossed her dirty jeans into her suitcase.

"What if he did?" Melissa questioned with huge eyes. "Can you see Mr. Caselli? He'd probably give that guy a lecture he'd never forget."

Ginger laughed, for she could easily imagine Tillie's father giving Noah an old-fashioned lecture.

"He's just so wonderful," Tillie breathed. She closed her suitcase and flopped herself on the bed. She gazed up at the ceiling. "His eyes are so *honest*. He wants to build things, and he wants to live in a cabin. There's *real goodness* inside of him. I think I've found a *real* knight."

The other three were astounded into silence, and they gathered around Tillie for seats on the bed. They'd heard the story of *The Knight & The Blackguard* many times from Tillie. Tillie had *never* acted like this about a boy, and *not even Alex* had ever been deemed a knight.

Sara's expression was near horrified as she cleared her throat and cautiously asked, "What about Alex?"

Tillie looked at Sara and answered simply, "Alex doesn't love me, and I've never been in love with Alex."

It was almost five a.m. when the girls heard loud banging on the door of their room, and then Mrs. Malone's voice called to each of them as she tried to roust them out of their sleep. Melissa hurried to the door and let Mrs. Malone inside.

"Get your things together, girls, as quickly as you can," she instructed in a frantic voice.

"Why?" Tillie asked as she sat up in the bed, rubbing the sleep from her eyes.

"There's a dreadful snowstorm headed for the Black Hills," Mrs. Malone explained. "We have to be out of town so we don't get stuck in it. We'll be boarding the bus in thirty minutes." And with that she left them to gather their things.

"I won't get to see Noah," Tillie whispered.

Sara got out of her warm bed, went to Tillie, and put a friendly arm around her shoulders. "It's okay. It just wasn't meant to be."

Tillie nodded, but her heart ached as she got dressed and then carried her luggage and art to the compartment on the side of the bus. She climbed on board, found Ginger, and slumped into a seat beside her.

"It's gonna be okay," Ginger reassured her.

"No, it's not," Tillie mumbled as she tried to swallow her tears away, and then she gasped.

"What?" Ginger asked.

"I have his number. I can call him before we go," Tillie said excitedly as she reached into her jean pocket and gasped again. "I left it in my other jeans! They're in the luggage—" Tillie got to her feet and was stopped in her tracks when she heard the doors to the bus close. Mrs. Malone stood in the front of the bus.

"Children, take your seats," she said. "We have a long drive ahead of us, and we have to get started now."

Tillie's heart felt like it would stop with disappointment, and she went back to her seat beside Ginger.

"It's still gonna be okay," Ginger reassured her. "We can call him from Sioux Falls." Tillie nodded as she laid her head upon Ginger's friendly shoulder and let her tears fall like the rain from the day before. Ginger put her arm around Tillie. "There, there, now," Ginger whispered. "It's gonna be okay. You just wait and see."

Chapter 4

Noah woke up before six on Sunday morning, amazed at how good it felt not to have a hangover. His head and neck didn't ache, and his thoughts were clear. He leapt from his bed, eager to start his new life—a life including Angel. So many things were yet to accomplish before she came back.

He knelt beside his bed, folded his hands, and bowed his head. "Father, thank you for showing me how *wrong* I've been. Thank you for Angel and this time we've had together. I promise to be a good husband and *always* love her, just the way You've always loved me. I'm so sorry for the way I've acted, Father. Please forgive me, and help me make this right with Josh and Mona."

After he'd showered and shaved and tied back the combed ponytail, he tiptoed to the kitchen to make breakfast for Mona and Joshua. It was the *least* he could do, considering the horrible way he'd treated them for the last several years. It probably wouldn't *fix* everything, but it was a start.

Mona and Joshua awoke with a start, smelling the cooking breakfast and brewing coffee.

"If he's got a bunch of his friends down there, I'm calling the cops," Joshua scowled as he threw on his robe and headed for the steps.

"He didn't even get his things out yesterday," Mona grumbled, following her husband.

They hurried downstairs to see who was in their kitchen, surprised to find Noah, clean shaven and wearing Mona's white apron as he set the table. Mona's mouth fell open in surprise as she realized what was going on. They rarely saw Noah, and *never once* had he served them. Not only that, but he appeared to be sober.

Joshua closed his own surprised mouth by swallowing hard, staring at Noah with confusion.

"I know, I know," Noah said with a smile as his blue eyes twinkled. "Why don't the two of you just sit down and have a cup of coffee. Breakfast is almost ready."

They nodded mechanically and made their way to the table. They were astonished as Noah poured their coffee and brought them a platter of eggs and bacon.

He took a seat as he smiled at the two of them. "I'm truly sorry. You've always been so good to me, and I've repaid you with heartache after heartache. And I'm sorry I blew you off yesterday and didn't get my things out, but I promise to take care of that today. In fact, I've already packed some things this morning. I'll be out before you guys get back from church—"

"Noah," Joshua interrupted...*He's trying to make amends...I can't make him leave now—*

Noah held up his hand and smiled. "No, Josh. I've taken advantage of you long enough. I'm twenty-three years old, and it's time."

"But, Noah," Mona whispered, "you don't have anywhere to go."

Noah raised his eyebrows. "I've got a plan. You know those little cabins for rent over by Canyon Lake?" Mona and Joshua nodded. "They've had a 'For Rent' sign up over there for weeks now. I've got some money in savings for a deposit, and most of the cabins are furnished. So I won't have to worry about furniture or anything—"

"Noah, what's gotten into you?" Mona looked lost and confused. This just wasn't like Noah at all. There he sat, his half-lidded, hungover eyes were gone, and in their place were bright, dancing, blue eyes. He was clean shaven, wearing clean clothes, and had combed his hair—and was that after-shave she could smell?

Noah laughed as he reached for Mona's hand. "Mona, darlin', I've recommitted my life to the Lord and decided to stop my drinking."

*****

Thankfully, Mona allowed Noah to take his bed and some linens, as they were the only furnishings not available at Canyon Lake Cabins. She even gave him an old set of dishes she had out in the garage. But there would be other things he'd need, which she pointed out as she watched him collect his things.

"What will you do for towels and a coffee pot, for instance?" she questioned. *How will you ever take care of yourself?* She couldn't believe he was moving out. *Even more unbelievable, he's not angry in the slightest.*

"I'm sure I can find some things at K-Mart," Noah assured with a smile.

Mona forced her tears away, got ready for church, and left with a very quiet Joshua.

Noah called Arnie and asked to borrow his pickup in order to move his things. Arnie was hung over, but he helped Noah the best he could. The temperature had dropped significantly in Rapid City since the day before, and heavy clouds loomed on the horizon as they loaded up the few boxes, bed frame, and mattress.

Noah had paid the deposit and his first month's rent on a one-bedroom cabin on Canyon Lake before ten o'clock that morning. It was a bit of a dump, but he thought he could fix it up with some hard work and serious cleaning.

The small living room contained an old, brown couch with a matching chair and some end tables. Tan curtains hung from the windows. It had an eat-in-style kitchen, complete with a stove and refrigerator. The bathroom was as small as a broom closet, but it held the basics—and that was really all he and Angel needed for now.

He sighed with contentment as he glanced out the living room windows. A mother duck guided her ducklings over the lake and through the sprinkles of snow that had started to fall. *Angel's gonna love this!*

"By the way," Arnie asked as he set down the last box, "where were you this weekend? Carrie had a great party last night."

Noah smiled as he glanced at his watch. "I'll tell you about it later," he answered as he buttoned his heavy denim jacket and ushered Arnie out of his new place. "I really gotta go somewhere right now." He locked his front door and hurried toward his motorcycle.

"Can I call you?" Arnie called out as Noah started the bike.

"I don't have a phone yet. Leave a message at Maggie's."

"Are you gonna get a phone?"

Arnie could see Noah laughing as he shrugged his shoulders and waved. Noah put on his gloves and glasses and headed into the snow that had just begun to fall.

By the time Noah got to the hotel, the visibility had been drastically reduced. He'd have to park the bike and call someone for a ride. He parked under the canopy of the hotel and turned off the engine. The snowstorm was turning into a blizzard, and his heart soared with excitement. *Angel will be stuck here for at least one more day. No one in their right mind would take off down the road in this mess.* Even though Noah realized he and Angel probably wouldn't be going anywhere, it would still be fun to sit in the lobby and talk.

He strode to the front desk where a man in a suit was writing into a ledger. "Can I help you, sir?"

"Yes. I'm looking for one of the artists staying here this weekend. Her name is Angel. Can you look up her room number?"

"Do you have a last name?" the man asked as he pulled out a thick book and opened it to the back section.

Noah shook his head. "No. But she was with a group of people that competed in some contest. One of them was a dancer."

"Oh, yes" the man acknowledged with a nod of understanding as he closed the book. "Junior Artists of America. Their chaperones were concerned about the storm, and they pulled out of here before six o'clock this morning."

Noah's happiness dissolved into despair and disbelief. "You mean they're *gone?*"

*****

Petrice and Marquette had promised to visit Sioux Falls on the day of Angel's return. Neither of them had been home in the last couple of months; and, in their lines of work, a vacation was *always* a good idea.

Petrice Caselli was a respected New York attorney. His flourishing business, however, had been more than he'd expected, leaving him with little time for a social life. His parents worried that, at the age of thirty-six, Petrice would never marry, but he had a surprise for his family.

Marquette and his beloved wife, Tara, lived between Como Lake, Italy, and Tyson's Corner, Virginia, just outside of Washington, D.C. They maintained a dual citizenship with Italy and the United States. Their security business had flourished over the last seven years, taking them all over the world. They were sought after by large corporations and governments with secret enemies. Wherever they went, Marquette and Tara Caselli were admired and respected for their ability to solve mysteries; uncover heinous, secretive plots; and even put the ledgers straight on a set of "fixed" books.

Vincenzo and Kate did not have far to travel. They loaded their small family into their new station wagon and made the hour's drive from Centerville to Sioux Falls, bringing their children and love for one another with them. Their daughter, Alyssa, was three and a half, and their son, Angelo, was two and a half.

Under Vincenzo's care and management, Reata had grown into a several-thousand-acre operation with cattle and crops. Uncle Angelo, from whom Vincenzo's son was named, would have been proud had he lived to see the progress Vincenzo consistently achieved on Reata. Beautiful Rosa was fifty-five by now, and her thick shoulder-length black hair was streaked here and there with silver. Her eyes were as black as they'd ever been and showed very little age around them. The accent with which she spoke had softened considerably since leaving Italy nearly nineteen years ago.

Guiseppi Caselli would turn fifty-nine in the fall, and he still spoke with a thick Italian accent. All of his hair had fallen out on top, and what remained on the sides had turned an extraordinary silver. He still worked long hours at Angelo's, the *ristoranti* given to him by his dear brother. Perhaps he'd retire next year, but for now, he was content to work hard, like a man should, for as long as he could.

Tillie spotted her and Ginger's families from her window in the bus. The families waited in a group at the corner of Twelfth and Main Streets, next to the school. The sun was shining in Sioux Falls; no snowstorm yet.

"They're already here," she groaned

"It's gonna be okay," Ginger said. "You don't have to tell them anything yet. Let's just get through this, and then sneak up to my house. We can call him from there." Her eyes narrowed as she gazed at the group waiting for them, and her tone changed to curiosity. "Who's the tall blonde with Patty?"

Tillie shook her head. *Who is that?* Her skin was as white as snow, her hair so blonde it glowed in the sun, and she was taller than all of them—even Marquette.

Tillie made her way out of the bus, meeting her family at the bottom of the steps. They threw their arms around her and began their ritual of kisses and greetings. Those dear brothers, all in their mid-thirties by now, were dressed nearly identical in Italian navy-blue suits. They had matching silk scarves in their breast pockets and shiny black, wing-tipped shoes on their feet. Navy felt fedoras with trim hat bands were poised perfectly atop their handsome heads. They all talked very fast and very loud and yet spoke with gentle but very well-educated accents, giving a poetic quality to everything they said. They were, perhaps, a little overwhelming to the rest of the crowd around them with their spirit, grace, and fluency. However, to each other, they were what they had always been—the most important thing in the world.

They welcomed her with happiness and tears, uncontrolled in their ethnic passion, embracing her in the only way they knew how. It made her smile with relief to be back with them. But for the very first time, a part of her heart no longer belonged exclusively to them.

"Auntie Tillie!" Tillie felt little arms around her legs and stooped to embrace her niece and nephew. She laughed at them and their excitement to see her.

"Did you bring us a present?" Alyssa's tiny voice questioned, her black eyes wide with excitement. She looked so much like her mother, Kate.

Tillie laughed again. "Of course I did." Little Angelo clapped his pudgy hands, and Tillie hugged them again. "They're in my suitcase. We can get them out when we get over to Nonna's house." She gave them each a kiss and stood up.

Vincenzo embraced his little sister and held her close one more time. Tillie caught the wonderful aroma of pipe tobacco. Papa was always after him to stop puffing on the thing, but it gave Vincenzo a grace and style all his own.

Kate embraced her with a smile and a kiss, whispering into her ear, "Angel, you spoil my babies!"

Tillie laughed and kissed Kate's cheek, smelling the familiar soft perfume that always reminded her of when she was very small. Kate and Vincenzo's romance had blossomed before Tillie was even born. In fact, Tillie could not remember a time when the dark-eyed Kate wasn't with them. Tillie had many wonderful memories of stories told on Kate's lap and walks between Vincenzo and Kate on warm summer evenings. There were trips to the DQ and french fries at the Barrel, weekends on Reata to visit the baby pigs, and buggy rides behind Old Platinum into the apple orchard.

Marquette and Tara caught her in their arms, embracing her at the same time. "My dear Angel," Marquette said as his dark eyes glistened with tears of joy. "You have safely returned. We were so worried when we heard about the storm." He kissed each of her cheeks, accidentally brushing his long ponytail into Tillie eyes. She smiled. Papa had begged him to cut that thing off for years, but Marquette would only threaten to grow it longer. He was the most handsome of the Caselli sons, and the elegant, black tail gave him a very exotic and foreign look.

"Precious girl," Tara exclaimed. She kissed Tillie and looked into her eyes with a sudden frown. She leaned close to Tillie and whispered, "You look tired."

Tara was the most gentle and gracious creature Tillie had ever met. She was Italian, like the rest of Tillie's family, and she spoke with the same soft accent. Her dark, wavy hair fell soft upon her shoulders, and her round, black eyes lit up her beautiful face with joy and contentment.

"They got us up at five a.m.," Tillie said as she glanced over Tara's shoulder, spying the tall stranger with Petrice.

"My little Angel," Petrice greeted. He took his little sister into his arms, giving her a soft kiss on the top of her head. "There is someone I want you to meet."

Tillie looked into Petrice's eyes and saw an unfamiliar sparkle. Everything else about him was the same—his dark hair softly grayed at the temples, the friendly smile, the warm embrace. Yet when she looked into his eyes, she saw something new.

He gestured to the beautiful, tall blonde standing beside him, and Tillie let her eyes glance her way. She was a good head taller than Petrice and very thin. *Ma`ma's gonna want to get some noodles into this woman right away.* Her hair was the most beautiful hair Tillie had ever seen, and it hung perfectly behaved on the woman's shoulders—unlike the wild curls atop Tillie's head that refused to be tamed. Her eyes were an exquisite blue, and they sparkled with excitement when she looked at Petrice.

Tillie heard Petrice say something in Italian, a language only Tillie did not speak. To her surprise, the woman responded in *his* language, almost in an admonishing tone. The other brothers and Tillie's parents laughed.

"I am sorry," Petrice chuckled. "This is Elaine, but you may call her Ellie. She is my wife—"

"Your wife!" Tillie exclaimed, extending her hand in greeting. She couldn't help but notice how her parents were glowing on the sidelines.

Elaine took Tillie's hand. "It's nice to meet you," she said, her English perfect.

Tillie nodded, unable to take her eyes off of the woman. *American.* "You're…" She hesitated. "You're so…" Tillie was clearly taken off guard, and her family laughed around her. "You're beautiful."

"Thank you, my dear," Elaine responded with a smile.

Tillie stood silent and nodded as she stared into Elaine's deep blue eyes. *Patty loves a woman with blue eyes.*

Tillie's parents held her then, pretending an enthusiastic greeting, but they saw the disappointment in her eyes. Petrice was Tillie's favorite.

Guiseppi felt a measure of pity for the child. He held her close as he whispered, "He will still love you." He patted the top of her head and gave her a kiss.

Tillie forced away her tears. She pretended to be pleased about Petrice's new wife, but inside she couldn't believe he'd done such a thing. *How can he go off and get married without telling any of us? How can he go off and get married to someone we don't even know? What's wrong with him?*

They helped her get her things together and stopped to cheer when they saw the blue ribbons on her paintings.

"We are having a party this day!" Guiseppi shouted with exuberance. "There is a meal waiting for us at Angelo's!" He threw his arms into the air and then around Rosa. "Come, everyone, and celebrate with us, for we have much to be thankful for!"

Tillie's brothers cheered, and Marquette and Vincenzo slapped Petrice on his back. It was how they had celebrated for years.

During the celebration at Angelo's, the story of how Petrice met Elaine unfolded with all of the eloquence and dignity characteristic of Petrice. He claimed he fell in love with her the moment she walked into his New York office. Elaine, herself, admitted she'd been quite swept off of her feet by the mannerly Italian and just couldn't resist his proposal. This resulted in a small wedding at the office of the Justice of the Peace on the day before their arrival in Sioux Falls.

And Elaine was quite a catch, according to Guiseppi and Rosa, who were obviously as enamored with her as Petrice. She was a full ten years younger than Petrice, and she not only spoke Italian fluently, but Spanish and French as well. She already had her own business designing and modeling clothing. She'd also traveled the world over with her late father, who'd been a General in the United States Air Force, and she shared many wonderful stories about that.

Guiseppi and Rosa glowed when Elaine spoke. They gave her the most admiring and approving looks, as they bestowed blessings upon blessings with just their eyes.

Tillie watched her parents, and the resentment stormed around inside of her. She felt herself wanting to frown but forced it away. She had found someone too. Would they be as approving if she had drug Noah home on the bus? She glared at Petrice. *Traitor.*

"How's it goin' over here?" Ginger whispered beside Tillie, making her jump. She hadn't even noticed Ginger come over.

Tillie looked at Ginger, rolled her eyes, and grumbled, "She's just *fabulous*. She speaks three different languages, not including English, and she's seen every country on the planet, including Communist China, which she traveled to with her father, who was none other than special envoy to President Nixon. No one *ever* has been this fabulous."

Ginger giggled. "When are we gonna get out of here? We gotta get over to my place and call Noah."

Tillie sighed, her face relaxed, and she afforded Ginger a small smile. "I suppose as soon as the 'fan fest' is over." She frowned in Elaine's direction, narrowed her eyes, and glared at the pretty lady when no one was looking. "Jeez. This was supposed to be *our* party. But good ol' Ellie shows up and steals the show."

*****

Arnie met Noah at Maggie's, where they drove Noah's bike up a ramp and into the bed of the pickup. The streets were too slippery to drive on, and visibility was at zero. Maggie hadn't opened her bar today. She, like the rest of the town, was at home, waiting out the storm.

"What's with you, man?" Arnie asked as he got into the pickup with Noah and turned up the heater. "Why would anybody strike out in the middle of a blizzard on a bike?"

Noah shook his head and looked away from Arnie and out the passenger window. "Just take me home, to my new place."

Arnie sighed and put the truck into drive. "Whatever you say, man."

Traffic had piled up all over town behind accidents and blocked roads, and it took a while for Arnie's truck to make it safely to Canyon Lake. They unloaded Noah's bike next to the cabin and placed a tarp over it.

"Come on, Noah," Arnie said with a smile as Noah went up the steps and put his key into the lock. "Let's go see Theo. He's got some good stuff this weekend."

Noah shook his head. "You go ahead. I gotta hang on to my money."

Arnie frowned. *That* wasn't like Noah at all. Noah was the life of the party, and he'd been missing all weekend. Now he was turning down an opportunity to party?

"What's your problem, Noah? Don'tcha wannna get high?"

Noah unlocked the door and turned to look at Arnie. He smiled a little and shook his head. "I don't want to do that anymore. But you have a good time." And with that Noah stepped inside of his little cabin and closed the door behind him.

*****

The sun had slowly disappeared, and the clouds rolled in, delivering the predicted blizzard to Sioux Falls by late afternoon. The weather service calculated the entire state would be paralyzed with blizzard conditions by early evening. As a result, Petrice and Elaine caught the next flight back to New York. Vincenzo left immediately, upset with the second severe spring blizzard in a period of less than two months. He had to meet with his ranch hands and again collect whatever cattle they could. Marquette and Tara, on the other hand, were content to stay for a few more days, as they did not have to be anywhere until the end of the week.

Guiseppi started a fire in the living room to take the chill out of the house, pausing to listen to Rosa humming a tune in the kitchen.

Marquette and Tara sat on the living room floor as they went through a file, making highlights and jotting down notes.

Guiseppi frowned as he watched them. "And where will your adventures take you *this* week?" he asked in Italian, for they always spoke in their first language when Tillie was not with them.

Tara looked up at Guiseppi and smiled. "We have gotten a tip from the Swiss. They believe to have had contact with a Ponerello in Zurich."

"You are *still* chasing those fiends?"

Tara nodded, and Marquette laughed.

"Have you not chased them since 1968?" Guiseppi remembered the old case well. Since 1955, Italian and Sicilian authorities had pursued the most notorious Mafia family Sicily had ever known: The Ponerello Family. Marquette and his former associate, John Peters, had to break off their chase of additional Ponerellos after capturing thirty-eight of the family members in Ustica in August of 1968. In the end, the Ponerellos had attempted to shoot their way free but could not escape.

A small freighter was used to ship them all back to Sicily, where they were to be jailed while awaiting trial. Still missing were fifty loose diamonds allegedly heisted by the Ponerellos from a jeweler in Palermo, Sicily. As the freighter began its departure from Ustica, Salvatore Ponerello Jr. escaped his bonds and threw himself upon the rocks near the shoreline. Even though a body was never recovered, it was assumed he died. Salvatore's father cursed Marquette that day and promised revenge upon him and his family for years to come.

Salvatore's curse didn't take, because it was at that same moment Marquette discovered the location of his beloved Tara and began a search for her in the opposite direction. She'd been "missing" for twelve years, and Marquette and John abandoned the Ponerello case in order to seek her out. As a result, they lost the trail of the missing

Ponerellos. As far as they knew, two of the Ponerellos had escaped the family in 1964 and were still alive somewhere in Europe.

Marquette sighed as he looked into his notes. "They will be tough to catch at this point, but we must try."

"I will pray for you." Guiseppi turned for the steps and made his way upstairs.

Tillie had retreated to her bedroom and hadn't had the chance to get away to Ginger's house. With the snowstorm bearing down upon them, she wouldn't get up there until tomorrow, *at the earliest.* She flung her suitcase upon her bed, just ready to open it and get the phone number out of her jeans when her father knocked on the door.

"Angel," he said, and she could tell he was smiling by the tone in his voice. "Can Papa come in?"

"Come in."

Guiseppi opened the door and gave her a smile. He reached for the suitcase and set in on the floor, taking a seat on the bed and patting the place next to him. She sighed and took a seat beside him.

"Tell me about your time in Rapid City." He put his arm around her, giving her a tender embrace.

"It was good," she answered as she looked at the floor.

"Is there something you need to be telling your Papa?" he questioned. Tillie's guilt made her stomach feel like she was going over a hill really fast. *What's he talking about? Does he know? Did Ginger tell? Who told?*

Tillie shrugged, and it made Guiseppi laugh. "You are upset with Patty."

"How could he do that to us, Papa?" she grumbled.

"Your brother is thirty-six years old. Perhaps he thought it best not to wait any longer."

"But she's a *stranger*, Papa. He should have brought her home *first.*"

Guiseppi nodded. "Yes, he should have brought her home first, but he did not. It does not mean he loves us any less. Your brother is a man, Angel, and men must make their own decisions. This was his decision to make, *not ours.*"

Tillie pouted, and it made Guiseppi chuckle.

"No, my little Angel. Do not make a decision to resent your brother. It is just that he spoiled you so terribly."

"He didn't spoil me."

"Oh, but he did." Guiseppi sighed and slowly stood up. He smiled down at his pretty daughter and said, "You pray about this, my little Angel. The Lord will reveal to you where your heart needs to be."

Tillie nodded obediently, and her father left the room.

*****

Tillie had fallen asleep on her bed, and when she woke up, she smelled coffee brewing. She saw the brightness shining through her bedroom window. *Is it morning already?* She was still in her clothes from the day before and realized her family must have let her sleep late. She got off the bed and went to the window, unable to see across the street because of the blizzard's whiteout. *Wow. There's definitely no school today. All too easy. I'll get up to Ginger's and call him.*

She opened her bedroom door and went down the hall. The house was quiet except for the sound of the washing machine in the basement. She descended the steps as she looked around for someone and saw Tara coming from the kitchen with a full cup of coffee. Tara smiled and turned around, heading back into the kitchen.

"I will pour you a cup, and we can have coffee together," she offered. Tillie followed her into the kitchen, where Tara had already gotten a cup and filled it.

"Papa lit us a wonderful fire this morning," Tara said, handing Tillie her cup. "Let us visit there." And with that, she headed back to the living room, curled up on the rug near the fireplace, and set her cup on the hearth.

Tillie sat down next to her and reached for the afghan on Ma`ma's chair. "Man, it's cold in here," she said with a shiver. "Where is everybody?"

"Ma`ma is doing some laundry, and Papa and Marquette have gone to check the restaurant."

"*In this?* I couldn't even see across the street."

Tara agreed, "I know. I told Marquette they should not go, but Papa insisted. He is worried about the old pipes, you know." She noticed the downcast look in Tillie's expression and reached for one of Tillie's hands. "We were so surprised. But she seems like a lovely girl."

Tillie feigned a smile as she looked into Tara's eyes.

Tara saw the unusual lack of sparkle in Tillie's black eyes. Her job involved detailed perceptions, something she'd learned well over the years. "Angel, he still loves you." She took a deep breath. "Is there something else?"

Tillie shrugged and looked away from her sister-in-law, but Tara followed Tillie's eyes.

"What in the world is going on?" Tara questioned with a frown.

Tillie sighed and hesitantly answered, "Well, it's *really* screwed up right now, but I think it'll be okay. At least Ginger says it's gonna be okay."

Tara shook her head as she reached for her coffee. "It must be a boy."

Tillie's eyes opened wide with surprise. "But *please* don't tell Marquette. He blabs *everything* to Ma`ma."

"Perhaps you should be telling Ma`ma."

"No. Now promise me, Tara."

"First tell me about the boy."

Tillie looked into the fire. "His name is Noah, and he's not a boy. He's a *man*." She looked at Tara in time to see her swallow very hard and her eyes open wide with surprise. She whispered, "He asked me to marry him."

Tara gasped. "You are not even old enough to date. *Angel!* What will Papa say?"

Tillie shook her head. "I didn't give him my *real* name, but I have his number upstairs. I'm gonna call him from Ginger's this afternoon. I'm not gonna tell Ma`ma and Papa until after I turn eighteen."

Tara's round mouth hung open and her eyes were big and round. "Angel, I have so many questions. I do not even know where to begin. Where did you meet this man?"

"In Rapid City. Tara, do you believe in love at first sight?"

"Well, *sometimes*. But love at first sight is also as heartbreaking as it is passionate. It is not a wise thing to allow yourself to fall in such a way."

"But it was an accident. He was just so wonderful."

Tara shook her head. "No, Angel. Love is *never* an accident. It is a *choice*."

Tillie shrugged. "Well, then, I *choose* to love Noah, and I'm gonna marry him when I turn eighteen. I feel like I've known him my entire life."

Tara's pretty face was a mixture of astonishment and horror, but she managed to whisper, "But what about Alex? Your parents think—"

"I was a little kid, and I carried on far too long about Alex. Somebody should've straightened me out on that a *long time ago*—"

"There you are!" Rosa exclaimed.

Tara and Tillie jumped in surprise and turned their heads as Rosa came into the living room with a basket of folded laundry.

"I hope you are all rested up," she said as she set down her basket. She stooped beside Tillie to kiss her head and took a seat on the chair close by. "It is so good to have you back home. We missed you."

Tillie smiled. "It's great to be home, Ma`ma."

"I have managed to get your clothes washed," Rosa continued. "They smelled so of pine."

"My clothes?" Tillie looked at the basket of folded laundry beside her mother.

"Oh, goodness!" Rosa laughed. "I do not know what you got into out there, young lady, but your jeans smelled so of pine. I had to wash them *twice!*"

Tillie thought she might faint as she stared at the folded pair of jeans at the top of her mother's laundry basket. She reached for the clothing and put her hand into the pocket, pulling out the tiniest handful of shredded, white napkin.

"What is that?" Rosa asked.

Tillie stared into the few shreds that lay in her hand. "Nothing, Ma`ma."

Chapter 5

"Why on earth did you put it in your pocket?" Ginger whispered over the phone. "Talk about leaving incriminating evidence just lying around. You really need to keep better track of your stuff."

"I just wasn't thinking, that's all. Now what am I gonna do?" Tillie whimpered.

Ginger snorted. "You're totally up a creek." She suddenly gasped, "I know! As soon as your folks will let you, come up here. We'll call information for Maggie May's number and leave him a message there."

Tillie's broken heart was relieved with the idea. "Okay, but I doubt Ma`ma will allow me to come up before noon. It's still really stormy, and Papa and Marquette aren't back yet."

"That's okay. We've got all day. He probably won't be expecting a call for a while anyway."

*****

Vincenzo and Guiseppi had built Tillie a developing lab in the basement two years ago. After her telephone conversation with Ginger, she went down to develop her Black Hills photos. Each one must turn out perfectly so she'd have a flawless memory of his face.

Tillie smiled as she looked into the developing face of Noah near Mt. Rushmore. "You're awesome," she whispered.

She heard a soft knock at the door and Tara's whisper, "It is me, Angel. May I come in?"

Tillie opened the door, and Tara stepped into the darkroom. When Tara's eyes adjusted to the darkness, she saw the photos of the young man hanging above Tillie's pans.

"Is that him?"

Tillie nodded.

"He is very handsome, Angel." Tara took a breath and looked at Tillie. "We have been going through a certain file, and I noticed something you might be interested in…" She hesitated. "Shortly after Marquette and I are finished in Zurich, we must go to New Castle, Wyoming, and Rapid City…Angel, perhaps you should come with us, if Papa and Ma`ma will allow it, that is."

Tillie's eyes filled with excitement and anticipation. "Oh, Tara, do you think they will?"

Tara frowned, knowing she shouldn't be conspiring in this way with Angel. However, the idea of marriage at such a young age shouldn't be taken lightly. Perhaps if Angel had the chance to visit with the young man again, she might change her mind.

"If we do not tell Papa and Ma`ma of your true purpose, they will allow it." Tara felt the sting of guilt to deceive her husband as she cleared her throat to continue, "And we will not be sharing these details with Marquette, because if this does not work out, we will not mention it to anyone ever again."

Tillie nodded eagerly and threw her arms around Tara. "Oh, thank you, Tara! But I'm positive everything will be great!"

*****

Petrice held his new wife in his arms and swung her around in a circle. They'd been looking at new apartments all day long and finally found exactly what they needed.

"I love this place," Elaine gasped as she held Petrice around his shoulders and kissed him. "It's going to be perfect."

Their new apartment was located on Park Avenue, on the uppermost floor of a very chic complex. Three large bedrooms with a bathroom in each, a large living area for entertaining, and a gourmet kitchen. Elaine loved to cook and entertain. The view from their living room window was the majestic New York City skyline, and Petrice knew he'd impress his family with the snapshots he was about to send home.

"Do you think your family will like it?" Elaine asked as she took Petrice by the hand and walked to the window overlooking the city.

"Almost as much as they love you." He smiled into her eyes, raised her hand, and gave it a gentle kiss.

Elaine held her breath and gazed into her new husband's eyes. She'd found the most romantic man in the world. "But I wonder if they will be as delighted with me when they find out you're not coming to your sister's graduation."

"They will just have to understand, Ellie—"

"But your little sister seemed so upset already. You know we could reschedule the trip," she persisted sweetly.

Petrice smiled and shook his head. "No. I have waited thirty-six years for a wife, and it is my duty and blessing to take care of you. We will go ahead with our trip." He sighed with contentment as he gazed past the Twin Towers in the distance. "And it will be so good to see *Italia* again."

*****

Marquette and Guiseppi returned home before noon, and Marquette went upstairs to change into something more comfortable. Tara followed him up to their room, closing the door behind them.

"I notice we will be passing through Rapid City, South Dakota, in a few weeks," Tara said.

"We are not *passing through*," he said as he hunted through the suitcase for a sweater. "I have been thinking of flying directly into New Castle. They have a small airport, and I have been able to hire a charter from Minneapolis."

Tara was quiet, and Marquette saw the expression of dismay on her face. "Why?" he asked, as he finally found a sweater, put it down on the bed, and removed his shirt.

Tara shrugged. "Angel has expressed some interest in going back to Rapid City."

Marquette pulled the heavy sweater over his head and sat down on the bed to look at Tara. "But she just returned. Why does she want to go back already?"

"She loved it there. And it would certainly be fun to have her along. She has never gone on a trip with us before."

Marquette frowned. "And what will she do with herself once we have her there? We have an important meeting with John Peters, and she *cannot* simply tag along."

"She can shop or sketch," Tara answered.

Marquette sighed and hesitantly agreed, "I suppose. But at the first sign of danger, she will be put onto a plane and sent home. These people we are following are quite dangerous."

"Of course," Tara agreed.

Their conversation was cut short when a soft knock was heard on the door. "Ma`ma has lunch ready," Guiseppi announced from the other side.

"We will be right down, Papa," Marquette answered.

*****

Guiseppi and Rosa gave their permission for Tillie to accompany Marquette and Tara to western South Dakota. Marquette would

63

rearrange his own plans and charter a plane from Sioux Falls that would take them directly to Rapid City and on to New Castle.

Tillie was beside herself with excitement as she bundled up and made a brisk walk through the whiteout still raging through Sioux Falls. She had to make it to Ginger's to place the call, and Ginger had an *excellent* plan.

Ginger's father had had a road construction team working in Rapid City for several months now. When the number showed up on the long-distance part of the phone bill, Ginger theorized her parents would assume the call was made to one of the construction crew. Ginger assured Tillie that her parents would not even check the number.

First they dialed information, whispered the name of Maggie May's into the phone, and jotted down the number.

"Okay," Ginger breathed as she peeked out of the narrowly opened door of her bedroom. "This is the big one. I'll watch for Mom, and you make the call. But hurry."

Tillie giggled and began to dial.

*****

Arnie came to Noah's cabin that afternoon. The snowstorm had started to clear off in Rapid City, and he'd heard Maggie's was opening. He begged Noah to come with him, and Noah protested, citing his new financial obligations toward rent being the reason. However, Arnie offered to buy Noah a few cold ones, and Noah reluctantly went along.

Maggie laughed when Noah stepped up to the bar and ordered a straight Coca-Cola. She opened the bottle and set it down on a cocktail napkin in front of him.

"Well, you sure *look* good," she said as she admired the handsome young man with the clean-shaven face and clear eyes.

Noah took a gulp of the soda. He glanced over at his buddies, who were already drunk in a booth not far from him. "What a bunch of idiots. Maggie, did I *really* act like that?"

Maggie guffawed. "You were their ring leader!" She shook her head. "And that was only last week. Is this big change in you all because of that girl?"

Noah blushed with a smile. "I *love* her, Maggie. I don't know what else to say. I asked her to marry me, and I want to be with her always."

Maggie's mouth dropped open. "Do you think you know her well enough?"

"I feel like I've known her all of my life—" He was interrupted by the ringing of the telephone beneath Maggie's bar.

"Hold that thought." Maggie winked and reached for the telephone. "Maggie May's."

Tillie excitedly took a breath and glanced at Ginger who was keeping watch at the bedroom door.

"Hello," she said in a small and shy voice. "I was wondering if I could leave a message for someone."

"What kind of a message?" Maggie asked gruffly.

"A message for my…" Tillie hesitated and bit her lip. She looked to Ginger, who rolled her eyes.

"Say Noah's name!" Ginger whispered. "And hurry up before someone catches us!"

Tillie cleared her throat. "The message is for Noah—"

"Who is this?" Maggie sounded irritated.

"Um…this is…um…this is Angel."

Maggie nearly dropped the phone. She handed the receiver to Noah. "It's for you, and you're *never* gonna guess who it is."

Noah frowned. "Hello?"

"Noah?" Tillie's heart began to pound in her ears, and she noticed the color draining from Ginger's face.

"Is it him?" Ginger whispered.

Tillie nodded. "It's me. Angel."

"Angel!" Noah smiled at Maggie. "It's Angel. Why didn't you call me?"

"Oh, my goodness," Tillie giggled nervously. "You'll never believe what I've been through. First I forgot the number in my jeans and packed them onto the bus. Then, after I got home, Ma`ma washed my jeans…*twice!* But then my friend Ginger called information, and we got Maggie's number. We were just gonna leave a message. I can't believe you were there!" She paused. "You're not drinking are you?"

Noah laughed out loud. "I'm having a Coke. I rented one of those cabins yesterday that I was telling you about."

"He rented the cabin," Tillie whispered to Ginger.

Ginger nodded and whispered, "Hurry! Tell him when you're coming out there."

"I have to hurry. I wanted you to know my brother and his wife are bringing me to Rapid City the weekend after next. Will you be around?"

"Yes," Noah answered, and in his tone Tillie could hear him smiling.

"I have so many things to tell you—"

"Here comes Mom!" Ginger whispered.

"I have to go," Tillie said.

"I'll be right here," Noah promised. "I love you, Angel."

Tillie smiled as she watched Ginger's eyes get even bigger. *Mrs. Engleson must be close.* "I love you too," she whispered into the phone, quickly hanging up before Mrs. Engleson walked past the bedroom door.

Noah sighed with a smile and handed the phone to Maggie. "She loves me, Maggie May."

Maggie frowned, turning her gaze to the mysterious portrait hanging at her bar and then back at Noah. *This is so weird...*

*****

Tillie threw her heart and soul into her sketches and paintings, creating beautiful portraits of Noah and their time together in the Black Hills. The watercolors and acrylics she chose for these masterpieces were the richest, most-intense colors she'd ever used. She kept the paintings on easels in her room, hidden under sheets until the timing was perfect.

The watercolor portrait was of Noah as he stood beside Bridal Veil Falls. The colors she chose were deep grays and blues for the waterfall and shades of tan and brown with traces of green in the budding trees. She'd managed to capture the exact likeness of Noah's dancing expression as he smiled into her eyes.

The acrylic was done to match the black-and-white photograph she'd taken of him at Mt. Rushmore. Beautiful brush strokes in white, black, and gray carved out the faces of the majestic monument behind Noah. Noah's vest-and-jeans attire made him look as if he'd just stepped off the mountain after a hard day's work of carving. The painting mirrored her innermost spirit, resulting in her finest work.

*****

On the other side of the globe, a very distressed Tara paced along her marble veranda overlooking the shores of Como Lake. The sun wasn't up yet, but she couldn't sleep anymore.

What on earth has gotten into me? Why am I even doing this? What was I thinking when I helped Marquette to persuade his parents to allow the little waif to come along?

Tara sighed as she dropped into a comfortable lounger, and her gaze fell to the moonlit peaceful waters. Her memories drifted back to a time when her own love life was in shambles. She was without her beloved Marquette, separated by the unfortunate circumstances of someone else's deception.

It was 1964, and she'd refused Luigi Andreotti's proposal of marriage. He, in return, and with great vengeance, refused to divulge the location of Marquette Caselli. Luigi *knew* she could only love Marquette, but he attempted to force her into keeping an old promise made during the uncertain heat of a World War II battle. For four long years, Luigi attended the university and endeavored to convince her at every turn that it was *he*, not a simple farm boy, promised to her in marriage. He was the one, he tried to assure her, to whom she belonged. Further, she would do well to honor her father's memory and submit to the marriage.

However, Tara wasn't in love with Luigi, nor had she ever been. Marquette was the one who belonged in her heart and in her life. Luigi left America, a bitter and vengeful thief, attempting to steal whatever happiness she may have had with Marquette by hiding her very existence from the only man she ever loved.

God had watched over Tara and blessed her abundantly for being true to her heart and waiting for Marquette. It was God Himself who revealed to Marquette where she waited and brought him to her in His own time.

Father, why am I so troubled? I know that You plan our course..."Father, have mercy on us. I have made these deceitful plans with Angel, and I fear for her heart."

*****

It had been two weeks, and Noah Hansen hadn't had a drink. He couldn't believe how easy it was to get up in the mornings, and he was surprised at his lifted mood. For years he'd awakened with headaches and an ugly humor. He used to snap at his coworkers, cussing at the drop of a hat. That old behavior had no place in his life anymore, and everyone noticed.

He cut off his long hair, joined Alcoholics Anonymous, and promised Joshua he'd attend church services regularly. The changes happened so quickly in Noah that his friends had little time to figure out what was going on before it was suddenly over with. He didn't go drinking, partying, or out with Carrie anymore. He only went to see Maggie, have a Coke, and go over his plans for Angel's coming weekend.

He signed up for evening classes at Rapid City Central High School in order to study for his GED, and he'd talked to an administrator about the GI Bill. Noah had gotten information on the building trades class offered at Western Dakota Vocational-Technical School.

He scrubbed his little cabin from top to bottom and purchased a coffee maker at K-Mart, along with some pretty, pink towels for the bathroom for Angel. Maggie gave him one of the photographs Estelle had taken of him with Angel. He had it framed and displayed it on one of the end tables in his living room. In the photo, they were looking into each other's eyes and smiling, and it made Noah's heart soar every time he looked at it.

Joshua and Mona were pleasantly surprised at the changes in Noah, especially when he came over after work nearly every day to help Joshua with the spring cleanup in the yard and in the orchard. The heavy, spring snow had melted as quickly as it had fallen, and Joshua's yard was in need of care.

It was Friday night and the day was unseasonably warm, prompting Joshua to start his grill out back and cook up some hamburgers for Mona and Noah. Joshua kept shaking his head and chuckling every time he looked at Noah, who sat on the back step of the house and watched him barbecue. Looking at Noah was like looking at a different person, and Joshua couldn't keep the delighted smile from his expression.

"What?" Noah asked.

"I just can't get over it" Joshua shook his head.

"What?"

"You. You cut all your hair off. You look great. What's *with* you lately?"

Noah shrugged and gave Joshua a sly wink. "Maybe I got a secret."

Joshua saw Noah smile with contentment. He sighed and looked back at his grill. "And you quit drinking. I can hardly believe that." His eyes opened wide, and he stared at Noah with surprise. "It's a *girl*, isn't it?"

Noah laughed. "Her name is Angel, and I love her. She's wonderful."

Joshua nodded, surprised with Noah's disclosure. Noah had been hanging out with a girl by the name of "Carrie," whom Joshua knew very well was "easy" and could get Noah illegal drugs if he wanted them. "Does this mean things are over with Carrie?"

"This girl is *so* different from Carrie, or any other girl for that matter. She's a *nice* girl, Josh. She doesn't believe in getting drunk, and she's a Christian. She's so beautiful. You won't believe it when you see her."

"Are we gonna meet her soon?" Joshua asked.

"Tomorrow. I'll bring her over tomorrow. Oh, and Josh, there's one more thing…" He hesitated, and Joshua looked up from his burgers to see another sly but excited expression creeping out of Noah's happy eyes.

"What is it, Noah?"

"I'm goin' back to school."

Joshua's mouth fell open with surprise. "She must be *some girl*."

"She's the one, Josh."

*****

Rosa hummed an old tune she'd learned from her own ma`ma while she dusted the rooms on the main floor and then worked her way up the winding banister, into the upstairs. The day had warmed in Sioux Falls, and she opened windows along the way to let in the freshness.

As always, the room Marquette and Tara had stayed in the night before was neat as a pin. They were such considerate houseguests. But it did need a good dusting, and Rosa bustled along as she sang her tune, sending prayers to God whenever she thought of them. It took a little while for Rosa to dust her way through the upstairs, singing and praying, but at last she'd made it to the room at the end of the hall— Angel's room. Rosa walked through her daughter's room, opening the blinds and the window, and looked around. It was what Tillie called her "organized mess," and only she knew where to find everything. Rosa slowly shook her head. Well, at least the child had made her bed before they left.

Tillie had two separate easels that were under cover, which seemed unusual to Rosa. Tillie also had a drawing table in her room, and there were several sketches left lying on the top. Rosa took a curious peek at the exposed projects and frowned. *I don't recognize that man…*

She felt the hair on the back of her neck begin to prickle as she raised her feather duster and started for the tall bureau. The bureau was higher than Rosa, and she could barely reach the top with her duster. As she began to brush the surface, she disturbed an unseen stack of photos. Startled, Rosa pulled her feather duster from the bureau, and the photos cascaded to her feet.

"Oh, dear," she muttered as she stooped to pick up the mess. As she began to scoop them up, she gasped.

She stepped back to the drawing table and looked through the sketches. *What! The same man!* Rosa looked to the covered easels and without hesitation removed one of the sheets to reveal an incredible watercolor of the same man. He stood beside a rocky waterfall, and the colors were done in the richest shades of blues and grays Rosa had ever seen. This was Angel's best work *ever*—far more lovely and elegant than even *Obedience*.

Rosa glanced at the bottom of the portrait and saw the words "The Perfect Knight." She gasped again, accidentally dropping the photos. When she stooped to pick them up again, she noticed writing on the back of the photos.

"Me and Noah at Maggie's," she read aloud, flipping the photo over to reveal Tillie standing beside a very handsome young man at the front of a—*Is that a bar?* Rosa thought she might faint. She flipped the photo over again and read the words, stopping for some reason on Noah's name.

"Noah," she said. Rosa swallowed and felt her knees go weak as old recollections and stories paraded themselves like flashing lights in the back of her memories. She slumped onto Tillie's bed and went through all of the photos in her hand. *The bar, the motorcycle, the long hair…*

Rosa's breath became short as she reached for the phone beside Tillie's bed and dialed Frances Martin's number. Frances had been Rosa's dearest friend since 1956, when the Casellis came to America. It was her husband, James, and his eldest son, Sam, who met them in New York when their ship arrived, helping the Casellis to travel to Sioux Falls by way of a long train ride. It was her daughter, Kate, who had married Rosa's son Vincenzo, and she'd always hoped their youngest son, Alex, would marry Angel. They'd lived just down the street from one another for nearly twenty years and had shared many things.

Rosa swallowed hard to compose herself. She put a purposeful smile into her tone before the line stopped ringing and Frances picked up on the other end.

"Frances?" Rosa greeted sweetly.

"Hello, Rosa. What are you up to today?"

"Well," Rosa began as she maintained her deceptive calm, "I was praying today and thought of Noah. You know, the boy your brother has told us so much about."

"Oh, yes, how long have you prayed for him now?"

"Since Christmas of 1960," Rosa answered, forcing her breathing to be normal. "But I was wondering…do you have a photo of the boy? It would certainly be nice for me to know what he looks like."

"As a matter of fact, Mac *did* bring some photos from out West on his last visit. He's been friends with Noah's brother for years, you know."

"Yes, I understood that."

"Tell you what," Frances said, "why don't you brew us up a pot of tea, and I'll see what I can find and bring it down."

Rosa's heart flooded with expectation. "Okay, thank you, Frances. I will see you soon." She hung up and stared at the photos in her hand. Over the last fifteen years they'd heard horrific stories about Noah from Frances' brother, Mac, who lived in Rapid City and managed the Martins' law office there. He'd been a dear friend to Joshua Hansen, the boy's brother, since the accidental death of their parents in 1956.

Rosa frowned and whispered, "And if you *are* the same boy, may God have mercy on your soul."

*****

Marquette and Tara's room at the hotel in Rapid City had two full-size beds, while Tillie's room had one giant, king-size bed. Tillie thought it was strange when Marquette had sent her to the room with the one bed, but as she watched them unload their files, his reasons became clear. He needed the extra bed for desk space. He and Tara systematically spread their files on the extra bed and onto the table nearby, checking details here and there and taking notes. The two of them were fascinating to watch, and Tillie smiled. *It's just like "The Rockford Files"!*

Soon Marquette began making telephone calls and asked for a man named John Peters. He seemed to become very agitated during the last conversation and suddenly he said, "No." He turned around when he saw Tillie in the room. That was her signal to move along; her mysterious brother was at it again. She went back into her adjoining room and closed the door so Marquette could finish his conversation in private. She wanted to check Maggie's parking lot anyway. She slipped out of the adjoining room, down the hall, and into the lobby of the hotel. From the entrance of the lobby, Tillie could see all of Maggie's parking lot. No motorcycle yet. She sighed and made her way back to her room.

*****

Rosa's tea kettle whistled almost the moment Frances rang the front door bell. Rosa put on her best smile and hurried to the door, eager to let Frances in and take a good look at that photo. She led Frances to a chair by the kitchen table, noticing the white envelope she carried with her, which she laid next to her place at the table.

Rosa wanted to grab it and tear it open, *knowing* it would reveal the dirty blackguard conspiring to steal Angel's innocence. Nonetheless, she kept her calm, gracefully placed her tea tray on the kitchen table, and took a seat across from Frances.

Frances was in a very chatty mood that day, and it seemed she'd forgotten why she came to Rosa's house. Rosa didn't want to draw

Frances' attention to her odd request, so she didn't ask if the photo was, indeed, enclosed in the white envelope. Instead, she visited with Frances for an hour before Frances announced she had a hair appointment and needed to leave.

"Oh," Frances said as she stepped out the door and onto the porch, "your photo is in that envelope."

"Oh, thank you," Rosa replied graciously. "Have a good day, Frances."

"You, too, Rosa," and with that, Frances turned and hurried away.

Rosa slammed the door and locked it. She ran all the way back to the kitchen where she ripped open the white envelope, as she'd fantasized she would do for the last hour, and pulled out the photograph. She gasped as she sat down on the chair and stared into the familiar face.

"Noah Hansen, you *wretched devil!* And just think, I actually prayed for you to make something of yourself. You will *not* have my Angel!"

*****

"I will not take my Tara with me," Marquette insisted into the phone. "No, John. I will go alone. If the beast is there, then one of us will see him tonight."

As Tara listened to Marquette's side of the conversation, she got the impression John Peters needed to be in two places at once tonight. If he could get Marquette to take one of the leads, they could then meet and compare notes tomorrow at New Castle.

Marquette exchanged a few more words, hung up the phone, and turned to face Tara, who sat on the bed with a very quizzical expression on her face.

"You will not take me where?"

Marquette frowned and tugged at his necktie, which only resulted in making the knot even tighter.

"Let me help you before you strangle yourself." Tara got to her feet and loosened the knot with ease.

"Thank you, my love." He threw the troublesome tie onto the bed and unbuttoned the top two buttons of his shirt. "John has gotten himself into a fix of sorts." He threw one of his hands into the air and rubbed his forehead. "He says two separate meetings are planned for this evening, and I must go to one of them, along with a Rapid City Police Detective—I think his name is Morris—so I may identify a Ponerello should one be seen. John will attend the other."

"And you do not want me to go?"

Marquette shook his head. "These people have shot at me before. They will stop at nothing if they feel they have been trapped."

Tara nodded.

Marquette sat down on the end of the bed and began to remove his shoes. "An old-fashioned stakeout," he muttered. He reached for the pistol he'd conceal beneath his jacket. "But the problem has never been with their guns."

A short time later, Marquette knocked on Tillie's door to let her know he had to leave for a little while but that Tara might be interested in doing something. He was surprised to see that Tillie had been "fixing up," as she called it. Her hair was brushed into combs on the sides, and her lashes looked thicker and longer than usual. She wore a feminine, sleeveless white blouse, showing off her dark shoulders; new blue jeans; and dainty leather boots.

"I was just going to let you know I have to leave for a meeting," he said. If he hadn't been so agitated about the coming events, he would have allowed himself to suspect why she'd "fixed up" to sit in a hotel room. Instead he frowned and asked, "Are you wearing *lipstick?*"

Tillie smiled. "I thought I'd try a new look. What do you think?" She gave a graceful, little spin in front of him.

He relaxed his tense expression and gave her a faint smile. "I think you look lovely, Angel."

"Thanks, Marq." She noticed the handle of his pistol beneath his coat. "Must be *some* meeting."

He rolled his eyes and covered the pistol by closing the front of his jacket. "Do not tell Ma`ma."

"I haven't yet," she replied with a wink.

Marquette took a breath and gave her a soft kiss on the cheek. He pointed his index finger at her and instructed, "Be good."

"I will," she promised.

As Marquette hurried away, Tillie looked down at her bare ring finger on her left hand and sighed.

*****

"I think it will be alright, my Rosa," Guiseppi said as he tried to assure his wife that Angel would not come to ruin during her most recent trip away from home. He admired the new watercolor, *The Perfect Knight*, and then the acrylic he'd unveiled when he came home. It was a magnificent painting of the man now identified as Noah, sitting upon the rocks at Mt. Rushmore. Tillie had simply entitled that one *Noah*.

Guiseppi looked at his teary-eyed wife, who had revealed all of her afternoon's discoveries to him when he returned home from work.

"But they are standing *in a bar*," she persisted, dramatically flinging the photo at her husband.

Guiseppi picked up the photo. "But, my dearest Rosa, they do not appear to have been drinking." He raised his eyebrow. "One thing about our little Angel is that she is smart, like her ma`ma, and she has been taught the difference between right and wrong. She may be in the middle of disobedience and rebellion, but she will *not* make a worse decision. That we can be sure of. Besides, she is with Marquette and Tara. Even in her own sin, she will be safe."

"But what if he forces himself…" Rosa couldn't even continue the question, her words mingling with tears of fear in the back of her mouth.

"He will not." Guiseppi looked at the new portraits before them. "If she thinks he is a knight, then she will be safe. Angel knows the difference."

*****

Tara followed Tillie with stealth through the shadows of the parking lot. She'd followed lots of people, and Tillie would never know she was there; but she wasn't going to let Tillie do this alone. She hid herself behind vehicles, side walls, and dumpsters as they walked along.

Noah waited anxiously at the bar, sipping on a bottle of Coke, and looking at his watch every few minutes. He wore a clean shirt and untorn jeans, and his new haircut was washed and combed; Angel would be so surprised.

Noah, Maggie, and Estelle had carefully planned the event. A white cake decorated with pink roses waited in the refrigerator, and Noah had remembered the ring. The diamond was small, but it was all he could afford. It sat in a box in his shirt pocket, just waiting to be placed upon Angel's pretty hand.

"She'll be here," Maggie assured as she dried glasses behind the bar.

"What's taking so long?"

Maggie laughed. "You've only been here for about ten minutes. What are you so nervous about?"

"I don't know. Just excited I guess—"

Noah's old drinking buddies burst loudly through the door, laughing and joking, as drunk as ever, and they had Carrie with them.

"We brought you a surprise, Noah!" Theo yelled, giving Carrie a push in Noah's direction.

Carrie laughed hysterically, obviously just as drunk as they were, and staggered to Noah's side at the bar. Her strawberry-blonde hair hung in her face, and there were dark circles beneath her gray eyes. She put her hand on Noah's thigh and looked alluringly into his eyes.

"I've missed you, Noah," she slurred. "Where ya been?"

Noah shook his head and removed Carrie's hand from his thigh.

"What's a matter?" she whined as she stood very close to him and began to touch his face. "*That* never bothered you before."

"Knock it off, Carrie," Maggie growled.

Carrie sneered, "Shut up, Mammie." She looked at Estelle, who was standing next to Maggie, and spat.

Maggie pointed her index finger at Carrie. "You know, I *never did* like you."

"Good!" Carrie shouted. " 'Cause I never liked you either."

"Come, on, Stellie!" Theo yelled loudly from the booth. "Set us up!"

"Hurry up, Stellie," Maggie whispered. "We'd better get those jokers settled down before Angel shows up and they scare her away."

Estelle nodded. "And we've gotta figure out a way to get that tramp, Carrie, out of here—"

The door opened again and in walked a tall, thin gentleman dressed in a suit. He had bright red hair, and he came to Carrie's side.

"Thank God the babysitter's here," Maggie muttered.

"Come on, Carrie," he said, taking her by the arm. "We need to be getting you home. Your folks are worried about you."

Carrie jerked her arm away from him and slapped his face. "Get away from me, Roy. I ain't goin' nowhere with you."

"Come on, Carrie," he insisted, again taking her by the elbow. "Say good night to your friends."

"Alright then!" Carrie screeched, and she suddenly turned and put a full kiss onto Noah's lips. "Now we can go," she smirked.

By this time Tillie had made it to within a few feet of the glass doors. She gasped in horror. *He kissed her! He changed his mind! But he promised me…We promised each other.* Tears flooded her black eyes as she backed away, shaking her head. *Unbelievable.* She turned around and sprinted towards the hotel.

Tara almost darted after Tillie, but she was curious as to what had gone wrong inside of the bar. She positioned herself to have a better view, gasping when she recognized John Peters sitting in one of the booths near the door. *What in the world?*

Tara watched John leave his booth and follow the staggering girl and her tall, red-headed companion out of the bar. They didn't see him back there, or at least it didn't appear they'd spied him. They got into the back of a black limousine, and John waited in the shadows until it pulled out of the parking lot. Then he jumped into a dark sedan and followed them.

Chapter 6

Tara caught up to Tillie in the hallway of their hotel. She hurried her into the room and wrapped her arms around her. "There, there now. Tell me what happened."

"He was kissing another girl," Tillie sobbed.

Tara gasped. "Are you certain? Perhaps there has been a misunderstanding."

Tillie shook her head. "There are some things I didn't tell you about Noah. He's a drunk, Tara. I thought maybe he wanted to change, but I was wrong and *stupid!*"

"Oh, my goodness," Tara breathed. *Thankfully Marquette is away for that meeting. This is God's grace in the matter.*

"I don't ever want to see him again. I just want to forget about this," Tillie cried. "I can't believe I was such an idiot. All the signs were there. He's a blackguard."

Tara stroked the soft curls upon Tillie's head, wondering how the girl made such a misjudgment. The young lady was an *excellent* judge of character and could usually see a blackguard from a mile away. It was difficult to believe she was so fooled into thinking Noah was a knight. But if he was kissing someone else, that was a sure sign of a fickle heart...*and knights are not prone to fickle hearts.* And then there was the drinking. Oh, how Tara wished she'd known about the drinking before encouraging the whole fiasco.

*****

As the clock struck midnight, Noah was forced to realize Angel wasn't coming. He'd waited patiently at the bar, drinking Coke after Coke, watching Maggie's customers come and go without a single sign of Angel.

"I can't believe it," he said as he watched Maggie clear away some glasses. "What happened to her?"

Maggie shook her head and frowned. She *hated* it when people got stood up, and she *really* hated it that it had happened to Noah. "She probably changed her mind," she grumbled as she took a cloth from below the counter and wiped off the bar.

Noah shook his head. "She wouldn't have changed her mind. She *loves* me. Something must have happened. Her parents stopped the trip from happening or there was some kind of an accident, but she'd never stand me up. She'll call." He stood up from his stool and gave Maggie a tired smile. "I'm goin' home, but you be nice and understanding when she calls. Tell her I waited and I'm not mad."

Maggie hid her disbelief behind a gruff smile. "No problem, Noah."

"Thanks, Maggie," and he left the bar.

Estelle set down a tray of used glasses near Maggie's sink. "What happened, Maggie?"

Maggie shrugged. "That poor kid. I hope he doesn't start up with that drinking again over this deal. He was lookin' so nice."

Estelle nodded, emptied her tray, and returned to her work.

*****

Tillie wept bitterly until nearly midnight before Tara was able to calm her down and coax her into her covers.

"*Please* don't tell my family," Tillie begged.

Tara was anxious as she held Tillie's hand and tried somehow to comfort the distraught girl. *How will we keep this from our family? Angel is a mess. Thankfully we have separate rooms, but Marquette will see his fretting sister in the morning, and he will want an explanation.*

"Promise me, Tara," Tillie pleaded between sobs.

Tara slowly nodded her head, hearing the door open and close in the other room. *Marquette is back.* She tucked the covers around Tillie's chin and kissed her forehead. "I will tell him you are not feeling well," she whispered, "but you must pull yourself together by morning, or he will know."

Tillie sniffed. "Okay. Thanks, Tara."

Tara looked worriedly at her young sister-in-law, gave Tillie another kiss, and whispered, "I love you, Angel, and I do not know how, but some way we will get through this." Tillie sniffed. Tara patted her hand and left the room through the adjoining door, closing it behind her.

Marquette looked up when he saw his wife enter the room. He sat on the end of the bed, took off his shoes, and tiredly smiled. He frowned when he saw her distressed expression. "Is everything alright?"

Tara shook her head. "Angel is not feeling well."

Marquette took a weary breath, stood to remove his jacket, and off came the holster strapped beneath his arm.

"How did it go this evening?" Tara asked.

"Dreadful," Marquette answered as he lay the holster down on the small dresser. He began to unbutton his shirt. "A *complete* no show. The police are so frustrated with this case, and frankly, Tara, so am I. I have chased these people all over the world, and I am about to give it up."

"Did John call you?"

Marquette shook his head. "And he was supposed to call a few hours ago. He had promised Detective Morris that he would contact them shortly after ten o'clock. One cannot imagine what has gone wrong with *his* end of the investigation."

"I saw him this evening," Tara said. "I was walking toward the shopping center, and I watched him follow two people out of the bar across the street."

"And you are sure it was John?"

"I am positive."

"And the people he followed?"

Tara shook her head. "I have no idea. I do not believe we have received any information on them. They got into a limousine and drove south on LaCrosse. John followed them in his own car."

"Do you think they knew they were being followed?"

"It did not appear they knew."

"Did they see you?"

Tara shook her head again. "I am certain I was well hidden."

Marquette sighed and scratched his head. "Well, perhaps John will shed some light on this tomorrow when we meet with him in New Castle."

*****

The three of them left for New Castle early Saturday morning by way of a small, four-seat airplane. Marquette explained it would be much quicker than having to take the highways through Custer State Park and Black Hills National Forest.

Tillie rode along in one of the back seats, wearing dark sunglasses and appearing to nap for most of the trip. Marquette frowned with concern. "Angel, are you not feeling any better?"

"I'll be fine, Marq," she answered.

"It is just some flu or something," Tara quickly offered with a smile. Marquette nodded and said no more. Had he not been so deep in thought about his case, he would have noticed his wife was feeling rather poorly as well but just putting on a very good show.

Tara had not slept at all the night before as she struggled with whether or not she should tell their family what she and Tillie had gotten themselves into or just let the matter go, as Tillie requested. It seemed Tillie would need the love and support of her family during this time, but then again, telling them would mean upsetting Rosa and Guiseppi to no end. Also, Marquette would surely seek out Noah, and that was trouble none of them wanted.

They waited on the tiny airfield for John Peters for two hours. It was like a desert, with heat growing more intense as the minutes passed, baking the dried dunes of dirt and an occasional tumbleweed. The landscape was surprising, considering the landscape only a few miles east was covered with lush trees and Black Hills greenery that flourished into a beautiful paradise.

Marquette paced in front of Tara and Tillie, where they sat in hard folding chairs beneath a torn vinyl awning. Earlier, he'd compared the dilapidated little place to an airfield where he'd waited to meet with a terrorist informant on one of the Philippine Islands. Tillie managed a small smile during her brother's diatribe, thankful for his passion and the unfortunate set of circumstances that was taking her mind off her troubles.

"Do you *suppose* they might have a phone?" Marquette asked in exasperation as he paced around under the awning, pausing to gaze down the gravel road beyond them.

Tara shook her head. "I believe all they have provided to us is this *miserable*, small awning." She looked above her at the holes allowing some of the midmorning heat to pass through and complained, "Pray no large flocks of birds happen upon us this morning."

Tillie actually snickered at that point as the situation was suddenly very comical. Here they were, out in the middle of nowhere, waiting for a man who was obviously not going to show, and Tara was worried about whether or not a flock of birds might happen by.

Marquette laughed, took off his dressy hat, and tossed it to Tara. She caught it with a smile. He raised one eyebrow. "Put that on your pretty head so the birds will not get you."

Tara adjusted the hat on her head. "Perhaps we should return to the bar. Someone there may be able to give us some information."

Marquette nodded. "I had that same thought myself." He gazed again down the gravel road and then back at the pilot who waited for them in the plane. "Let us go back to Rapid City."

*****

It was just after noon when the tall, dark man strolled into the bar, exuding an aura of mystery that fit him every bit as well as his custom-made suit and hat. Maggie was in her usual place behind the counter, taking advantage of the slow Saturday afternoon by putting figures into her monthly ledger. The place was empty today, probably due to the warm weather.

She looked up when the door opened and saw his long-legged, leisurely gait approach her with purpose. *What a handsome man.* Beautiful, dark olive skin and eyes as black as could be. And then she saw the gold flash of a wedding band as he removed his hat, exposing his well-kept ponytail...*Lucky girl...*

Marquette smiled and took a seat on one of the stools at the bar.

"What'll ya have?" Maggie asked in her typical gruff voice.

"Some information, if you please," he began with a smile as he pulled a photograph out of his inside breast pocket and laid it upon the bar. It was John Peters. "I understand this man was in this establishment last evening?"

Maggie looked at the photograph and tried to swallow away her surprise. She'd seen him skulking around in the back of the bar the last two times Roy had been in to fish Carrie out of the place. Noah told her that Carrie's family was into dealing drugs. Maggie's thoughts progressed from there and went immediately to the implication of Noah if Carrie's family were brought in for their illegal activities. After all, he may have been one of their best customers.

She narrowed her eyes and looked at Marquette. *He's some kind of a fed or something, here to uncover that nightmare on the other side of town and take Noah down with them. I sure won't miss Carrie, but Noah, on the other hand, just straightened himself out.*

"Never saw him before in my life," Maggie lied.

Marquette acknowledged her reply and surprised her with another photo. This one he and Tara found only that morning in an envelope John Peters had sent to them the week before. He laid it on the counter, and Maggie recognized Roy, a shady-looking character who worked for Carrie's stepfather.

"How about this man?" Marquette questioned.

Maggie just shook her head. "Sorry. Can't help you today, mister."

Marquette sighed, picking up the two photographs and placing them back into his pocket. Just then, he saw Tillie's painting hanging on the other end of the bar and smiled. "A nice painting."

Maggie nodded. "I bought it from one of those Junior Artists that was out here a couple of weeks ago."

Marquette smiled. "You will never believe this, but my baby sister created that portrait."

Maggie's mouth fell open in surprise. *Angel's brother?! Well, where's Angel?!* She quickly recovered her composure. "I did meet her the day I bought the thing," she gruffly sputtered. "I understand she won some awards."

Marquette noticed Maggie's suddenly strange demeanor, and he tried to reestablish eye contact with her. "She is quite talented, and we are very proud of her,"

Maggie's eyes twinkled as she suddenly recognized the person at her bar. She decided to bring up a subject to get him out of there…*Vietnam vets rarely enjoy discussing their service.* "You're the refugee, aren't you?"

Marquette sighed, "One of many."

"She had a blue ribbon on that one," Maggie continued. She looked Marquette up and down once again, stopping at the neat pony-tail that hung down his back. "But I'm sure you didn't have *that* when you served."

"Oh, no," Marquette chuckled as he gracefully placed his hat back upon his head. "I will call upon you if I require further information. Thank you so much for your courtesies in this matter."

"Anytime," Maggie responded with a smile, relieved the conversation was winding up. "And tell that baby sister of yours hello."

"I will do that." He turned and left the bar as gracefully as he had entered, and Maggie sighed with relief as she watched him stroll across the parking lot and into the hotel.

*****

Tillie and Tara had stayed behind, saturated with worries of what Marquette would uncover in the tiny bar. They wanted solid leads on the Ponerellos, but at the same time, they didn't want Marquette to learn of Angel's "fling" with a sleazy biker.

Tara shook her head. "I cannot believe you could make such a mis-judgment of the man. Angel, what if it was a mistake? Perhaps you simply misunderstood the situation—"

"I did *not* misunderstand the situation," Tillie insisted from her curled-up position on the bed. "There was full lip-to-lip contact."

Tara frowned. "But, Angel, in my line of work, I have often come across things that are not as they appear—"

"Then there's the drinking. He was drunk the night we met. The warning signs were there, Tara. I just didn't want to see them." Fresh tears flooded her black eyes. "I just want to go home and forget about this. Thank God He made this opportunity available to me so I could see what a rotten and disobedient child I am and what a horrible mistake I was getting ready to make."

*****

Noah walked the same path at Canyon Lake as he'd taken with Angel on their first date. The day had warmed, drawing the heavy pine scent out of the trees, reminiscent of the night they'd walked this path together. He remembered how her pretty hand had felt so perfect as it nestled into his own, the soft fragrance of her perfume, the gentleness in her smile... He took a deep breath of the dry, spring air and tried to sort out what may have gone wrong. *It's not June yet. She won't turn eighteen until June, so that's probably the problem.* He sighed and shook his head. *Maybe she's just too young to make this kind of a commitment. Maybe she told her parents and they kept her from coming back...*

Whatever...I'll wait for her to contact me until I'm positive she's not returning. No matter what her age or whatever the misunderstanding, I still love her.

"Oh, please, God," he prayed as he walked along, "bring her back to me."

*****

Marquette felt Tillie's "illness" was more intense when he returned to the hotel and decided to take her home. There was no longer any reason for him and Tara to stay in Rapid City. Besides, Angel would be more comfortable with Ma'ma. He called their parents and told them they were on their way.

As they sailed through the South Dakota skies on their way back to Sioux Falls, Marquette put a friendly hand upon his sister's shoulder and said, "Oh, by the way, the lady in the bar says to say hello."

Tillie's heavy sunglasses hid her surprised expression.

"I saw your painting in the bar, and it looks lovely there," Marquette continued as he tried his loving best to comfort his sister.

Tillie only nodded, thankful that Maggie hadn't spilled the beans.

*****

Rosa and Guiseppi met them at the airport in Sioux Falls. Rosa took Tillie into her arms when she came through the gate. Tillie laid her head on her mother's shoulder, and tears of relief spilled from her eyes.

"What is it, my Angel?" Rosa whispered.

"Don't make me say here, Ma'ma. I'm just so happy to be back home with you and Papa where I belong."

Tara sighed with relief as she watched them embrace. Angel was safe again, back with her parents where she belonged.

*****

Midafternoon Maggie saw the familiar Harley pull into her parking lot. He was only the second visitor that day. The nice weather was keeping everyone away, and that meant she'd be really busy that night.

Noah strolled through the front door and up to the bar. "Hear from anybody?"

Maggie nodded as she reached below the counter for a bottle of Coke, opening it and setting it before him. "I got the strangest visitor in here today."

"I'm sure you see a lot of strange people, Maggie," Noah attempted a joke. "You work in a bar."

Maggie feigned a smile. "This guy was *weird*, and you'd better be careful, Noah, 'cause he was looking for Roy." Noah looked surprised at her information. Maggie nodded and opened a bottle of Coke for herself, took a long gulp, and set the bottle down with a thud. "Tall, dark guy with a ponytail, dressed in a fancy suit. Just happened to mention he was Angel's brother."

"Angel's brother?" Noah's eyes danced with anticipation. "They must've come after all. When is she coming over?"

Maggie raised one black eyebrow. "Noah, the guy is a fed or something. And he didn't ask for you or even say your name. I'm tellin' ya, Noah, it was spooky. He had some kind of a foreign accent, and he had a picture with him of that guy that's been followin' Roy around whenever he's pickin' up Carrie."

Noah sighed in anguish and rolled his eyes. "Oh, Maggie, do you think he told her about the dope?"

Maggie shook her head. "I don't know, but I lied my tail off. I told him I'd never seen either of them in my life. Doesn't Angel know about the drugs?"

Noah shook his head. "I thought the drinking was probably bad enough. Besides, I haven't been high since before I met her. I'm done with that stuff, Maggie."

"How much of that stuff did you buy from Carrie's father?" Maggie asked with a frown.

"I never bought anything from Jack. Whatever I got, I got from Carrie. She already had it. I got some stuff through Theo a time or two..." He hesitated. "Do you think they're getting ready to bust Jack for drugs?"

Maggie shrugged. "Don't know. We always wondered where he got his money. I hope they don't haul you in with 'em."

Noah took a breath and asked, "Now, Maggie, back to this brother. Where did he go after he left here? Did he leave a card or something?"

"I don't think this guy leaves a calling card," she dryly answered. "He said he'd be calling me if he needed anything further. He walked into the hotel right over there."

Noah put some change on the counter for his Coke and smiled at Maggie. "I'm going over there. Maybe the guy is still there."

"You're looking for trouble, Noah," Maggie cautioned as she frowned. "I go and lie like the devil, and you run right back into the thick of things."

Noah laughed. "They can't get me on anything. I'm clean as can be, Maggie. It'll be okay."

Maggie rolled her eyes. "Just watch your back, Noah."

Noah hurried out of the bar, across the parking lot, and into the hotel lobby. The same suited man he'd visited with before was waiting at the front counter.

"Hello," the gentleman greeted Noah with a smile.

"Hi." Noah's face flushed with excitement. "I'm looking for someone. Tall, dark guy with a ponytail? Have you seen him?"

"He left a couple of hours ago."

"Is he coming back?"

The man shook his head. "His little sister got sick, and he checked out and left. Anything else I can help you with?"

"Can you give me his name?"

The man shook his head again. "I'm sorry, but that information is restricted."

*****

Tillie lay on her bed and stared up at the ceiling. *This is going to be tough. Why did I do this to myself?* She glanced at the covered easels and groaned. *I don't ever want to see him again—not even the photos or the sketches.* She rolled over on her side and caught a glimpse of the corner of one of the photos she'd stashed beneath her bed. *I must have lost my mind...*She heard a soft knock on her bedroom door and quickly dried her tears with a corner of the bed-spread. "Come in."

Ma`ma came smiling into the room. She held a tray with a cup of soup and a saucer of toast. She sat it down on Tillie's nightstand and closed the door.

"I thought perhaps we should visit," Rosa said as she took a seat on the bed and reached for her daughter's hand. "And I thought you might want to put something into your stomach. Marquette tells me you have not eaten anything since Friday morning."

The warm, tender touch of Ma`ma sent a river of fresh tears streaming from Tillie's eyes. She sat up and folded herself into the arms of her mother.

"Oh, Angel," Rosa began feeling the tears beginning in her own eyes. "*Please* tell me what happened. We found the paintings and photographs while you were gone."

Tillie felt more relief than she ever had in her whole life. She softly sobbed, "I'm so sorry, Ma`ma. I hate myself for what I've done. He just seemed so wonderful."

"I know, my Angel," Rosa soothed as she held her daughter.

"I saw him *kissing* someone else. He must have changed his mind. I just can't believe what an idiot I was."

"Oh, my Angel, you have *never* been an idiot. He must have been a gifted actor to make you believe such things."

Tillie sniffed. "Please, Ma`ma, don't tell my brothers. I've been such a sinful, wretched child and am so embarrassed."

Rosa's eyes opened wide with surprise. "Marquette did not know?"

Tillie shook her head. "And he's the *last* person I want to find out about this. He'll make a bigger deal of it than anybody should, and he'll be going back to Rapid City to work on this stupid case. This is *my* sin, and I don't want anybody else but you and Papa to know what I've done." Tillie's words trailed away as she started to sob again.

Rosa drew the child back into her arms. "I will not tell."

An hour later, Rosa emerged from the room with the empty cup and saucer. Guiseppi was waiting just outside the door. He took the tray and allowed Rosa to descend the stairs in front of him as they made their way to the kitchen.

"Marquette and Tara are in their room," he whispered. "What did she say?"

"She is very repentant and has asked us not to tell her brothers," Rosa whispered. "She said Noah changed his mind."

"Changed his mind?"

Rosa sighed. "After all that we have shown her, Guiseppi, is it not a strange thing that she should make a misjudgment such as this?"

Guiseppi took a deep breath. "We will pray about this, my Rosa, but if this continues to bother Angel, I want to find the young man and see for myself that she has made such a dreadful mistake."

"Guiseppi," Rosa whispered, "I know it is hard for you to accept, but perhaps our daughter has, indeed, made such a mistake. Blackguards can be crafty, and she may have been fooled. Perhaps her judgment was clouded in her disobedience and sin."

Guiseppi wanted to agree with his wife, but in his heart something was amiss. Angel was far too sensible to allow a deception of this nature. And it seemed more than mere coincidence to Guiseppi that his own godly Rosa had prayed for the same young man for so many years.

Chapter 7

"Put it right here, please," Alex instructed politely as he showed the men where, *exactly*, to position the beautiful piece of furniture. The brand new cherry wood desk was a graduation present from his parents.

Alex Martin had returned from Massachusetts over the weekend. After seven long years, the last two being the most difficult, he was done with it. In a mere matter of months, he'd ace the South Dakota bar and be a real attorney and not just some flunky running errands in a law office.

Alex was handsome, much like his father and brother, and stood at least five inches over six feet tall. He had the Martin's masculine build of wide shoulders and a small waist. His hair was so black it shone blue when he stood in the light just right. His skin was evenly smooth olive and without any kind of blemish. His eyes were as black as coal, and his perfect, white teeth dazzled when he smiled.

Like all of the Martin men, Alex dressed flawlessly—from his perfectly pressed white dress shirt to the black slacks and black tie. The Martins did not wear the stylish and popular leisure suits of the time, but rather the professional, straight-cut and pleated Italian suits that fit their handsome bodies to a tee.

The women at Harvard had thrown themselves at Alex, but he'd refused them all in order to stay focused on his studies and preparations for life. Law was Alex's life, and nothing in the world could compete with his love for the profession.

Like his older brother, Sam, Alex was encouraged to study law the same as all of the Martins for generations before him. But Alex was different from the other Martins. While Sam and his father simply "practiced law," Alex had the unique gifts of memory and discernment.

The propensity with which he was able to memorize things the first time through and then apply them to specific instances was enviable. He also had the rare and often nerve-racking ability to look into someone's eyes and extract the truth. Public defenders had hated him at the small law firm where he interned in Boston because he knew immediately who was guilty and who was not, and he gave that information without even being asked for it. Sudden confessions of those presumed innocent were *common* when Alex performed his questioning.

Sam poked his head around the corner and smiled at his younger brother. He was thirty-seven, twelve years Alex's senior, but they were as close at two brothers could be. They looked almost identical, except for the soft strands of silver just starting to run through Sam's black hair.

"Nice desk," Sam said.

Alex nodded. "It is, isn't it."

Sam stepped into the new office. "So how do you like your new digs?"

Alex looked around at the richly paneled office; the plush, gray carpet; and expensive drapes hanging on the fourth-story corner windows. "I can see the Shrivers' building from here…and…" He walked to the opposite side of the office. "I'm going to put the conference table over here. Perfect."

"Mr. Martin," came a female's voice from the doorway, and Alex and Sam turned to see Shondra Payne, poised perfectly with her pad and pen. She had worked at the law firm since 1968 as their senior office manager. Shondra was a top-notch attorney, and she ran a tight ship. Alex's father had already told him he'd be spending quite a bit of time with Shondra until he'd "learned the ropes."

"Yes, Shondra," Sam and Alex answered at the same time, and they laughed at each other.

"Sam," Shondra clarified with a smile, "your ten o'clock is here. Would you like me to show them in?"

Sam nodded. "Sure. I'll be there in a second."

Sam gave Alex a pat on the shoulder. "It's great to have you home, Alex," and then he followed Shondra out of the office.

"It's great to be here," Alex said to himself. He nodded and smiled at his new surroundings.

*****

It had been a wonderful Saturday with little Alyssa and Angelo. Tillie took them to Dennis the Menace Park, while Vincenzo and Kate helped Papa and Ma`ma paint their living room. Alyssa carried her little Indian dolly with her the whole day, and Angelo beat upon his drum like a maniac. After they'd played themselves out at the park, Tillie took them to McDonald's for their favorites: burgers, fries, and chocolate shakes. Toward the end of the meal, Angelo became upset with his older sister and threw what was left of his burger at her. The scene was intensely comical, and Tillie tried her best not to laugh as she scolded Angelo. Being just two and a half years of age, Angelo instantly lost himself in a fit. His little voice rang through the McDonald's like a fire siren. Alyssa was so embarrassed of her brother that she crawled under the table.

It was all Tillie could do to maintain her composure. She'd witnessed Angelo's fits before, but he'd never had one in public. It was obviously time for a nap. She gathered her little charges, put them into the old 1955 Chevy Bel-Air her father had kept running since his arrival in America, and drove them back to Nonna's. She sang little songs to them all the way across town in an effort to quiet Angelo's screaming. He passed out before they reached the driveway.

Tillie put the old car into park and breathed a sigh of relief. *Thank God that's over with.* She had enjoyed the day (up to the point of Angelo's fit) as the sweet children and their busy activities took her mind off of Noah. And she would have thought of him just then, but Vincenzo had heard the car in the drive and was coming out of the front door to help them into the house.

He opened Tillie's car door for her and noticed the tired but happy expression on her face. "Hello, Angel," he said with a smile. He glanced into the backseat and saw his sleeping little boy. "How did things go?"

"It was a great day—" Tillie began to reply, but Alyssa clamored over Tillie and into her father's arms to better explain.

"Angelo threw the biggest fit *ever*," Alyssa informed as she looked into her father's eyes. Vincenzo looked to Tillie for an explanation.

Tillie sighed and smiled at her brother. "Well, it really wasn't *that* bad. And he didn't throw it until the very end—"

"He threw his hamburger *right at me*, Papa," Alyssa said.

Vincenzo gently placed his finger over Alyssa's mouth and smiled. "Shhh. Do not interrupt Auntie."

Alyssa sighed with obvious despair and sat quietly on his hip.

"It really wasn't *that* bad," Tillie continued with a tired smile. "He just got a little cranky. We had a big day."

Alyssa spied her mother coming out of the house and wriggled to be released from her father's arms.

"Alright, you little stinker," Vincenzo said. He gave her a soft kiss upon the head and gently set her on the ground. She scampered to her mother.

Vincenzo offered his sister a hand out of the car. "Thank you for taking them today. I am quite sure he was a handful."

Tillie laughed, "He's great, Vincenzo."

Vincenzo scooped his son out of the backseat. The little tyke didn't even stir as he was sleeping so soundly. Vincenzo took him into the house, up the stairs, and tucked him into a bed in one of the guest rooms.

After trying to diminish Alyssa's dreadful report on her brother to Kate, Tillie followed them into the house where Guiseppi was talking on the telephone.

"Oh, she is right here," Guiseppi said when he saw Tillie walk into the house. "Angel, it is your brother. He wishes to speak with you."

Tillie took the phone, expecting it to be Marquette, but instead she heard the voice of Petrice.

"Hello, Angel," he happily greeted. "I hear you were with Vincenzo's babies today."

Tillie sighed. She didn't want to talk to him and *hadn't* talked to him since he'd been in Sioux Falls with "Miss Fabulous" a month ago. She wondered what news he could possibly have *this* time.

"Hi, Patty." She dropped her tired body into the kitchen chair next to Guiseppi. "What's up?"

"Well," Petrice began, "I wanted to let you know we will not be coming to your graduation—"

"Why not?" Tillie's pretty face twisted into a frown. "I'm giving the commencement."

"Yes, I know," Petrice replied. "Angel, Ellie and I have not had the chance for a honeymoon yet. We are going to *Italia*—"

"Of all the people I thought would dump on me," Tillie snapped. "I can hardly believe *you'd* be the one."

Guiseppi watched his usually angelic daughter turn on her favored brother, and he was astounded. Not only had he *never* heard her talk this way to another member of their family, but to hear her speak this way to her Patty was something he would have never expected.

"And what about Andy's ordination?" Tillie was suddenly on her feet and spoke as sharply as she dared but not yelling. No one wanted to awaken Angelo. "I suppose you're gonna just blow him off *too*. Marq's speaking about Vietnam. What are you *thinking?*"

Guiseppi put his hand on Tillie's shoulder. Vincenzo and Kate stared in wide-open-eyed amazement, and Rosa hurried into the room to see what on earth had gone wrong.

"You are such a *creep!*" she finished, handing the phone back to her father. "*I hate him.*" With that, she frowned and stomped out of the house.

Guiseppi put the phone to his ear as he watched Tillie leave through the front door and head down the sidewalk in the direction of Ginger's house.

Rosa's mouth hung open in amazement as she watched the spectacle, and Vincenzo and Kate just stood very still.

Little Alyssa reached up to hold her mother's hand. "Auntie is really mad," she whispered.

"Angel…are you there?" Petrice asked.

"No," Guiseppi answered. "She has gone to Ginger's. I think perhaps you should try to call again later. Did you want to speak with Vincenzo?"

"Certainly. Put him on."

Guiseppi handed the phone to Vincenzo, who covered the mouthpiece and whispered, "He is not coming to the graduation?" Guiseppi shook his head in answer, and Vincenzo whispered again, "Is that the *best* decision he can make?"

Guiseppi shrugged. "He and Ellie wish to visit *Italia* on a honeymoon trip."

Vincenzo rolled his eyes and wished they were still young so he could sufficiently thrash his brother for this offense. "Petrice," he said sternly into the phone. "You have decided *not* to attend Angel's graduation and Andy's ordination?"

"It cannot be helped. It will be the only chance I have to get away. I go to trial shortly after we return, and my summer is completely booked. I had arranged to be away for Angel's graduation early on in the year—"

"And so now you take that special time for another event?"

"I am sorry, Vincenzo, but it cannot be helped."

"This is devilish of you," Vincenzo growled. He turned away so his daughter would not see how angry he had become and continued, "I cannot believe you would do this to someone who loves you so much. Of all of us, she has loved you the most."

"She does not," Petrice argued. "And do not attempt to use guilt on me. I have made my decision. I will go to *Italia* with Ellie, and that is final."

"Have a wonderful time then!" Vincenzo slammed the phone into its cradle on the wall. He turned around and faced the rest of his quiet family. "He is taking her to *Italia,* and that is final."

Rosa sighed and shook her head. Tillie had had a hard enough time these last few weeks, and Petrice could have made a better decision. Of course, had he known, he would never have considered skipping her graduation.

*****

Alex sat on the front porch, half dozing in the afternoon sun, when he heard the door open behind him. Sam sat his large frame into the seat beside Alex and sipped a cup of coffee. From this very place on their porch, they'd watched the Casellis for years, and it was a wonderful memory for both of them. Alex remembered when he was too small to see over the bushes and Sam would hold him up high enough to watch their sister, Kate, and Vincenzo on the Casellis' front porch. Now they were big men and could easily see the comings and goings from a seated position.

"Wow," Sam whispered, "she looks mad." He waved at Tillie as she walked by on her well-worn path to Ginger's house. Tillie politely waved back, but she did not smile, and it made Sam chuckle. "She's *really* mad. Wonder what happened."

Alex shook his head. He'd been napping and didn't see Tillie walk by until Sam came outside.

"Listen," Sam chided with a faked frown, "if you're gonna do this, you gotta do it right. Now what's the haps down there?"

"I fell asleep," Alex chuckled.

"*You fell asleep?*"

"You've worked the daylights out of me for two weeks now. I'm exhausted." Alex let his eyes follow Tillie up the hill. "Where's Becky-Lynn?"

"Her mother's in town," Sam answered. "They're doing something together today. I swear that old woman *hates* me."

Alex had to laugh. Sam married Becky-Lynn twelve years ago, just a few days after they'd graduated from law school. Becky-Lynn's parents lived in one of the Carolinas, where they farmed, and Sam was convinced early on that her mother disliked him.

"I can't believe how tall Tillie has gotten," Alex commented as he watched her ascend Ginger's porch steps.

"She has." Sam smiled and gave his brother an elbow. "Didn't you notice when you were dancing?"

Alex smiled. "Yes, I noticed."

Sam nodded and took another sip of his coffee. "She graduates in a couple of weeks, and Mom says she delivers the commencement this year."

Alex nodded. "Just like Petrice. Remember that?"

Sam remembered the passionate, Italian-flavored speech Petrice delivered at Washington Senior High School in 1957. His accent was so thick back then.

"Where's she going to college?" Alex asked.

"Augustana, here in Sioux Falls," Sam answered as he watched his brother watch Tillie disappear into Ginger's house.

*****

Ginger was overjoyed to see Tillie on her porch, and she pulled her into the house.

"You'll *never* guess what happened to me today!" she said with an excited smile and a giggle. Before Tillie could make a guess, Ginger continued, "I tried to call you, but the line was busy. *Bobby Maxwell asked me to the prom!*" She let out a little squeal, melting Tillie's frown into a smile.

"That's great, Ging." She put her arms around her best friend. This was excellent news, considering Ginger had been in love with Bobby Maxwell since their sophomore year. This was the first time Bobby had ever asked her out.

"Can you believe it?" Ginger breathed. "Mom's gonna take me to JCPenney for a new dress." She noticed Tillie's half-sad expression and asked, "What's the matter?"

"Oh, that *stupid* brother of mine."

"Which one?" Ginger asked. Usually Tillie spoke so highly of her brothers.

"Petrice and 'Miss Fab' are going to Italy for a honeymoon trip and skipping my graduation."

"No!" Ginger's mouth hung open in amazement.

"She must be *really* wonderful," Tillie sighed as she flopped herself on the couch.

Ginger sat down next to her lifelong buddy and sighed. "And just think, this whole time I thought Petrice was gonna turn up queer."

"Far from it," Tillie mumbled.

Ginger put her arm around Tillie's shoulder. "It'll get better. You'll see."

*****

Noah smiled as he watched the foamy water rushing down the rocks. The trees were full of leaves now, and the pine scent was stronger than ever. It was hot in the Black Hills today, and he had taken his bike for a ride to his favorite place. If he closed his eyes, he could see her. She was standing just over there, holding that wonderful, old camera as she captured the beauty of Bridal Veil Falls. She'd loved the story about the Indian warrior who saved his bride, and she'd loved him…*She told me so, so what happened? Where is she? Why hasn't she called?*

Noah shook his head and opened his eyes. She wasn't standing there after all, and he'd tricked himself once again. "There's gotta be a way to find her," he whispered to the Lord as he looked up into the clear heavens. "Please help me."

*****

Just a few miles away in New Castle, Wyoming, someone found an abandoned rental car and notified authorities. Upon investigation, it was learned the car was rented to John Peters weeks before. There were obvious knife slashes in the upholstery, and the backseat was covered with dried blood.

Marquette and Tara Caselli were notified, and they dropped everything they were doing to rush to Wyoming. They went through the blood-covered car, praying to find a clue as to John's whereabouts.

"This amount of blood indicates that whoever met their demise here had their throat slashed," Tara proffered.

Marquette could only nod in agreement. The Ponerellos were *known* for their skill with a knife. He narrowed his eyes as he studied the random slashes…*This is just not right*. He shook his head and took a breath. "A Ponerello would never miscalculate like this, Tara. They *never* stab."

Tara shrugged. "Then how do we explain this amount of blood? It is an obvious Ponerello kill. Mario is getting older. Perhaps his eyesight is failing him."

"Fifty-seven does not make an old man." Marquette reached for something glinting between the seats and pulled out a metal key. "What do we have here?"

Tara raised one of her eyebrows. "It appears to be a motel room key…perhaps John's."

Marquette held the key to the light and read the narrowly engraved words aloud, "Fountain Motor Inn."

They obtained a warrant to search the motel room and question the employees.

"I'm tellin' ya," the manager of the hotel said, "I never saw the guy. He checked in, but he never checked out. He took everything with him. The room was empty the next day."

While Marquette and Tara combed the room for the tiniest of clues, two police officers questioned all of the staff. They showed them photographs of John Peters and the tall, red-headed man whom Tara had watched John follow out of Maggie May's.

A police officer came into the room, where Marquette and Tara were seated on the edge of a bed. "A couple of the maids saw your John Peters on the day he checked in. But nobody saw the other character. That's all I got."

Marquette bit his lip. *What on earth led John to New Castle?*

"Listen, mister," the officer continued, lowering his voice. "There's this old story around here that everybody talks about—and I don't even know if it's true or not—but up by Beulah, there used to be an old Mafia hide-out. It's owned by Game, Fish and Parks now; it's called 'The A Ranch.' "

Marquette and Tara looked confused.

The officer sighed and continued, "You're chasing people from Sicily or something, right?" They nodded, and the officer went on, "Well, maybe your Sicilian thought he could hide out up in Beulah, and when he got up there and found out the feds own it now, he wound up over here."

Marquette nodded in understanding. "Perhaps."

The officer shrugged. "Just an idea." He took a breath. "We're short a man today, so I'm pulling double duty. If you don't need me anymore, I really need to get going."

"Of course." Marquette stood and extended his hand. "Thank you for your help. We appreciate it."

The officer smiled and shook Marquette's hand. "No problem. Give us a call the next time you're in town." He left the motel room, and Marquette turned around and looked at a very tired Tara.

"That makes you the last person to see John," he said

Tara looked at the floor and shook her head. "I should have followed him."

"That would have really messed things up. You know that. And perhaps you would be missing now as well." His black eyes shone cleverly as he took a seat on the bed near her. "And I have been through *that* before. It was a dreadfully unpleasant experience and not worth repeating."

"Agreed."

Marquette sighed. "With this latest information we must assume John to be dead." He swallowed, and Tara saw the grief in his dark eyes. John had been Marquette's friend since high school. They'd solved their first case *together* more than fifteen years ago, and they had truly been best friends. Marquette had been the one privileged to lead John to the Lord in 1968.

He took a deep breath and slowly let it out. "I will call his wife."

*****

Prom was planned for the day before graduation. Not a single boy had asked Tillie, so she was surprised when Billy Fairbanks Jr.'s flashy blue 1968 Chevelle pulled into her driveway one evening. Billy was the handsome captain of the football team and had dated a girl by the name of Renee Collins for years. It was recently rumored they'd broken up, and her parents wouldn't allow him to see her anymore.

Billy was the first boy ever to show up at the Casellis' house and ask for a date. Everyone at school knew the Caselli rules, and *The Wrath of Old Man Caselli* was legendary. A lot of boys had been attracted to Tillie but lacked the courage to approach her father. It was also rumored Tillie wasn't really interested in any of the boys at school anyway. She was in love with some rich guy at Harvard.

Billy was tall and stocky, built to play football. His blonde hair and blue eyes, along with a charismatic smile, made him very popular, especially with the girls.

Tillie was aghast as she watched Billy from her bedroom window upstairs. "This is really weird," she whispered to herself, easing open her window to eavesdrop.

Guiseppi was watering his beloved flower beds bordering the sidewalk around the front porch when Billy approached the older man with a smile. "Mr. Caselli?"

Guiseppi frowned at the young boy but accepted his hand with a firm shake.

"I'm Billy Fairbanks," he introduced. "I understand you have a special rule for asking your daughter out."

"Oh, really?" Guiseppi quipped.

Tillie watched from above and almost laughed out loud at her precious father's antics. She covered her mouth to squelch the uproar threatening to bubble out of her. She didn't want to go to prom at all, let alone with someone as conceited as Billy Fairbanks.

Billy nodded. "The rumor is whoever wants to escort Tillie somewhere has to ask her father first, so I'm asking if I can take her to our senior prom."

Guiseppi scowled, "My daughter will not be eighteen on that evening. You will have to have a chaperone."

"That will be perfectly fine," Billy agreed.

Guiseppi stared hard into Billy's eyes. "You will have to ask my daughter's permission as well. The decision is not mine alone."

Billy nodded in agreement, and Guiseppi told him to wait on the porch. He took Rosa from her hiding place near the narrowly opened door, and they went up to Tillie's room.

Tillie was still standing by the window when her parents came into her room. She gave them a small smile. "He's kind of a jerk," she whispered.

Guiseppi's expression reflected he'd already sensed something *blackguardly* in the young man's personality. "But it is your prom," he reminded, "and people make such a big thing out of it."

Tillie bit her lip. "I don't know. What would *you* do, Ma`ma?"

"Well," Rosa sighed, "we did not have *the prom* in *Italia,* but if we would have, I would have at least utilized the young man's company for an escort. He does have a lovely car, and it might be fun. Kate and Vincenzo enjoyed their prom. Also, you have other friends, like Ginger, who will be going. It will not be like a *date* at all."

"And I am certain one of your brothers would be more than happy to chaperone," Guiseppi added. "That is, if you do not want little, old me dragging along behind you."

Tillie giggled and reached for her father's hand. "I'd love to take you, Papa."

Guiseppi smiled into his daughter's eyes. "Well, what will you have me tell the young fiend on the front porch?"

Tillie hesitated. "I guess…I'll go."

Guiseppi sighed and put his most serious face back on as he turned and left. Tillie and Rosa scampered to the window above the porch to listen to the rest of the conversation.

"That poor child," Rosa whispered.

"Don't feel too sorry for him, Ma`ma. He could be the devil."

Rosa covered her mouth and stepped away from the window, snickering and shaking her head.

In the end, Guiseppi decided it would be alright for Tillie to go with Billy, alone, to the prom, as long as he had her home by midnight. He'd done all the right things by asking Tillie's father *and* automatically agreeing to having a chaperone. Those were good signs, and Tillie would only be a few days away from her eighteenth birthday.

*****

Rosa wanted Tillie to shop for a new dress for the event, but Tillie said, "No…I think I'll just wear that blue thing I wore to Alex's party."

"Oh, my little dear," Rosa fretted, "should we not buy something you will cherish?"

"I only wore that blue dress once, and I really liked it."

Rosa let the matter go with Tillie, but she worried to Guiseppi a few days before the event was to take place. Tillie just wasn't her happy, joking self anymore. She'd grown quiet, hadn't spoken to one of her brothers, and stopped painting altogether. Rosa thought a date for the prom, especially with such a handsome, young character, would have perked her up a little, but Tillie seemed to be getting worse instead of better.

Rosa and Guiseppi lay in their bed, whispering to one another in the dark. The house was quiet, their door was shut, and Guiseppi felt safe enough to speak of the events that had taken place nearly a month ago. "Has she spoken of Noah and what happened?"

"Not one word, Guiseppi. And she has packed away all of the beautiful sketches and paintings. She stashed them beneath her bed and said it would keep the mice away."

Guiseppi sighed. "Oh, my Rosa, what can we do for her? I imagine she is still sick at heart and just not speaking of it."

"And she will *not* speak to Petrice. He tried to call several times before he left for *Italia,* but she would not come to the phone. He sent a letter last week, and I saw it ripped to shreds in the kitchen trash this morning."

"She is very upset," Guiseppi whispered. "Perhaps we should have explained to Petrice—"

"No, Guiseppi. I promised her we would not tell her brothers. She is very embarrassed."

Guiseppi moaned. "I cannot believe she is so embarrassed about this. Everyone sins from time to time."

"She feels she was disobedient and rebellious by spending so much unchaperoned time with the young man. She does not want her brothers to know that she did something they would have never done."

"Well, it is not as if they are without sin," Guiseppi snapped. "Remember the trouble Marquette gave us when we left *Italia?* And those boys think we do not know, but remember the time Vincenzo carried himself away with the champagne? And look at Petrice? Going off and marrying someone before even bringing her home—"

"Guiseppi, settle down. You need to allow her time to grieve. And those boys do not need to know about this. Perhaps all will correct itself with time."

*****

Marquette and Tara arrived ready to celebrate all of the events over the weekend. First Tillie's prom, then the commencement, and then Andy's ordination. It would be wonderfully busy, and Guiseppi's staff at the restaurant had planned two meals—one for after the commencement and one for after Andy's ordination.

Rosa and Tillie were upstairs in her bedroom, working the last of Tillie's thick, curly hair into a wonderful arrangement beneath Rosa's gifted hands. Tara was in the kitchen, getting their supper together, while Guiseppi and Marquette whispered something to one another as they sat in the chairs before the fireplace in the living room. Tara sensed her husband and father-in-law were up to something, especially when they began to laugh hysterically.

Unbeknownst to any of the family, Billy Fairbanks Jr.'s father had been acquainted with the Casellis when they first came to America. He'd done a blackguardly thing in high school, and Marquette and his brothers never forgot it. Billy Fairbanks Sr. had coerced Marcia Witten into compromising her honor during their junior year of high school. As a result, she became pregnant and they were married. Marcia was only Billy Fairbanks Sr.'s *first* wife. Everyone in town knew he was now going through his fourth divorce, and his son, Billy Fairbanks Jr., had remained in his custody for the child's entire life. Marquette conveyed all of this information to Guiseppi, and they began to scheme.

Billy arrived a little later than his scheduled time, stepped up to the front door, and rang the bell. Guiseppi frowned into Marquette's eyes and gave him one nod. Marquette nodded in return, rose from his seat, and put on his most dreadful scowl before he answered the door. He took his time to open the door and looked into the blue eyes of the captain of the high school football team. Billy had left his fast car idling in the driveway behind him, obviously for a quick getaway. He was dressed in a black tuxedo and carried a pretty corsage of simple white carnations, tied with a pale-blue ribbon.

"Yes?" Marquette asked as he raised one eyebrow and looked very mysterious.

Billy was suddenly taken off guard. He'd never met Tillie's famous brother, and he backed up on the porch to check the numbers on the house…After all, he'd only been there once before. He gulped and stammered, "Is this Tillie Caselli's house?"

"Yes," Marquette answered as he continued to stare the poor boy down, never offering to let him inside.

Guiseppi hid his old head behind his paper and shook with laughter. He swallowed as hard as he could and tried to force his humor away. It was important for the young blackguard to be filled with a good scare before he took their little Angel away, alone, in a car.

"Well..." Billy hesitated. *This is really weird. Who is this guy?*

Tara realized what was going on at that point and hurried to the door. She extended a friendly hand toward the young man on the porch. "You must be Billy. Please, come in."

Billy sighed with relief and stepped inside.

From behind his paper, Guiseppi rolled his eyes and shook his head. *Women could be so nice.*

"Tillie is nearly ready," Tara said. She turned toward her husband, who was still frowning in the shadows of the doorway. She narrowed her eyes at him as if to say, *"Behave yourself!"* And then she smiled and looked at Billy, "I will get her." She hurried up the steps and down the hall.

Once Tara was gone, Guiseppi rose from his chair and walked to the entryway with a frightening frown. He slowly circled the tall, young man waiting nervously in the foyer.

"I see the *boy* is here," he said as he looked young Billy up and down.

Marquette nodded and gave the boy a very critical stare. "I hope you plan on treating my sister *honorably* this evening."

Billy gulped and stared at the floor. "*You're* her brother?" He'd heard *those* rumors as well, and he wondered if Marquette had his gun tonight.

Tara informed Rosa and Tillie of what was going on in the entryway below, and they giggled and hurried down the stairs to save the lad. By the time they descended the stairs, they saw poor Billy in front of two very intense interrogators. Tillie couldn't help but smile, but she tried to pretend she was concerned, quickly putting herself between Billy and her brother and father.

Rosa had put Tillie's hair up into a feminine twist, weaving tiny faux pearls all throughout it. She was dressed in a sleeveless pale blue taffeta gown and wore elegant white gloves pulled past her elbows. Delicate pearls dangled from her ears, and the matching strand glimmered against her dark neck. Vincenzo and Kate had given them to her for her birthday the year before.

"Here," she said sweetly to Billy, "I have a boutonniere." She pulled out the pins and expertly fit it onto his lapel, replacing the pins and attaching it securely where it belonged.

Guiseppi's heart melted as he watched his beautiful daughter's graceful movements. There was not a more perfect creature in the entire universe, except perhaps for her mother. He didn't like this young character she was going out with, but it was probably only for the one time; and Guiseppi could live with that.

"I have this," Billy offered in a nervous voice as he pulled out the pins as Tillie had done. As he approached the left side of her dress in order to pin it on her, Marquette's hand shot out in front of him. Billy halted the procedure.

"Does that not have a wristband?" Marquette questioned.

Billy slowly nodded, and Tillie raised her left hand. He awkwardly slipped the corsage over her glove.

"Much better," Guiseppi said with a nod.

"We should be leaving," Billy said abruptly. If he'd known about Guiseppi's imaginary scorecard, he would have seen several points subtracted from the knight's column, doubled, and placed into the blackguard's column. One must never rush a beautiful lady.

"Perhaps we could take your photo," Rosa suggested as she wound her camera.

Billy resisted the urge to run from the house and stood politely where Rosa instructed. He allowed her several shots of the two of them.

"Now you may go," Guiseppi dismissed.

"Thank you, Papa," Tillie said with a smile.

Guiseppi kissed his daughter's cheek. "Remember. Home by midnight."

Tillie smiled, and Marquette and Tara each gave her a kiss before Rosa threw her arms around her daughter.

"I cannot help it," she quietly cried. "You look so beautiful tonight."

Tillie chuckled as she returned her mother's embrace, and it made Guiseppi's heart sigh with relief. *Angel will be okay. She just needs some time.*

Billy ran ahead and opened the door of his car for Tillie, but he didn't help her tuck the long dress safely into the car. Tillie thought that was a little blackguardly, but she dismissed the omission because she wasn't looking at anyone, *especially boys*, in a very good light these days.

The car ride to the prom was uneventful. They talked about school and how excited they were to be graduating. Billy had gotten a football scholarship to Nebraska State, and he was pleased about that. He planned on majoring in economics, but what he really wanted was to be a football coach.

When they pulled into the parking lot of the prom, Tillie saw him slip something into his jacket pocket. It wasn't clear what he'd done, but she thought perhaps it was just his wallet.

"Well, we're here," Billy said with a smile as he looked toward the decorated hotel. Trees and bushes, glowing with tiny white lights, lined a path all the way around. It was a well-known place for hosting large gatherings and receptions in Sioux Falls, and Tillie remembered Kate and Vincenzo mentioning that their own prom was held at the same place.

"Should we go in?" Billy asked.

"Sure," Tillie answered…*Isn't that what we're here for?*

Billy jumped out of the car, slammed the door, and hurried along up the path…*without Tillie.*

She watched him with disbelief. He hadn't *waited* for her, and that wasn't even the *beginning* of his second mistake. Her father and her brothers had always opened the doors for their wives, whether they be doors on cars or doors on buildings. Good ol' Billy blazed right out of the car, leaving his date behind to fend for herself.

Tillie snorted and opened the car door, gathered the full dress into safe handfuls, and helped herself out of the car. By this time, Billy was well on his way to being halfway down the path. By the time she caught up to him, he was visiting with some of his football buddies. They were all surprised he'd managed to bring the untouchable Tillie Caselli with him.

"Did your dad threaten him or anything?" one of them asked her sarcastically.

"No," Billy laughed. "But her brother sure scared me. What kind of a spook is he anyway?"

Tillie was horrified at his remark. "What are you talking about?"

"Well, jeez." Billy rolled his eyes. "He questioned me like I was some kind of a criminal."

Tillie glared at him…*Well, maybe you are.* She shook her head and went into the prom to find Ginger. She didn't have to hang around Billy all night long.

"*Spook*," she muttered to herself as she pressed through her class-mates. She snorted and shook her head.

After visiting with several people along the way and beginning to enjoy herself, Tillie spied Ginger and Bobby over by the punch bowl.

He was behaving like a true gentleman as he dipped some punch into a cup and handed it to Ginger.

"Hey, you," Ginger said with a smile when she saw Tillie. "Are you having fun?"

"Sort of." Tillie raised her eyebrow. "I think I might have to call Marq for a ride though. That Billy's really a jerk."

Ginger looked confused. "Really?"

Tillie nodded and whispered, "Are you guys having fun?"

Ginger giggled. "He's *great*. And he passed all of the tests."

Tillie smiled. At least somebody was having a good time.

Tillie was surprised at how many of her male classmates wanted to dance with her, including Billy. He actually approached her later on in the evening and apologized for the remark about her brother. Tillie forgave him and agreed to one dance, still certain she'd be calling Marquette for a ride home.

The rest of the evening went along, and Tillie had a good time. She had many dances with boys surprised to see her there, and she visited with classmates she would not be seeing in a very long time. Lots of them shared their plans for college or work in another state, and it was an exciting night to find out about the next chapters planned in everyone's lives.

As the night continued, the dance hall grew warm. Tillie and Ginger decided to step outside for just a short time. Ginger had danced with Bobby the whole night and was having the time of her life.

"He's just so cute," she said as they whispered beneath the trees in the back of the building. They shared a small bench, enjoying the cool breeze of the evening.

"I'm happy for you," Tillie said with a sad smile, wishing she could have brought Noah to her prom. But then she mentally slapped herself. That would have been a disaster. *He probably would have spiked the punch and led several young ladies into sin along the way.*

"Hey, Bobby and I can give you a ride home," Ginger offered. "That way you won't have to get Marq all riled up."

Tillie laughed. "Okay. We don't want to rile Marq."

Ginger stood from her place on the bench. "I'm gonna find Bobby because it's almost midnight. You can wait for us here."

"Sure."

Ginger went back inside to find Bobby. Tillie sighed and leaned back, being careful not to hook any of the material on the bolts of the

104

bench. She looked down at the pretty dress and smiled. It was a nice dress, and it had been a nice prom. At least she'd gotten to go.

Someone suddenly sat down next to her, and she looked up to see Billy. "Hi, Billy."

Billy smiled, but it was a weird smile—nothing like Tillie had ever seen before. When he opened his mouth to speak, she understood.

"Hello, Tillie," he slurred. He reached into his pocket to pull out the unidentified object she'd only caught a glimpse of earlier. It was a flask. "Wanna drink?"

Tillie shook her head. "I don't drink."

"You are such a little prude, Tillie Caselli," he laughed as he slipped the flask back into his pocket.

"You're ridiculous," she muttered as she stood from the bench and attempted to walk away.

Billy grabbed her by one of her white-gloved arms and roughly pulled her back onto the bench. He yanked her body up against his and forced a wet kiss upon her mouth.

"Gross!" she yelled and pulled away. She gave him a stinging slap to his face and asked, "Was that your tongue?"

She struggled to her feet and attempted to get away from him, but Billy caught her arm again. This time Tillie leveled one of her gloved fists as hard as she could right into his nose. He held her arm and laughed.

"Come on, Tillie," he coaxed as he pulled her closer to his body again. "Everybody does it. You need to try this."

Billy suddenly let go of her arm and spun to the ground. Out of nowhere, Marquette appeared standing above the drunk body of the captain of the football team. "Not *everyone* does it before they are married. And when a young lady says no, she means it." He was wearing dark clothing and one of his favorite hats. He adjusted the brim and reached for his little sister. "Are you alright, my Angel?"

Tillie's mouth hung open with surprise. "When did you get here?"

"I have been here all evening," Marquette answered.

Tillie frowned with confusion.

Marquette sighed as he looked at Billy. He'd found his way into a seated position and was rubbing the arm Marquette had wrenched behind his back.

"Sometimes," Marquette began, "a blackguard will come to a young lady's house and do all of the right things, expertly fooling her into an evening alone." He let out a heavy breath and shook his head. "And only the *most perfect* of knights knows a blackguard in disguise."

Tillie laughed. "You're the most perfect knight and brother in the whole world."

Marquette only shook his head and smiled. "Papa sent me."

Chapter 8

Noah sat on the rickety wooden steps of his cabin, watching the sun light the lake while ducks glided along the mirrored surface. He held her photograph and looked longingly into her face as he remembered their conversation. He'd asked her, "When do you think you'll be back?", and she'd promised, "The very latest will be June." *Just one more day until June…one more day…*

*****

The last day of May 1975 dawned in perfect splendor over the Black Hills of South Dakota. From Mona's porch swing, she watched the easterly sun bathe its light over the hills and trees in the early morning. Mona called this her "special time"—that certain part of the day when she talked to the Lord, gave Him whatever weighed upon her heart, and asked Him for guidance and wisdom. She heard a soft noise behind her and turned to see Joshua as he padded along in his stocking feet, carrying two steaming cups of coffee.

"Good morning, Joshua," she greeted with a smile as she took one of the cups. "What are you doing up so early?"

Joshua sat down in the swing beside her and draped his free arm over her shoulders. "Do you really think you have the market cornered on getting up early?"

Mona shook her head, gave him a soft kiss on his chin, and looked into his brown eyes. She sighed and returned her gaze to the hills as she took a careful sip of the coffee.

"And what are you so deep in thought about this morning?" Joshua asked.

"Your brother, Noah. I think somethin's wrong with that kid."

"Oh, Mona," Joshua attempted to brush off her worry. He took a sip of his coffee and followed her gaze into the hills before them.

"Nothing's wrong with that kid. He just has to adjust to living alone and having a different sort of lifestyle."

Mona shook her head. "He's got a heartache. Can'tcha feel it, Josh?"

"You mean the girl?"

Mona nodded. "And why is he being so mysterious about her? Why doesn't he just bring her over?"

Joshua shrugged. *That* part was a little weird, but he was used to Noah doing strange things. At least he'd stopped seeing Carrie.

"I don't know." Mona shook her head and sipped her coffee. "I think somethin's gone wrong with that deal."

*****

Tillie Caselli was poised before the lectern in the Washington Senior High School auditorium. Her curly hair spilled from beneath her cap and rested on her shoulders. She wore the flaming orange robe the girls had all complained about but no one had done a thing to correct. Orange and black were the school's colors. The boys wore the black robes, and the girls were stuck with the orange.

She saw her family seated together and smiled at them. That rotten Petrice hadn't even shown up at the last minute, but she didn't care. Let him have a life if he really wanted one.

Billy Fairbanks Jr. was seated with the other graduates, dressed like the rest of the boys except for one distinct difference: Billy sported two black eyes this morning. Tillie swallowed to keep herself from laughing. *I must have hit him harder than I thought.*

The Martins were just behind her family. Sam sat with Becky-Lynn and that "mean old woman" Tillie had heard about. Alex sat next to his mother, and Frances was next to James. Next to them were Ginger's parents, and way on the end was Andy, who'd be an ordained minister tomorrow.

"My family came to this country shortly before I was born," Tillie began. She felt her voice shake and swallowed in order to continue. "They became citizens of the United States on the day of my fifth birthday. But I was born privileged. I am an American by birth. Never will I have to wait five years or take a naturalization exam. I was born *here,* and that gives me great power.

"My oldest brother gave the commencement address in this very room eighteen years ago, and I hope my message will be delivered with the same eloquence. My brother is a gifted speaker, poetic and powerful. His words here eighteen years ago have been remembered by my family and our friends since he said them from the same place I stand today." Tillie seemed to sigh as she smiled into the audience. "I have looked at Petrice's old commencement notes, and I see he spoke of *pressing toward the mark*, which he has done in a most impressive way. He has gone from this place to speak to famous diplomats, congressmen, and even the United Nations.

"But what *I* ask of you, my dear classmates, is that whatsoever things are true, honest, just, pure, lovely, and of good report; if there be any virtue, and if there be any praise, *think on these things*, for it's what guides our life into its *best* conclusion and keeps us safe and solid. True nobility, righteous purity, and lovely admiration are the things my family raised me to believe in, and what I believe to have brought me to this place here today." She paused to smile, and her dark eyes sparkled with mischief. "Of course, it has become unpopular to speak of the Christ from these public podiums, but I will veer from the lowered standard and risk my words when I say we should all desire the excellence of Jesus. Seek Him out, no matter what the insignificance of the situation at hand, and follow Him into Truth, for it is His desire we all be saved and none of us lost. And I know it was His perfect desire that brought me into being and what places me before you today.

"My Papa says our time is here and now, and what we decide to do with these privileges will affect the rest of our lives. Decide carefully, my friends, where you will go and who you will be going there with, for if you go with Jesus, you will be assured of His will and glory in your lives.

"Ma`ma says God holds our future in His hands and if we know God, we know our goals and we know where our future will lead us, and that is heavenward."

Tillie nodded to her classmates and smiled. Everyone began to clap, and she looked at her family. Ma`ma was crying and so was Papa. She waved and blew them a kiss from the palm of her hand. Truly, there were no greater parents, or examples, in the entire world.

Guiseppi's staff had planned a reception for Tillie and Ginger, laying out a feast fit for kings. They roasted beef for the noon celebration, cooked sweet potatoes, mashed white potatoes, whisked the gravy until it was as smooth as rich cream, and glazed carrots with brown sugar and honey—*and that was just for the American guests!* For Tillie and her family, they roasted capons, fried cauliflower, tossed zucchini with tomatoes and basil, and prepared Tillie's favorite: canolli. In the center of the banquet table stood a four-tiered white cake, decorated in black and orange and topped with a graduation cap and two tassels.

"You have done an excellent job," Guiseppi said as he gave Georgie a pat on his shoulder. Georgie had been one of the first people hired by Guiseppi in 1956, and he had an interesting history.

Georgie was a homosexual in a time that did not accept such behavior. His entire family disowned him in the early fifties, and Georgie had attempted suicide. Marquette found him drunk in the alley behind the restaurant shortly after that and told him to clean himself up and get a job. Georgie took Marquette's advice and was still working for Guiseppi after nearly nineteen years. Guiseppi didn't approve of Georgie's lifestyle, and he made it clear that he didn't want Georgie's "friends" around the place. However, Guiseppi felt pity in his heart for Georgie because of the way his family had treated him. Georgie thought highly of Guiseppi and admired him for the way he'd raised his sons and daughter. There were many things Guiseppi's children had done over the course of the last nineteen years that Georgie knew his own father would have disowned them for. But Guiseppi took the responsibility of "raising them up in the way they should go" to heart. He loved and taught his children at the same time, a thing Georgie had never had with his own father.

"This food is delicious," Ginger said with a smile as she helped herself to another plate of the mashed potatoes and gravy.

Tillie nodded. "*That's* one thing we've never been short of."

"What?"

"Food. Have you ever known my family to have a get-together without food? It's just one big, happy supper."

Ginger laughed, nearly choking on her mashed potatoes.

"Don't make 'em come out your nose," Tillie teased as she remembered a dreadful incident with cookies and milk when they were younger.

Tillie's joke sent Ginger into near hysterics. She forced down the mouthful of mashed potatoes and let herself laugh out loud. "*Nobody* is this funny."

Tillie laughed at her own joke and noticed Bobby Maxwell just entering the restaurant. He looked very lost and nervous when Andy and Mr. Engleson approached him.

"Hey, he's here," Tillie whispered. "And he looks pretty nervous. Better get over there and save him from the interrogators. I saw those two getting advice from my brothers after the commencement!"

Ginger giggled and hurried off to see her new beau.

Vincenzo and Marquette walked over to their sister when they saw Ginger hurrying away.

"Is that Ginger's new boyfriend?" Vincenzo asked.

Tillie smiled. "He's really nice."

"No drinking?" Marquette raised one eyebrow.

Tillie shook her head.

"No groping?" Vincenzo asked.

Tillie's mouth fell open in surprise.

Vincenzo chortled, "I heard about the prom disaster. Dear Marq pointed him out to me today at the commencement. Wow, you must pack some power into those little lady hands."

Tillie laughed and shook her head. "I can't believe I did that."

"I cannot either," Marquette said with a smile and a shake of his head. "I am certain the young man learned a lesson he will *not* soon forget."

Tara touched her husband's elbow, and he turned to see his beloved wife had joined them.

"Georgie needs help with some trays," she said with a sweet smile. Marquette and Vincenzo nodded and hurried off to give Georgie a hand, leaving Tara and Tillie alone.

"Finally!" Tara rolled her eyes and smiled at Tillie. "First your big dance, then graduation. We haven't had the chance to visit, and I have missed you!"

"Me too," Tillie replied.

"Marquette said the two of you got some pretty unusual looks when he took you to the *DQ* last night after prom."

Tillie grinned. "Oh, Tara, it was *so* funny! Here's Marquette, all dressed in black and wearing one of his hats. He looked just like a mobster. And then here I am in a formal. We laughed and laughed. Can you imagine? I can just see him skulking around behind the trees, peeking at me and Billy. I didn't even know he was there!"

Tara laughed. "He is quite good at his job. I learned everything I know from him." Her voice lowered and her round eyes became very concerned. "Please know I have not stopped praying for you. Are you okay?"

Tillie's smile faded, and she slowly nodded. "It's gonna be okay. You said so yourself."

"Are you still thinking of him?"

"All of the time, Tara. He's always there, in the back of my mind. I'm trying to put it behind me, but it just doesn't feel *right* to do that." She shrugged and sighed, "I don't know. I guess it was just a weird deal."

Tara put her hand on Tillie's shoulder. "Is it possible you misunderstood?"

"No way. He was just a blackguard in disguise."

At that moment, Alex Martin walked up to the two of them and extended his hand to Tillie. "Congratulations, Tillie."

Tillie reached for his hand. "Thanks, Alex."

"Great commencement speech," he said in his deep voice, the voice that used to just melt her.

"Thanks," she replied, noticing his brilliantly white teeth. *How does someone's teeth get that white?*

"Kate tells me you won two blue ribbons. One for *Obedience* and one for *Refugees*," Alex went on. "You do fine work."

Tillie feigned a smile, surprised that the very cool and aloof intellectual had taken the initiative to speak with her.   He'd never given her more than ice-skating lessons and the two dances at Mulligan's Spring Ball. *So, why is he talking to me now? Why is he even here?*

From their place just outside of the kitchen, Marquette nudged Vincenzo and whispered, "Look at *that*. Would you just *look at that*. He is back barely a month and already making a move on our little Angel."

Vincenzo turned and examined the situation. Alex was visiting with Tara and Tillie, and it looked innocent enough. He smiled at Marquette. "They have known one another for many years, *all of her life*, Marquette. Why does it bother you?"

"I do not care for the way he looks into her eyes." Marquette narrowed his expression and glared at Alex.

Vincenzo laughed and slapped Marquette on the back. "Did you forget? He is the brother of my wife, and he is fine man, Marquette. Do not be so suspicious."

*****

Christ the King Church was filled to overflowing the next day. The entire church had turned out for Andy's ordination. They'd watched him grow from a small child into a man, prayed him through his tour of duty in Vietnam, and then saw him dedicate his life completely to the Lord. His best friend was Alex Martin, and Alex spoke at the ordination as well.

"I remember when we were small," Alex said from the podium. He was dressed in a sharp, black suit and spoke like an expert. "Andy and I would always pretend to be soldiers and watch my sister and her boyfriend from behind the bushes at my place." Soft laughter from the congregation interrupted for a moment. Alex smiled and continued, "But when it came time to fight for our country, Andy did the right thing, while I stayed behind. Andy has a brave heart, and he trusted God to keep him safe, just the same as he trusts God now to help him lead this church and save others along the way.

"Jesus said, 'Greater love hath no man than this, that a man lay down his life for his friends.' And Andy has done *exactly* that in more ways than one. First, he laid down his life for his fellow soldiers and unknown citizens of a country not his own, in the name of freedom and in the name of God. Secondly, he laid down his life for this church, forsaking all others, so he may lead and guide us, shepherding his friends as he believes Jesus has commanded him to do." Alex paused and smiled at Andy. "No greater friend have I than the friend I have in you."

The congregation applauded as Alex returned to his seat, and Marquette arose to be the next speaker. From the front row in the choir, Ginger and Tillie sat side by side, where they'd been seated for years.

"He's still *really* cute," Ginger whispered as they watched Alex's long legs carry him gracefully across the platform.

Tillie rolled her eyes and shook her head. "He's not *that* cute," she whispered as Marquette started to speak.

"It was a place of tremendous uncertainty," Marquette was saying. He looked more glamorous than ever, dressed in a double-breasted, pin-striped navy suit with a silk scarf folded into his breast pocket. He wore no hat in the church, exposing his elegant ponytail.

"I remember wondering to myself many times," Marquette continued in his soft accent, "why did God make me a citizen in a new country, only to have me leave it and fight for another? Andy and I have spoken of this many times. I thought God had fallen asleep and forgot about those of us who believed in Him. We would be hiding in the jungle, and our new best friend would suddenly be dead before our very eyes. We went days without food and without sleep, and I wondered what had happened to the Lord.

"My purpose became clear, as I struggled each day between somehow trying to survive the battles or simply ending my own life. I realized we were in this place of sin and destruction, but God was still with me in my heart. I called upon Him, and He convinced me to survive so I might serve whatever task He had chosen for me.

"Andy's purpose became clear as he struggled in battle as well, but his purpose was far different from my own. Andy left his comfortable and safe home in America to fight an unseen enemy, an enemy he did not know, only to return and continue another great battle. The battle of good and evil. Now he will combat the tremendous uncertainties of how many shall follow and how many shall fight him for what he believes in, choosing either their death and destruction or complete freedom in Christ."

Marquette smiled at Andy. "God blessed us in America, but he gave us our purpose on foreign soil." He nodded at Andy and returned to his seat while the congregation applauded.

Ginger saw Tillie's eyes fill with tears, and she whispered, "What's wrong?"

Tillie shook her head and whispered with a smile, "That's the first time I've ever heard Marquette talk about Vietnam."

They feasted for hours at Guiseppi's restaurant, where his staff had prepared yet another wonderful meal. The neighborhood had never celebrated for two days in a row before, but no one seemed the wearier from it.

"This is how *every* weekend should be," Sam declared as he gulped down a canolli. He and Alex had refilled their plates twice and were considering another trip to the buffet table.

Alex smiled and shook his head. "We'd get fat."

Sam leaned close to whisper, "By the way, did I misunderstand something, or were you looking at a certain little member of the choir today?"

Alex rolled his eyes and shook his head.

Sam's eyes shone with mischief. "Yes, you were, Alex! I saw the *whole* thing. Pray Marquette didn't catch you."

Alex laughed nervously and whispered, "I couldn't help it. She's changed so much. She's really…really…" Alex hesitated.

"Pretty?" Sam finished as he followed Alex's gaze into Tillie's direction.

Alex whispered, "What do you think? Is she too young, or would it be okay?"

Sam shrugged. "Depends. She might not even give *you* the time of day."

"And why not?"

"Marquette might kill you."

"That lunatic has *never* liked me, even when I was little."

Sam laughed. "He's not a lunatic, is he?"

"Well of course he is," Alex scoffed. "God only knows what he *really* does for a living."

Sam laughed again and gave Alex's shoulder a friendly pat. "Here's a little brotherly advice for you, Alex. Pray like crazy before you do anything." He glanced Tillie's way and frowned softly.

"'Cause I think something weird happened there, and more than just the prom disaster. She's just not her old, chipper self these days."

*****

Tillie tried to fall asleep but was just too uncomfortable. The day had been hot and humid, and no one had remembered to turn on the air conditioning. She tossed and turned for quite a while before she finally got up and went down to the kitchen for a can of soda. She quietly let herself out the patio door and nearly screamed when she saw the silhouette of a man in one of the loungers. Thankfully, it was her father, and she laughed at her own scare.

"I'm glad that was you," she said as she took a seat close to him. She opened her soda can and took a big gulp. "Can't sleep?"

"It is hotter than Hades in that house," Guiseppi said.

Tillie took another gulp of her soda. "Want me to get you a can?"

Guiseppi shook his head and lifted his empty can into the air. "This is my second."

Tillie leaned back on the lounger and looked into the starry night above them. "What would you think, Papa, if I said I wanted to travel with Marquette and Tara? You know, learn what they do. Maybe I could do that."

Guiseppi laughed as he reached over for his daughter's hand. "I would think you were being crazy and short-sighted."

Tillie wrinkled up her nose. "Papa, that's not very nice."

"Listen to me, my Angel. For one thing, it is a miracle the two of them yet live. Why put your young, wonderful life in danger?"

Tillie shrugged.

"Are you trying to run away, my Angel?"

Tillie shook her head. "No. No, Papa."

"You know this thing with Noah will pass." He gave Tillie's hand a soft squeeze. "It just may take some time."

At the mention of Noah's name, Tillie felt her eyes burn with tears. She tried to fight them away, but her Italian passion was far too strong. She felt them fall from her eyes and down her cheeks.

Guiseppi touched one of the tears with his index finger. "Do not be afraid to cry, my little Angel. God has given you tear ducts, just the same as He has given you a heart."

"But why did He let this happen to me?" Tillie whispered as she felt a sob beginning to grow in her chest.

"He did not *let* anything happen to you." He got out of his chair and sat down beside his daughter. "You, my little Angel, *chose* this thing. And it was not a very wise choice."

"I'm so sorry, Papa," she cried.

Guiseppi's heart broke for the girl, and he took her into his arms. She laid her head on his chest and wept.

"Everything will be okay," he assured as he caressed her back. "We will pray for you, and everything will be alright."

*****

Tillie went to work with her father every morning that summer, like her brothers had done years before her. Ginger was busy with Bobby every day of the week, and Tillie had nothing better to do. Besides, the restaurant was fun. Georgie was comical and so was the old cook, Doria. Doria had been at the restaurant since 1955, the year before the Casellis came to America, and he was getting on in years. Tillie guessed him to be at least sixty, but he was still fit and able to work hard in Guiseppi's kitchen.

"Nobody *really* knows how old he is," Georgie said one day as Tillie chopped vegetables. "He keeps it a secret so we'll all be surprised when he finally drops dead in one of his cauldrons."

Tillie laughed. Georgie always made Tillie laugh.

She waited on tables, washed loads of dishes, and helped out wherever they needed her. Sometimes she'd lose herself in a daydream over a big sink of dishes, remembering the romantic rides on the back of his bike, the soft scent of his Old Spice, and the gentle expression in his eyes. Then she'd realize her dishwater had gotten cold and admonish herself for thinking of him at all. It was a moment in time, and she didn't need to waste any more of her life on *that* nonsense.

By now Marquette and Vincenzo had noticed the unhappiness in her spirit, even though she tried very hard to hide it. They blamed Petrice's continued absence and lack of communication between brother and sister. As a result, Marquette surprised Vincenzo in late June by showing up at the ranch unannounced.

Kate sent a hand into the pasture to find Vincenzo, and he soon rode into the yard, his horse kicking up dust under its thundering hooves. Vincenzo jumped off of his horse and gave his reins to the hand. He stretched as he walked toward his flashy brother, frowned, and attempted to brush the dust from his jeans.

"What is so important that I must come in from the field?"

"I have chartered a ride for us," Marquette answered.

"A ride?" Vincenzo's frown deepened. "Where?"

"To New York City. I believe it is high time we paid our blackguardly brother a visit."

Vincenzo's frown softened and he began to laugh. "Alright, then. When do we leave?"

Tara stayed behind with Kate while the two brothers headed for New York. They'd been there many times to visit Petrice but had yet to be invited to his new place.

Petrice was surprised, to say the least, when the dusty cowboy and the fancy gentleman appeared at his new apartment door. Obviously, Vincenzo hadn't even taken the time to change his clothes.

"I cannot stay long," Vincenzo said as he walked past Petrice and into the apartment. He took off his straw cowboy hat when he saw Elaine seated on the couch. "Hello, Miss Ellie."

Elaine smiled in polite greeting and got to her feet.

"Nor can I." Marquette walked into the room and looked out of the giant picture window at the Twin Towers. "Hello, Miss Elaine. Nice view."

"And to what do I owe this little surprise?" Petrice asked, sensing the anger in his two younger brothers.

"Angel is not yet well," Vincenzo said as he, too, looked at the magnificent sight before him.

"What is wrong with her?" Petrice asked with a frown. "She will not answer my letters, and she will not speak to me on the phone."

"You broke her heart," Marquette answered.

Petrice shook his head and turned from them, walked toward Elaine, and touched her hand. "Please leave us for just a moment—"

"No," Vincenzo interrupted. He turned from the view at the window and said, "Ellie is our sister now. This involves her as well."

"But the responsibility for this mess rests totally upon *your* shoulders, Patty," Marquette said as he looked at the two of them. "You should have forsaken yourselves the trip and attended Angel's graduation."

"Well, it is too late to point fingers now," Petrice retorted. "The damage has already been done. I have tried to apologize to her, but she will not listen to a word of reason."

"A woman's heart is difficult to reason with," Vincenzo narrowed his eyes. "You are the one responsible for this hurt, and you are the only one that can make it right—"

"You must humble yourself, Petrice," Marquette interjected. "Go to her and humble yourself. Take whatever tongue lashing you deserve and make this thing right with Angel, for we cannot bear the burden of her pain any longer."

Petrice sighed. Marquette had always been such a dramatic fellow, but he knew in his heart he *could* do more to make the situation better.

*****

Noah sat on his rickety steps, watching another sunset glow behind the hills. June had almost come to a close and still no word from Angel. He looked to the heavens and prayed, "Father, I don't understand. What's gone wrong?"

Chapter 9

Noah sat on a stool at Maggie May's, studying the beautiful portrait of *Obedience*. He looked at the snapshot Maggie had tucked into one corner of the frame—the precious photo Estelle had taken on the last night they were together. As he looked into Angel's sweet smile, Noah was lost in her memory—the softness of her skin, the way she smelled, and the tenderness in her eyes...*She really loved me.*

Maggie came out of the kitchen, surprised to see someone at the counter. She hadn't heard the door bell signal someone had entered the bar. "When did you come in?" she asked in her usual gruff manner.

"Couple of minutes ago," he answered as he looked at the painting. "Your bell is broken again, but I'll fix it before I leave."

Maggie nodded. "How's class?"

Noah turned his eyes toward Maggie. "Good."

Maggie took a deep breath and shook her head. He looked *terrible* today. Sober, but terrible. The sadness in his expression had steadily gotten worse over the summer. The longer Angel stayed away, the more depressed Noah became.

"So what's goin' on for you today?" she asked as she opened a bottle of Coke and set it on the counter.

Noah sighed and reached for the bottle. "I'm meeting Joshua out behind the fish hatchery this afternoon. He says he's got something to show me."

Maggie took a breath and asked, "So do you see Carrie anymore?"

Noah frowned. "What kind of a question is *that?*"

Maggie shrugged. "Just askin'. Curious I guess."

Noah's frown deepened as he shook his head. "What would I want with *that* tramp?"

Maggie raised her eyebrows. "Sorry. Little touchy today, are we?"

Noah sighed, relaxed his frown, and looked at the portrait. By now, June had come and gone, and he'd heard *nothing* from Angel. "I just can't believe it's taking so long, Maggie," he moaned. "I should have heard from her by now."

It was a hot summer day in the Black Hills as Noah rode his Harley up the gentle incline of Highway 44 and into Rimrock Canyon. The crag along the highway had been blasted through to make room for the road, and it was quite an impressive drive. It twisted and turned through the jagged, cliff-sized stones on either side; but, without Angel to share it, Noah didn't even care.

Less than ten minutes into the canyon was The South Dakota Fish Hatchery, set into a tiny valley between the rocks and hills. All around it were high mountains and trees, and Rapid Creek rushed through with water from Pactola Reservoir down into Canyon Lake.

Noah saw Joshua leaning on the side of his car as he pulled into the parking lot surrounding the fish hatchery. He waved and parked beside him. "Hey, Josh," he greeted as he got off his bike.

"Hey, Noah," Joshua said with a smile. "Let's take a little walk down by the creek."

Rapid Creek gushed along, full to nearly overflowing. The rushing was so loud one could hear the creek before it could be seen. As they walked deeper into the trees and grass, the creek came into view. Just on the other side of the creek was a beautiful, clear meadow.

"Let's cross here," Joshua said as he led Noah over an old wooden bridge.

They continued across the meadow and up a soft hill until a sculpturesque view of the Black Hills was before them. Noah could see for miles from this vantage, and he took a surprised breath.

"Wow," he breathed, "I didn't even know this was back here."

Joshua smiled as he looked out into the hills. "Dad and Mom left this land to you, Noah. You receive full ownership on your twenty-fourth birthday."

"No kidding?" Noah looked at his brother with surprise. "Why didn't you tell me before?"

Joshua shrugged. "I'm not really sure why I kept it from you. I think I was afraid you'd beg me to sell it…you know, for the money."

Noah took a soft breath and promised, "I won't sell it, Josh."

Joshua turned around and pointed downward, back toward a small meadow closer to the fish hatchery. "That's where Dad and Mom and I lived for a long time, before I went to Korea."

"But there's nothin' there."

Joshua nodded. "There used to be houses all through there. Of course, Dad and Mom moved out and sold our place to someone else before you were even born. Then everything was wiped out in the flood of '72." Joshua returned his gaze to the hills in the distance. "I'm really glad you're not gonna sell it."

Noah followed his brother's gaze, inhaling the strong pine scent. The Black Hills spruce bordered the area, even as far down as the rushing creek. Beyond the jade tree tops, the *Paha Sapa* (as the Sioux Indians had named the hills) reminded Noah of the brief life he'd shared with Angel. The clear meadow before him danced with singing birds and the fluff of old dandelions…*She would have loved this*.

Joshua noticed the intense sadness in Noah's expression. "Mona says you're going to work for Denis Construction," he started, hoping to get some conversation out of Noah.

Noah nodded and allowed Joshua a faint smile. "Yep. I start there next week. The pay is better than the packing house, and I'll be able to learn inside carpentry in the winter. That goes along with my trades class I'm gonna be taking at the technical school."

"I imagine you're pretty excited about that."

Noah shrugged. "I guess."

Joshua put his hand on Noah's shoulder. "Noah, you seem so down lately. Is something wrong?"

Noah averted his eyes and looked back to the Hills. "Not really."

Joshua frowned. Noah *was* hiding something, and hopefully Noah would tell him when he was ready.

*****

Elaine sat on their new white couch, watching her husband pace back and forth in front of the window with the most coveted view in town. She hadn't felt right about what they'd done, even while they planned the trip. She would have *never* just skipped a special day for one of her own siblings, if she'd had any, but she'd allowed her passion for Petrice to make her decision.

"We have made a dreadful mistake, Petrice," she said.

"Bah!" Petrice growled and threw one of his hands into the air as he continued to pace. "They have wives! They should be more understanding."

Elaine slowly shook her head. "This was different. We didn't even invite them to our wedding." She sighed and looked at him. "Petrice, I don't know your family at all, but what little time we spent with them in Sioux Falls, I get the impression they'd do anything for each other."

Petrice stopped his pacing and looked at his beautiful wife.

"And then," she continued, "your brothers show up here. Out of the blue. It looked like Vincenzo left whatever he was doing to fix this situation. How many people actually do things like that? We're not *there*. We don't see what your sister is obviously going through every day." She shook her head and frowned. "And if I'm responsible for hurting her, I want to remedy that. I plan on being your wife for a very long time, Petrice Caselli, but we've done something wrong and need to make amends."

Petrice slumped down beside his wife. "It is very difficult for a man to admit when he has been wrong."

Elaine nodded...*I can see that.*

*****

Across the Atlantic, Marquette and Tara had just finished a very troubling interview with a man they'd located in a Viennese prison. Alonzo Dimetris had forged a false passport for a man he identified as Mario Ponerello. However, he'd done the forgery in 1964—a good four years *before* Marquette had even begun his search for the man and more than eleven years ago. To make matters worse, he claimed to have no recollection of what name he'd put on the passport.

To Marquette and Tara's surprise, Alonzo was able to identify the tall redhead who'd followed John out of Maggie May's. He was a German named Dr. Schneider Rauwolf, and he'd helped Mario escape Sicily in 1964. Rauwolf not only facilitated Ponerello's escape, he also hid him in Berlin until Alonzo could affect the false passport that allowed him to slip into the United States. According to Alonzo, there was a complicated network of operatives within the United States government who obtained and sold Social Security numbers to foreigners. Again, Alonzo had no recollection of their names. Of course, Marquette and Tara realized Alonzo was serving a life sentence for his crimes and had probably decided to "forget" the details.

The wind was chilly as they walked along the pathway in front of Bergtheater, situated on the famous Ringstrasse Boulevard. The stone architecture of the Bergtheater never failed to impress Marquette, and he always made a point of seeing it whenever they visited Vienna. Great columns of arched windows placed between strong stone beams reached several stories above them, while morning church bells could be heard chiming from nearby Votivkirche.

Tara was dressed in a long leather coat and knee-high boots, with her head topped off with a warm beret and gloves on her hands. She shivered in the wind and tucked her arm into Marquette's, snuggling closer to him as they walked along.

"And America requires no papers to move about from state to state," she reminded as she chattered through her teeth. "Good grief, but it is cold! It is supposed to be *warm* here in the summer!"

Marquette replied, "So there is no way to find out where Mario eventually relocated." He pulled her close and rubbed his own gloved hand up and down her back to make her warmer. He wore a long coat and hat as well, but this chilly spell in Vienna was even making him shiver.

"Obviously John pieced together a trail that led him to New Castle, but where from?" Tara questioned.

Marquette took a chilly breath. "And we know that 'The A Ranch' no longer hides for the family, so Mario was most certainly sent away at some point."

"Or perhaps it was already federally owned by the time he got there, but he decided to remain in the area anyway?"

Marquette grinned. "Imagine Mario's surprise."

"The Rapid City and New Castle police have all of our information," Tara chattered. "They will contact us if they should come across anything."

Marquette sighed and shook his head. They'd been going through this particular scenario for years now. "We were so close, my Tara. Now it seems our leads have dried up once again."

*****

Tillie sat in her mother's window seat in the living room. The cushions were soft and comforting as she snuggled herself into them and watched the raindrops slide gracefully down the glass.

"What are you thinking, my Angel?" Rosa's soft voice came from behind, and Tillie turned to see her mother with a tray of tea.

She smiled. "That will perfectly hit the spot, Ma`ma, and I was thinking that I'm just gonna go into work today."

Rosa nodded with a smile, pouring a cup for Tillie and handing it to her. "Papa will be happy to see you. He thinks you are a hard worker."

Tillie took the cup. "Thanks. Does he really?"

Rosa nodded as she poured herself a cup and seated her tiny body in the window seat beside her daughter. "Papa always says, 'No one works like my Angel.' "

Tillie giggled with satisfaction and took another sip of the tea. Orange and spice. "Mmmm. My favorite. Thanks, Ma`ma."

"I saw you received a letter from Ellie?" Rosa raised one eyebrow. "What was that all about?"

Tillie sighed. "She apologized. Ma`ma, the woman can really write. You should read the letter. It was the most incredible thing I've ever read. She went on and on about how sorry she is for putting her own selfish passions ahead of my own and asked me for forgiveness, like a thousand times."

"Will you ever forgive Petrice for what he has done?"

Tillie turned back to the window and shrugged her shoulders. "Probably. It's just too weird right now. I mean, there he is, living with this chick we don't even know, and he hasn't come for a visit in months. I just feel so unattached from him right now."

Rosa nodded and sipped at her tea. She had to admit she'd felt the same way. "There was a time when he was your best friend," she reminded.

Tillie frowned. "Well he's not anymore. He's got a *new* best friend."

Rosa chortled. "I think you might be a little jealous."

"Humph! I'm *not* jealous. What's to be jealous of?"

"Oh, I do not know. Maybe it is that he chose someone while we were not looking? Or perhaps it is something else?"

"Oh, Ma`ma," Tillie scoffed. "She's so different from the rest of us. Just look at her. Marq and Vincenzo chose girls that *look* like us. Know what I mean? This chick is as white as a ghost."

Rosa laughed and gently admonished, "Angel! Our Lord does not show favoritism, and neither should you."

"I'm not, it's just that she *is* different. You must have noticed."

"Well of course I noticed," Rosa admitted. "But her difference is probably one of the things that attracted your brother. You cannot deny that she is a *very* beautiful woman."

Tillie shook her head. "I know. She's gorgeous."

"And you have very good reasons for being so upset with your brother, but you are just a tad jealous of his new bride." Tillie looked sick and Rosa laughed. "Well that is what she is, and we all need to get used to this *new bride* because I am quite certain they will be together for at least as long as I live." She took a breath and added, "And do not think it has been so easy for your Papa and I. We would have liked to have had at least the tiniest preview or been included in their celebration, but they have not allowed us even a cookie break—"

Tillie laughed. "Okay, Ma`ma. I'll speak to him the next time he calls."

Rosa nodded. "That is my good girl."

*****

The choir at Christ the King practiced every Saturday morning, and Tillie and Ginger sat next to each other in the bottom row of the sopranos.

"Bobby is *so* awesome, Tillie," Ginger whispered before the practice began.

Tillie smiled and whispered back, "So where's he going to school?"

"Oh, my goodness!" Ginger exclaimed. "*That's* the best part. He changed schools this week. He *was* going to Nebraska, but now he'll be going to Mankato with me!"

"Oh, my goodness!" Tillie gasped. "Did he change just for you?"

Ginger nodded. "I can't believe how *great* this is working out!"

Tillie smiled, deliberately hiding the sadness she still carried in her heart. She wasn't about to rain on Ginger's parade.

In the marble vestibule of the church, Sam snuck up on his younger brother, placed a hand on his shoulder, and laughed hysterically when Alex startled.

"What are you doing here?" Alex whispered with a frown.

"I went to pick you up for our golf game," Sam answered. He raised one eyebrow as he continued, "Mom said you were over here— *joining the choir?*"

Alex narrowed his eyes at Sam as he tried to find the perfect words for response.

Sam chuckled, "Is choir practice being held in the vestibule this week?"

Alex rolled his eyes and peered around the corner at the choir as they started practice. "I don't want to look too obvious."

Sam laughed again. "And you don't think creeping around in the vestibule is the least bit suspicious looking?"

Alex took a deep breath and let it out. "Listen, Sam, I'm sure you're up on all the great techniques, but I'm new at this. I'll just go about it in my own way."

"Listen, Alex, instead of *stalking* her, why don't you just ask her out. You know, like on a date."

"Would you please just shut up." Alex turned his eyes away from the choir and frowned at Sam. "I can't just *ask her out.*"

"Why not?"

Alex turned his eyes back on the choir. "I'm twenty-five years old, for Pete's sake. Don't you think her family will have something to say about that?"

"No. They *like* us—"

"Marquette hates my guts," Alex interrupted.

"I don't think he *hates* you."

Alex nodded. "He *hates* me."

"I wouldn't let that bother me," Sam encouraged. "It's not like you're asking *him* on a date." He laughed at his own joke and went on as he tried to talk through his laughter. "Can you imagine? Marquette comes along. He'll be sitting in the backseat, wearing his suit and hat." Sam mimicked Marquette's soft accent, "You are driving like a blackguard. Slow down."

Alex shook his head. Sam's comments would have been funny had they not been so close to the truth.

"Hi, guys." Alex and Sam both jumped and turned to find Reverend Andy Engleson standing behind them. How long had he been there? Neither of them could even begin to guess, and they wondered what he'd heard of their conversation.

Sam smiled at Andy and mischief leapt from his eyes as he said, "Alex wants to join the choir."

"And so does Sam," Alex quickly added.

*****

Rosa lay in the sun while Guiseppi watered his precious flower beds. When he was finished, he went into the house, found the iced tea pitcher and two glasses, and brought them out to the patio.

"I could use a cool drink about now," Rosa said as she watched Guiseppi pour her a tall glass. "Thank you, Guiseppi." She took a long drink and added, "It is just what I needed."

Guiseppi poured himself a tall glass and took a seat in the lounger next to Rosa. "The flowers look beautiful this year, do they not?"

Rosa smiled with approval as she looked out over Guiseppi's cherished flower beds. "You do a wonderful job."

Guiseppi raised his glass at Rosa and smiled. "Thank you." He sipped at his glass for a moment, and his expression became thoughtful. "Has she spoke of him?"

Rosa slowly shook her head. "Not with me."

Guiseppi nodded and sighed. "She asked me if she should travel with Marquette."

Rosa laughed. "What on earth for? It is amazing they yet live."

"That is exactly what *I* said. I asked her if she was trying to run away. She says 'no', but who knows."

"He must have been a wonderful man, at least in the beginning." Rosa looked at Guiseppi curiously. "Do you think I should tell her of the fifteen years of prayers I have offered for Noah?"

Guiseppi shook his head. "Not yet. I do not feel comfortable at all in giving her that information—"

"But, Guiseppi, he did not ask her, not even once, to compromise her honor, and he did ask for her hand in marriage."

"But she saw him with another," Guiseppi reminded. "And I am not comfortable with that—"

"But, Guiseppi, look at how she suffers. Do you not think it strange how many years I prayed for *this* particular young man before he came into her life?"

"Of course I think it strange," Guiseppi answered with a frown. "*And I think it every day*, Rosa, my love. But I cannot make myself comfortable with risking her feelings one more time. I am afraid for her tender heart. Say, for instance, we contact this young man and bring him back into her life. She would be so hopeful, only to possibly have her hopes dashed again." Guiseppi shook his head. "No, my Rosa. We will not risk our Angel's heart again."

*****

Vincenzo took a comfortable seat on the porch swing and dipped his favorite pipe into the pouch of tobacco he kept in his shirt pocket. Kate's mother had called, but Kate had promised to join him on the swing just as soon as she was through with her conversation. The kids were tucked into their beds, the dishes were done, and the sun was setting in the South Dakota sky. Vincenzo struck a wooden match against the railing of the swing and put the fire into his pipe. He shook the match out and set it into the glass ash tray Kate *insisted* he use. He would have rather tossed it into the yard. He heard the front door creak open and expected to see Kate. Instead, he saw his two little children sneak out with their precious blankets in tow.

"Alright, my little babes," he said trying not smile, "what are you doing?"

Angelo was the first to scamper to his father. He threw his blanket into the swing beside Vincenzo and leapt in on top of it. Alyssa followed, giggling along the way. She flung her blanket into her father's lap and then jumped on him.

"Are you not supposed to be in bed?" Vincenzo questioned as he clasped the pipe between his teeth and put one arm around little Angelo, who had snuggled close beside him. He took ahold of Alyssa with the other.

"Ma`ma is on the phone," Alyssa whispered.

"We want a story," Angelo said.

Vincenzo smiled at his children, removed his arm from Angelo, and took the pipe from between his teeth. He asked, "What kind of a story?"

"Tell us about the soldiers again," Alyssa coaxed.

"The soldiers," Angelo echoed.

Vincenzo nodded. "Well, okay. But very fast because Ma`ma will want you back in the bed very soon."

They nodded and shivered with excitement. Vincenzo smiled, took a serious puff from his pipe, and blew the smoke away from them.

"They were powerful men of God," he began, "and they came to us as the war raged all around—"

"And they worked hard, like men should," Alyssa interrupted.

"Yes," Vincenzo agreed with a nod. "They worked very hard milking the goats, collecting the eggs, and brushing beautiful Delia."

"Nonna's horsy," Angelo reminded.

"Yes, Nonna's horsy," Vincenzo continued. "And they loved us so much! They watched over us while we played outside and kept us safe from the bombs and the Nazis."

"Because the Nazis were evil," Alyssa whispered.

"Very evil," Vincenzo said with narrowed eyes. "One day the soldiers had to leave us, and we cried."

"Why *did* they have to leave?" Alyssa asked.

"You know the answer, my Alyssa," Vincenzo gave her a gentle hug. "Why do *you* not finish the story? You seem to know it better than your Papa."

"No," Angelo protested. "Papa tell it."

"Well," Vincenzo began again, "there was a great battle."

"In *Italia*," Alyssa whispered.

Vincenzo nodded. "Many soldiers were required because there were many evil Nazis waiting to kill them. But the good soldiers fought bravely, in the name of God and freedom."

"And in the name of America," Alyssa whispered.

Vincenzo nodded. "And in the name of America, and they won. They set us free from the evil Duce so that we might escape and come to America."

"Where you met the princess," Alyssa giggled.

Vincenzo laughed. "Yes. Where I met the princess."

"What did she look like, Papa?" Alyssa asked.

"Oh, she was beautiful," Vincenzo said with a soft smile as he remembered. "She had black hair and shiny black eyes. Her shape was graceful and her voice like a song, and her name was Kate Martin."

Angelo giggled as he snuggled close to his father, and Alyssa put her arm around his neck. "And she loved you," she whispered. She gave her father a soft kiss on his cheek.

"And I loved her," Vincenzo said as he looked from child to child and smiled. "And here we are. Now we have a little prince and a little princess of our own!"

"And they're supposed to be in the royal bedchamber," Kate's soft voice surprised them from the doorway. The three of them looked up and gasped.

"What's going on out here?" she said in a pretended cross tone.

Alyssa and Angelo responded with giggles, and Vincenzo smiled. "I was telling them the story of how I met the beautiful princess."

Kate smiled. She remembered the day well.

Chapter 10

Noah's skin turned golden brown from his long days in the summer sun, and his sandy-brown hair became the color of cream. His arms grew strong and his chest broadened with the muscles of his labor. But even though his physical appearance was that of a strong man, the heart within him was not bearing up under the ache of Angel's absence. His eyes had lost their sparkle and dance, and seldom did he smile.

The months of spring passed, and the dry heat of July came to the Black Hills of South Dakota. Noah had worked for Denis Construction for three weeks and was pleased with his new job. The work was physically demanding, but he enjoyed it far more than cutting meat. There were heavy boards to lift, nails to pound, and wood to saw. In the end, if you performed your job with care, there was a beautiful structure to show for your efforts.

He stopped by Maggie's at least two or three times a week for lunch and to ask if Angel had called. Of course, Maggie always answered with a no. Over the past several weeks, she'd watched his mood slide steadily. He was quiet and withdrawn on most days as he ate his lunch at the bar, staring into the haunting portrait. He told Maggie more than once he was praying for a second chance with Angel, and he hoped God would answer soon. It troubled Maggie to see him carry on so much about the girl; but, on the other hand, he'd stopped talking about Carrie, and *that* was a relief.

Maggie saw the uncharacteristic spring in his step as he hopped off his bike out front and fished something out of one of the saddlebags. She narrowed her eyes for a better look. *What does he have?* Noah smiled as he walked through the glass doors, up to the bar, and laid down what appeared to be blueprints.

"Hello, Maggie May."

"Hey, Noah," Maggie greeted, frowning at the blueprints as she reached beneath the counter for a Coke. She opened the bottle and set it before him. "What's this?"

"I'm gonna build this house," he announced as he unrolled the plans on the counter. He grabbed the Coke and took a long drink. "Man! It's hot outside!"

Estelle saw them huddled at the bar and peered over Noah's shoulder. "Want the special? It's meat loaf."

"Yep," he answered.

"You're gonna need a whole pocket full of money to build *that* house," Maggie said gruffly. "The thing has about six bedrooms."

"Seven, actually, if you count this little room over here. But..." and when Noah looked into Maggie's eyes, she thought she saw a little sparkle, "*that's* gonna be her studio." He pulled some snapshots out of his shirt pocket. "And look at these, ladies." He spread the photos out over the top of the blueprints. Estelle and Maggie looked at the photos of the beautiful meadow in the Hills. "This land is all mine. My folks left it to me. I don't have to purchase a lot or anything. All I have to do is come up with some money. I'll be learning to do all of the carpentry work myself."

Estelle humphed and hurried into the kitchen to retrieve Noah's order, leaving him and Maggie alone at the bar.

"What does a single guy like you need with a big house like that?" Maggie frowned.

Noah's face glowed as he reached into his jean pocket and pulled out a crumpled bright pink flyer. "Look at this, Maggie."

Maggie took the flyer and carefully uncrumpled it. Her eyes opened wide when she saw what it had to say. "Junior Artists of America," she read aloud. She let out her breath...*Noah thinks she's coming back*...She swallowed hard and tried to be gentle. "Noah, you've gotta stop this nonsense. That girl ain't comin' back."

"Oh, Maggie," Noah laughed, "I don't know what went wrong, but she'll be back."

Maggie shook her head and dropped her gaze back to the flyer in her hands. The convention was only two weeks away. "Have you talked to Joshua about this?"

Noah looked away from Maggie.

Maggie felt so much pity for the poor fool that she had to fight away her tears. She took a breath, "Maybe you should just mention it to him."

Noah shrugged. "I don't know. We'll see."

Estelle returned with the special and set it down beside Noah, so as not to disturb the precious plans before him. "It's a nice place, Noah," she said with a smile. "She's gonna love it."

Noah smiled and looked from the blueprints to the photos of the meadow, and then at the portrait that hung at the bar.

*****

"My little Angel," Petrice said to get her attention.

She was very deep in thought and hadn't noticed him come in. The suddenness of his voice made Tillie jump, and she looked up with surprise.

Her wild hair was in somewhat of a ponytail, and there were stray suds caught in the curls. The apron she wore over her t-shirt and jeans was soaked, and her feet stood in a puddle of water. She frowned at her brother and mumbled, "Oh, it's you." Then she went back to concentrating on the pots in her sink.

Petrice had found his little sister scrubbing pots and pans in the kitchen at the restaurant. He hadn't seen her since April, and they hadn't visited on the telephone since May. It was now almost August. She hadn't returned any of his phone calls, and she hadn't sent him anything all summer—not even a thank-you for the birthday gift he'd sent her in June.

In just the moment their eyes had met, Petrice saw the change in his sister's expression. He hadn't noticed it in April, but it was certainly there now. The lively sparkle was gone from her lovely black eyes, and sadness wrinkled her brow.

"Can we sit for a minute?" Petrice asked with gentleness.

"No, Patty." She slammed a heavy pot into the rinsing sink. "I'm too busy for you."

Petrice sighed, "Angel, can you please forgive me for what I have done?"

Tillie looked at her oldest brother, and her angry heart began to melt. He'd always been so patient, so kind, in every situation when it had anything to do with her. She really wasn't so angry with him as she was at the circumstances. She'd had a horrible summer— beginning in the spring with her rebellious mistake—and had no Patty to run to for justification. Only her parents had been available, and they'd lovingly affirmed her disobedience. Patty would have made an excuse for her behavior.

"Please, Angel," he begged as he looked into her sorrowful eyes.

The gentleness in his voice and the softness of his accent is what she remembered most about her childhood. He would hold her and tell her she was the best and everything would be okay...

She fought her softening heart by frowning. "Good grief, Patty. Is she even as old as I am?"

Petrice smiled. "Yes. Even older. She is twenty-five."

Tillie rolled her eyes, stepped away from the sink for a towel, and grumbled, "She's as white as white can be. What on earth do you see in her?" She flung the towel into the laundry bin beside the sink, put both of her hands on her hips, and gave him a scowl.

Petrice's black eyes sparkled. "I love her, Angel. Her color makes no difference to me."

Tillie swallowed hard, and her frown began to fade. Her eyes filled with tears...*he loves her?* She shook her head. "Why didn't you tell us?" Tears began to slip from her eyes.

Petrice reached for one of her hands. "I am so sorry. More sorry than you can ever know. We *should* have waited. I became so caught up in the new love I felt for this woman, I forgot about where I came from and how much you all mean to me. Especially *you*, my Angel. Please forgive me, for I have done a dreadful thing."

She went into his arms and sobbed against his chest.

"It does not mean I love you less," he whispered as he gently stroked the soft curls on top of her head. "And you will always be my Angel, no matter what."

Tillie only nodded, unable to answer through the sobs she couldn't calm. He was finally there, and that was all that mattered at the moment.

He touched her tears with a tender hand and wiped away as many as he could while she continued to cry. "There, there, now. Please let us go out for a very fun time this night. What do you say? Ellie has come with me, and she is excited to see the Midwestern metropolis of Sioux Falls."

Tillie laughed through her tears and looked into her brother's eyes. "Where in this town could you possibly impress a girl from New York City?"

Petrice smiled and raised one brow. "Let us take her to the Arkota. I hear there will be a dance there this evening, and we will invite Ma`ma and Papa."

Tillie nodded. "Doria made tons of ravioli today. We could eat here first and then just walk over."

Petrice quietly agreed and stepped back from his sister. He noticed his soaked suit jacket and laughed. "I believe I will need to change my suit before we go. When can you leave?"

"I have to ask Papa," she answered. "I know he's around here somewhere. We rode together today."

They left the dish room and went into the kitchen area of the restaurant. Doria was stirring in one of his "cauldrons," and Georgie was busy with a giant bowl of salad greens.

"We're looking for Papa," Tillie said.

"Dining room," Doria answered.

Tillie and Petrice headed in that direction. Guiseppi was sitting in a booth with a man dressed in a suit. The man had his back turned to them, and they didn't recognize him at first. As they got closer, they saw a file and some papers spread out on the table. As Guiseppi looked up and got to his feet, it prompted the man with him to turn his head. A very surprised Alex got to his feet as well.

"Alex!" Petrice said with a smile as he extended his hand. "How good it is to see you here."

Alex took Petrice's hand, "Hi, Patty." He looked at Tillie. "Hi, Tillie."

"Hey, Alex," she greeted with a smile. "What are you doing here?"

"We needed your father's signature on some papers," he answered.

"And just think," Guiseppi said excitedly, "I did not even have to go to the office. Alex brought them right to me."

"Very thoughtful." Petrice smiled approvingly at Alex and then shifted his gaze to Guiseppi. "Papa, Angel and I were wondering if you and Ma`ma would like to come dancing with us this evening."

"That is an excellent idea," Guiseppi answered with a smile. "At the Arkota?"

Petrice gave Alex a friendly slap to the shoulder. "And why do you not come along, Alex? You look like you could use a little fun."

"Yes, Alex," Guiseppi encouraged, his black eyes sparkling. "And tell those parents of yours to join us."

"And call Sam and Becky-Lynn," Tillie added excitedly. "I'll bet they'd have a great time."

Alex smiled. He'd love to go dancing with Tillie.

*****

Tillie and Petrice headed for home to change their clothes. Elaine and Rosa were seated in the living room when they arrived, and Elaine got to her feet when Tillie came through the front door. Rosa had noticed that Tillie and Petrice smiled at each other on their way up the sidewalk, and she sighed with relief. They seemed to have ironed out their differences. Now how would it go with Elaine?

Elaine approached them where they stood, smiled shyly at Tillie, and reached for one of her hands. Tillie was amazed, again, at the woman's height as she looked up into Elaine's blue eyes.

"Can we visit for just a moment?" Elaine asked. Her tone was so unsure and shy, and it touched Tillie's heart.

"Sure," Tillie answered as she continued to look into Elaine's pretty eyes. *Wow, they're really blue.* "I got your letter. Thanks. You're a great writer."

"You think so?" Elaine asked with surprise.

"I do," Tillie answered honestly.

Elaine took a deep breath. "Tillie, I am so sorry for my part in this. Please forgive me."

Tillie saw Elaine's amazing eyes fill with tears. She squeezed Elaine's hand and smiled into her eyes. "It's okay. Let's just forget about the whole thing and start over."

Elaine drew Tillie into her arms. "Oh, thank you, Tillie."

"My *family* calls me 'Angel,' " Tillie whispered with a smile.

*****

Alex couldn't have planned the event more perfectly if he'd set things up himself. Marquette was busy somewhere in Europe, and there'd be no one looking over his shoulder tonight. His parents were delighted to join the impromptu party, as were Sam and Becky-Lynn. Vincenzo and Kate asked their foreman and his wife if they'd watch their two little ones, and they were in Sioux Falls in time to join everyone for dinner at Angelo's.

Guiseppi and his two sons looked nearly identical, dressed in flashy, double-breasted black suits and ties, topped off with black hats. The three of them together were impressive, to say the least. As they entered the restaurant that evening accompanied by their beautiful women, they captured the attention of every customer in the place.

Rosa was dressed in a full black dress that came to just below her knee. It was a sleeveless halter style, perfect for dancing, and it framed her petite figure perfectly. She'd pinned up her thick hair to show off the pretty pearls dangling from her ears, and on her feet were tiny black patent leather pumps.

Tillie was also dressed in a halter-style dress with a full skirt, but hers was pastel pink, which accentuated the dark color of her pretty shoulders. She put her hair up as well, showing off the delicate curve of her neck and the feminine shape of her face. Guiseppi whispered something to her as they walked in, and she laughed.

Sam was seated next to Alex, and he whispered into his brother's ear, "*Man,* she's cute!"

Alex only nodded as he watched the pretty young lady come in, looking forward to every minute of the night ahead of them.

Kate wore a yellow chiffon—Vincenzo's favorite summer dress. It was a sleeveless tank, tight at the waist, and fully pleated to her knees, and Vincenzo said she looked like a precious flower upon his arm.

Elaine's tall but perfect body was dressed in an elegant navy, straight-cut dress without sleeves. It was form fitted to her flawless figure, just past her knees, and she had worn flat shoes so she didn't look so tall next to Petrice. Her golden hair was twisted into a figure eight, and diamond earrings dangled from her earlobes. Petrice glanced upward into his new wife's eyes and smiled. Certainly there was not a more beautiful creature on the face of the earth.

Alex and his father and brother stood from their seats when the Casellis arrived and extended their hands for greetings. Alex pulled out the chair next to him and looked at Tillie. "Would you like to sit here?"

"Thanks, Alex." She smiled and accepted the offered chair.

Sam tried to watch without being too obvious, and he whispered into his wife's ear, "I think he likes her."

Becky-Lynn's green eyes smiled at Sam. She stole a careful glance in Alex's direction and gave Sam an acknowledging nod.

As usual, the food was superb, with more than enough to go around several times. Sam and his father entertained the Casellis with story after story of the different cases they were working on. They gave one hilarious detail after the next, bragging of how they regularly outsmarted their opponents. Alex managed to tell a few stories as well; and Becky-Lynn, having practiced law with Sam and James for nearly fifteen years, added her two-cents' worth from time to time. She affirmed their success but put their stories into a more *truthful* light. Frances laughed at Becky-Lynn, which encouraged the woman to interject even more anecdotes. Rosa laughed until she had to wipe tears from the corners of her eyes.

After they'd had their fill of visiting and delicious food, they walked over to the Arkota, where the dancing had already begun. The Arkota Ballroom was the most popular place in Sioux Falls for dancing. It boasted the largest dance floor in the state and hosted superior big-band entertainment.

They secured two tables near the dance floor, and Guiseppi whisked Rosa into his arms. They gracefully stepped into the fox-trot already in progress. Tillie laughed at her cute, little parents. They were so *perfect* for each other.

Petrice showed Elaine to the dance floor. Even with her height, they were a remarkably graceful couple, and Tillie watched with a sigh. She fought off the pangs of jealously rattling around in her heart. *He loves her…Don't forget…He loves her…*

"Would you like to dance?"

Tillie turned and saw a very tall Alex Martin smiling down at her. Had she known what was going on inside of the poor man's head, she would have been surprised. Alex was beside himself with the prospect of being able to spend the entire evening with Tillie, uninterrupted by her controlling brother.

"I'd love to," she answered with a polite smile.

He offered his hand, and she placed her own into his palm. He nodded like a gentleman and escorted her onto the dance floor.

They had nearly every dance together for the next several sets. Both of them were excellent dancers and stepped together in time as they waltzed, fox-trotted, and finally jitterbugged with the best of the older crowd. They sat together during the breaks, and conversation flowed out of Alex, comfortable and easy.

Petrice and Elaine decided to take a break and took a seat next to Sam and Becky-Lynn. Petrice noticed Alex Martin's attentions toward his younger sister, and he smiled as they watched them. "How long has this been going on?" he asked of Sam.

"Couple of months…for Alex anyway," Sam answered as he smiled at the couple on the dance floor.

"But only for Alex?" Petrice asked.

Sam leaned forward as he confided, "Tillie's been a little quiet over the summer. You did hear about the prom disaster, didn't you?"

Petrice nodded but inwardly blamed himself. She had been quiet because of *his* actions. He sighed, shook his head, and looked out onto the dance floor where Alex waltzed her around once again.

"They make a lovely couple," Petrice said.

"Now if Alex could just get her attention," Sam commented.

"I cannot imagine that to be too difficult. She has always had a heart for your brother."

Sam shrugged. "Well I'm not so sure about that anymore. She hasn't given Alex a drop of hope all summer."

"I think things will be getting better now."

Sam nodded and watched the couple on the dance floor as the number ended and they headed in his direction. "How about some club sodas?" he offered as he waved down a waitress.

Alex held a chair for Tillie as she seated herself. "That would be great. We're thirsty."

Sam gave his order to the waitress and then looked at Petrice. "So where's Marquette?"

"Oslo, I believe," Petrice answered.

"And Tara doesn't like the weather there," Tillie giggled. "Norway is not her favorite place. It's too humid there."

"How long will he be away?" Alex asked.

"He won't be home until Thanksgiving," Petrice answered.

"I talked to him a couple of days ago, and he said it's gonna be long and drawn out," Tillie added.

Alex fought the urge to laugh hysterically. *No Marquette for three whole months!*

*****

Tillie watched them load the last of Ginger's belongings into the cavernous trunk of her parents' black Ford LTD. It was hard to believe summer was already over and Ginger was on her way to school in Mankato. Tillie would start college in just a few short weeks at Augustana in Sioux Falls.

"I hardly saw you at all this summer," Ginger said as she and Tillie prepared for their good-bye.

Tillie felt tears begin to burn in the back of her eyes. For once, she wished she was *not* so Italian. *Why do we always have to cry at the drop of a hat?*

"Now don't do that!" Ginger whispered with a hug. "I'll be writing you."

"You'll be too busy with Bobby," Tillie cried. She gulped away her tears and tried to give Ginger a smile.

Ginger shook her head. "I'll make time for you." Her eyes became thoughtful and she whispered, "I'm sorry things didn't work out with Noah."

Tillie nodded and shrugged. "Well, I guess it just wasn't meant to be."

"But Alex Martin is still a really nice guy, and he seems to really like you a lot."

Tillie smiled and shook her head. "He doesn't like me. He's just being nice."

"Hey, Ging," Mr. Engleson called from the car. "We gotta get on the road."

Ginger gave Tillie one last embrace. "I'll miss you."

"I'll miss you, too," Tillie said, as she held Ginger as tightly as she could. "When will you be home?"

"Christmas for sure," Ginger answered, and then she began to step toward the car. "Write me. Okay?"

Tillie sighed as Ginger got into the car. They slowly backed out of the driveway and headed down the street...*Everything is changing...It will all be different now.* She wiped the tears from her cheeks and plodded slowly toward home.

*****

Frances poured Rosa another cup of tea and returned the pot to its place on the stove. They hadn't gotten together for months and decided to indulge themselves in a leisurely visit.

"And did I tell you about Noah Hansen?" Frances said as she took her seat, not noticing the alarmed expression in Rosa's eyes.

"No," Rosa managed to answer. She lifted the tea cup to her lips and took a sip.

"Well," Frances continued, "I talked to Mac last week, and that kid has made a total turnaround. He's stopped his drinking and running around and has gone back to school. He's recommitted his life to the Lord and never misses church anymore. Apparently your prayers have done the trick. He's a changed man."

Rosa forced a smile. "That is wonderful, Frances." Inwardly, however, she was worried. *Noah a changed man? After fifteen years of committed prayer, he has reconciled with his Creator and begun a new path...Father, did You intend that path be shared with Angel?*

Chapter 11

"This is an odd thing," Marquette said as he narrowed his eyes and read from the letter he'd just received from his mother.

"What is it, my love?" Tara asked as she hung the dry cleaning in their temporary quarters in a fourth-floor apartment overlooking the Oslofjord.

"Ma`ma says Angel has changed her major and they are very *pleased*." He frowned as he continued to read aloud from the letter. "She seems to be very impressed with her Russian History professor." He shook his head and looked up at Tara. "*Russian* History? What in the world?" He began to read again, "She has also taken a class devoted to the study of major English poetry." Marquette pretended to gag.

He read silently for a few more moments, and Tara heard him gasp. She had finished with the dry cleaning and walked to where he sat, knelt down beside him, and peered into the letter.

"What now, my love?" she asked as she tried to quickly scan the words.

"That rotten Alex Martin," Marquette growled through clenched teeth. "Just listen to this!" He began to read verbatim from the letter, "We had a wonderful party at the Arkota while Patty and Ellie were in town. The Martins came along, and Vincenzo and Kate drove up. Alex and Angel had a wonderful time, dancing until the band would play no more. She smiled so while she was with him, and Papa and I think they make a lovely couple." He gave Tara a bewildered look. "A *lovely couple?*"

Tara giggled at Marquette's comical expression.

"Why do you laugh at me?" he questioned with a frown.

"Because you are so funny. And why do you fret so?"

140

Marquette shook his head. "Because he is ambitious, and I do not care for the worth he places upon his career and himself. For years Angel has gone on about the wonderful Alex Martin. I thought she had finally forgotten about him."

"Do not worry so much, my love. Alex *is* a wonderful man, and your family has always loved him so much. Would it truly be such a terrible thing if it were Alex who made your sister happy?"

Marquette took a deep breath and slowly let it escape. *Yes. It would truly be a terrible thing. Alex's vaulting drive to succeed will surely bring ruin into Angel's precious life, and why the rest of them cannot see it absolutely astounds me.*

*****

Noah Hansen received notice that he'd passed his GED exam, but it did little to raise his spirits. He'd attended the Junior Artists of America activities but found not one sign of his precious Angel. Something serious must have happened, he reasoned. He now worried she no longer existed, because the possibility she'd stopped loving him or had decided for herself not to return was unacceptable. But, for just a little longer, he'd follow through on the decision he'd made all along. He'd love Angel and wait for her return, no matter what the painful consequence turned out to be.

Mona offered to throw a little party for him when he brought them his certificate, and she invited the church and his friends. The guys and Carrie showed up but stayed only for a short while. They had another party they had to get to, and they were already drunk. Noah was relieved when they left.

After the guests and Noah had left, Mona and Joshua relaxed on the front porch in the old swing. The evening had been a pleasant one—and had even offered some entertainment when Noah's old friends staggered through the party.

Joshua put his arm around Mona's shoulders as they rocked in the swing. A warm breeze stirred the quiet Black Hills evening, rustling the leaves in the orchard and carrying the wonderful scent of pine through the air.

"Somethin's wrong with that kid," Mona drawled.

Joshua nodded. "But what is it? Is it the girl?"

"I think so. I've seen this before. That boy has gone and fallen in love, and something has gone terribly wrong."

"But with *who?* It doesn't seem to be Carrie, praise the Lord."

"Oh, it's definitely *not* Carrie. This reminds me of what happened to my cousin, Bif. You've met Bif, right?"

"Is that his real name?"

Mona shook her head. "His real name is Buford Ignatious Franklin Spencer, but we call him Bif because it's shorter, and *that's* another story all by itself." She took a breath. "Ever wonder why Bif is single?"

"I just thought maybe he was a confirmed bachelor."

Mona shook her head again. "No. He met a girl when he was a very young man, I suppose about Noah's age. The way the story goes is he met her one day in the library. They visited the whole day, and when it was time for the library to close, she promised to meet him there the next Saturday. Well, Saturday came and Bif went back to the library. He waited the whole day and she never showed up. For years Bif has been goin' back to that library on Saturdays, Joshua. But she never came back, and he never found anyone to replace her in his heart."

Mona's stories always made Joshua laugh, except for this one. He squeezed Mona's shoulder again and felt her head rest against him. "I'm so happy I found you," he said as he tenderly kissed the top of her head.

"Me, too, Darlin'," she agreed. And then they were quiet for a long time as they listened to the crickets and frogs and the soft breeze in the orchard.

*****

Alex received notice from the South Dakota State Bar that he'd been admitted. He headed toward his father's office at the end of the hall and entered unannounced.

"I did it, Dad," he said as he came through the door with a wave of the letterhead.

James looked up from his work and smiled at Alex. "Did what, son?"

Alex set the letterhead on his father's desk.

James focused on the notice and raised one eyebrow. "Well, was there ever any doubt?"

Alex likewise raised one black brow. "Not really."

James smiled at his son and handed him the letter. "Congratulations, son. You'd better call your mother." Alex nodded and began toward the doorway. "Oh, Alex," James added, causing Alex to turn around to look at his father. "I'll have Shondra plan an announcement party at the Minnehaha Country Club. We'll invite the lawyers from around town so you can get familiar with everybody."

Alex nodded. "Thanks, Dad." He hurried back to his office, clutching the notice in his hands while he walked to the window and gazed out over Sioux Falls. "I did it, and I did it *better* than everybody before me." He sighed contentedly. "This is only the beginning."

*****

The colored leaves of late September were starting to drop to the ground. The air was cooler and the summer humidity had faded, making the Sioux Falls climate more comfortable.

Tillie's last classroom had been hot and sticky, and she headed to the outside of the campus. She brushed some leaves off of a bench and took a deep breath of the cooler air, enjoying the breeze upon her warm face. That felt much better.

She looked at the stack of books beside her and impulsively picked up the old, tattered, red cloth-covered book she'd found in the school's bookstore. In it was a collection of very old poems, and she wouldn't have purchased it except the collection included a very special poem: *Annie Laurie.* She opened the book and read the words to the song Noah sang to her while they danced in the little cowboy restaurant. In an instant, she felt his tender arms around her, smelled the soft scent of his Old Spice, and saw the dancing in his blue eyes when he told her he loved her…*He actually told me he loved me and wanted to marry me.*

She angrily snapped the book shut, set it down, and picked up *The Barretts of Wimpole Street.* This was her assignment, and she might as well get started.

Elizabeth Barrett Browning was the current English poet of focus, and Tillie was intrigued. Mrs. Browning had been heavily involved in the fight for the liberation of Italy from Austria. Tillie was drawn into the dramatic love story of Elizabeth Barrett and Robert Browning, their correspondence, and his love of her poetry. She sighed at their romantic adventure, looked away from the book, and gazed into the traffic of students walking along the path. Here and there, she saw couples holding hands and smiling into each other's eyes. *Her* brief romance had had the *opposite* conclusion.

In the crowd she saw the familiar shape of Alex Martin, and she caught his eye. He waved, appeared to change direction, and took a seat on the bench. "Hey, Tillie."

"Hey, Alex. What are you doing on campus?"

"Oh," he began as he took a breath and looked away from her for a moment, "I had a little business to take care of." He looked at her and smiled again. "I'm surprised to see you out here."

"I'm between classes," she answered.

Alex looked at the book in her lap. "What are you reading?"

Tillie frowned as she closed the book and showed him the cover.

"*The Barretts of Wimpole Street*," Alex read aloud. He noticed her frown. "Aren't you enjoying it very much?"

Tillie shrugged. "It's okay. Just a little fanciful, I guess."

"It's a true story, you know."

"It's probably overdramatized." She placed the book back on the stack beside her.

Alex was surprised by her comment. Most women loved the story of how Robert Browning fell in love with Elizabeth's poetry, married her, and whisked her away to Italy. He found himself without words to reply and searched himself for a change of subject—something to strike up any kind of a conversation. "Have you had lunch?"

Tillie shook her head in answer.

"Well, how long before your next class?" he asked.

"A couple of hours."

"I've got a great idea. You should go to lunch with me. I don't have an appointment scheduled until this afternoon."

Tillie reluctantly agreed.

There was a small café located on the corner of 26th and Minnesota Streets, and it served soup and sandwiches over the lunch hour. It was casual but clean, and Alex chose the place because he didn't want her to think he was coming on too strong. She'd been extremely quiet since the *prom disaster*, and he didn't want to do anything to frighten her away. Besides, he had three months to work his way into her heart, without opposition from her obsessive brother.

"So," he said as he smiled at her across the table, "you think the Brownings' story is a bit overdramatized?"

Tillie rolled her eyes and set down her sandwich. "Come on. It's *not* really like that."

"I think it can be," Alex shared with a scholarly and thoughtful expression. "After all, her work did gain substance and distinction after she married Robert."

"But don't you think she was just a touch on the long-winded and scattered side?" Tillie raised an eyebrow and smiled mischievously. "Like scatterbrained?"

Her comment took him by surprise, and he laughed out loud. There he was, trying to have an intellectual discussion, and she made a joke. He looked into her eyes as he watched her chuckle at her own humor. "You're funny."

Tillie smiled as she looked back at the handsome Alex Martin, noticing the sparkle of his white teeth. *He thinks I'm funny, and he seems to really enjoy my company. What I'd have given had he paid me just a little more attention last year at Christmas, or even at the Mulligan's Spring Ball last March. Now, here we sit, directly across the table from each other. He's buying my lunch and laughing at my jokes. How things have changed.*

She looked into his dark, smiling eyes and wondered how in the world she'd gotten to this place—and why she didn't feel the thrill she'd imagined would be there when she'd finally arrived.

*****

Since September of 1962, Vincenzo and Kate had hosted Reata's Annual Apple Picking Party. This year was the fourteenth time the event was scheduled, and preparations proceeded as they always had. Rosa, Tillie, and Kate, along with the foreman's wife, Barbara, got together the weekend before the event and baked buns for roasted meat sandwiches. And they made delectable pies for dessert, created from whatever apples were frozen the year before. Tillie had to admit that she and Kate chased the babies more than they'd participated in the actual bun and pie baking, but Rosa and Barbara didn't seem to mind. Frances Martin and Diane Engleson prepared twelve of their now-famous chocolate sheet cakes, and Doria and Georgie made giant tubs of coleslaw and pans of baked beans.

Guiseppi ordered the restaurant closed, as he had from the beginning, so everyone could attend the apple-picking festivities. There was still the story-telling contest for the men and the apple-pie contest for the ladies. The top prizes of twenty-five dollars had been upped to fifty dollars several years ago, enticing more participants every year.

In 1962, the entrance fee onto Reata was fifty cents, and each family could have all of the apples they could carry out of the orchard. In 1970, Vincenzo raised the fee to two dollars, and everyone thought it was quite a deal, including Vincenzo, who would have had to hire someone to pick the apples and sell them for him. This way, he got rid of the apples and, after he'd subtracted out the cost of the roasted meat sandwiches, made a small profit on the side.

The entire orchard was open for everyone, except for the special place beneath some smaller trees on the west end. That place was roped off and no one was allowed there, for that was where Uncle Angelo and Aunt Penny rested.

When Uncle Angelo was still alive, he and Vincenzo designed a roasting pit from memory identical to the one their neighbors in Italy, the Andreottis, had. As in years past, Doria and Georgie would use the pit to roast two hogs and a side of beef. They sliced the meat thin and laid it into the fresh buns the ladies had prepared the weekend before.

In 1975, the grand event took place on the third Sunday in September. It attracted hundreds of apple pickers from Centerville, South Dakota, and surrounding counties. Marquette and Tara were still in Oslo, but they called to wish Vincenzo good luck. This was the first harvest they'd ever missed. Petrice and Elaine, on the other hand, rearranged their schedules and flew in to stay on the ranch and help Vincenzo and Kate with preparations.

Vincenzo designated and mowed a large portion of grassland where the participants could park. That way cars would not come too close to the main house where the eating, pie contest, and storytelling took place. Two young hands were mounted on prancing geldings at Reata's entrance gate, directing the large amount of traffic as it wound its way in and out of the ranch.

Great barrels of water and ice were set on the property and in the orchard to protect the people from dehydration while picking apples on the hot, late-summer day.

Tillie looked around at the hundreds of people as she remembered the event from her childhood. Uncle Angelo's dog, Duchess, always had puppies about this time of year, and once a sow had perfect little baby piglets. Uncle Angelo used to carry her through the barn, introduce her to the horses, and let her down to touch the puppies. However, she held on tight to Uncle Angelo's neck while she took the most cautious peek into the pig pen, as the mother pig would bite!

Kate asked Tillie to serve the cake, so she stood at attention at one of the tables while people filed by for their piece. She smiled at each one as they would say "Thanks" or "Great party" and move along. Last year she'd gotten to help the hands at the gate, but this year she hadn't arrived early enough and was stuck on cake detail. Worried about the heat of the day to come combined with Tillie's thick, curly hair, Rosa had insisted they put it into a tight French braid. Already, the heat and humidity had forced tiny curls out of their place in the braid, and soft tendrils were sticking to the back of her neck and the sides of her face.

"Angel." Vincenzo's voice was beside her and she turned to see her brother with a handful of small paper plates. "Kate says you might need these."

Tillie smiled at her brother, took the plates from him, and set them down on the table next to the cake. "Thanks, Vinzo," she said, surprising them both. Where had *that* come from?

Vincenzo was taken aback and his eyes flew open in surprise. "Why, Angel, you have not called me that in years."

Tillie laughed and shook her head. "I'm sorry. I guess I was just remembering Uncle Angelo and the pigs and puppies. I must have had a little stroke or something and reverted back into my childhood."

Vincenzo laughed, put his hand on his sister's shoulder, and gave her a gentle kiss on the cheek. "Do you need a cool drink?"

Tillie shook her head. "No. I'll be fine."

Vincenzo put his arm around her and flagged down a very young hand walking by. "Tracy, come over here please," he said, and Tracy instantly headed in his direction. "Wash your hands," Vincenzo instructed. "You will be taking over here for just a few moments while my sister gets herself a drink."

"Yes, sir," Tracy answered. He nodded at Vincenzo, tipped his hat toward Tillie, and then hurried off to wash up.

Tillie giggled at the cowboy's hat tipping. "I can't believe he just did that. I didn't know men still did that in real life."

"They do if they work for me," Vincenzo said.

"Oh, I see," Tillie acknowledged with a smile.

"Now you get yourself a drink, Angel. I will watch this cake table until Tracy returns. And get yourself one of Doria's sandwiches." Vincenzo closed his eyes and smiled. "Mmmm, you will not be sorry."

Tillie placed the cake server into her brother's hands. "Thanks, Vinzo." Vincenzo laughed, and she wandered off in the direction of the pit.

Smoke billowed from the fire in the pit where Georgie and Doria were doing their usual preparation of the meat. They frowned as they concentrated on their work, occasionally looking up to see how long the line had gotten. Rosa and Guiseppi were near the pit, passing out the sandwiches as fast as they were prepared. Doria's mouth was moving, but Tillie couldn't hear what he said. Whatever it was, it made Rosa laugh heartily. She repeated the remark to Guiseppi, who, in turn, laughed as well.

"What's so funny over here?" Tillie asked.

"Oh, dear," Rosa laughed again. "Doria says if he does not die today, he will surely live forever."

Tillie laughed, and Rosa placed a sandwich in her hand. "Take this, my Angel, for we have so many guests today I do not know if there will be any left for later."

Tillie took the sandwich and stepped back from her parents. She took a bite and looked out around Reata. What a great life: the orchard, the cattle, the crops. No wonder Vincenzo and Kate were so happy. She saw Kate with her babies as she held each one by the hand and led them carefully through the cake line where Vincenzo dished them up some dessert. Kate smiled into his eyes, and Vincenzo gave her a soft kiss on the lips. They held up the rest of the line, oblivious to the crowd waiting around them.

Tillie smiled, shook her head, and looked around again. She found Petrice and Elaine sitting under a tree. They were absorbed in a conversation and looking only at one another. Tillie sighed...*I guess she's not so bad...She's a pretty nice lady—*

"Hello, Tillie," came a familiar voice from beside her, and she turned see to Alex. He had his own sandwich and held two paper cups of water with one hand. "Vincenzo said you needed a drink."

Tillie smiled and took a cup. "Thanks, Alex."

"No problem." Alex looked around. "One time Andy and I hid along the drive," and he pointed to the main entrance of Reata. "You know, when we were into our soldier thing. Vincenzo used to leave the grass tall along the sides, and we hid in it with our binoculars. We were like ten or something, and Marquette had set up this date for Georgie with a girl named Marta. Did you ever hear about this?"

Tillie looked curious. The story was vaguely familiar.

"We named it 'Operation: Big Date,' " Alex continued. He shook his head and laughed at the memory.

"But Marta and Georgie were already acquainted," Tillie remembered.

Alex nodded. "Boy, were we all surprised. We thought she'd save the day and change ol' Georgie."

Tillie smiled as she recalled bits and pieces of the story.

"And do you remember Duchess?" Alex asked with a wistful smile toward the barn.

"I remember," Tillie answered. "And I remember her puppies."

"I wanted one *so* bad," Alex said. "I think I begged my parents every night for a year. Mom still said—"

"No livestock in the house," Tillie finished, and then she had to laugh because it's what Guiseppi had always said to her.

Alex smiled as he looked into her sparkling black eyes. *She's so pretty. I wonder if she even knows.*

Tracy had taken over the cake-serving duties just in time for Vincenzo to have dessert with his family, and they took a seat on a blanket in the shade of a full hayrack. Kate noticed Alex and Tillie talking, and she tapped on Vincenzo's knee.

"Look at that," she whispered.

Vincenzo followed her eyes and saw the brother of his wife, looking into Angel's eyes, smiling as if he'd been drinking.

"Do you think she notices?" Vincenzo asked.

Kate shook her head. "I'm not sure."

"Well, the rest of us do!"

"Sam says he really likes her," Kate whispered. She didn't want her little ones to take any of the conversation back to their family.

"Oh, really?" Vincenzo raised one eyebrow.

"And apparently he has joined the choir."

"They are expert dancers together as well."

Kate smiled. "They *do* make a lovely couple."

Vincenzo agreed with a sigh and looked into his wife's eyes. "Marquette will, undoubtedly, become unglued when he returns from Norway and finds out what has happened."

Kate shook her head. "I don't know why. Alex has turned into a wonderful man. In fact, he's an awful lot like Marquette."

Vincenzo smiled and replied, "And therein, my love, lies the problem."

James and Frances were seated on a blanket not far from Alex and Tillie, watching the two as well.

"I remember a time when she couldn't get enough of him." James frowned as he watched his son look into the eyes of Tillie Caselli.

"Well, that was *before* the prom disaster." Frances patted her husband's knee. "But Alex is certainly interested, and I think he'll change her mind."

James's sigh was heavy, and Frances frowned. "What's the matter?"

He shrugged and took another breath as he watched the two. Slowly he began to shake his head. "I don't know, Frances. Why would he take the time to court someone now? His career's just off the ground, and he's planning on getting into politics. I just don't think he has the time or desire required to be a husband."

*****

Tillie was tired. It had been a long, hot day. When she and her parents returned home that evening, she left them to visit on the porch and went to her room. She sat down in front of her vanity and began to undo the tight French braid her mother had insisted on that morning. When she'd finally removed all of the knots, she reached into her drawer for a wide-tooth comb, catching a glimpse of the corner of a photo. Curious, she took it out of the drawer. It was the picture she'd taken of Noah at Bridal Veil Falls, the one she'd turned into a portrait and stowed beneath the bed.

Tillie felt tears begin as she laid the photo delicately on the vanity and looked down into his dancing, wonderful eyes. It was like a lifetime ago. *Maybe it didn't really even happen—*

"Angel?" said her mother's soft voice, and Tillie looked up to see Rosa in the doorway of her room.

"Yes, Ma`ma," Tillie replied without realizing her tears had already been seen by Rosa.

"What is wrong, my dear?" Rosa questioned tenderly, and then she saw the photo.

Tillie looked sadly back to the photograph and shook her head. "I thought I'd gotten rid of these, but I found this one in my drawer."

Rosa swallowed hard and put a tender hand on Tillie's shoulder.

"You know, Ma`ma," Tillie continued, "it's funny. He was *white*, like Ellie, but I didn't even notice until just now. His color meant nothing to me."

Rosa was silent and knelt beside Tillie. She looked up into her daughter's sorrowful eyes and almost cried. "What can I do for you, my Angel?"

Tillie shook her head and looked back into the photo. "Nothing. It's my consequence. We'll just have to wait for it to go away."

*****

Guiseppi looked into Rosa's eyes as she stood in the doorway. She didn't say a word, but he knew what she was about to tell him. Quietly, Rosa closed the door and took a seat beside Guiseppi.

"She spoke of him," she whispered. She looked into her lap and shook her head. "I have to tell her."

Guiseppi shook his head in adamant disagreement. "No. Let us wait—"

"For what, Guiseppi?" Rosa whispered as she fought the tears of frustration. She wanted to end this nonsense. "Let us go to Noah. Let us get an explanation and bring him to Angel. It *must* have been a misunderstanding, and I can no longer bear her sadness pressing upon my heart." Rosa's tears escaped and trailed their way down her cheeks. She took quiet breaths as she sobbed and put her hands over her mouth so that her daughter wouldn't hear her crying.

"No, my Rosa." He put his arm around her shoulders and pulled her toward his body. "I do not want to take the risk."

"Please, Guiseppi, before this thing with Alex goes any further, she should be told. Is it not more than mere coincidence that we have prayed for Noah for nearly fifteen years before their *chance* meeting?"

"Disobedience combined with coincidence," Guiseppi said with a frown. He shook his head and locked his jaw. His Angel's heart would *not* be risked again, no matter what the explanation. Alex Martin, on the other hand, was an honorable man and obviously in love. She would be safe with Alex, and her heart would mend with his charming attentions.

Chapter 12

Noah was deep in thought as he chewed Maggie's famous burger. He had a *new* plan, and his hope was ignited once again. *Now, if I could just figure out a way to tell Maggie without worrying her too much.*

Noah had immersed himself in his building trades class, and his interest was reflected in the quality of his work. When it became too cold to build, Denis Construction did carpentry and wood-working inside homes that had either been constructed during the warmer months or for those who wanted to remodel their existing homes. Pete Denis, the owner of the construction company, was impressed with Noah's excellent workmanship and praised him constantly. Noah always blushed with embarrassment and wished Pete wouldn't carry on like that. However, Pete's comments were very encouraging, and Noah found himself planning his days away as he carefully put together the perfect house for Angel in his mind.

It will have wooden shutters on paned windows, an oak front door with beveled glass, hardwood floors, and Victorian chandeliers. The staircase into the upstairs is going to be open and winding, and there will be lots of bedrooms for our kids...

Maggie noticed how quiet Noah was that afternoon when he came in for lunch, but the bar was busy and she hadn't the time to come over and visit with him. When she finally had a moment, she walked over to where he sat, placed her hands on her hips, and knowingly accused, "I know you're up to something."

Noah stopped chewing and looked up at Maggie. He swallowed, reached for his glass of water, and took a gulp. "I'm not up to anything," he answered, taking a big bite of the hamburger.

"What are you doing, Noah?" Maggie frowned.

Noah swallowed again and looked at Maggie. "Tomorrow's Thanksgiving."

"Happy Thanksgiving, Noah."

"Thanks, Maggie."

Maggie saw the familiar sparkle of anticipation and expectation in his eyes. "Oh, no." She shook her head. "*Don't you dare.*"

"There's another conference at the hotel—"

"Noah!" Maggie snapped and wagged her index finger. "She ain't comin' back. Her bein' here the first time was a *mistake!*"

Noah shook his head. "I'm going over there on Saturday. Just in case."

"In case of what?!" Maggie scolded quietly so as not to draw the attention of her other customers. "Noah, you've gotta get yourself under control. Every time you start feeling a little better you find some art conference to take yourself to so that you can start this pathetic nonsense all over again!"

Noah smiled faintly. "But she might come back."

Maggie rolled her eyes and stalked away.

*****

Alex had made a habit of "having a little business" on the campus at Augustana College. Tillie noticed that the frequency of his visits had increased to nearly every day of the week. In fact, she thought it strange if Alex *didn't* show up shortly after her Major English Poets class. She did enjoy seeing him, but her heart still ached for Noah. She wanted him to somehow show up and explain everything, beg her to marry him, and whisk her out to the beautiful Black Hills where she belonged. However, she spoke of this desire only to the Lord.

Alex, for his part, did everything he could to come up with excuses for being near her, taking great care not to overwhelm her with his interest. Joining the choir was an especially beneficial stroke of genius as Alex could now pick her up on Saturday mornings for practice. They might as well ride together, he'd reasoned. After all, she lived only a few houses down and was on her way to practice anyway. She had agreed to the rides, and he pushed it no further than that.

On the Wednesday before Thanksgiving, a gentle snow started to fall on the Augustana Campus. Tillie smiled when she saw Alex along the familiar path. His long, black trench coat was spotted with fluffy, white snowflakes and his black hair and broad shoulders dusted with winter whiteness. He smiled at her, and she noticed he was carrying a white rose.

What on earth is he doing with a flower? He's not going to give that thing to me, is he?

Kate had given Alex the idea to ask Tillie out on a *real* date. She told him specifically what to say and added that the white rose would be a nice touch. She promised to pray and encouraged him to take this next step.

"Hi, Tillie." He smiled confidently and presented her with the flower.

Tillie took it hesitantly from his hands. She half-smiled into Alex's handsome, black eyes. "What's this for?"

"It's for you. Granddad used to give Grandmother a white rose when he was about to ask her for a special favor. To Granddad, a white rose was symbolic of hope."

"The hope of what?" Tillie raised one eyebrow.

"The hope we have in Christ, that we will always follow the path He wishes us to take."

Tillie's heart softened just a touch at the romantic story. "So, what's this special *favor?*"

"I bought tickets for a benefit on Friday, the day after Thanksgiving," Alex answered. "It's for the Crippled Children's Home. There will be dinner at the Minnehaha Country Club and then a production at the Sioux Falls Playhouse. The package includes a limousine. Would you accompany me?"

Tillie was astounded. She knew something like this had to happen sometime. Every day he seemed to get a little more courageous. However, he hadn't said the word *date;* he just didn't want to attend this benefit alone. His actual words had been *accompany me.*

"What's the production?" she asked…*I don't know about this…*

"*The Sound of Music*—" he began, hearing her soft gasp.

Tillie recovered her surprise, upset with herself for the little gasp. *The Sound of Music* was her favorite story. She smiled into Alex's eyes and then looked into the snowy petals of the rose. "Okay, I'll *accompany* you to the benefit."

Alex managed to restrain the intense urge he had to take her into his arms and passionately kiss her. "How 'bout lunch?"

"Sure," Tillie replied with a smile, and they left the campus for their favorite café.

*****

Alex removed his trench coat and hung it on the rack behind his office door. He pulled out his comb and worked the leftover snow-flakes out of his hair. The snow had started to melt and run down the back of his shirt. Funny, he hadn't even noticed it until he returned. As he straightened his tie, Sam poked his head in the door.

"So, how did it go?" he asked.

Alex smiled. "Everything was perfect, and she will be *accompanying* me to the benefit on Friday."

Sam nodded with approval and took a seat in one of the chairs in front of Alex's desk. "How'd she like the white rose?"

Alex seated himself behind his desk. "She loved it." He noticed the file Sam was holding and pointed to it. "What's that?"

"Oh." Sam sat up and tossed the file onto Alex's desk. "Remember Noah Hansen?"

Alex nodded. *Who could forget him?*

Alex and Sam's uncle, MacKenzie Dale, managed their branch office in Rapid City, South Dakota. When Mac returned from World War II, he went to work for his best friend and his sister's husband, James Martin. Shortly thereafter, he and his wife, Charlotte, relocated to Rapid City, South Dakota. There he met Earl Hansen and started taking care of his legal work. The Hansens were killed in a car accident in 1956, leaving their entire estate and young son, Noah, to their older son, Joshua, and his wife, Mona. Mac befriended the grieving young preacher and his wife, and they'd been friends ever since.

Whenever Uncle Mac was in Sioux Falls for a holiday or other special occasion, he told all kinds of stories about Noah, the little rebel poor Joshua was trying to raise. At first, Noah just threw snowballs at passing cars and sometimes let fly with bad words, but during his adolescence, his behavior escalated into skipping school, cigarettes, and petty theft. By the time Noah was drafted and sent to Vietnam, he was drunk every day. Everyone thought the military would straighten him out, but he was even worse when he returned.

Alex opened the file and glanced into the neatly stacked papers. "What about Noah? Is he in jail?"

Sam shook his head. "Surprisingly, no. Uncle Mac tells me he's been sober for months. Joshua thinks he was jilted by some girl, but nobody knows what happened to the guy. Anyway, he turns twenty-four in December, and we need to do a transfer on that land trust. Do you want to take care of it?"

Alex began to go through the file. "Why can't Uncle Mac or one of his associates take care of it?"

"He and Aunt Charlotte are going to Arizona for a couple of months. She hasn't been feeling too good," Sam answered. "The

Hansens have been clients for thirty years, so he doesn't want just anybody to handle it."

"Do I have to go out there?"

"Probably should," Sam answered as he got to his feet. "Good P.R. never hurts. Besides, with Uncle Mac out of the office for a while, it won't hurt to have someone check on things while he's away."

Alex looked into the file…*After all these years, I'm finally meeting the infamous Noah Hansen.*

*****

Late Wednesday evening, Petrice, Elaine, Marquette, and Tara arrived in Sioux Falls. They smiled as they walked to where Rosa, Tillie, and Guiseppi waited. Rosa stepped into her sons' embraces, threw her arms around the both of them at the same time, and showered kisses upon their faces. Marquette and Petrice laughed, returning her embrace. Rosa then moved on to their wives. She embraced Tara first and then Elaine. As she held Elaine, she looked up into her eyes and smiled.

"Do you have a secret?" Rosa asked, her black eyes shining with excitement.

Elaine could barely contain the thrill of the secret she and Petrice had already shared with Marquette and Tara. She looked at Petrice, who was embracing his father and sister, and then she looked at Tara. Tara only giggled and turned her face away.

"You *do* have a secret," Rosa gasped with a smile. "Patty!"

Petrice turned his attention toward his mother. "Yes, Ma`ma?"

"Tell me what makes your Ellie so happy this night."

Petrice took Elaine's hand into his own. "May I tell them?"

Elaine nodded, and her face blushed a deep red.

Petrice looked at his family and announced with a smile, "My Ellie and I will have a baby in May."

"Praise the Lord," Guiseppi cried with a smile as he reached to embrace his daughter-in-law. Elaine bent so that Guiseppi could kiss her, and he looked into her eyes. "I am so happy for you."

"Thank you, Guiseppi."

Tillie plastered a fake smile onto her face and put her arms around her sister-in-law. "Congratulations," she said sweetly…*I was just getting used to the fact that he loves you.*

They arrived at the Caselli home, unloaded their things, and gathered around a fire in the living room. Rosa poured hot cups of apple cider and dipped a cinnamon stick into each one. She'd prepared cream puffs with chocolate filling and icing for just this occasion, and Tillie helped her mother serve the delicious treats to everyone around the fire.

"And how was Oslo?" Rosa winked mischievously at Tara.

"Oh," Tara replied as she rolled her eyes, and Marquette began to laugh. "It was awful. The humidity was worse there this year than any other time we have visited. I felt like a clam."

"It was not so bad," Marquette laughed as he took hold of Tara's hand. "She is just so fragile when it comes to the humidity."

Tara humphed and sipped at her cider.

Guiseppi chuckled and looked at Petrice. "And what of this Senator's seat that is coming available next year?"

"I have officially thrown my hat into the ring," Petrice answered. "If I win the spring primaries, I will attempt to take the junior Senator's seat in New York."

"How cool," Tillie commented as she smiled. "My very own brother will be a Senator."

Petrice sighed with a smile. "Please pray for us." He looked at Elaine and said, "Sometimes we feel as if we have bitten off more than we can chew." He took a breath. "And tell us, Angel, how is your first semester going?"

"Good," she answered as she took a bite from her cream puff.

"I was surprised to hear you changed your major," he continued. "What prompted that?"

Tillie nearly choked on her cream puff, swallowed hard, and answered, "I guess I was just tired of art."

Marquette's eyes were wide with surprise. "*Tired* of art?"

Guiseppi could see where this was leading and cleared his throat loudly. "Sometimes we all need a change." He smiled at Tillie. "Besides, preparing for all of those exhibits was becoming a tiresome thing for Angel."

Tillie nodded in agreement and smiled at her father. "It's nice to have some time to myself."

"Perhaps you will change your mind again next semester," Petrice suggested.

"Perhaps," Tillie replied as she took another big bite of her cream puff.

"Angel will be attending a formal benefit on Friday," Rosa blurted out.

"Oh?" Marquette smiled curiously at his sister.

Rosa continued, "It is a benefit for The Crippled Children's Home. There will be the use of a limousine, dinner at Minnehaha, and then a production of *The Sound of Music* at the Sioux Falls Playhouse."

"Wow," Petrice said with a wink. "I tried to get tickets for that benefit, but they were sold out in October. When did you manage to get them? You must have paid a fortune."

Tillie nearly choked again. "Alex Martin invited me. He had the tickets."

Marquette's handsome face knit itself into a terrible frown. "Alex Martin?"

"Now, Marquette," Guiseppi began as he leaned forward in his chair, "they have been seeing one another for quite some time—"

"Not exactly *seeing one another*," Tillie corrected quickly. She could tell just by the look in Marquette's eyes that he wasn't pleased. "We just have lunch occasionally. He asked if I would accompany him, probably so he wouldn't have to attend alone."

Petrice winked at his little sister. "Angel, Alex would have had to secure those tickets some time ago. He has probably been planning to ask you for quite a while."

Tillie frowned. "Are you sure?"

"Of course he is sure," Marquette snorted, and Tara put her hand on his knee in an attempt to calm him down. However, it didn't work, and Marquette ranted, "He has been planning this for months."

Tillie stared at her brother in open-eyed amazement. She'd always known Marquette didn't particularly care for Alex, but his reaction had been a little over the top. "He's very kind to me, Marquette," she said with a frown.

"He is a wonderful man, Marquette." Petrice laughed as he tried to calm the tense situation. "Do not begrudge Angel this lovely event."

Tara chuckled as she patted Marquette's knee. "And he is *so* handsome." She smiled at Tillie and changed the tone of the conversation. "Is it a formal event?"

Tillie nodded. Had her skin not been so dark, her family would have seen the hot flush upon her cheeks. Why had Marquette been so aggressive?

"What will you wear?" Elaine looked from Tillie to Marquette and then back to Tillie. This obvious feud between Marquette and Alex was news to her. Petrice had never mentioned it before.

Tillie took a breath and feigned a smile. "I have a straight-cut, long black formal." She placed her hand delicately upon her chest and explained, "With a white v-neck and long sleeves."

"What is the length?" Elaine asked.

"Just above my ankles," Tillie answered, beginning to relax. "I'm going to wear my pearls, and Ma`ma will put my hair up." Tillie gathered her thick curls into her hands and demonstrated for them how she would look with her hair up. "Like this, so you can see my earrings."

"The pearls Vincenzo and Kate gave you for your birthday?" Tara asked quickly so that Marquette would not be tempted to butt in further.

Tillie nodded.

"And what for shoes?" Elaine asked.

"Black patent-leather pumps," Tillie answered, and she looked at her mother. "I will have to borrow Ma`ma's. And I have this *really cool* black cape in case it snows."

"Ooo, a really cool black cape," Guiseppi teased as his eyes sparkled. "How fashionable."

Everyone laughed, except for Marquette, who only pretended to smile.

*****

"I cannot believe this. I am away a mere three months and that *fiend* has set his sights upon my baby sister," Marquette ranted in a whisper as he got into the bed with Tara later on that evening. He hadn't commented further and stayed very quiet during the rest of their visit. Everyone finally decided to go to bed, and he was relieved to get away from them so he could express his own opinion to Tara.

Tara snuggled close to him, put her hand on his chest, and softly kissed his cheek. "Do not be jealous, Marquette."

"I am *not* jealous." He took his wife's hand into his own. "I have *never* been jealous of Alex Martin a day in my life."

"Your sister seems happy about this, and you know, Angel has had a hard time of it this year. She seems so much happier now. Perhaps it is Alex who is bringing her around."

Marquette rolled his eyes. "Why can he not fool someone his own age? Why does he set his sights upon a babe who does not know better?"

"She is not a babe," Tara snapped. "And he is not *fooling* her. Look at the trouble he has gone to in order to win her attention."

"Oh, please, Tara," Marquette scoffed. "Of course he is fooling her—"

"And you will *not* be following them around on Friday night," Tara interrupted, placing her hand delicately over Marquette's mouth. "Now turn off the light, my love, for I must awaken with Rosa to help with the turkey in the morning."

Marquette opened his mouth for further response, but Tara increased the pressure of her hand.

"No," she whispered with a frown. "Not another word. Now turn off that light!"

Marquette snorted, rolled away from his wife, and turned off the light beside their bed. *Even she has thrown in with the rest of them! Must they rally around Angel and actually encourage this unholy debacle she is about to embark upon? Have they completely closed their eyes to the truth apparently only I can see?*

By morning, Sioux Falls was covered in a thick blanket of white snow. It was so bright outside that Tillie had to squint as she gazed out of her mother's kitchen window and into the empty field behind their house. "But no sun," she observed, and then she smiled. "That probably means more snow." She looked at her niece and nephew who were at the kitchen table with Ellie, eating some crackers and cheese. "Which means that we get to play outside!"

The two little ones clapped their hands.

Kate laughed. "And you're the only one that's happy about *that*." She and Vincenzo had just arrived and brought with them several homemade pies and another two gallons of apple cider. Kate was pouring one of the gallons into a kettle on top of the stove at that moment so everyone could have some of their favorite holiday drink. She'd spend Thanksgiving with the Casellis, and then she, Vincenzo, and the babies would go to her family's house for another dinner. Uncle Mac and Aunt Charlotte had traveled from Rapid City to Sioux Falls for a visit before they left to winter in Arizona. James' only living sibling, Ruth Martin Morgan, was also in town for the holiday. She and her husband, Luke Morgan, lived in West Virginia.

Rosa had kept everyone busy with jobs in the kitchen. Tara peeled the baked yams, and Tillie prepared raw vegetables, pickles, and olives for a relish tray. Kate would soon begin to peel the white potatoes. Ellie, however, sat quietly on a kitchen chair, watching them all bustle around and taking a sip of the iced club soda Rosa had offered her.

"Do not fret, pretty Ellie." Rosa patted Elaine's shoulder and encouraged, "This dreadful time will soon pass. Here," and she handed Elaine a toasted biscotti, "nibble on this, my dear."

"Thanks, Rosa," Elaine replied. She put the biscotti to her a mouth and bit off a cautious amount.

Tillie felt pity for the poor girl and wanted to kick herself for all of the mean things she'd thought of Elaine over the past several months.

"Angel," Rosa instructed, "please get me the punch bowl for this cider."

"Yes, Ma`ma. Where is it?"

"The closet in the billiard room."

Tillie passed through the living room and noticed her father and Petrice deep into a humorous discussion. Heaven only knew what they were talking about because they spoke in Italian, as they often did when she wasn't around. They smiled politely and waved as she passed through the room, not missing a beat of their conversation.

Vincenzo and Marquette were in the billiard room, and they each held a que. They were visiting in Italian as well, and Tillie hesitated outside of the doorway before they saw her. It was fun to listen to their foreign language, even though she didn't understand it. Marquette's voice sounded angry, but Vincenzo laughed a few times. *They must be arguing*, she guessed, and then she heard Marquette say "Alex Martin" as clear as a bell.

She stepped into the doorway and confronted Marquette, "You were talking about me and Alex's d…d…thing…that we're going to."

Vincenzo smiled and looked at Tillie. "I, for one, am excited for you. You will have a wonderful time." He feigned a scowl at Marquette. "With the dear brother of my lovely and devoted wife."

Tillie confronted her brother with a frown, "Marquette, you're jealous of Alex the way I was jealous of Ellie."

Marquette shook his head. "I am *not* jealous."

Vincenzo nodded and taunted, "You are jealous, Marquette—"

"Listen to me," Marquette interrupted, "Ellie is a lovely girl. Alex is—"

Tillie held up her hand and shook her head. "Don't even say it, Marquette." She smiled hesitantly and embraced her tall brother, giving him a soft kiss on the cheek. "I love you, Marquette, and I'm so thankful that you're my brother. Now this benefit is for a good cause, and I really want to go and see the play. Be *happy* for me."

Marquette looked down into the sparkling black eyes of his little sister, sighed, and relaxed his angry expression. "Alright. If you insist."

"I insist."

"Well then," Vincenzo turned from the two of them and realigned his cue on the billiard table, "let me finish beating you."

Marquette gave Tillie a tender kiss on the top of her head. "I am sorry, Angel. I will attempt to restrain myself."

Tillie smiled into Marquette's face. "Thanks." And then she retrieved the punch bowl and left them alone to finish their game.

Ellie's queasiness had disappeared by the time Thanksgiving dinner was on the table, for which she was relieved. She'd watched the delicious food being prepared for hours—turkey and stuffing, mashed potatoes and gravy, sweet potatoes, buttered corn, homemade buns, and cranberry sauce.

Rosa called everyone into the dining room where they circled the table and stood politely as they waited for Guiseppi to pray. He looked around at his family and smiled as he realized the drastic differences the last nineteen years in America had brought.

"Nineteen years ago, this was the first day in our new home in America," he began. Tillie saw his eyes mist over with the memories, and she found herself getting emotional as well. Guiseppi took a deep breath and bowed his head. "Thank you, Father, for your glorious blessings upon us. Thank you for growing our family so abundantly. To think, we were only five terrified people on that day nineteen years ago, and now, here we are, having more than doubled our family, and You are still adding on, Father. Thank you for the safe travels of my sons, and thank you for this food you provide to us each and every day of the year. Please continue Your blessings upon us and guide us through the rest of our lives. In the Name of Jesus. Amen."

*****

Rosa hadn't missed a single after-Thanksgiving-Day sale since she'd come to America in 1956. Aunt Penny had taken her on her first shopping trip, and she spoke of it every year as they all headed out to the stores. This year, as in years past, Rosa chattered in the passenger seat of the vehicle while someone else drove. Rosa had never learned to drive and had no desire. If Guiseppi or Frances were not available, Rosa could count on Tillie.

Today, Tara drove, and she giggled at Rosa's wonderful memories. Ellie, Kate, and Tillie were in the backseat, and the babies had been left with Frances, who opted to stay home this year and visit with her brother and sister-in-law. Guiseppi and his sons reconciled inventory at the restaurant on this day every year, and that is where they would be for most of the day.

After hours of shopping and eventually a late lunch at Angelo's, the ladies returned home with their packages and hid them in Tillie's developing lab in the basement. Rosa put on some tea, and Kate called Frances to say she'd be up to get the babies in a few minutes.

"Well they're both napping right now," Frances informed, "so why don't you stay there until Alex comes to pick up Tillie?"

"Is he nervous?" Kate whispered into the phone.

"He's scared to death, though he'll admit it to no one," Frances giggled. "But he'll look sharp as a tack. He's wearing his black tux."

Kate whispered into the phone, "I think Tillie is really excited. She talked about it a couple of times today—" Rosa appeared in the room, and Kate smiled and said, "Okay, well, thanks, Mom. I'll see you later." She hung up the phone and looked at Rosa. "The kids are taking a nap, so I guess I'll just stay and have a cup of tea with you guys."

Tillie took a hot bath, washed her hair, and wrapped a towel around her head to keep it wet enough for Rosa to work with. She put on the elegant black dress with the white v-neck and sat down in front of her vanity to put on her make-up. There was a soft knock on her bedroom door, and she said, "Come in, Ma`ma." She reached for some powder and was surprised to see Tara's smiling face.

"Hey, you," Tillie said with a smile as she began to apply the powder to her face. "Are Papa and the boys back yet?"

Tara nodded and took a seat on a chair by the vanity. "Papa and Marquette are reading the paper, and Petrice and Vincenzo are playing pool." She looked into Tillie's eyes. She *did* seem happier, but… "I am wondering about Noah," she whispered.

Tillie put her hand on Tara's arm, smiled into her eyes, and assured her with a lie, "I'm just about over that whole episode. Don't worry about it anymore."

Tara smiled and replied, "Okay, Angel."

The door to Tillie's room opened again, and it was Rosa. "Let us get started, Angel," she said with a smile. She set a plastic bag filled with bobby pins on the vanity and started to unwrap Tillie's wet hair.

Tillie sat very still and watched her mother weave and pin her rebellious curls into place. She piled them onto Tillie's head in the shape of a curly bun, leaving delicate tendrils to dangle femininely on her neck. She was sure to expose Tillie's ears so the tiny pearl earrings Vincenzo and Kate had given her would show. When Rosa was finished, Tillie's hair was dry.

"We did it," Rosa chuckled. "We have outsmarted your hair once again." She clasped the pretty strand of matching pearls around Tillie's neck and stood back for a look. "I have done a wonderful job."

Tillie smiled as she looked at the pretty hairdo her mother had created. "It's great, Ma`ma," she admired, giving it a soft pat. She turned her head from side to side and looked at Tara. "What do you think?"

Tara stood back to gaze upon Tillie. "Lovely!"

Rosa reached into her apron pocket and pulled out a black bottle of her favorite potion. "I almost forgot!" she exclaimed as she took off the lid. "Chanel No. 5." She misted a tiny bit of the perfume on the back of Tillie's neck and inhaled deeply. "Ah. That smells wonderful. *Now* you are ready."

There was a knock on Tillie's door, and Tara rose from her seat to pull it open. In the doorway stood a very serious-looking Guiseppi. "He is here."

Tillie was surprised at her sudden excitement. She got up from her vanity and looked out of her window. In the driveway below waited a long, white limousine. A man dressed in tails and a top hat waited beside one of the back doors.

Guiseppi turned his eyes to Tara. "Please leave us alone for a moment. We must speak with our daughter."

Tara nodded and left the room, closing the door behind her.

Guiseppi smiled at his pretty daughter. "You look beautiful."

"Thank you, Papa."

Guiseppi drew in his breath and handed Tillie a small red box with a gold bow. "For you, Angel. And forgive us for not thinking of having this little talk at an earlier time."

Tillie's eyes were confused as she reached for the dainty box. "Thanks, Papa." She opened the lid and gasped when she saw its contents. The most delicate band of gold and tiny diamonds rested inside a black felt box.

"For your purity, Angel," Rosa said. She took the tiny band out of the box while Guiseppi reached for her left hand. Rosa slid the band onto Tillie's ring finger and smiled mischievously into her daughter's eyes. "Because you may be tempted."

"Alex won't tempt me," Tillie said as she admired the ring upon her finger.

Guiseppi nodded. "You have not seen him yet." He took Tillie's other hand into his own. "Please, Angel, if you should be tempted on this evening, or any other evening when you are with Alex, please call us so that we might talk you through it."

Tillie looked into their earnest eyes. *They're amazing.*

"This will be our special pact," Rosa said as she squeezed the hand that wore the ring. "And it can be our secret. No one needs to know of this. Now, promise us, Angel, you will call if you are tempted."

"I promise."

"Then we must not keep the young man waiting." Guiseppi opened the door for Tillie and Rosa.

As they descended the stairs and the foyer came into view, they saw all three of Tillie's brothers exchanging what seemed to be pleasant conversation. Marquette was even smiling, and Tillie thanked God. Then she saw Alex and almost stumbled on the steps. He stood tall and strong, dressed in a black tuxedo with a stiff, white shirt and black, shiny buttons. His black hair shone blue beneath the light in the foyer, and when he smiled up at her, she was sure his white teeth sparkled. She smiled in return, and she and her parents continued down the steps to join her brothers and Alex in the foyer.

"You look magnificent, Angel," Petrice whispered into her ear as he gave her a soft kiss upon the cheek. Vincenzo and Marquette stood side by side and nodded in agreement.

Tillie saw all three of her sisters-in-law peek from the kitchen and then heard their soft laughter. She swallowed hard and tried not to be nervous. *Why do they have to make such a spectacle over everything? It's just a benefit for children.*

"Hello, Tillie," Alex greeted, sounding more confident than ever. "You look lovely."

"Thank you, Alex." She smiled, feeling her face flush. Rosa slipped something into her hand, and Tillie looked down to see she was holding the boutonniere they'd picked out at the florist's earlier that afternoon. "May I?" she asked politely as she held the boutonniere before him.

"Of course," Alex replied with a smile.

Tillie forced her hands not to shake as she pulled the pins out of the boutonniere and secured it perfectly on his left lapel. She noticed the soft scent of his cologne, and it made her face flush again. *Thank you, God, for making me so dark.*

Alex held a pretty corsage made of white sweetheart roses and baby's breath, but he handed it to Rosa with a smile. "Would you be so kind as to help me with this? The florist neglected to attach a wristband."

"Of course." Rosa gave him an approving nod and then pinned the corsage on Tillie's left side.

"You mustn't forget your cool black cape," Guiseppi whispered as he draped it over her shoulders, being careful not to disturb the pretty corsage.

"Is it snowing?" Tillie asked.

"Yes, it just started," Alex answered. "And we should be getting along. The driver has asked me for extra time on the icy roads."

"Okay," Tillie said as she looked at her sweet, little parents and then over at her brothers, who stood together near the kitchen entrance. Vincenzo gave her a sly "thumbs up," and she almost giggled.

Alex opened the door and looked at Rosa and Guiseppi. "I promise not to have her out too late. Would you like her in before midnight?"

"Midnight is fine," Guiseppi answered.

"Very well, then," Alex said with a smile. He opened the outer door and stepped onto the porch, pausing to offer Tillie his hand. "It's quite slippery. Please allow me?"

Tillie nodded bashfully and placed her small hand into Alex's bigger one. He grasped a gentle hold to lead her through the door, down the steps, and to the door of the limousine where the patient driver waited, covered completely in snow by now.

"Ma'am," said the driver as he politely tipped his hat and opened the car door. Tillie stepped into the limousine, while Alex helped her with the trailing cape. He seated himself next to her, and the driver closed the door.

From the living room window inside of the house, Guiseppi and his sons watched the fancy limousine back out of the driveway and head down the street.

"What a show-off," Marquette mumbled.

"Very smooth," Petrice said with a soft slap to Marquette's back.

Vincenzo smiled. "You are in *big* trouble, Papa. This could be the start of something."

Guiseppi smiled and raised his eyebrows. *I certainly hope so.*

*****

The house was dark, and Vincenzo's car was gone. The dinner and play had been excellent, and they'd been able to visit comfortably throughout the entire evening. They'd exchanged good-humored stories about English poets and Russian language, and Tillie had made Alex laugh several times with her quick wit and comical spirit.

"Kate and Vincenzo must have gone home," Alex noted as he slowly walked Tillie to the doorway.

"And I think everyone else must have gone to bed," she added.

They were at the front door, and Alex wanted to kiss her but knew the overture would be out of the question. He'd have to wait.

"Thank you," he smiled down into her eyes. "I had a really nice time."

"Me too. Thanks for inviting me."

Alex reached for one of her hands, lifted it to his lips, and placed a delicate kiss on top of it. *Is this okay? Or will she punch me in the nose?*

Tillie only smiled into his eyes and stood very still.

"I hope we can go out again," he said, keeping a gentle hold of her hand.

Tillie slowly nodded. "That would be nice."

"I was hoping you'd say that." He reached behind her and opened the door. "May I call?"

Tillie smiled with a nod and stepped through the door, noticing he still held the hand he'd kissed.

"When would be good?" he asked.

"Will you be picking me up for choir practice in the morning?"

Alex nodded. He had completely forgotten about that.

"We can talk about it then," she offered.

"Okay," Alex said, releasing her hand. "Goodnight, Tillie."

"Goodnight, Alex."

He turned and walked back to the limousine, where the driver waited beside the open door. He looked up and saw her watching, and he waved before he got inside.

Tillie closed the door and leaned against it with a heavy sigh. *He's the perfect knight!*

Chapter 13

Noah stood in Maggie's bar and stared at the haunting portrait. Where was she going? And why did she have such a determined expression on her face? *Angel's mother...or at least that's what she said. She does look like Angel.*

Estelle watched him from the kitchen as his eyes searched every detail. She'd thought about asking Maggie to take the thing down because the poor kid just tortured himself with it. She shook her head and bit her lip as she recalled the past seven months. *Noah wants Angel*, and that felt unexplainably *right* to Estelle.

With nowhere else to turn for help, and unbeknownst to Maggie, Estelle had started to pray. Every day she got down on her knees and begged Noah's God to bring Angel back. She wasn't sure she believed it would work, but she felt *compelled* to perform the oddly comforting ritual. Maggie would've never understood because she thought Noah was behaving like an idiot, but Estelle felt there was something more.

Maggie came out of the back room and paused beside Estelle, following her gaze to where Noah was standing before the bar.

"He's been starin' at that thing for ten minutes," Estelle whispered.

Maggie groaned and went to the bar. "Noah!" she barked, startling him from his thoughts. "What'll ya have?"

Noah eased back onto the stool. "What's the special?"

"Ribs," Estelle answered. She scribbled onto a ticket, hung it on the wheel behind the counter, and disappeared into the kitchen.

Noah rubbed his chin and took a seat at the bar. Maggie pulled a Coke out from under the counter, popped off the top, and set it down on a cocktail napkin. She raised one eyebrow. "Did you go over to the hotel?"

Noah tipped the bottle and took a long drink. "Yep. Nothin'." He shook his head. "Why can't I find her, Maggie? I just can't imagine what's happened. Why didn't she come back?"

Maggie looked at Noah with feigned disbelief. "You can't possibly be serious. Did you actually believe she'd come back and you'd live happily ever after?"

" 'Course Maggie didn't see her over there this mornin' either," Estelle informed as she marched past them with a tray of salt and pepper shakers.

Noah frowned at Maggie.

"Listen, Noah," Maggie continued as she rolled her eyes, "I was gonna give that girl a good shaking for what she's done. Nobody deserves to be treated this way." She gave him her most tender pat on his forearm. "I'm sorry. But you must've known it would be a long shot."

"I did," he admitted. "What can I do now? I have no idea where to look. There must be a million little towns in this state, and what if she's living in Sioux Falls? That place is so big, I'll never find her if she's there."

*****

By the middle of December, Alex and Tillie had gone on real dates. They saw a few movies and the symphony, each time enjoying each other's company. Alex was always the perfect gentleman. He never got too close and never tried anything more than to offer to hold her hand while they crossed slippery pavement. He didn't try to put his arm around her in the theater, and he *never* attempted a kiss, even though he wanted one. He only kissed the top of her hand, and only at the very end of the evening.

Alex came to the campus every day for lunch, scheduling himself around those precious few hours Tillie had free after her morning class. Sometimes he'd take her to the small café on Minnesota and 26th Streets, and sometimes he'd bring sandwiches for them to eat in the car. McDonald's was her favorite

"You know," she said one day as they sat in his Mercedes eating hamburgers and drinking chocolate shakes, "I'll only have about twenty minutes for lunch next semester." She laughed at his stricken expression and added, "Come on. You need to save some money anyway."

"Can't you reschedule something?"

Tillie shook her head. "I have Major American Poets and then a class on the Bolsheviks right after that."

"I guess then...that...maybe..." He hesitated. "Maybe I'll just have to try to see you more often in the evenings."

Tillie smiled and nodded. "Okay."

Alex took a sip of his shake. "By the way, I'm going to Rapid City tomorrow, but I'll be back in the late afternoon. I have to do a land transfer for one of my uncle's clients. They've been clients of our firm since 1945. Uncle Mac wants either me or Sam to go, and I'm low man on the totem pole."

"Will you drive?"

Alex shook his head. "No. I've chartered a small plane. In fact, we could probably have dinner at The Normandy when I get back, if you want to."

Tillie smiled. "Sure."

*****

The snow was falling at Rapid City Regional Airport when Alex's charter landed. He found their shuttle service, which consisted of a rusted out Volkswagen van and a chain-smoking driver who careened down old Highway 44 into Rapid City. Alex was amazed to still be alive when he was dropped off at the First Federal Bank Building on the corner of St. Joseph and West Boulevard.

"What time do you want me to pick you up?" the driver growled out of the window as Alex walked around the front of the van.

"Don't worry about it," Alex said politely, slipping him a five dollar bill through the window. "I'll call a taxi when I'm done."

"What's this for?" the driver questioned with a frown.

"The tip?"

The driver laughed hysterically. "Oh, yeah. Ain't never got one of those. Thanks, mister."

"You bet." Alex nodded and turned toward the building.

He walked into the open lobby, passed by the familiar lighted fountain (now shrouded in Christmas greenery), and pushed the button by the elevator. Alex brushed the snow from his black trench coat while he rode to the eighth floor, where Mac's offices were located.

He stepped off of the elevator and strode down the hall, heading for the double glass doors at the end. There was a pine wreath hanging there, and the smell almost took his breath away as he opened one door and entered the office.

"May I help you?" greeted a friendly-looking woman seated behind a receptionist's desk. She was dressed in a professional navy suit and wore her dark brown hair short around her head. A small pair of spectacles rested at the end of her nose. Above her was professional lettering that read Martin, Martin & Dale, A.P.C.L.

"Yes." Alex smiled as he set down his briefcase and extended his hand in greeting. "I'm Alex Martin."

The woman gave his hand a gentle shake. "I'm Lori." She stood behind her desk. "We've been expecting you. Why don't you follow me, and I'll show you to your uncle's office."

Alex picked up his briefcase and followed her through some wooden doors. The perimeter of the large office was lined with separate offices and cubicles scattered within their borders. There were at least twenty-five cubicles, complete with equipment and secretaries. Lori led him past them to the office in the farthest corner and opened the door.

Alex gasped, unprepared for the decor he saw. Uncle Mac's office was done in *extreme* Western flare. Paintings of Sioux Indians and cowboys hung on the two available walls, as the other two walls were corner windows. A loud, red-and-black wool blanket was draped over the arm of a leather couch, a buffalo head hung on the wall next to the door, and there was some kind of cattle horns mounted on the front of Uncle Mac's desk.

Alex stared in amazement. *I don't remember any of this.* "Wow," he breathed, taken aback by the appearance of the room. *I'm actually related to this guy.*

"I know." Lori smiled in understanding. "He's a cowboy at heart."

Alex sat down his briefcase and started to take off his wet coat. The situation became even more awkward when he realized there was no place to hang his coat.

"Oh, here," Lori offered as she took the coat from his hands and hung it on one of the buffalo's horns.

Alex's mouth fell open, but he closed it and said, "Thank you."

"No problem. I'll send in Mac's secretary. I'm sure you'll want to get started. The Hansens will be here at two o'clock, and there's a meeting scheduled with the rest of the lawyers at three. They'll brief you on what's going on while Mac's away."

Alex nodded, and she left. He strolled over to the corner windows and looked out across Rapid City. There wasn't much to look at from this angle because the Black Hills were in the other direction. However, he could see "M" hill, which was a hill of whitewashed stones in the shape of an "M" for the South Dakota School of Mines & Technology. He could also see through the "gap," which was the curve of Main Street as it wound through two small ridges and into

Baken Park on the west side of town. Memorial Park was right over there, and he could almost make out frozen Rapid Creek running through the middle of it.

Someone cleared their throat behind him, and he turned to see another woman. She was short and plump and wore a cross expression between her hazel-colored eyes. Her willowy blonde hair was drawn into a very messy bun at the back of her head and held in place with an unsharpened pencil. She was dressed in a professional-looking tan suit, but Alex noticed she wasn't wearing any shoes.

"I'm Bonnie," she introduced. "What do you want me to start with?"

Alex walked to where she stood and extended his hand in greeting. "I'm Alex Martin. How do you do?"

"Fine," she said with a confused look, shaking his hand hesitantly. "I thought we were gonna do a land transfer?"

Alex picked up his briefcase and walked to the desk. He pulled out the Hansen files, shuffled through a few of his neat notes, and looked at Bonnie. "I guess I need a Quit Claim Deed for the trust—"

"Who'll be signing for the Trust?" she interrupted, scribbling onto a steno pad.

"I will," Alex answered, and she looked at him with surprise.

"What did you say your name was?"

"Alex Martin."

She glanced back at her steno pad. "Do you have a middle initial or any i's at the end of your name?"

"I's?"

"You know, like the second or the third?"

"Alex J. Martin, the third," he answered. *How in the world does Mac get anything done with this nut? Shondra's much more professional. In fact, Shondra would have had the papers all ready to go by the time I got here.*

"And what else do you want?" Bonnie brusquely questioned.

"Well, a Certificate of Transfer would be nice," Alex answered with a forced smile. "And why don't you throw in a Warranty Deed with a homestead clause for good measure."

"Don't need a homestead," Bonnie said, not even looking up but continuing to write on her pad. "Noah's not married."

"But Joshua is," Alex corrected curtly, and she looked at him. "And prepare an Affidavit of Receipt for Noah as long as you're at it."

"Alright. You're the boss." And with that, she turned on her heel and left the office.

"Weird," Alex mumbled as he took a seat behind the desk and began to get his file in order.

A short time later, a huffy Bonnie produced the completed documents and dropped them on Alex's desk.

"Anything else?" she asked, with her nose turned up slightly, avoiding eye contact.

Alex looked through the deeds to make sure they'd been prepared correctly and shook his head. "No, thank you. That will be all."

As Bonnie turned to walk away, she said over her shoulder, "The Hansens are here. Do you want 'em?" Before he could answer, she disappeared around the corner of the door.

She is so strange. He shook his head and reached for the intercom button that was so familiar on his own phone, quickly realizing Uncle Mac did not have one. He got to his feet and walked out to the reception lobby where two men in sturdy Western coats and a pretty woman with red hair and a leather coat were seated. The men wore heavy blue jeans, cowboy boots, and deerskin gloves. The woman, on the other hand, wore dress slacks and shoes and a black beret atop her striking red hair.

The older man looked to be about forty or so. He had smiling, brown eyes and graying brown hair. The woman next to him was probably his wife. It was hard to tell how old the younger man was because of the intense sadness reflected in his expression...*He must be Noah.*

"The Hansens, I presume?" Alex asked with a smile. He extended his hand first to Joshua. "How do you do? I'm Alex Martin, and this is a pleasure."

"I'm Joshua, and this is my wife, Mona, and my brother, Noah," Joshua introduced. He pulled off his gloves and shook the friendly, young lawyer's hand.

"Please follow me," Alex instructed, turning to open the wooden doors for them. He swung his arm in the direction he wanted them to go, and they followed. Alex led them back to Uncle Mac's office and showed them inside. "Can I take your coats?" he asked, but they shook their heads. "Well, have a seat then. Coffee?" He regretted his last remark. Bonnie would *never* bring coffee. Thankfully they all shook their heads again.

Joshua, Mona, and Noah seated themselves in the chairs in front of the desk, and Alex seated himself. He took another quick look at the papers and handed the set to Joshua.

"You'll need to sign here," Alex explained as he pointed. "And the Trustee, that will be me, will sign here. Noah will sign this Affidavit of Receipt, and Mrs. Hansen will have to sign the Warranty Deed where indicated." Alex looked up and smiled. "And we'll need a notary to seal this. Can you wait just a moment? I'll be right back." He hurried out of the office, leaving the Hansens alone for a short time.

"He's seems awfully young to be a lawyer," Mona whispered as she looked over her shoulder.

"He just graduated this year," Joshua whispered. "I think Mac said he's twenty-five."

"He looks more like twelve," Noah whispered.

They quickly quieted themselves when Alex returned with Lori, who held a silver seal in one hand and a black pen in another.

"Lori is a Notary Public," Alex explained as they positioned themselves on the other side of the desk. "She will notarize your signatures. Normally you'd have to produce identification, but Lori assures me she's known all of you for years."

The Hansens nodded with smiles. Lori had been at the front door for as long as any of them could remember.

"Do you need any of these documents explained?" Alex asked.

The three of them shook their heads and began signing where they'd been instructed, setting their pens down on the desk when they'd finished. Lori signed and stamped her notary seal on the papers and then left the office.

"Congratulations and happy birthday, Noah," Alex said as he extended his hand, and Noah shook it.

"Thanks," Noah said.

"Now, if you need anything or if you have any questions, please don't hesitate to call me," Alex said as he reached into his inside breast pocket. He pulled out a tiny, leather billfold holding his business cards and gave one to Noah. "This is my number in Sioux Falls. I'll be handling everything for you while my uncle is away."

Noah took the card but was confused. "You mean you're not *staying* in Rapid?"

Alex shook his head. "I have to get back. But I can be out here on a charter if you need additional work, or you can call me if you have any questions."

"Mac told me, but I forgot. When will they be back?" Joshua asked curiously.

"Probably in April or May," Alex answered. "Aunt Charlotte is very ill and needs to stay in the drier climate for awhile."

"We were very sorry to hear that," Mona acknowledged.

Alex nodded. "They were through Sioux Falls over Thanksgiving, and she said she's feeling a little better."

Joshua began to get to his feet, and Noah and Mona rose almost at the same time.

"Well, can we buy you a late lunch?" Joshua offered.

"No, but thank you." Alex replied with a smile. "I have a meeting here at three o'clock, and then I'm flying home shortly after that. But I'll be having an early dinner with my—" he hesitated. He didn't want to call her his "girl friend," because she was definitely something far more special than that. He pretended to swallow and then he finished, "my dearest friend."

"Oh, I heard about her," Joshua said as he smiled. "Mac said you're seeing a young lady. Tillie?" Alex nodded and smiled. "What does she do? Is she a lawyer too?"

Alex shook his head and just about laughed. *Tillie a lawyer? That would really be something else.* "No, she just started college. She's studying comparative literature."

Joshua extended his hand to Alex. "Well, it was sure nice meeting you, Mr. Martin."

"Please, call me Alex." He took Joshua's hand and gave it a firm shake. "And let me know if you need anything else."

"We'll do," Joshua replied.

"Nice to meet you," Mona drawled with a smile, extending her feminine hand.

"Thanks, Alex," Noah said as he extended his hand, and Alex again saw the horrible sadness in his eyes.

"It was my pleasure," Alex said.

*****

Nothing is more beautiful than the Black Hills blanketed in snow. Noah hiked along next to Joshua as they made their way across the meadow. Snow had covered the hills as far as their eyes could see, and more was falling by the moment. Mona made them promise not to stay out too long, but once they were out in it, it was hard to leave.

"What on earth is *comparative literature?*" Noah wondered aloud as they hiked along.

"Beats me," Joshua answered with a shake of his head. "And how 'bout that guy? He came clear out here just to do some paperwork for *us*. That's pretty impressive."

Noah shrugged. "Seems like a nice guy."

They'd hiked a little further when Noah began to speak again. "You know, Josh, I've got this idea." He stopped in the snow and waited for his brother to stop as well.

Joshua turned, waited, and looked at Noah. "What idea?"

"Well," Noah began, "I've been watching this builder, and he loves my work. I think I can do what he does."

"What do you mean?"

"There's a real estate class starting next week," Noah explained. "I can get my license, sell some stuff, and make some money in this town."

"I think you can too," Joshua agreed.

"I have so many ideas," Noah continued as he started to walk through the snow again. "I just need some extra money to get the thing off the ground. I don't have all of the bugs worked out yet, but maybe I'll give that Alex Martin a call and find out what I've gotta do." Noah sighed and looked at the snow-covered land before him. "But I'll *never* sell this property. I'm gonna *live* here some day."

Joshua looked at his younger brother. He'd changed so much in such a short period of time, making Joshua believe Noah could do anything. But questions remained. For instance, how had Noah been able to walk away from his old lifestyle and never return? And what had left that horrible sadness in his eyes?

"Noah, how did you do it?"

"Do what?"

"Get sober so fast and stay that way."

Noah chuckled and looked at his brother. "I had to buy groceries instead of booze. Funny how that sobered me right up." Noah chuckled again at his own humor.

Joshua smiled and shook his head. "No, what I mean is, Noah, you're different now. You're sensible, and you're making great plans."

"My head is clear." He gave Joshua a slap on the back and asked with a smile, "Isn't that what you always wanted?"

"But what's making you so *sad*, Noah?" Joshua looked into Noah's eyes for a long moment before Noah turned away and focused on the snow-covered Hills around them.

Emotions swelled in Noah's heart and her memory was everywhere—her sparkling eyes, the sound of her voice, the warmth of her presence. "Do you believe in love at first sight, Josh?"

Joshua sighed and slowly nodded. "Sometimes. I think I fell in love with Mona the first time I laid eyes on that woman. What's going on, Noah?"

Noah looked at Joshua with a small, sad smile. "I met someone, Josh."

"The girl you were going to bring over last spring?"

Noah nodded. "We spent the whole weekend together, but it wasn't like how it used to be with other girls. She was *special*." He took a deep breath. "There was no drinking and no sex. We went up to Mt. Rushmore and hiked all over Spearfish Canyon..." Noah hesitated and looked away. "I asked her to marry me."

"You what?" Joshua gasped with surprise.

Noah sighed. "And she said yes, but I don't have her number or her last name. The only thing I know about her is that she paints and belongs to Junior Artists of America. Maggie's got one of her paintings at the bar."

Joshua's eyes were wide with surprise. "How did you wind up without her name?"

"Turned out she was only seventeen."

"Oh, dear," Joshua moaned.

"But she said she'd turn eighteen in June. In fact, she called Maggie's once and told me her brother was bringing her to Rapid City. That was before May, and I haven't heard from her since."

Joshua stared down at his boots for a moment and shook his head. So *that's* what had done it. Amazing. He'd heard about things like this before, but he was never quite sure he believed it until now. He looked into Noah's sad eyes, put his hand on his brother's shoulder, and smiled. "You've done such an incredible thing with your life, Noah. I just want you to know how proud Mona and I are of you."

"Thanks, Josh."

Joshua took a breath. "And let me tell you a little something about love. You can *choose* to love someone, but it's extremely difficult, if not impossible, to change your mind later. Sometimes infatuation can fool us into believing that we're in love—"

"I really love her, Josh."

Joshua nodded. "*Charity suffereth long.*"

"What are you sayin', Josh?"

Josh sighed. "You're suffering because this girl isn't around anymore. You're still here, loving her, but possibly she didn't make that same commitment to you. What I'm trying to say is that maybe she wasn't willing to *suffereth long* for you."

Noah shook his head. "No. She loves me, Josh. She told me so."

Joshua took a deep breath. "You've got a *real* future now, Noah. You're twenty-four years old. The same age I was when you came to live with us. Let me tell ya, Noah, you're gonna just keep on gettin' older. It's already been eight months, and you haven't heard from her. I think you'd better prepare yourself for reality."

Noah sighed sadly, and Joshua patted his shoulder.

"Time will heal this thing for you, Noah," Joshua assured. "Just give it to God and let Him work on it."

*****

The Christmas season that year was romantic and wonderful for Tillie Caselli. Alex increased the frequency of his attentions by way of phone calls, humorous cards, Christmas candy, and lunch every day. Tillie liked the way Alex looked into her eyes but fought the feelings growing in her heart. And, more than once, she considered ending the relationship with Alex. Sure, Alex was fun and he cared about her, but whatever they shared never felt quite *right*. Instead of being honest with herself, Tillie buried her feelings deep inside her heart. More than anything, she desired to talk to Noah, perhaps work things out and try again. But fear controlled her decision, and she pushed the memory of Noah as far away as possible.

On Christmas Eve morning, Alex stopped by with Tillie's gift. She was surprised and without words when she opened the wrapped box and found an old book inside: *A Masque of Mercy*. As she opened the cover, she saw it was signed by the author, Robert Frost.

"Where did you get this?" Tillie whispered.

Alex smiled. "When I was in Massachusetts. I came across it in an old bookstore. I thought you might like to have it because you're switching to Major American Poets."

"Thanks, Alex," Tillie whispered, giving the cover of the old book a delicate pat. "That was very thoughtful."

Alex smiled sweetly, gave her hand a tender kiss, and then he was off—like the gallant knight from some fairy tale—to fulfill all of his obligations in a perfect way.

That afternoon, fluffy, white snowflakes began to fall on Sioux Falls, making everything sparkle with brilliance. Tillie sat on the window seat in the living room, reading the old play off and on, sometimes watching the snow fall. She looked to the west and thought of Noah, wondered what he was doing, who he was with, and if he was enjoying his Christmas. Tillie was enjoying hers, but something was missing. Something was *always* missing, and it tugged constantly at her heart.

"Your brothers will be here soon," Rosa said from behind her, and Tillie turned to her mother. Rosa looked into Tillie's eyes and shook her head. "Oh, my Angel, you have that look again."

Tillie swallowed hard and felt tears in her eyes. "I'm sorry, Ma`ma."

Rosa took a seat next to Tillie and put loving arms around her daughter.

"I just can't forget him," Tillie whispered. She laid her head on her mother's warm chest and gave in to the comfort of Rosa's arms.

Rosa fought away her own tears of frustration and regret. "I do not know what to tell you, little one." She brushed a tear from Tillie's cheek. "It has been eight months. I think it is time for you to lay his memory aside once and for all. Perhaps your interests should lie elsewhere now."

"Oh," Tillie whispered with a nod, "you mean with Alex?"

"I think he loves you, and he has been very gentle with you."

Tillie looked pleadingly into her mother's eyes and cried, "But something is missing. Something just isn't right."

Rosa increased the strength of her hold on her daughter and whispered into Tillie's curls, "I know, Angel, and we will continue to pray for you. That you will get over this, whatever it is, and move on with your life. But, Angel, please do not pine away for a man you do not intend on ever seeing again."

Tillie tried to nod and fight off the intensity of the emotions within her. She rested in her mother's arms and wished she could make the feelings go away.

Rosa held her daughter as tightly as she could. *Why will Guiseppi not tell the child? Should she not at least have the chance to decide for herself?*

Of all the decisions Guiseppi had made in their nearly forty years of marriage, Rosa disagreed with only one. Guiseppi's decision came from the tender heart he had for his daughter and not the God-given wisdom he had in his brain. In her spirit, Rosa *knew* he was wrong to keep Angel away from Noah, and she feared it would eventually trap them in something deceitful and desperately wicked.

PART II

TY

Chapter 14
May 1976

Noah had received his real estate license in February and listed a few properties under the builder he worked for, who was also a real estate broker. He performed his regular carpentry duties during the day and showed properties at night. His continuing carpentry classes at the technical school were also scheduled for the evening, but Noah managed to handle everything like a professional. He didn't wear expensive suits or drive a flashy car like the rest of the realtors he'd become acquainted with. Nonetheless, people looking for homes and businesses were drawn to the enthusiastic young man who wore jeans and boots to work.

The first property Noah listed sold within a month. Pete Denis said it was a miracle because no one ever sold their first listing that fast. Within the next month, however, Noah sold four more listings, including a pricey office building downtown. Pete couldn't believe it. But Noah had asked the Lord for a break, and he felt he'd been answered with a yes. The sales provided him with enough cash to get his own business started.

Over the winter months, Noah had called Alex Martin several times with questions on where to begin his new business. Alex had also made a few trips to Rapid City to meet with Noah to discuss exactly what his plans were for his business and its development.

By March 1976, Hansen Development, LLC, was in business and Noah had started to work for himself. After having worked for such a popular builder, Noah was acquainted with other builders, subcontractors, plumbers, and electricians. He'd met an architect who designed the layout of what Noah planned to be his first strip mall, inclusive of ten leasable spots. He then had Alex make the offer to purchase the land. The offer was accepted, and construction began toward the end of March.

By mid-April, all ten spots had been leased, and Alex traveled to Rapid City once again to make sure everything went along smoothly. By this time, the two men had developed a friendship based on admiration and mutual respect. Uncle Mac would be returning to Rapid City in May, but Noah preferred doing business with the young, snappy dresser from Sioux Falls. Alex, for his part, couldn't wait to hear about Noah's next plan of action and made the commitment to continue to represent Noah's interests even after his uncle returned.

Before making an offer on the second piece of land, Noah reviewed the cost of building a home on his own land behind the fish hatchery. He had just enough to dig and pour the foundation and have it framed. He prayed before making the decision and then hired the best cement contractor he knew. The foundation was finished before the middle of May, and another contractor was ready to begin the framing.

*****

Elaine Caselli gave birth to a blue-eyed baby boy in the middle of May, and they named him Michael Petrice. He had tons of black curly hair, and Petrice reported that the babe hadn't stopped crying since he was born. They promised to bring Michael to South Dakota in June, as Vincenzo had invited everyone to the ranch for a family barbecue in celebration of their fourteenth anniversary as United States citizens.

In a stroke of incredible blessing the previous December, the partners in Petrice's law firm asked him if he would be interested in relocating to Cape Vincent, New York. The New York law firm was growing, and the older partners wanted to put satellite offices in small towns all over the state. Petrice and Elaine took a weekend to the tiny northern town located on the shores of Lake Ontario, looked around for a suitable home, and decided to make the move.

They found an old, three-story brick house on Tibbett's Point Road, heading westerly toward the old lighthouse. There was a considerable amount of private beach available to them, and, from their front windows, they could watch ships from all over the world pass through the clean, blue waters of the St. Lawrence River and Lake Ontario. Originally built in 1854, the home was in desperate need of repair and restoration.

Petrice had received an inheritance, as had all of his siblings, when their Uncle Angelo passed away in 1964. For the last eleven years, he hadn't dreamed of touching it, but, with the new baby on the way and a house they wanted to turn into a home, he was more than happy to liberate some of the funds.

Earlier that spring, Petrice had won his Senatorial primary, which put him in the running for a seat in the United States Senate. In November he was confident that he'd replace one of the Liberal Senate seats with himself and his Conservative Party principals.

*****

Sam Martin passed by Alex's open office door and looked inside. Alex was leaning back in his chair with his feet up on the desk, staring out the window with a blank expression on his face.

"Hey," Sam said in a low voice that made Alex startle. Sam laughed and stepped into the doorway. "How was Rapid City?"

Alex took his feet off the desk and sat up straight. "Great."

Sam nodded. "How's Noah?"

Alex raised one eyebrow. "If he keeps going at it like this, he'll be a rich man in a couple of years. Man, he's a hard worker."

Sam shook his head and smiled. "Who'da thunk it?" His face grew serious as he asked, "Is he still sober?"

"Yes, but he looks a little rough, like he's depressed or something. I don't know. I guess he looks better than he did last winter. He's coming to Sioux Falls this month."

"Maybe after he's been off the sauce for awhile he'll look better," Sam offered. He stepped inside of the office, closing the door behind him. "Hey, I just have to ask you about something. How are things going with Tillie Caselli?"

Alex smiled and sighed. "I love her, Sam."

Sam took the seat in front of Alex's desk and leaned forward. "Have you told her?"

"Told her what?"

Sam rolled his eyes. "That you love her!"

"No. I can't do that, Sam. I just don't know how to say that without scaring her away. She's only nineteen years old, and she's barely finished her first year of college. She's too young."

Sam laughed and over-pronounced his words, "You say it like this…Tillie…I…love…you…See how easy it is? Then you give her a little smooch, and she'll say the same thing."

"Jeez, Sam." Alex rolled his eyes. "I haven't kissed her yet either." Sam's mouth fell open in surprise, and the look on his face made Alex chuckle. "I know," he laughed. "And that's not the half of it. I'd really like to ask her to marry me, but I'm not sure she's ready for that. It'll probably take a year to plan the wedding, and she'll be twenty by then—"

Sam grimaced. "Wow. You sure know how to hit with both barrels." He took a breath. "Let me tell you something, Alex. She's a really nice girl—" He interrupted himself with spontaneous laughter and then attempted to look serious. "You haven't *kissed* her yet?"

"Well, I've kissed her hand."

"But no lip-lock?"

Alex shook his head. "No lip-lock."

Sam tried to stifle his humor as he said, "Well, she's got a nasty right hook—" and then he burst into laughter.

Alex glared at his brother. "Sam, help me for once."

"What do you want me to do?" Sam laughed. "I could walk by and pretend to accidentally push your faces together."

"Okay, leave," Alex ordered with a frown. "I'll figure this out myself, like I do everything else."

"No." Sam calmed himself. "I'm sorry." He cleared his throat and, even though still smiling, he spoke seriously. "Okay, here's what you do. It worked with Becky-Lynn, and it'll work with Tillie."

"How many dates did you go on with Becky-Lynn before you kissed her?"

"Lots," Sam answered. "Just look into her eyes and slowly, but not threateningly, lean toward her, maintaining eye contact until your lips touch." Sam closed his eyes at that point and his tone became sweet and wistful. "Close your eyes and let the Lord do the rest. Then whisper, 'Tillie, I love you.' " Sam opened his eyes and looked at his brother. "I can guarantee, she's gonna say the same thing. Might even kiss you back."

Alex's expression relaxed a little and he began to nod. "I'm gonna do it."

"Now don't go crazy and ask her to marry you," Sam cautioned as he wagged his index finger. "Remember how they do things over there. You gotta ask Mr. Caselli *first*."

"I remember," Alex recalled. Vincenzo had asked James before he asked Kate.

Sam got up and walked toward the door. "I gotta get to court, but you remember what I said, and don't be afraid. It's gonna be okay." He opened the door just in time to see his pretty wife hurrying by. He caught her gracefully with one arm around her waist and held her in Alex's doorway. "Here's a little inspiration for you, Alex." And with that, he took Becky-Lynn into his arms, looked into her eyes, and kissed her lips passionately. "I love you, Becky-Lynn."

Becky-Lynn almost laughed, but she smiled into Sam's eyes as she replied, "I love you too, Sam."

Sam looked at Alex and said matter-of-factly, "See. It'll be easy."

*****

Tillie Caselli had finished her first year of college, but she hadn't painted anything in over a year. With great purpose and resolve, she'd managed to squelch the creativity God Himself had bestowed upon her. Thankfully, her brothers and sisters-in-law had stopped asking for her work. She was running out of excuses.

She saw Alex Martin on a more-than-regular basis. He was kind and gentle, and the time she spent with him mended her broken heart. She loved the feel of his hand around hers when they went walking, the sound of his voice over the phone, and the special way he looked into her eyes—thoughtfully, lovingly, admiringly. The pain of whatever had happened with Noah just the year before was becoming nothing more than a bad memory, for she had allowed it to be chased away by the tender courtship undertaken by Alex.

They rode to choir practice together the morning of Vincenzo's celebration. Ginger and Bobby were both home from Mankato, and Bobby had joined the choir as well. Ginger whispered to Tillie during the practice that she and Bobby were engaged and were going to announce it tonight after everyone got home from the barbecue. Ginger was pleased with the new love in Tillie's life, and she didn't give the memory of Noah a second thought. It had *always* been Alex. Noah had been just a little bump in the road.

After practice, Alex and Tillie rode along in his Mercedes, while Ginger and Bobby followed behind in Bobby's dilapidated old 1960 Ford pickup.

Alex looked in the rearview mirror and wondered if the young man was going to make it. "Oh, that poor guy," Alex said with a grin. "I know what he's going through. You should have seen this old clunker my dad made me drive around Massachusetts. I'm amazed I lived through it."

"What kind of an old clunker?" Tillie asked as she looked out the back window of the car to check on her friend. Fortunately they were still back there.

"It was a 1952 Ford something," Alex replied with a playful frown. "I sold it the day I left town. Half the time it wouldn't run, it was terrible in the snow, and it guzzled more gas than I could put into it."

Tillie laughed at the funny story, and Alex saw the sparkle in her pretty eyes. She was dressed in the loveliest white lace sun dress he'd ever seen, and she'd looked like an angel during choir practice. He almost said it, but then he locked his smile and kept his eyes on the road.

The hot, humid air around the ranch smelled of plowed dirt; however, as Alex turned his car into the winding driveway, the aroma of farming gave way to the fragrance of the apple orchard in full bloom. Alex put his car into park, and Bobby pulled in next to them. The old pickup rattled, shook, and backfired before it was done. Alex smiled mischievously at Tillie. "It's *exactly* like my old Ford." Tillie laughed out loud as they got out of the car to join the rest of the party.

All those present on the day the Casellis were sworn in were invited to Vincenzo's party. His list included all of the Englesons, all of the Martins, Georgie, and old Doria. There was excellent grilled meat in Vincenzo's pit and the ladies' finest of dishes. Guiseppi and James Martin had cranked out several quarts of homemade ice cream earlier in the week and stored them in plastic buckets in Vincenzo and Kate's freezer.

Everyone was gathered around Petrice's new baby, who screamed for all he was worth as he lie in his mother's arms. The three families were crowded beneath the largest stand of trees in Vincenzo's yard, where tables and lawn chairs had been set in the cool of the shade. Marquette thought perhaps the babe might be hot, so he fanned him gently with his hat. Petrice stared at his new son and scratched his chin with wonder. Vincenzo smiled. New fatherhood could only be experienced once.

Tillie heard the baby crying and took hold of Alex's hand, attempting to hurry him along. "Come on," she said as she put a little spring into her step. "He's so sweet. You'll just love him."

Alex picked up his step, and soon they were making their way through the crowd of people gawking at the crying baby.

"Hi, Ellie." Tillie smiled at her like they were old friends. "Can I hold him?"

"Sure, Angel," Ellie answered, placing her baby into Tillie's arms.

Tillie cradled the precious bundle and looked down into the little, screaming face with a smile. "There, there now," and she began to rock back and forth. "You look just like your papa." She looked at Elaine and added, "Except for his blue eyes." She smiled into the baby's face and said, "Now, Michael, you mustn't cry. Look at everyone that has turned out for your party." And as she cooed and swayed, the baby began to settle down.

"She has had a lot of experience with my babies," Vincenzo whispered to Petrice, who was stunned as he watched a repeat episode of what had happened the night before at his parents' house.

Guiseppi heard Vincenzo's comments, and he chuckled as he shook his head. "No, Vincenzo," he corrected, looking into the peaceful face of his new grandson. "Angels know one another." The crowd around them "awed" at Guiseppi's comment but were mystified, nonetheless, at how Tillie could calm the baby so quickly.

"I don't know how you do that," Elaine said, smiling as she watched Tillie sway with the baby.

"It's all in the hips," Tillie whispered with a smile. She looked at Kate, raised one brow, and said, "Kate actually had to hula for Alyssa."

Everyone laughed, and Kate nodded her head.

After the baby had gone to sleep, Tillie laid him in the small, portable bed Kate had brought outside.

"Hurry up and eat," Kate coaxed Elaine as she handed her a plate that had already been filled. "They always wake up in the middle of your meal."

Everyone nodded their heads in agreement, except for Tara, who was always very quiet when a new baby came home. Her family pretended not to notice, and Tara had gotten good at hiding the sorrow of not being able to have children. Marquette's bout with the mumps in his early twenties had destroyed whatever hope they may have had to have babies.

Guiseppi's old, black eyes sparkled with mischief as he gave Tara a gentle pat on the shoulder. "I saw your beautiful picture on the front page again."

Tara smiled at her father-in-law. "The Anthony Cooke arrest. The Police Commissioner was delighted."

"And you are *so* smart!" Guiseppi exclaimed. "For they chased him nearly three years before finally calling in an expert on the case!"

"Well, it was actually Marquette who found the love letter," Tara said, smiling at her husband.

"No matter," said Marquette, as he put his arm over her shoulders. "You were there with me, like you always have been."

After dinner, Elaine and Petrice took the baby inside for awhile. Ginger's father, Burt Engleson, Marquette, and Vincenzo took Alyssa and Angelo to the horseshoe pit to begin their "training," while Tara and Kate discussed the finer points of canning with Frances, Diane, and Rosa. Georgie and Doria left; and Guiseppi, Sam, and James were laughing about something over by the barn. Andy had gone back to the church, and Ginger and Bobby left to do some shopping in Sioux Falls.

"Hey, how about a walk?" Alex whispered into Tillie's ear. Tillie nodded, and they got up from the table. As they started to walk toward the orchard, Alex took her hand into his own, and she smiled into his eyes.

From Vincenzo's horseshoe pit, Marquette watched them disappear into the orchard, holding hands, and looking dreamily into one another's expressions. He attempted to storm off after them but was held back by a strong hand on his shoulder.

"Marquette, be still," Vincenzo said with a serious look. He gave Marquette a traditional slap to the side of his head. "Do not be so anxious to stir up trouble, my brother."

"He is a foolish boy and barely *that*," Marquette grumbled in Italian so the little ones would not repeat anything they'd heard.

Vincenzo frowned and shook his head. "He is a *man*, Marquette. A man of honor, and he loves the Lord. He works very hard, and he loves our Angel so much. Can you not see it in his eyes?"

Marquette snorted in response. He wanted nothing more than to follow that dastardly Alex Martin into the orchard and thrash him once and for all for whatever impure thoughts he was having about his little sister. But instead he forced his thoughts away, turned toward the little ones before him, and pretended to have fun playing with the horseshoes.

*****

"Georgie and Doria did a good job on the barbecue," Alex said as they walked along.

"And how about Mrs. Engleson's potato salad?"

"Delicious," Alex agreed. "But what really amazed me is how you settled down your nephew."

Tillie smiled. "Babies like to swing. Believe me, I've done a lot of swinging with our niece and nephew." For a second, Alex looked so surprised, and Tillie laughed. "Did you forget? You're an *uncle* to Alyssa and Angelo. We share a niece and a nephew."

"Oh, yeah," Alex recalled with a faint smile. "They were born while I was at school. Sometimes it's still a little hard to get used to all of the things that happened while I was gone."

"Seven years makes a big difference," Tillie pointed out.

The warm breeze was refreshing as they walked through the shade of the apple blossoms. Every now and then a gust would carry several of the delicate flowers through the air, and they would catch in Tillie's curls.

Alex stopped beneath one of the apple trees, and Tillie stopped beside him. "What?" she asked, looking curiously around them. *If*

*Marquette followed us…*and then she realized Alex was smiling down at her.

He brushed a stray curl away from her face and put his hand on the soft skin of her neck. He lowered his lips to hers and kissed her softly. It was a sweet, wonderful kiss, and Tillie was taken by surprise. He took her tenderly into his arms and held her close. "I love you," he whispered.

Tillie thought she might faint, but she smiled into the handsome dark eyes of Alex. When had *this* happened? When had she fallen in love with Alex Martin? She stood on her toes and kissed his lips in return. "I love you, Alex."

Chapter 15

Noah left for Sioux Falls on a warm Friday morning in the middle of June. He told Joshua he had an appointment with Alex Martin and wouldn't return until Sunday afternoon. In *truth*, Noah did have an appointment scheduled with Alex on Friday, but his time on Saturday served a very different purpose. There was a Junior Artists of America conference and show to be held at the Sioux Falls Arena on Saturday morning. *Just one more show, just to be sure.*

He arrived in Sioux Falls before one o'clock and followed the directions Alex had given him. This was Noah's first trip ever to Sioux Falls. Nothing looked familiar, the traffic was horrible, and there were too many people. No beautiful hills to border the outskirts, and no fresh pine floating on the air. Instead, heavy humidity hung like a haze over the big town, carrying the aromas of farming, growing crops, and dirt.

Noah finally found the office building. The lobby entrance on the main floor reminded him of the lobby on the first floor of Mac's office building. However, when he reached the offices of Martin, Martin & Dale, A.P.C.L., on the fourth floor, he was impressed. Gone was the wild, wild west decor he'd become accustomed to in Rapid City. Alex's offices had obviously been decorated by professionals. Elegant draperies covered their windows, rich cherry wood and leather furniture seated their clients in the waiting room, and classy paintings of colorful still life hung on the walls.

"Can I help you, sir?" a young lady's voice interrupted Noah's gawking, and he turned to see the smiling receptionist, Jan.

"Ah, yes," Noah hesitated with a smile as he tried to be as professional as possible. He was suddenly self-conscious about his blue jeans, cowboy boots, and work shirt. Alex would show up in one of his billion-dollar suits. "I'm here to see Alex…Martin."

"You must be Noah Hansen?"

Noah acknowledged with a polite but bashful smile.

"You're just a little early," Jan said. "Mr. Martin should return shortly. Please have a seat, and would you like me to get you anything to drink?"

Noah was surprised. He didn't receive *this* type of service in Rapid City. He thought about it for a moment. He *was* thirsty. After all, he'd just pulled off the road after a six-hour trip.

"Well, what do you have?" he asked.

"We have available an assortment of soft drinks; iced tea; water, of course; or coffee," she offered.

"Iced tea, please."

Jan nodded. "Well, have a seat, and I'll be right back," and with that she left her desk. Noah found his way to one of the leather chairs in the beautiful lobby. Jan returned with a tall, icy glass filled with tea and some magazines.

"Alex picked these up for you," she said. "His assistant said you should take a look at them." She hurriedly returned to her desk, where the phone had started to ring.

Noah looked at the magazines the receptionist had just handed him. Both of them were devoted to the subject of building and remodeling, and Noah smiled. *Alex is such a nice guy.* He took a sip of his tea and opened the first magazine. He became so engrossed in what he was reading that he didn't notice when Alex had returned.

"Hello, Mr. Martin," Jan greeted with a smile. "And how was Miss Caselli today?"

Alex gave her his usual smile, reached for his messages, and answered, "Perfectly wonderful."

Jan glanced toward Noah. "Mr. Hansen is here."

Noah was aware someone had said his name and looked up to see Alex had arrived. He got to his feet with a smile. Sure enough, another billion-dollar ensemble.

"Sorry to keep you waiting," Alex apologized as he extended his hand in greeting.

Noah shook his head, got to his feet, and gave Alex's offered hand a shake. "No problem. Thanks for the magazines."

"How was your trip?"

"Good," Noah answered. "But is it always this humid here?"

Jan chuckled behind them, and Alex gave her a sideways smile. "She *hates* the humidity, but yes, it's always pretty humid here." He stepped aside and gave a graceful wave of his arm toward the long hall behind Jan's desk. "Why don't we go back to my office."

Noah fell in beside Alex, who showed him down the hall and into the very different office. Noah gawked again. There were no bull's horns mounted on the front of Alex's desk, and Noah couldn't imagine drilling holes into the beautiful wood anyway. Alex had a *real* coat rack by the door instead of the buffalo head Mac used, and his office was expensively paneled. There were only two paintings on the walls. One was a portrait of an old man who strongly resembled Alex, and the other was some sprawling brick buildings.

"Wow," Noah breathed, "this is really different from Mac's office."

Alex nodded and made a gesture toward one of the chairs in front of his desk. "Have a seat."

Noah took the seat in front of Alex and looked back at the portrait of the old man. "Who's that guy?"

"That's my great grandfather, Arturo Martinez." Alex pronounced the name with a perfect Spanish accent. "He came to America in the eighteen hundreds and changed his name to 'Martin' so he could attend formal schooling. He was the first of my ancestors to graduate from Harvard Law." Alex looked toward the other painting and explained, "That's a painting of Harvard in about the mid-1920's. Arturo left it to my father, and he gave it to me."

Noah swallowed. *This guy's really smart…and rich.*

*****

Bright and early Saturday morning, Noah left his hotel room and followed the directions Alex had given him to the Sioux Falls Arena where Junior Artists of America had set up their show. The arena was huge, and this show was three times the size of all the other shows he'd been to. This would take quite a while to go through.

Noah wandered through the arena for hours, examining each booth and display and stopping to watch the dancers on the stage. She'd had a red-headed friend with her, and Noah thought perhaps *she'd* have some information on Angel's whereabouts. But after he'd watched several sets and no red-head appeared, Noah gave up and went back to scouting the art booths.

By the time supper time rolled around and the artists were beginning to pack up their belongings, Noah was extremely discouraged. He found his old pickup and drove the entire way back to Rapid City that night. He threw himself into his bed when he got home and stayed there until Monday morning.

*****

Vincenzo relaxed in the swing and looked up into the starry night. *Perfect. Angel should have named her sketch "Perfect Life."* He took a long draw from his pipe and exhaled slowly. It was nearing the end of August by now, and plans were again underway for Reata's Annual Apple Picking Party.

The front door creaked, and Kate looked at him with a smile. She closed the door and took a seat beside him on the swing. He put his arm around her and kissed her cheek.

"Will those bambinos be staying in bed this time?" he whispered.

"They're both fast asleep," she answered. "By the way, I saw my little brother today."

"And how is Alex?" Vincenzo asked as he took a thoughtful draw from his pipe.

"He's very happy. He's in love, you know."

Vincenzo raised his brows. "I believe that we have all had *that* information for some time."

Kate took a breath. "I know. But…" She became serious as she continued, "He's kind of worried about Marquette. You know, they've never gotten along very well."

Vincenzo looked at his wife with a serious expression. "You tell your dear brother not to worry of such things. Marquette has proven to be an unreasonable man in this circumstance. And tell him that Petrice and I have taken care of the matter and that he may visit with Papa at the time of his choosing."

Kate smiled into her husband's eyes as she felt the weight of uncertainties slip from her shoulders. "Thanks, Vincenzo."

"Anything for the brother of my beloved," Vincenzo whispered, and he placed a delicate kiss upon her lips.

*****

From his office at home, Petrice heard the front door open and close. He smiled. Ellie had returned from town. He'd stayed home with little Michael so she could run a few errands and pick up some groceries. He heard her familiar footsteps come through the kitchen and down the hall.

"Hi," she said softly from the doorway. "How did it go?"

Petrice looked into her blue eyes and smiled. "It went well." He glanced at the bassinet in the corner of his office. "He was the *best* little boy."

Elaine smiled and made her way to the bassinet for a peek inside. Michael's behavior had improved over the summer months. He rarely fussed anymore, and he slept through the nights now.

She turned around and smiled at Petrice, and it was then that he noticed the playful sparkle in her eyes. She knelt beside his chair, placed a loving hand upon his knee, and looked into his eyes.

"I don't know if you can handle this or not," she chuckled.

"And what is making your eyes smile so today?" Petrice asked as he placed a tender hand upon her cheek and looked into her pretty expression.

Elaine giggled. "I'm pregnant again."

Petrice's black eyes flew open in surprise, and his mouth was frozen in the strangest expression. "Pregnant? Again? So soon? How did *that* happen?"

Elaine laughed. "I imagine the same way it happened the first time."

Petrice rolled his eyes and chuckled. He got out of the chair and knelt on the floor beside his wife to take her into his arms. "God is a great God."

*****

Noah was watching the old trailer house being unloaded at his Canyon Lake job site when an expensive rental car pulled onto the lot and a familiar man got out, briefcase in hand. Noah smiled when he recognized Alex. He grabbed a hard hat from the pile on the hood of his pickup and walked toward him.

"What on earth are you doing out here?" he asked with a surprised smile.

"Well," Alex replied as he placed the hat upon his head, "I got some really good news this morning, and I just happened to be able to catch a charter, so here I am." He looked around at the construction workers and glanced at the trailer. "What's *that* for?"

"Oh," Noah moaned and rolled his eyes. "I've got so much paperwork, and the men don't have a place to review their plans. It's gonna be like a little office, and I'll just haul it from site to site. It was my sister-in-law's idea. What's the good news?"

"Remember the offer we made to the Texan?" Alex said with a raised eyebrow.

Noah remembered. He and Alex had made an offer, without expecting to get the job, but agreed it was time to get Noah's name out there in the business world.

"He's more than satisfied," Alex informed. "Do you think we're ready to handle it? Two sites up at once?"

Noah thought he might faint. He already had two sites up at once, but Alex didn't know about the second one. He began to shake his head. "I don't have enough men."

"We've got some time before you have to begin construction," Alex said. "How long do you think it will take to assemble an additional crew?"

"A couple of weeks at least. I'll have to have more equipment; materials; and, of course, additional cash flow for payroll and supplies."

Alex took a breath and asked, "Did you get a secretary yet?"

Noah shook his head. "Mona's been helping me. I suppose I could ask her to give me a hand with hiring."

Noah seemed to be hesitating, so Alex gave him an encouraging smile. "Listen, Noah, let's just have a look at your books and see what you have on hand."

"My books?" Noah asked with a confused expression.

"You know." Alex felt his heart drop into the pit of his stomach. Had he been mistaken, or was Noah completely oblivious to the word *books?* He swallowed and asked cautiously, "Your ledger?"

"My ledger?" Noah was really lost now. No one, at any time, had ever used the word *ledger*, not even Mona.

Alex bit his lip and stared at Noah. "Well, where do you keep your money?"

"Oh." Noah's expression relaxed and he smiled. "In my checking account."

Alex's dark eyes were wide with surprise. "In your *personal* checking account?"

Noah laughed at Alex's expression. "Well, yeah. Where am I supposed to keep it? Under the mattress?"

Alex shook his head and forced himself to smile. "Noah, we gotta talk."

After a grueling two hours at the bank, Alex had straightened everything out by setting up two separate accounts for Noah's business. One account was to be used for equipment and materials and the other specifically for payroll. But the payroll issue was going to run them into some problems. Noah had been paying his men in cash and hadn't filed a single wage report with the State of South Dakota. The next appointment they had was with an accountant's office in the same bank building where the law offices were located. Alex, himself, would straighten out the mess with the State.

"You have to withhold taxes and social security," Alex explained as he drove away from the bank. "An accountant can take care of these things for you. He or she will file the reports and pay the taxes."

"But what about the cost?"

Alex laughed out loud. Noah already had so much in his checking account, and with the collateral he offered for his Rimrock property, the bank agreed to extend him a good line of credit for cash flow.

"Noah," Alex said with a smile, "you're going to be fine. And you've got Mona to help you organize and schedule things."

"But I want to build," Noah persisted. "I don't want to spend my time running around town, signing reports, and playing with money."

Alex understood Noah's dilemma and replied, "You'll be able to spend as much time as you want at the sites if you have the proper people in place to take care of everything else."

Noah shook his head. "I don't know, Alex. Where do I find more men?"

"Job Service," Alex answered matter-of-factly. "We'll start there."

By the end of the day, an exhausted Alex Martin boarded his charter back to Sioux Falls. He laid his head back against his seat and reviewed everything they'd accomplished that day. From memory, he checked off every necessity he could think of with regard to Noah's new business. Bank accounts, a line of credit, a new ten-man crew, a trustworthy accountant, a new equipment order, and an order for new materials. He smiled as he remembered the old trailer house being set level that afternoon. That had been important to Noah, along with the coffee maker his sister-in-law delivered later on for an "office warming" gift.

Noah was such a simple, uncomplicated man with only a desire to build things. But the lonely sadness hidden behind Noah's eyes bothered Alex. He couldn't help but wonder what in the world had happened in the man's life that had caused such a revealing and yet mysterious mark on his expression. Was it just his wild and crazy days of drinking, or was it something more?

*****

Water, electricity, and a telephone line were hooked up to the trailer, and Noah was pleased with how comfortable he could be while he managed the site. The utility hook-ups were temporary, so when this project was finished, he could relocate the trailer to the next job site.

He went to K-Mart and purchased several card tables, brought them back to the trailer, and filled them with papers, blueprints, and plans. The men on the site didn't seem to mind the chaos, but it drove Mona crazy. She strove to help him put things together in some kind of an orderly fashion. She found Noah a used desk, a few filing cabinets, and some chairs and had them delivered to his new "office" at the Canyon Lake job site. She thanked God for Alex Martin. Without him, Noah would have surely been jailed for his unorthodox business practices. For a short time, Mona agreed to help him with his scheduling and orders he needed to place. However, she said she was looking for a "nice girl" to take her place. Naturally, that girl would have to be patient and organized.

In the evenings, Noah went to the secret job site on Rimrock to check every detail of construction and carpentry that had happened during the day. He trusted only himself with the woodwork, certain fixtures, and other delicate details. He worked until after midnight most nights before he went home to his tiny cabin on Canyon Lake and dropped into his bed. He was up early the next morning, arriving at Rimrock before anyone else and doing particular things that could be left to no one else. The house was coming along beautifully and would be finished in just a few short weeks. The only people he dared trust with his secret were Maggie and Estelle.

"And this is the window for the studio. It faces west," Noah explained as he laid the snapshots out on Maggie's bar one afternoon while he ate his lunch.

Maggie stared in disbelief at yet another set of photos from Noah's building site. *He's really gone off the deep end.* She forced a smile and praised, "It's lookin' really good, Noah."

"And when the sun comes up in the morning," Noah said with a wistful smile, "it lights up the front porch first, and then it moves over the glass in the dining room, then into the hall." He laid down another photograph so she could better understand and pointed. "See. Right here." He sighed with a smile. "Well, anyway, I gotta get back to work." And with that he picked up the glass of water next to him and took several big gulps."

"What do you want me to do with these?" Maggie asked as she looked at the snapshots on her bar.

"Those are yours," Noah answered. "Just put 'em with the other ones."

Maggie tried to smile as she replied, "Okay. Thanks."

"See ya, Maggie," he said with a smile as he hurried out the door.

Maggie looked down at the photos before her, and Estelle peered at them over her shoulder.

"The poor man," Estelle breathed. "Do you think we oughta call Josh?"

Maggie shrugged. "I don't know what to do, Stellie. I can't believe he's doing this. He ain't never gonna see that girl again."

Estelle gazed at the photographs of the beautiful home. "It's sure a pretty place though. Wouldn't it be nice, Maggie, if he could find her and bring her back?"

Maggie swallowed hard but didn't reply. She scooped up the photographs and put them with the others in the envelope beneath her counter.

*****

Noah was surprised one morning when he came to the trailer at the Canyon Lake job site and found Mona waiting for him with a fresh pot of coffee. She was sitting behind his desk, sipping from a Styrofoam cup.

"Mornin', Mona," he greeted with a smile. "What brings your lovely little self in so early today?"

Mona raised one of her eyebrows, and the expression in her green eyes told him she'd discovered something. "Thought we should talk before the rest of the men get here," she drawled.

Noah turned toward the coffee maker, grabbed a cup, and tried to remain as calm as possible. *There's no way she knows…This is just leftover acid paranoia.*

"I was drivin' up along Rimrock yesterday afternoon," she began.

Noah nearly dropped the coffee pot at her words. He steadied his hand and finished pouring his cup. He set down the pot, sauntered to one of the chairs in front of the desk, and took a casual seat.

Mona looked curiously into his eyes. "You buildin' somethin' up there, Noah?"

Noah's jaw almost hit the floor. *She knows.* He nodded slowly. "I'm buildin' a house up there."

"Uh huh. I saw Maggie yesterday afternoon. I saw the painting, the picture. I know *everything.*"

Noah took a deep breath. *What can I say? The house is there, and it's almost finished. What can be done about it now?*

"Joshua thinks you're all over that," Mona continued with a frown. "But I know you been takin' some trips out to Sioux Falls and the eastern part of the state. I'm gonna bet you ain't just been meetin' with Alex Martin. You been lookin' for that girl—"

"Mona, I really think she was the one. I really think I'm gonna find her…" He stopped himself…*I sound like an idiot.*

Mona saw the horrible sadness around his eyes and knew now what had put it there. She felt compassion for him, but also frustration. He'd carried on about this for long enough, and she just wanted to shake him for it. It was as if he'd replaced one addiction for another.

"Does Joshua know about the house?" She hadn't mentioned it to Joshua, just in case he *didn't* know about it. That would have to be Noah's duty. Noah shook his head in response, and Mona swallowed.

"He loves you so much, and we are so proud of you, but you can't keep this from him."

"I know, Mona."

"It's been more than a year, according to Maggie," she went on. "You *have* to give up on this thing before it ruins the rest of your life, Noah."

"I know, Mona."

*****

It was nearing the end of the summer now, and Tillie would soon start her second year of college. The last few months had been filled with romantic evenings hosted by the knightly Alex. They walked hand in hand to the DQ or attended performances of the Summer Symphony. There were drives to Reata to see their niece and nephew, and long, dreamy walks in the orchard. Noah couldn't have been pushed further from her mind, as her hand rested in Alex's and she looked into his handsome, dark eyes day after day. His kisses were gentle and loving, and he never once tried to compel her to compromise anything more.

Tillie had also delighted in yet another comical season with Georgie and old Doria, and she was melancholy at having to leave them behind to attend classes for another nine months. Marquette and Tara stopped in Sioux Falls for a short surprise visit on Tillie's last day at the restaurant. Marquette found her chopping vegetables as she sang along with one of Papa's old Dean Martin records. She looked just like an angel as she stood at the pile of assorted greens. Her curly hair was tied tightly on the top of her head, and her white apron was splattered with juice.

"There is my little Angel," Marquette said with a smile, and Tillie looked up to see her brother in the doorway of the kitchen. She smiled and reached for the towel tied at her waist.

"What are you doing here?" she asked as she attempted to hug him without ruining his beautiful suit.

"Tara and I are on our way to Denver," he answered with a soft kiss on her cheek.

"Where is she?"

"She is with Ma`ma. I wanted to see you alone."

"Why?"

Marquette sighed and gently took one of her hands into his own. "The answer to my prayer is that I must settle something within myself immediately. Our Lord has prompted me to ask you certain questions, so that I may make decisions to please your good heart."

Tillie smiled politely. Marquette could be *so* dramatic, and she had to fight the urge to giggle. But she wouldn't disrespect his loving personality in such a way. She maintained a serious expression, intent on hearing what he had to say.

"Angel, I am wondering about Alex. Papa says he is a good man."

"He is. He's very good to me, Marquette."

Marquette swallowed, obviously uncomfortable with whatever the next question was about to be. "Angel, does Alex have good manners with you?"

Tillie nodded.

Marquette swallowed again. "What I mean to ask…Angel…This is so very difficult for me. Has he been *honorable* with you?"

Tillie stifled her humor and put her arms around Marquette's neck. What a gentle, precious soul, trying his very best in the most uncomfortable situation of his life. How hard it must be for him to "settle something within himself." He was trying to lay aside his intense dislike for Alex for no other reason than for the cause of her feelings. "Marquette, he hasn't even asked."

Marquette sighed with relief and allowed himself a small smile as he took his sister into his arms. "Then I will bring myself to love him as you do."

*****

It was toward the very end of September when Noah completed Angel's house, and it was truly magnificent. It sat just above the meadow, looking out into the Black Hills. It was a wonderfully old-fashioned, two-story, Victorian home with a brick front and a sweeping, wrap-around porch. Wooden shutters were hung on the paned windows, and a hand-carved oak door with beveled glass would have greeted their guests at the front door.

Inside, on the first floor, was a large kitchen and a formal dining room with a built-in hutch, complete with glass doors and inside illumination. Across from the large entrance hall, a dainty parlor and a great room waited to be filled with furniture. The first floor was also where a very special room was located—Angel's studio. It was a nice-sized room, and Noah had found the perfect glass for the windows. They reached from floor to ceiling, facing the west so she could see the hills they loved while she worked on her paintings.

An open winding staircase led the way to the upstairs, where there was a master bedroom, complete with bathroom and a walk-in closet. There was a small adjacent nursery so the baby wouldn't be too far away. There were five other oversized bedrooms upstairs, along with two more bathrooms.

The floors were hardwood, except for the bedrooms, and each piece of woodwork trimming the doorways and floors was cut and finished by hand—Noah's hands. He hung the lights, the shutters, and the front door, leaving not one detail undone, and he spared not an ounce of perfection for his finished work.

He stood before the finished but empty home with Joshua. The workmen had finished a few days before, and not a soul besides Noah and Joshua were there to see the beauty of his accomplishment. The fall wind whistled woefully by as it carried the season's changed leaves into the front yard and dropped a few on the roof. It would have been the perfect place to bring home a new bride and start a family, but that wouldn't be happening. His hope of finding Angel had faded, and his heart was heavy with despair and regret.

"How's business?" Joshua asked as they gazed upon Noah's mansion. He had other questions, but they didn't seem appropriate right now.

"Good. Alex got enough business to keep us going through the winter. We've framed up the new site so the men can work inside, but I'm worried Mona's working a little too much."

"I heard she found a nice girl. Melinda? Is that her name?"

"Yep," Noah answered. "She'll start in a couple of weeks. I guess I gotta get a typewriter and a couple of other things for her." He turned to look at his brother. "What am I gonna do with this place, Josh? I can't believe I did this."

"Do you wanna live in it?" Joshua asked.

Noah shrugged, looked back at the house, and shook his head. "Not without Angel."

Joshua swallowed and put his hand gently on Noah's shoulder. "I'm sorry, Noah."

Noah saw the unfamiliar mist of tears in Joshua's eyes.

"It's been so long now, Noah," Joshua continued as he tried to keep his emotions under control. "I think you need to move on."

Noah nodded. Joshua was right. It was time to forget about Angel.

Chapter 16

Alex had done exceptionally well as a "first-year" lawyer. He'd set up more corporations and limited liability companies than all of the other lawyers in the firm combined, including Sam. His memory capabilities were impeccable. Everything he read or researched remained etched permanently into his recollection. If another lawyer couldn't locate a certain citation or remember where a specific code could be found, they'd hurry to Alex's office with a few particular questions. They left with the answer and the location of the cite a few minutes later.

Alex also held the only "all-wins" record in the firm, which meant the decision was favorable to Alex every time he went before a judge.

"You've only been at it for a year," an older lawyer teased. "Your turn is coming."

Sam even joined in on the jeering. "You'll lose one some day. We all do."

Alex was good natured and laughed at their teasing, but he was very confident about himself and his abilities. The idea of his *not* winning was buried so far back in his brain that he didn't even consider it to be a *real* possibility. That fact gave him the courage to proceed with the next phase of his plan.

He knocked on the door of his father's office and let himself inside. James looked up from the file he was reading, took off his glasses, and smiled at Alex. *Funny*, Alex thought, *Dad sure doesn't look seventy-seven.*

"Alex, what can I do for you?" James asked with a smile. He stretched and leaned back in his chair as he looked into his son's happy but apprehensive expression.

Alex looked at his father with a sigh. "Dad, there's something I want to do."

James raised an eyebrow. "What are you up to, Alex?"

His dark eyes shone. "I'm going over to see Mr. Caselli...about Tillie."

James' eyes were surprised, but he forced himself to smile. "Guiseppi will be impressed. You'll get the blessing for sure."

Alex saw the hesitation in his father's expression and frowned. "What's the matter, Dad?"

James shrugged...*About a million things, but I know you'll never listen to me.* He took a deep breath. "Alex, she's really young, and there's a lot of things you'll have to give up in order to be a good husband. She's used to living a certain way." As he spoke he saw his son's body stiffen. He swallowed and took another breath. "Listen, Alex, you've got a lot of plans for a career in politics—"

"I know that, Dad, but lots of politicians have wives, and Tillie—"

"There are better choices to make when you become a husband and eventually a father." James took a breath. "You can't be working from sunup until sundown when you've got a wife and children at home, not to mention the fact that she hasn't even finished school yet."

Alex shook his head angrily. "Listen, Dad, I know you put the brakes on your career to become a husband and father—"

"And I've *never* regretted it," James retorted.

Alex shrugged and started to back toward the door. "I don't think I have to do things that way."

James held up his hands and pleaded, "Please, Alex, don't get angry. Let's try to talk about this."

Alex shook his head. "No thanks, Dad. I'm going to see Guiseppi—"

"You mean *Mr. Caselli.*"

Alex rolled his eyes, turned with a huff, and stormed out of his father's office, slamming the door loudly behind him.

James let out the breath he didn't realize he'd been holding and stared at the closed door. Their discussions about politics had always ended this way...*This is what makes Marquette dislike my son. He's seen the relentless ambition in Alex since he was a little boy, and, if confronted, Alex will choose his own desires over everything else.*

*****

Alex parked his Mercedes in the parking lot at Angelo's and looked at the busy lobby of the restaurant. He could just make out Guiseppi's suited figure, standing near the door with a handful of menus as he greeted customers and sent them off to their table with the hostess. Alex sighed heavily, took out his handkerchief, and delicately blotted up the sweat collecting over his brow.

Dad's wrong about this, as usual. If he were honest with himself, he'd admit that he's been bitter and resentful about not pursuing a career in politics. It's what he always wanted.

"God, give me strength," he whispered as he climbed out of the car and walked to the lobby.

Guiseppi looked at Alex with delighted surprise and walked over to greet him. "Alex Martin!" he exclaimed as he took a firm grip on Alex's hand. "Will you be meeting my Angel here this day?"

Alex shook his head. "I came to see you, Mr. Caselli."

Guiseppi seemed to gulp, and he flagged down the hostess. "Margaret!" he called with a wave of his hand. A smiling young lady hurried toward Guiseppi and Alex. "Seat him near the kitchen, where we will not be disturbed," he instructed with a serious expression. He reached up to give Alex's strong shoulder a pat. "I will join you in a moment."

Alex followed Margaret to his quiet table, off by itself, behind the kitchen door. He thanked her, seated himself, and began the wait. *Why do I have to do it this way? It's not like we're living in Italy for Pete's sake.* Alex rolled his eyes and shook his head. *This is horribly awkward and old-fashioned. Why can't I just ask Tillie and she can announce it to the families?*

Guiseppi came along shortly and took the seat across from Alex. "And to what do I owe this pleasant surprise?" His black eyes sparkled as a playful smile began to tug at the corners of his mouth.

"Mr. Caselli," Alex began, "I need to ask you about something."

"Of course."

Alex clasped his hands together and set them on the table as if he were about to approach a judge in chambers. "I have come to ask for your blessing. May I marry your daughter, Tillie?"

Guiseppi raised one brow and questioned, "Have you asked Angel yet?"

Alex shook his head. "I thought it more honorable to speak with you first." He sighed inwardly. *Give the old man what he wants because we're probably going to be related for a very long time.*

Guiseppi's old eyes became like shiny marbles as he looked at Alex. "Alex, do you promise to always love my daughter, no matter the trials? Are you willing to stand beside her for the rest of your life, never consider another, and return only to her at the end of the day?"

Alex nodded. "There could be no one else for me."

Guiseppi smiled and gave Alex's hands a firm pat. "Alex, you are the last gentleman left on the face of this earth, and I gladly give my blessing. However, I am sure you know the rule, and that is the final decision must come from Angel. I will not force her into anything she does not want."

"Thank you, Mr. Caselli."

Guiseppi chuckled with delight. "You will call me Guiseppi from this day."

*****

Students streamed out of the buildings, down the sidewalks, and onto the dry fall grass at Augustana. Alex parked his car in its usual spot and went to find Tillie. The crispy, fall leaves along the cement path crunched beneath his feet as he strode excitedly to their usual meeting place. She was on the bench beneath the trees, where they'd met on that first day. Her soft curls floated delicately on the wind as she paged through a new book, smiling at whatever she'd read. Alex smiled as he watched her...*I do love her so much, and she'll make the perfect wife because she'll be proud of me.*

Guiseppi's words began to play over in Alex's head, "...*the final decision must come from Angel...I will not force her into anything she does not want...*" Alex took a deep breath, let it out slowly, and continued on his way...*she'll say yes.*

He sat down on the bench beside her, and she looked up in surprise. He presented her with the white rose and looked into her eyes. Tillie laughed as she took the pretty flower, put her nose into the blossom, and closed her eyes. "Mmmm." She looked at Alex. "What are you up to?"

Alex leaned closer to her and placed a delicate kiss upon her lips. He looked into her eyes and spoke softly in the words of Elizabeth Barrett Browning, "How do I love thee? Let me count the ways. I love thee to the depth and breadth and height my soul can reach, when feeling out of sight for the ends of being and ideal grace—"

Tillie giggled and interrupted Alex with a soft kiss on his lips. "You've always had a thing for Elizabeth, haven't you?"

"I think theirs was the most perfect of love stories," he said with a smile. "You have stolen my heart, with one glance of your eyes, with one jewel of your necklace. How delightful is your love, my dearest friend, you cannot imagine what it does to me when we're together."

Tillie looked into his handsome eyes. "Song of Solomon. Goodness but you're romantic today!"

Alex took a breath. "It will be hard for me to put into my own words what I'm feeling at this moment. I love you so much, Tillie Caselli, I can hardly bear the days I'm not able to spend at least a moment with you. You're smart and funny, and you make my heart feel like it could live forever. I love the sparkle in your eyes and the softness in your smile. I love the way you move and the way you laugh. I guess you're just perfect. A perfect match for me."

Tillie smiled into his eyes. He'd always made his feelings clear, whether it be in his manners or his gestures. But he'd never put them into words, and she found herself without response.

"Tillie," he began again as he looked earnestly into her eyes, "I saw your father today, and he has given me permission to ask you a certain question."

Tillie's heart began to beat so hard she heard it in her ears.

"Tillie Caselli, will you please marry me? I cannot imagine myself with anyone else but you for the rest of my life."

Tillie stared at him with amazement. How could she possibly resist? "Yes. Yes, I'll marry you."

Alex reached into his suit pocket and pulled out a tiny, black velvet box. "I'm so glad, because now I can give you this." He opened the box to reveal the two-carat diamond solitaire he'd carried around for the last couple of months. He plucked it from its safe nest in the box and reached for her left hand. Tillie gasped, and her hands shook as she watched Alex place the diamond ring on the same finger as the purity ring her parents had given her. "I want you to leave your parents' ring on your finger and wear mine at the same time," he said. "Would that be okay?"

Tillie nodded as she stared down at the magnificent diamond upon her hand. "Alex, it's so beautiful. Thank you."

Alex touched the soft skin on her face and kissed her lips. "I love you, Tillie Caselli," he whispered as he took her into his arms and gave her another tender kiss. "I want to be with you always."

Chapter 17
October 1976

Alex was shocked when he received the land appraisal on Noah's collateral, and he called him immediately.

"I think they sent me the wrong appraisal," he began as he reread the document in front of him. "They've added over a half million dollars in structural value, and you've *never* had a structure out there."

Noah swallowed hard and stared out the window of his little trailer office. He looked at the men on the job site, squinted, frowned, and bit his lower lip, thankful Alex couldn't see his telling expression. It had never dawned on him that Alex would find out about the house. *Alex is so smooth and cool...He's the last person I want to explain that deal to.* "Why did they send you the appraisal?" he questioned, trying to buy some time for an explanation.

Alex heard the uncertainty in Noah's voice and started to panic. *What's going on out there? I thought we straightened out the crazy stuff in August.*

"Because of the collateral that's attached to your line of credit at the bank," he explained. He loosened the knot on his tie. He hadn't dealt with surprises like this. Alex's clients and colleagues turned over *all* of the information—the *first* time around. Alex was organized, he had a certain order in his life, *and* he had everything memorized. *This isn't how things work in my world...*"I'm your lawyer," he continued as he pushed himself away from his desk to bend over, hang his head, and attempt to catch his breath. "They'll be sending me *everything*. And by the way, how were the men on that site paid? You didn't just go up there and start doling out the cash did you?"

"No," Noah answered, "I got their social security numbers and stuff and took it to the guy at your uncle's office."

"The accountant?"

"Yes."

"Well, what kind of a structure do you have up there?" Alex asked as his heart began to return to a more normal beat.

Noah took a breath and decided to just come clean with a portion of the truth. "Well, Alex, you see, I decided to do a little experiment up there—"

"A little *experiment?* There's more than a little *experiment* going on up there. Do you know what kind of a place it takes to get a half-million-dollar valuation?"

Noah wrinkled his nose as he thought about that. *Well, I know now.* "It did turn out awfully nice." *Half a million? Wow! I did a better job than I thought.*

Alex took a deep breath and attempted to start over. "Noah, it's okay if you want to have little *experiments* here and there, just let me know about it so I don't have to have a heart attack the next time a half-million-dollar house floats across my desk."

"Okay, Alex," Noah agreed in his friendly tone. He didn't understand fully all that Alex Martin had just gone through, but he was sorry he'd caused it just the same. He cleared his throat and continued hesitantly, "I suppose I oughta tell ya then that I have a lady who wants to lease it and run a business out of it. Like a little bed and breakfast. Will that be okay?"

"Of course. I'll get a lease together on that for you—"

"Well, she doesn't want to sign anything."

Alex's mouth fell open in surprise, and there was complete silence on the line.

For a moment, Noah thought they'd been disconnected. "Alex? Are you still there?"

"Oh, she'll be signing, or she won't get the property. In fact, you tell her your lawyer will be bringing the lease to town. And don't let her have the keys to the place until I'm there."

Noah laughed. "She's just a little old lady, Alex."

"And that's why she's gonna sign a lease," Alex responded. "You can't afford to let someone use a half-million-dollar property and then attempt to get squatter's rights on the place."

"Squatter's rights?" Noah laughed again. "What's *that?*"

Alex rubbed his forehead. "I'll explain it to you when I come to Rapid."

"When are you coming?"

"As soon as I can get there."

*****

Less than a week after that, Alex chartered a flight to Rapid City and was standing inside of the beautiful home Noah had built. He was impressed with the quality of work Noah had done. So much so that, before Ms. Vivian Olson arrived, he recommended *not* leasing it. But Noah said he didn't want to live there, and he didn't want it to be empty. Alex showed him the appraisal and explained what kind of a profit Noah would turn if he sold the property, but Noah didn't want to do that either. The best Alex could do was get a lease signed and collect a significant deposit.

On the outside, Ms. Olson appeared to be just an ordinary, little old lady, as Noah had described her. She was small in stature and wore her hair in a blue-dyed, ratted style. Her eyebrows were penciled-in, heavy and black, and her lips were coated with bright red lipstick. Alex thought the color of her lips perfectly matched the color of the Cadillac he saw her climb out of. She was no ordinary little old lady, and that was obvious to Alex. In fact, she reminded him of Cruella Deville, and she was more than just a little irritated about having to sign a lease.

"I'm just not comfortable with the terms," she said as she thumbed through the lease Alex presented her.

"Lots of people lease the buildings that house their businesses," Alex coaxed with a frown. *She's nothing more than a common criminal. Why wouldn't she want to sign a lease? Because she's trying to take advantage of Noah's kind demeanor.* "Tell you what, you lease it for six months, and if it's not working out for you, we'll let you off the hook."

Ms. Olson seemed to mull it over and began to nod her head. "Alright, as long as I get my deposit back—"

"*If* you haven't damaged the place," Alex interrupted. He reached inside of his suit coat for a pen and realized he didn't have one. "I'm going to run out to my car. I need a pen." He hurried out of the house, leaving Noah and Ms. Olson alone for a short time.

Vivian looked at Noah, raised one of her old eyebrows, and grumbled, "He's a smarty pants."

Noah smiled at her comment. Alex was, indeed, a bit of a *smarty pants*, but Noah liked him and was glad to have his help.

Ms. Olson looked around at the kitchen, admiring the woodwork and beautiful view of the hills directly out of the windows. "It's beautiful up here," she commented.

Noah nodded. "By the way, what are you gonna call it?"

Ms. Olson shrugged. "I don't know. What do *you* call it?"

"I always called it 'Angel's Place.' "

The front door opened and closed, and Alex rejoined them with a pen. "Here you go," he said as he handed her the pen and smiled at Noah. He looked at Ms. Olson. "Now, if you'll just give us your deposit, I'll have you sign and you'll be ready for business."

Ms. Olson frowned at him, handed him an envelope and waited. Alex opened the envelope to be sure she'd paid them with a cashier's check instead of some bouncing, paper check, and he smiled. "Thank you. You can sign right here."

Ms. Olson sighed and signed her name begrudgingly. Noah signed for his company, and Alex signed as a witness.

"It's been a pleasure doing business with you," Alex said, extending his hand.

Ms. Olson shook his hand. "Will you be sending me a copy?"

"Of course," Alex confirmed.

Ms. Olson extended her hand to Noah and offered him a smile. "You're a nice kid. Too bad you gotta hang out with such a troll."

Alex half-smiled. *A troll. That's nice. What a gal.*

Noah chuckled. "He's a *great* lawyer."

Ms. Olson frowned. "Right." She stomped out of the house, and they heard the door close behind her.

"Feisty little thing," Alex commented as he folded the lease and tucked it safely into the inside pocket of his suit. He handed Noah the check and asked, "Do you know what to do with this?"

Noah smiled faintly. "Nope."

Alex laughed. "Let's set up an escrow account. We're going to be getting lease deposits in from your strip mall tenants pretty soon anyway."

"Another account?" Noah's expression was bewildered.

Alex laughed again. "I know this seems like a lot right now, but after awhile, you'll get used to all of the things that go along with managing a business."

Noah shook his head and breathed, "I don't know if I'm ever gonna get used to this."

"You will. In fact, I'd bet it just becomes second nature."

As they headed for the door, Noah asked, "How long are you staying in town?"

"I have to leave tonight."

"To see your dearest friend?" Noah teased with a wink.

"To see my *fiancée*. We were engaged last week."

"Congratulations, Alex. That's great."

"Thanks, Noah."

*****

Tillie's family was happy for her, *except for Marquette*. In front of Tillie, he praised their decision and congratulated her several times. However, when he had Guiseppi alone, he voiced other concerns troubling him to his very core.

"She is *so* young, Papa," he said as his eyes filled with tears. "How can she *possibly* know what she wants yet?"

Guiseppi smiled and tried to reassure Marquette. "He loves her Marquette, and she loves him. You *promised* us you would come to terms with this relationship."

"*That* was before you gave her into marriage," Marquette argued. "She is only a babe. How can you let her go?"

"She will be twenty by the time she marries," Guiseppi reminded. "The same as your Ma'ma when Petrice was born. And Ellie is young—"

"But Petrice knows how to care for a wife." He shook his head. "And what of Alex's blinding ambition? I cannot believe you have done this."

Guiseppi frowned and spoke with authority. "Marquette, I have already given the blessing. What is done, is done. You can do nothing else now but honor the promise you made to me, your brothers, and your sister. You must come to terms with this."

Marquette scowled at his father but said nothing. *Come to terms with your blessing upon a doomed union? Why can you not see it, Papa? What is cloaking your godly judgment?*

*****

For their wedding gift, James and Frances Martin gave a large sum of money to Alex when he announced his engagement to Tillie. This gift was intended for the purchase of their first home. Even though James disagreed heartily with his son's decision to marry, he stayed oddly quiet on the subject. To comfort himself, he reasoned that, if there were any danger in the union, Guiseppi would have *never* granted his blessing. And James had long assumed Guiseppi to be the most godly of men. His sons, after all, had long deemed him the most perfect of all knights.

Alex and Tillie found a real estate agent, Ed Brown, who took them all over town. He showed them expensive houses with every amenity imaginable and located in the most posh of neighborhoods. Naturally, he was under the impression that the son of the wealthy James Martin Jr. and the sister of the elegant and famous Marquette

Caselli would want to live somewhere with class and status. However, the longer they looked for a home, the more discouraged Tillie became. Nothing seemed to appeal to her, and Alex wasn't about to make her live just anywhere.

"Why don't you tell me what you have in mind," Ed coaxed one Saturday morning. He'd been meeting with the young couple for two weeks and was surprised they hadn't settled for anything yet.

Tillie sat in the chair in front of the man's desk with a pensive frown. This looking-for-a-house business was really starting to get to her. Maybe they should just find a nice apartment and forget about the house. She knew *exactly* what she wanted, and she'd described it to Ed about a thousand times.

Isn't he listening? She took a deep breath and began to explain again. "Something that's older," she said with a feigned smile. "Something I can put some of *myself* into. I don't want someone else's home. I want my own."

Ed bit his lip thoughtfully. "How *older* are we talking?"

"How 'bout a hundred years," Tillie answered, and Alex's eyes flew open in amazed surprise. Tillie saw his reaction and laughed.

"Okay," Ed replied as he paged through his listing book. "There's a little place over by the Vet's Hospital..." He hesitated and looked at the two of them. "It's about that old, but it's been abandoned for some years. It's in a nice neighborhood, and I'm sure the neighbors would appreciate someone doing something with it. It might really be a nightmare to work with, but it's *old*. Electricity and water were updated about twenty years ago, but it got a new roof around five years ago."

Alex and Tillie agreed to at least have a look at the place, and to Alex's surprise, it was *exactly* what Tillie had in mind. And Ed was right. The older, two-story Victorian home was in desperate need of repair. The white paint was chipped and peeled, and rotted shutters hung askew from their loose hinges.

"But look at those awesome columns and the entry door." Tillie pointed out the three wonderful, tall, white columns out front; a double-entry door; and the romantic, covered front porch.

"And how about the four-foot weeds in the front yard?" Alex said sarcastically. The yard looked like a small wheat field.

"But there's a garage for your car," Tillie countered.

Alex sighed and looked at Ed. "Go ahead and take us through the place," and they followed the realtor inside.

On the main floor was a large kitchen, formal dining, living room, guest bathroom, and an oversized master suite. The master suite was complete with bathroom and an adjacent office. *Adjacent office or nursery...* The second story was smaller and had only two bedrooms and a tiny bathroom. Everything inside of the home was wholly unsalvageable, except for the structure itself. The cabinets and woodwork were broken and cracked, there were holes in the walls, and the carpets were filthy.

The backyard was perfect, according to Tillie. She saw something wonderful hidden within the out-of-control forest.

"That tree is just beautiful," she whispered with a smile as she took Alex's hand gently into her own and led him through the dried weeds and piles of leaves.

Alex looked up at the bare branches of the tremendous oak tree above them and frowned. "It doesn't have any leaves."

Tillie laughed and squeezed his hand. "It's the middle of October, Alex. It will have leaves in the spring, and the shade will cover the whole house." She pointed to the cement patio, oblivious to its cracks and chips, and then looked dreamily into his eyes. "When the weather is nice, we'll put a swing there and have coffee together in the mornings."

Alex looked at the barren tree and then at the dilapidated house. "You want to *live* here?"

Tillie nodded and looked into her husband-to-be's eyes. He saw the hope and animation in her expression, but he was more than just a little hesitant. After all, Alex was *not* a handyman, and he wondered who would be performing all of the work that needed to be done just to make it livable.

"We'll spend only a fraction of your parents' gift," Tillie coaxed. "The rest of it will be used for repairs."

"But who's going to *do* the work?" Alex asked cautiously.

"Papa knows lots of people," Tillie answered, and Alex sighed with relief. "And I can do lots of stuff myself."

Alex began to nod his head, and Tillie squealed softly with delight. She put her arms around Alex's neck and stood on her toes to give him a soft kiss on his cheek.

"I love you," she whispered.

Alex held her in his arms and looked at the crumbling house... *Home, sweet home?*

*****

Guiseppi's eyes sparkled when he saw the old house. It looked *exactly* like something Tillie would choose. The creativity and artistry that had been absent in her life would soon be reborn and set free upon the broken house. *It is just what she needs*, he thought, *and like her beautiful paintings, it will soon come to life and shine with a radiance only Angel can give it.*

"He gives her heart wings," Guiseppi whispered to Rosa as they watched the young couple walk through the old, falling-down house one more time.

Rosa smiled at her husband. Yes, they *seemed* perfect together, and yet her heart was heavy with unexplainable dread.

*****

In his sleep, Noah heard the telephone ringing and ringing. He rousted enough consciousness to grope around on the nightstand beside his bed and put the phone clumsily to his ear.

"This is the Pennington County Jail," a man's voice said on the other end. "This Noah Hansen?"

"Yes," Noah said as he rubbed his face and struggled into a sitting position.

"Got your girlfriend down here on a drunken disorderly," the man continued. "Wanna come and get her? She says you'll post bond."

"Angel?" Noah asked, still half asleep and bewildered.

"Says her name is Carrie Miller."

Noah sighed. "I suppose. I'll be there in a few minutes."

He got out of bed, hurried into some clothes, and jumped on his bike. He hadn't seen Carrie since last May, and she'd been strung out bad. She'd offered him some marijuana, and he'd *almost* taken it. It was then he'd decided to distance himself permanently from her and the rest of that old clan. The temptation to get rip-roaring drunk one last time was just too great.

Noah didn't know Carrie very well, except that she'd had a tragic childhood, and that was the reason she gave for drinking and smoking pot. He knew her real father had died while working on an oil rig in the Gulf of Mexico and that there'd been no life insurance to cover the loss. Mrs. Miller married again a short time later, this time to a suit-wearing, almost colored-looking man with an accent.

Carrie's stepfather, Jack Nelson, had a young son whom they referred to as "Tony," and Noah had never met him. Jack and Carrie's mother, Della, had a daughter together named Charise, and she was ten or eleven years old. Mr. Nelson bought a large house on Rapid City's west side, where they all lived. He was obviously well-off because there was the limousine and the men who worked for Mr. Nelson. Carrie had first said he was into the stock markets, but then said he was into drug dealing, and *everyone* became her new best friend.

Noah went into the stuffy, little jail where Joshua had waited way too many times for him. After he posted the small drunken disorderly bond, one of the officers brought Carrie out of holding. She ran to Noah and threw her arms around him.

"I'm so glad you're here," she cried happily.

He returned her embrace reluctantly and showed her to his bike. Hopefully she wouldn't be too drunk to ride.

"Don't take me to my house," she slurred. "I don't wanna go there anymore."

"Then where am I supposed to take you?" Noah asked disgustedly.

"Take me to your place…I know you got your own place now."

Noah sighed. He didn't have time for this. He had to get up early, and most of the night was already gone. He had about a million things to get done this week, and that new girl was starting.

"Okay," he said hesitantly. "But you gotta go home when you sober up."

Carrie nodded in agreement, and Noah started his bike.

By the time they reached his little cabin, the sun was creeping across the lake. It was later than he'd realized, and he shook his head. He parked the bike and helped Carrie stagger up the steps.

Noah sat her down on the old couch in the living room and started a pot of coffee. While that perked, he brushed his teeth and washed his face. He wasn't going to have time to shower or shave this morning.

"Here," he said as he handed her a hot mug of coffee. "Drink it." She took the cup from his hand, and he sat down on the coffee table in front of her. "Young lady," he scolded as he shook his index finger at her, "you have got to straighten out your life." He paused and frowned. *Wow. I sound just like Josh.* He took a breath and continued, "You're gonna kill yourself with that stuff."

"I know," Carrie replied as she hung her head and looked at the floor. "It just makes me feel better."

"Humph." Noah shook his head. "Don't I know it. But it's just not worth the lost time. And the booze makes you do crazy things you wouldn't normally do if you weren't so tanked up."

"I know." She began to cry and looked into Noah's eyes. "Noah, I'm pregnant."

Noah jumped to his feet and stood on the other side of the table. "How'd that happen?"

She looked up at him and answered, "How do you think it happened? Didn't Mona ever tell you about the birds and the bees?"

Noah rolled his eyes. "Of course she did…I mean…um…who…?"

"Roy Schneider, and he doesn't have a clue."

"*Roy Schneider?*" Noah snorted and shook his head. "That is the *ugliest* man alive. What on earth came over you?"

Carrie shrugged. "I love him."

"Oh, brother." Noah rolled his eyes and shook his head again. "You don't *love* Schneider."

"And what do you know about love, Noah?" Carrie shouted with a frown. She suddenly spied the photograph Noah kept on the small end table beside the couch. "Is this your girl friend? Is she here?" Carrie's eyes began to dart wildly all over the room. She stood quickly and headed in the direction of the door.

"No." Noah frowned and took ahold of Carrie's arm. "She's not here, and you're not in any shape to go anywhere. Sit down."

Carrie sighed and took her seat again. She picked up the photograph for a better look, smiling through her drunk tears, touching the faces in the picture. "She's pretty, Noah. Do you love her?"

Noah was uncomfortable with the direction the conversation had taken, and he took the photo gently from Carrie's hands. "Why doesn't Schneider have a clue?"

"Jack sent him away," she answered as she rolled her eyes. "He caught us...*you know.*"

Noah nodded. "I get the drift. Does your mom or Jack know about the pregnancy?"

Carrie shook her head. "They'll kill me. I think I'll just get an abortion. Can you borrow me some money?"

Noah couldn't hide his horrified expression, and he almost dropped his coffee. "Why?" he managed to croak out in a whisper.

She stretched out on the couch and put her hand over her eyes. "Noah, I'm a drunk. I can't raise a kid."

"I won't borrow you money for *that*," Noah said. "And I don't think it's any kind of an answer for anybody."

"What do you know about it, Noah?" Carrie questioned stubbornly. "You don't have to carry the kid for nine months. It's *my* choice now. Remember? It's been legal for a couple of years now."

Noah moaned. "Well, there are certainly *better* choices you could have made. Like not being with Schneider for one."

"Oh, quit with the lecture," Carrie snapped. "I'll do what I want. You sure had a different point of view when *you* were the one with me."

Noah clenched his jaw together. *You've always been such a mean drunk. You won't even be fit to talk to until you've been sober for a few hours.*

"Tell you what," he said. "Why don't you stay here today and get yourself sobered up. I gotta go to work. If you're still here when I get back, I'm taking you out to see Mona. She has stories and stuff, and maybe she can help you."

Carrie just waved him away, and Noah left for work.

*****

Mona had hired a beautiful young woman named Melinda Smalley. She had a tiny, graceful body; raven-black hair; soft brown skin; and round brown eyes. Her smile was open, as was her demeanor, and she seemed quite interested in digging into Noah's out-of-control office and getting the thing organized. Mona and Joshua knew Melinda very well, as she'd attended church with them for quite some time. She'd graduated recently from business college with a degree in office management, but Noah didn't let that fool him for a second. He knew what they were up to. *Young, single, smart, pretty.*

Noah looked terrible when he showed up at the trailer the next morning. Mona and Melinda were already waiting for him.

"Are you sick, Noah?" Mona asked as he got himself a cup of coffee.

Noah rolled his eyes and shook his head. "I just had a really early morning." He looked at Mona and asked, "Can I bring a friend over to see you tonight?"

Mona's eyes were curious. "Sure. Who?"

"I'll tell you about it later," he answered as he turned toward Melinda, who was sipping her own cup of coffee, waiting to begin whatever her new job would be. "I know this looks *really* bad," he attempted to apologize with a gentle smile. "But *I* know where everything is—" He was interrupted when the phone rang. He walked to his desk and began a search through the stacks of papers and plans as the phone continued to ring.

"Except for the phone," Mona said under her breath.

Melinda spied the cord at the wall and followed its trail to a place beneath Noah's desk. She pulled it out and answered the phone, "Hansen Development."

Noah looked at Mona and raised his eyebrows. "I think she's gonna work out."

Mona gave him a half smile in response and sipped her coffee.

The first order of business was to hire someone to get the trailer moved onto the next site, which was the Randall Jackson project located on Campbell Street. Before the trailer could be moved,

Melinda and Mona would have to organize the "files" and mail. Noah had been just putting things into boxes, helter-skelter. When one box was full, he just shoved it under a table and found another empty box. Mona and Melinda began going through the boxes, looking over each item carefully and attempting to place them in some kind of order.

"Why didn't you use your file cabinet?" Mona barked. *This is ridiculous.*

Noah scowled softly and handed Melinda a small file. "I didn't have time, Mona. I was too busy *working.*" He paused and frowned thoughtfully. "Oh, I forgot to tell you about something. Alex thinks I should have an office separate from the trailer so we don't lose anything. I found a little place over on Sixth Street, above the Roger Frye Paint & Supply. We'll take everything over there, except for the trailer, of course, and we better leave the tables and the coffee maker for the men."

Melinda had just uncovered several envelopes that were already opened. Their contents were still inside. "These are checks," she observed as she pulled a couple of them out for a better look. "Cashier's checks. Do you want these deposited?"

Noah looked at the checks. *So that's where they went to.* He took the stack of envelopes from her. "Let's see…This one is Jackson's down payment. That goes into the equipment and orders account. These three are for lease deposits, and they go into the escrow account." Melinda took notes as fast as she could. Noah continued with a surprised grin. "Well, *there's* where it went to. This one goes into my business checking. It's a closing check…I get to keep it."

Mona's eyes were wide with wonder. He probably didn't even know how much he had floating around in this place.

Noah looked at his watch and groaned. "I gotta go, ladies. Are you gonna be okay?"

Mona replied, "I think so. Where are you going to be?"

"Let's see." Noah scratched his head as he thought about it. "Well, first I gotta get over to the Campbell site and meet with Jackson. Then I've gotta meet with another guy out on LaCrosse. I'm giving him an estimate. I'll probably have lunch with Maggie around one or so if you need to catch up to me for anything."

"I'll just talk to you tonight," Mona said as she went back to her sorting. "What time will you be out?"

"Probably pretty close to six o'clock," Noah answered as he headed for the door. He paused and turned around to say with a smile, "Thanks. I really appreciate this. I know it's a wreck."

Melinda and Mona looked at him with wry smiles.

After a long and drawn-out meeting with Jackson, Noah hurried to meet with the man who wanted an estimate over on LaCrosse. By this time, it was well after one o'clock. If Mona had tried to meet him at Maggie's, they would have missed one another.

Shortly before four o'clock, a very tired and hungry Noah parked his old pickup out in front of Maggie May's and strode inside. It had started to snow at about three o'clock, and he was cold.

Noah took a seat at the bar, looking at the haunting portrait and then at the photograph still tucked into its corner. He shook his head and wondered briefly if it had all *really* happened. Something must have happened, for her photograph was right there in the corner of the very portrait she claimed to have painted.

"Hey, Noah," Maggie greeted as she came from the kitchen. "Where ya been all day?"

Noah rubbed his face. "I've had a busy day. No breakfast. No lunch."

Maggie reached under the counter for a coffee cup and set it before him. "Just made a fresh pot," she said as she reached for the glass pot on the hot plate beside her. She filled the cup, put the pot back in its place, and asked, "Do you want a sandwich or something?"

Noah replied, "Yeah. Just a sandwich. I'm going to see Mona and Josh for supper, but I gotta eat something before I pass out."

Maggie smiled and turned to yell at the strange man working in the kitchen. "Get me a ham and turkey on wheat, no cheese." She turned back to Noah, who looked very surprised to see the new guy. "That's Mel," she said as she pointed a thumb in his direction. "We're so busy I had to hire a cook." She shook her head and asked, "What did you do all day?"

Noah sipped at his coffee and answered, "I met with that Texan this morning, and then I met with a guy just down the road from here. He wants to build an apartment complex." Noah sighed tiredly. "I don't know about that. It's the biggest project I've had to bid on yet. I'm gonna talk to Alex before I take that one on."

Maggie shook her head. "This town is really growing right now. You went into business at just the right time."

Noah agreed with a smile. His expression changed to one of curiosity. "By the way, Maggie, have you seen Roy Schneider around lately?"

Maggie looked curious. "You mean the guy that works for Carrie's stepfather?"

"Yeah," Noah answered as he took another sip of his coffee.

"No. Why are you looking for him?"

Noah took a breath and answered, "It's a long story. Apparently Jack fired him. He caught him fooling around with Carrie."

Maggie raised an eyebrow and looked at Noah. "And who *hasn't* fooled around with Carrie?"

Noah shook his head. "Nobody I'm acquainted with." He hesitated and whispered, "She's pregnant."

"Good grief," Maggie groaned with a shake of her head. "I'm surprised it didn't happen sooner."

Noah nodded with a frown and whispered, "She wants an abortion."

"Ouch," Maggie replied as she squinted and shook her head. *Of all the mistakes I've made in my life, that's the one I wish I could go back and change. I would have been better off just giving that baby away...*

"I'm taking her out to talk to Mona tonight," Noah continued. "Hopefully she'll change her mind."

Maggie only nodded. *If I believed in your God, I'd promise to pray...*

Chapter 18

Noah was surprised when he returned home that evening and Carrie was still there. She was sober, showered, and had brushed her strawberry-blonde hair out of her face into a ponytail. She was wearing one of Noah's clean work shirts.

"Hope you don't mind," she said. "My other shirt smelled like the bar."

"It's okay," Noah replied. "I'm gonna jump through the shower and shave, and then we're gonna have a little talk. You gonna stay for a couple of minutes?"

Carrie nodded, and Noah went off to shower. He had changed his clothes and was just applying his shaving cream when he heard a knock on the bathroom door.

"Are ya decent?" Carrie asked from the other side. Noah opened the door. She saw he was fully dressed, but his face was filled with shaving cream. "That's something new. You never used to shave."

Noah shrugged, looked in the mirror, and began to draw the razor carefully up his chin. "So what do you wanna do? I see you're still sober."

As Carrie watched Noah she answered, "Not that I wanted to stay this way, but I got thinkin' about you and…" She looked at the photograph of Noah and Angel that she held in her hands and let out a heavy sigh. "And I just sorta put two and two together."

Noah looked from Carrie to the photo and then back into the mirror. "What are you doing with that?"

Carrie looked into the photograph and smiled wistfully. "I've never seen you look this way before. Who is she?"

Noah continued to shave. "I was gonna marry her."

"What happened?"

"Don't know," he answered, feeling the familiar lump in his throat. He swallowed it away and finished shaving.

"Is that why you dumped all of us?"

Noah nodded silently in answer, reached for a towel, and wiped the rest of the shaving cream from his face.

"She doesn't party, does she?" Carrie asked. Noah shook his head. Her expression was one he'd never seen as she gazed into the photo and barely whispered, "I wanted to be that for someone."

"What?" he asked with a frown.

Carrie looked into Noah's eyes, and her own filled with tears. "Whoever she was, she must have been very special, because you're not the same Noah Hansen I used to know."

Noah took the photograph gently from Carrie's hands and looked longingly into the eyes of the young lady who'd passed through his life. He shrugged. "Well, it's over now. I'm not going to be seeing her again. I should probably just get rid of this."

"No." Carrie shook her head. "I wouldn't."

"Come on," Noah said as he headed down the hall. "Let's sit in the living room and talk for a minute. You've got some stuff to work on, and we don't have the time for my defunct love life."

Carrie smiled as she followed him down the hall of the little cabin and into the living room, where she took a seat on the couch and he settled himself in a chair. "What does 'defunct' mean?" she asked with a curious smile. "And where did you ever learn a word like *that?*"

"My lawyer, Alex, and defunct means to be finished or dead," Noah answered, and he couldn't help but smile when he thought of Alex. He was always using words like that.

Carrie looked startled. "Why do you have a lawyer? Are you in trouble again?"

"Oh, I started this little business," Noah answered as he set Angel's photograph back into its place on the end table. "I need Alex to do up leases and papers and help me figure out the bank. Stuff like that."

Carrie looked thoughtfully at Noah. "How did you do it? I mean, quit the drinking and partying?"

Noah shrugged. "Well, for one thing I believe that Jesus Christ is my Savior, and He gave me strength. I go to AA a couple times a week, and I keep myself busy doing other things. For instance, I finished school and took some carpentry classes at the vo-tech." Noah hesitated and looked at Carrie with a stern expression. "And you can make that same decision too. It's just a decision, Carrie, and you're the only one that can make it. Don't drink any more of your life away." He shook his head disgustedly and added, "And you shouldn't be drinking right now anyway. You could hurt your baby."

Carrie became rigid instantly and looked away from him. "It's not a baby yet."

"Oh, come on!" Noah snorted and held up one hand. "Don't come at me with that feminut psycho drivel, because I won't even listen to it. It's just plain sin, and it'll wreck your life."

"Yeah, well, you don't have to carry the thing for nine months," she snapped.

"Oh, brother, you got some attitude. Go ahead. Go ahead and butcher yourself for all I care—" He stopped himself and swallowed hard. He *did* care. He didn't want Carrie to do that to herself or to what he considered to be her unborn child. He took a deep breath and began again. "Carrie, I'm sorry. I didn't mean that. I just can't believe you'd do that to yourself."

"It's an easy procedure," she insisted, looking away from him. "In and out of the hospital in a couple of days. Nobody needs to know."

Noah frowned. "No. It's not an *easy* procedure—"

"And just when did you get so worldly? What do you know about abortion?"

Noah took a breath. "My brother had to counsel a couple whose daughter had one. She died, Carrie."

Carrie looked surprised. "She died?"

"She couldn't live with what she'd done and killed herself a couple of years after the *easy procedure*. I don't think you realize what you put yourself through when you make that decision. Some of the stories she told her folks about the *easy procedure* sure didn't sound very easy. For one thing, her baby wasn't even dead when they took him out of her. The doctor held a plastic bag over his head until he stopped breathing. Is that really something you want to be involved in? Are you capable of taking another life like that?"

Carrie was very quiet and looked at the floor. "I really do love him," she said as she dropped her head into her hands. "I just know Jack would never allow it."

"Allow what, Carrie?"

"Me and Roy. You know. Being together," she answered in a soft weep.

Noah's heart was softened, and he left his chair to take a close seat next to Carrie on the couch. He put his arm over her shoulders, and she laid her head against him.

"I really do love him," she cried. "And I don't want to get rid of his baby, but I just don't see how I can take care of it. Mom's gonna be really mad when she finds out, and Jack will probably kill Roy."

Noah understood how she felt. Not being with the one she loved would be the hardest thing to overcome, including the drinking. "I know it's tough, but you'll be okay after awhile."

"You mean it finally goes away?" she cried.

Noah answered with reflections from his own experience. "For the most part. After awhile it's okay, and you just remember the good parts. It doesn't hurt like it did at first." He looked into her eyes and tried to smile. "Look at me. I'm as good as new."

Carrie laughed quietly through her tears. "You're a changed man. Think I'll turn out that good?"

Noah shrugged and smiled. "Depends. Come on. Let's go and talk to Mona and see if she has any words of wisdom for you." He got to his feet and pulled Carrie gently to hers. He handed her his handkerchief for her tears, and she laughed.

"You actually carry one of these?" She blew her nose and dried her eyes.

"Alex is *never* without one."

"Wow, I gotta meet this guy," Carrie said, and then they were on their way.

*****

Mona nearly fainted when she saw Carrie get out of Noah's old pickup and walk to the door with him. *I thought Noah was through with that girl. He hasn't even talked about her for more than a year.*

Even so, there she was. Mona feigned composure, put a smile on her face, and greeted her guests at the door.

"Haven't seen you since Noah's graduation," she said with a polite smile, noticing that Carrie's gray eyes appeared to be clear…*I think the girl is sober…How can that be…?*

"It's good to see you, Mona," Carrie said as she came through the door.

Joshua came around the corner and almost dropped the bowl of salad dressing he was whisking for Mona.

"Carrie?" he gasped. He looked so bewildered and confused, it made Carrie smile.

"Yep. I'm back, and it's worse than ever," she said in a cynical tone. She frowned deliberately at Joshua. "How the heck are ya, Josh?"

Joshua managed to respond, "Not bad. Can't complain. You?"

Carrie shrugged. "Well, I'm sober, and I don't like *that* very much."

Mona tried to laugh in an effort to ease some of the tension. "Well, that's nice. Why don't we just go into the dining room. Dinner is just getting to the table."

Carrie and Noah followed a very confused Mona and Joshua into the dining room, where the table was set for four. A steaming platter of roast beef and cooked vegetables waited for them. Joshua sat down the bowl of dressing, whisk and all, and then took his regular seat and stared at Carrie. *You're actually going to eat dinner with us? At our table? What's going on here? Did I miss something?*

"Why don't you pray, Joshua?" Mona suggested with a sweet smile as she took her seat next to her husband.

Joshua bowed his head…S*hould I pray for strength or go for the rapture?*

After Joshua had prayed, they began their awkward dinner. They spoke of the weather, how little it had snowed that year, and whether or not it would snow again soon. Noah mentioned the possibility of a new project on LaCrosse but that he had to talk to Alex before he committed to it. Mona mentioned she'd gotten a balance sheet from his accountant that afternoon, and he should take a look at it. Joshua talked about some new parishioners that were in to see him that afternoon, but Carrie talked about nothing. She stayed silent during the entire meal, and only occasionally looked up at someone if they were talking.

"Why don't Noah and I do the dishes," Joshua volunteered with a gracious smile. He got to his feet and picked up a few plates. "You ladies can go into the living room for a nice talk."

Carrie looked horrified. She didn't want to go anywhere. Why couldn't the talk just happen right here at the dining room table?

"Come on, Carrie," Mona said with her sweet smile, and she got to her feet.

Noah saw Carrie's hesitation. He put his hand on her arm and whispered into her ear, "Go ahead. It'll be okay. You gotta start somewhere." Carrie was uncertain, and she sat very still as she looked from Mona to Noah and then at her plate. "It's gonna be okay," Noah assured as he gave her arm a soft pat. "Just go with her."

Carrie swallowed very hard, got up slowly from her chair, and reluctantly followed Mona into the living room.

Mona took a seat on the couch, smiled at Carrie, and patted the cushion next to her. "Come on, darlin'. Sit over here. I ain't bit anybody in a long time." Carrie's hard face softened a little, but she took a seat on the opposite end of the couch.

Mona saw the fear and hesitation in Carrie's expression, and she wished Noah would have prepared her for whatever situation was about to unfold. Of course, there hadn't been time for that, and she'd have to go this thing cold. Thankfully, being the wife of a preacher, Mona was a crisis professional. Instinctively, she slid close enough to Carrie to put her warm hand on Carrie's knee. Looking into the young girl's eyes, she asked, "What's troublin' ya?"

Carrie almost winced. She felt the strange urge to hold Mona's tender hand, but she fought it. She didn't want to trust this woman with her problems. Carrie had never trusted anybody, and she wasn't about to start now. Why had she even let Noah drag her over here? These were *nice* people. They'd *never* understand.

"I'm sorry," Carrie stammered. "Me and Noah gotta get outa here."

"Please don't go yet," Mona said with friendly, Southern charm. She gave Carrie's knee a soft pat. "Ya know, we've never really gotten to know one another."

Carrie raised one eyebrow cynically. "You don't wanna get to know me."

Mona only smiled. "Don't be afraid. You got some troubles. I can tell."

"You'd never understand." Carrie shook her head and looked at her lap.

"You'd be surprised. Ya know, just because I'm married to a preacher doesn't mean I haven't seen a thing or two. Why, you don't even know where I'm from."

"Where *are* you from?"

"Atlanta. Georgia, that is," Mona answered. "I was born and raised there. I have three sisters and a brother, and they are *very* interestin' people. My daddy's a teamster, and he has very interestin' friends."

"I really don't have a dad," Carrie said slowly, and she seemed to become the slightest bit comfortable.

"How about that dark fellow with the accent?" Mona asked curiously.

"Jack?" Carrie said with surprise. "He's my stepdad, and he's really busy."

"Busy with what, Carrie?"

"Oh, you know, his stocks and stuff."

"How about your mama?" Mona continued.

"She's okay," Carrie answered. "But I really can't talk to her about this. She's busy trying to raise Charise right. She doesn't want her turning out like me."

Mona nodded. "Is Charise your sister?" Carrie acknowledged with a nod. Mona took a breath. "Well, what should we talk about, Carrie? Noah must have brought you out here for a reason."

"I'm pregnant," Carrie answered abruptly.

Mona's small mouth dropped open in surprise, and she gasped, "Oh, my goodness!"

"Are you mad?" Carrie asked, her face expressionless.

Mona shook her head and laughed nervously. "No. Why would I be mad?"

"Because," Carrie said as tears began to burn her eyes, "you're so *nice*, and I'm such a *monster*."

Mona's eyes were wide and round, and her mouth fell open again. She cleared her throat and stammered, "Well, I don't think you're a *monster*, and I'm sure you didn't do this by yourself." Mona frowned and growled, "And Noah knows better—"

"Noah didn't do this."

Mona couldn't hide the surprise on her face, but she spoke anyway. "Well, I think you're a person with some troubles and you're stuck in some sin right now, but ya know, we all sin every day, Carrie darlin', even me and Joshua and Noah. All you can do now is try and clean up your act and do the best thing for that baby."

"I've been thinking about an abortion," Carrie informed as she avoided Mona's eyes.

"Oh, dear." Mona attempted to breathe calmly through the bomb Carrie had just tossed into the conversation. She reached for Carrie's hand and squeezed it tightly. "Please don't do something like that. You'll regret it."

Carrie sighed, "I already regret what I've done."

"But what about the father? What does he have to say about this?"

Carrie shook her head as tears left the corners of her eyes, dropping onto her cheeks. She looked into Mona's pretty green eyes and whispered, "He wants me to just get rid of it."

Mona was moved with compassion for the girl and, with her index finger, gently touched the tears streaming down Carrie's face. "Do you got time for a story, Carrie?" Carrie nodded hesitantly, and Mona continued, "I have a cousin named Marla." She sighed heavily. "Well, Marla got herself caught in some sin when we were in our early twenties. She had an affair with a married man and wound up pregnant. She decided the best thing for her would be to have an abortion. Now, in them days, it wasn't all legal like it is now, and she had to sneak off somewhere to have it done. So she had her brother drive her to another town and went to the address they'd been given.

"Marla went into this little surgery-type room and was told to wait for the doctor. While she waited, she thought about what she was gettin' ready to do and changed her mind. Well, this big, ol' greasy guy comes walkin' in and claims he's the doctor. She said he was drinkin' whiskey, and he tried to force her onto the table to give her some sort of a shot. I guess there was quite a struggle, but she managed to get the metal bedpan and hit him in the head as hard as she could and knocked him out. Then she ran for her brother's car, and he brought her directly to our house. My mama hid Marla out until that baby was born, and then Marla gave him to one of my daddy's teamster friends and his wife, on account of they couldn't have kids."

"Well," Carrie cleared her throat quietly, "I don't want to give my baby away."

"A baby needs a father *and* a mother," Mona insisted tenderly.

"So, would you hide me out for awhile?" Carrie asked.

"If that's what it takes. And I could help you find a family for the baby. I know lots of people."

Carrie bit her lip and looked at Mona. "Can I have a few days to think it over?"

Mona nodded. "Do you pray, Carrie?"

Carrie looked confused. "What do you mean, Mona?"

"You know, talk to the Lord?"

Carrie shook her head.

"Well then, I'll say this as gently as I possibly can. Carrie, darlin', you gotta pray. You're in some sin here, and I'm not condemin' ya. I sin every day. But you could go to the Lord Jesus and ask Him for forgiveness and comfort and to give you peace. Then you will be able to think clearly and make a good decision. Carrie, Jesus *loves* you *and* your baby, and He'll steer you right."

"Mona, I just don't believe in that stuff." Carrie shook her head and looked away.

Mona sighed with a shrug. "You just think about it for a few days. Think about all of the terrible things you've done and whether or not you'd like to leave it in the Lord's hands, or whether you'd like to just tough it out on your own. Jesus will give you peace."

"What's Jesus got to do with me and my life?" Carrie asked with a frown.

"It's really hard to see sometimes," Mona continued. "But Jesus was God's son, and He knows what it's like to be human, what it's like to suffer, what it's like to cry. He died for us, Carrie. He put His own life aside so we could have salvation."

"What's salvation?" Carrie asked, and her frown softened slightly.

"It's when you believe your sins are completely forgiven because you asked the Lord Jesus for forgiveness. You believe that you will be in Heaven with Him someday. Because of Jesus, you believe that you will live forever and never die."

Carrie's expression was bewildered. She'd heard those preachers on the TV saying the same thing, and then they'd ask for a big check. It was just a little over the top and hard to accept—someone actually forgiving Carrie for what she'd done. *Besides, I really haven't been that bad. Everybody fools around, probably even ol' Mona herself. I just happened to get caught…*But then she looked at Mona, who appeared to be so sincere and honest. "I'll think about it," Carrie whispered.

Just then, Noah and Joshua walked into the room.

"I got a plan," Noah said with a nod and a smile.

*****

"Hansen Development on line seven. Can you take it?" Jan's voice came out of Alex's intercom, interrupting his conversation with Tillie. They were sitting in Alex's office, laughing and talking about their new house and what the subcontractor had discovered that morning.

Alex smiled and winked at Tillie, replying, "Sure. I'll take it real quick." He pressed the button for line seven and picked up the phone. "Hey, Noah, what's going on out there in the wild, wild west?"

Tillie smiled at Alex and lowered her head into the magazine on her lap: *Good Housekeeping, Special Publication.* After a few seconds, she didn't even hear Alex's conversation.

"What are you doing?" Noah asked, and Alex could tell he was smiling by the tone in his voice.

"I'm with my fiancée," Alex answered. "What are *you* doing?"

"Well," Noah took a breath, "I talked to this guy who wants to put up apartments on LaCrosse. What do you think? If I take it, I'll need to hire about twenty men, but we won't have to write leases or anything. It's just a slap-up job and somebody else takes over. It's big. I could make some good money."

"Can you find twenty men at this time of year?" Alex asked as he glanced out his window and noticed the big chunks of snow falling from the sky.

"I think so," Noah answered. "The weather's been so good out here this year, and we haven't even had a hard freeze yet. I bet we could get the foundation and frame up before December. Then the men could work inside for the rest of the winter."

"Do you want me to prepare an offer?"

"I guess so," Noah answered. "Do you want me to have Melinda give Shondra a call with the figures?"

"Yes," Alex answered. "And tell her not to forget the land appraisal. I want to see what the land is worth before we write the offer."

"Okay, Alex." Noah took a deep breath. "And Alex, I'm getting married two weeks from Wednesday. Do you and Tillie want to come?"

Alex's mouth dropped open in surprise. "Wow…Noah…I didn't even know you had a girl friend."

"Well," Noah said with a sigh, "we've known each other for awhile, and now seemed as good a time as ever."

Alex was surprised, but he smiled and shook his head. That was so like Noah to drop a bomb like that. Alex looked at Tillie and asked, "Hey, do you want to fly out to Rapid City for my client's wedding?"

Tillie looked up from her magazine, and her eyes held a thoughtful expression. "When is it?" she asked with a curious frown.

"Two weeks from Wednesday," Alex answered.

"That's the election," Tillie reminded. "I promised to fly to New York that week."

Alex nodded at her and said to Noah, "Well, I can come, but Tillie's flying to New York to be with her brother and their family. He's running for the junior Senator's seat."

Noah was surprised. "Petrice Caselli is her *brother?*" He laughed. "Boy, Alex, you sure know who to connect yourself to."

Alex laughed at Noah's comment, surprised he was that politically informed. "Yes, Petrice Caselli's going to be my brother-in-law."

"That's cool, Alex. Well, I gotta go. Tell Tillie I'll be prayin' for her brother. We need another conservative in Washington."

"I will," Alex replied. "Thanks for calling."

"You bet," Noah said, and then they hung up.

*****

At first, Carrie thought it was the dumbest idea she'd ever heard. However, after they'd left Mona and Joshua's house, they talked about it alone. Noah made the whole idea seem like the right thing to do.

"Neither of us really likes being alone," Noah urged. "It would be really nice to have someone to share time with…and…" He hesitated with a frown before continuing. "And I could help you stay away from the booze."

Carrie considered his statements thoughtfully. "I don't know…I always wanted to have a big church wedding and marry the man of my dreams. You know, like all girls dream about."

"I know," Noah sympathized, "but these are the circumstances you've created. The people from Josh's church will show up just because they think he's great. I'll give you some money, and Mona can help you find a nice dress." He sighed and smiled at her. "We can make the best of this situation—at least a decent memory."

Carrie shook her head. "But why would you do this? We don't *love* each other."

Noah shrugged. "I guess I would do it for the baby and a little for you." He smiled and added, "Maybe I need some purpose in my life. I've wasted so much time waiting for Angel to come back and for that whole thing to work out."

Carrie gave him a sad smile and looked into his eyes. "I'm sorry. She must have meant a lot to you."

Noah nodded. "But now we have the opportunity to make a bad situation better. Your baby can have a father *and* a mother. We'll raise him or her together, and you won't have to give him or her away."

"But what if Angel *does* come back?" Carrie wondered with tears. "Or what if there comes a day when Roy and I *can* be together and he wants the baby? Then what do we do?"

Noah shook his head. "Carrie, you and I both know better than that. The two of us got left behind, and Angel and Roy found other lives."

*****

Petrice drove with care along West Broadway as it turned into Tibbett's Road. The snow had started to fall earlier that afternoon, and the road was very slippery. The election was less than two weeks away, and he'd settled his last lawsuit, taking care of the final loose ends. Since Petrice was so much farther ahead in the polls, the partners of the law firm had already hired his replacement.

He sighed and smiled as he drove along, thinking about all of the appearances he, Elaine, and Michael had made over the past several months. At first the polls ran in favor of the liberal candidate, but for the last several weeks now, the poles had shifted, showing Petrice ahead by a long shot. His conservative values, open enthusiasm, and soft accent attracted the national spotlight. It seemed everyone in America was rooting for Petrice Caselli.

Petrice turned off Tibbett's Road and into the driveway of the beautiful old home he shared with Elaine. From the driveway, he saw her through the front window, rocking little Michael, and singing to him. He pulled into the garage, closed the door, and hurried inside.

"Hello, my love," he said with a smile as he peeked around the corner and into the living room where she sat. "How is the little bambino?"

Elaine smiled at her handsome husband. "He is turning into such a good baby," she whispered as she looked down into Michael's sleeping face. "And I can't believe how much he looks like your sister."

Petrice took off his coat, flopped it over a chair, and went to his wife and son. He placed his hand delicately on top of the baby's head.

"He sat up in the high chair today," Elaine whispered with a smile. "I had to pack him in with some little blankets, but he smiled the whole time. It was really fun."

Petrice looked into his wife's eyes and said, "I have something to ask you about, my love." Elaine looked curious and waited for Petrice to continue. "I have located a used Learjet and a pilot." They'd talked of buying a plane since Petrice had decided to run for the Senate in order to get around more efficiently and not have to rely on commercial charters or regular flights. "And," he added with a smile and a sparkle in his eye, "I settled the Donssell case today. There is more than enough to pay for the plane, so we do not have to go into debt for it."

Elaine agreed immediately. "Well, definitely, Petrice! Especially with the new baby coming along, and especially if you win the election. We need a more feasible way to get around. Let's do it!"

Petrice smiled and looked into her eyes. "And there is one other thing I feel compelled to ask you about." He waited for a moment before continuing. "Do you miss working, Ellie?"

Elaine laughed under her breath. "Heaven's no! Why would you even ask me such a thing?"

"Because I realize that, in marrying me, you gave your entire life to do other things, and being a Senator's wife will not be easy."

Elaine chuckled again. "I never really had a life until I met you, Petrice Caselli." She shook her head and smiled. "Now I've got everything."

*****

Tillie had worked on her "new" house for two weeks, and Alex was amazed at what had already been done. Since she was still in school during the days, she relied on Rosa to let the contractors inside. After her last class of the day, she'd hurry over to check on their work. In those first weeks, she'd arranged for all of the cabinets and carpet to be removed and hauled away. Much to Tillie's surprise, the removal of the carpets revealed hardwood flooring in excellent condition.

"We can have the floors refinished," she said excitedly as she led Alex through the old house one afternoon after school.

Alex observed the surroundings with a pensive frown. "It looks like a war zone in here."

Tillie took a tight hold of his hand and continued on enthusiastically. "And look at this, Alex…", and he followed her into what would be their formal dining room. There she'd thumb-tacked a sketch of a built-in china hutch. "I talked to a cabinetmaker yesterday," she continued. "He says he can make the hutch match the cabinets I ordered—"

"You drew that?"

"Well, I couldn't really find anything I had in mind, so I just sketched this out."

"Wow." Alex admired the sketch. "This is really good. Will it look like this when it's finished?"

"I hope so," Tillie replied with a smile as she looked at the sketch. She pointed to dishes she'd drawn inside. "And these will be the pattern of the china on our registry."

Alex nodded as he remembered the day they'd gone to Shrivers and were enrolled in their bridal registry. He looked into Tillie's happy eyes and smiled. She grew more beautiful as the days passed by, scheming and planning about the old house, and lovingly sharing with him all that was in her heart and mind…*She's amazing…She'll make a perfect wife.*

Chapter 19

"Now listen to me, little one," Vincenzo said as he smiled into his excited sister's eyes. "You must always remember to turn on your exhaust fan when you do this." Vincenzo had installed a heater in the garage at Tillie's old house so she could work on refinishing an oak table and chairs.

Alex looked apprehensively at the broken pieces of what would become a dining set... *We'll really sit at that and have meals?*

Vincenzo noticed Alex's stare and laughed. "Your hubby-to-be looks very worried about this."

Tillie reached for Alex's hand and assured, "It's gonna be great. Just wait and see."

Alex smiled at his excited bride. *She's been right so far.* In just a few weeks, he watched the house go from being a complete "war zone" to having finished walls and ceilings. The bathrooms had been given new tile floors, and all of the home's woodwork was refinished and reinstalled. The old wood floors were sanded and refinished, and the master suite on the first floor was covered with a soft, thick, white carpet. Next week the cabinetmaker would install the kitchen cabinets and the built-in china hutch in the dining room. Along with him would come the plumber, who'd install a sink and dishwasher in the kitchen and a claw-foot tub in the master suite.

"Have I showed you the fabric for the seats?" Tillie asked. Alex shook his head, and she gave an excited, little jump and ran into the house.

Vincenzo laughed and looked at his brother-in-law. "Your love for my sister has given her heart a new purpose."

Alex smiled at Vincenzo's comment. "Thanks, Vincenzo."

Vincenzo shook his head. "No. Thanks to *you*, my friend. She has not been this creative in a very long time. Your love seems to bring out the very best inside of her."

Tillie came back into the garage, holding the dark-blue Paisley tapestry she and Kate had ordered from a catalog. She took a piece of it and placed it over the seat of the only standing chair. Her graceful hands formed pleats like a skirt, and she looked up at Alex.

"Kate said she'd help me with this part, but see?" She looked back at the chair. "Won't that look nice?"

Alex smiled and nodded. She was wonderful.

*****

On the first Tuesday in November of 1976, an exuberant Petrice Caselli stood at the podium with Elaine beside him and his new baby in his arms. His brothers and sister, parents, and niece and nephew stood behind him as he thanked the people of New York for making him a United States Senator. Confetti and balloons rained down on them from somewhere above, and his excited supporters cheered and applauded from the floor.

"This is more than an honor for me to be able to represent you fine people in this way," Petrice said from the stage. The excited crowd interrupted with cheers and shouts, and Elaine laughed. They *really* loved her husband. "I cannot believe where my life has taken me," he began again. "From a tiny but wonderful place in *Italia* to this great country of America, where I will serve its people in the name of God and for the cause of freedom—"

Petrice was interrupted again by the excited crowd, and his brothers laughed. This reminded them of his commencement speech at Washington Senior High School nearly twenty years ago. He had the gift to rally a crowd.

"I will serve you well," Petrice promised. "With my voice, I will take your concerns to a liberal Washington and fight for what we know to be righteous and holy, and Washington will tremble with the fear of the Lord!"

The crowd erupted in whoops and cheers again, and Elaine smiled into her husband's eyes. If anyone could get their message through, it was Petrice Caselli.

*****

On Wednesday morning Alex chartered a flight for Rapid City. He had just enough time to attend Noah's wedding and then fly back to prepare for trial the rest of the week. Thankfully, Noah's wedding was scheduled for the morning, or he wouldn't have been able to attend because of his busy schedule.

He walked into the church on South Canyon Road and was greeted by a friendly red-headed woman he recognized.

"Alex Martin," she greeted with a smile as she extended her hand. She was dressed in a soft, green dress that matched her eyes to perfection.

Alex took Mona's hand. "How are you, Mrs. Hansen?"

"Just fine," she said in her Southern drawl. "Yourself?"

"Great," Alex answered.

"Noah tells us you're engaged! Congratulations!"

"Thank you, Mrs. Hansen."

"And when will you be getting married?"

"Early June," he answered.

"I watched the election last night. Noah told us that your fiancée's brother is Petrice Caselli?"

Alex nodded politely.

"Wow," Mona continued. "Did you hear his speech?"

"Yes," Alex answered with a smile. "And he's always been an incredible speaker. I heard his high school commencement address."

"You've known that family for a long time then."

"They've lived just down the street from us for about twenty years," Alex replied. "By the way, where's Noah? I'd like to say hi before the wedding gets going."

"And he wants to see you about something too. He's upstairs in the men's dressing room." She smiled and pointed toward the steps. "Just go up the stairs, down the hall, and into the second door on your left. He's in there with Joshua."

"I'll bet he's nervous by now."

"Oh, I'm sure he is," Mona agreed.

Alex headed for the steps, and Mona turned to greet some other guests that had arrived.

"You know, you don't have to go through with this," Joshua reminded as he watched Noah adjust his black tie in front of the mirror.

"I know," Noah said with a serious expression. "But I want to."

"Marriage was intended to be so much more," Joshua insisted. "I admire what you're doing for Carrie and the baby, but what about *your* life, Noah?"

Noah shrugged. "You just don't understand, Josh. Neither of us has anybody, and she doesn't want to give the baby away. It's a good plan."

"And what about *intimacy?*" Joshua whispered, almost afraid to talk about it.

Noah chuckled. "It's not going to be like that, Josh. We don't love each other. We're just doing this for the baby…and…" He hesitated as he looked at Joshua. "And so we don't have to be alone."

Joshua shook his head. "That's the worst reason I've ever heard."

"Well, it's my reason, Josh, and I feel good about it, so be happy for me."

Joshua rolled his eyes, and they heard a soft knock on the door. Joshua opened the door, and Alex stepped into the dressing room, extending a friendly hand toward Noah.

"You look great," Alex commented, admiring Noah's black suit and tie and noticing the black cowboy boots exposed at his pant leg. "Love the boots."

Noah laughed, and Alex noticed that the horrible sadness that had been present in Noah's eyes from the time they'd met had softened. In fact, his blues eyes danced with excitement and anticipation.

"Congratulations, Noah," Alex said as he gave his friend a pat on the back. "You look really happy."

"I am," Noah said with a smile. He then lowered his voice as he spoke to Alex. "Say, I've got a little bit of a favor to ask of you."

"Sure," Alex said with a nod, and Joshua started to laugh.

"Joshua is performing the wedding, of course," Noah began, and he flushed with embarrassment. "My best man was jailed over the weekend. Would you mind standing up for me?"

Alex wanted to laugh. *This* was so typical of Noah. He took a breath and nodded his head. "I'd be honored."

In Carrie's dressing room, her mother and sister helped her button the white gown and set her lacy veil into place. It was a simple satin gown with a flowing train and long sleeves, and Carrie looked beautiful as she stood before her mother and her younger sister. She hadn't had a drink in more than two weeks, and her family was astounded at the change in her appearance. Instead of the dark circles and the sunken eyes, Carrie's face glowed with expectancy.

"You'll be safe with Noah," Della assured as her shaky hands adjusted the cap of the veil on Carrie's strawberry-blonde head.

Carrie looked at her aged mother. If she didn't know better, she would have guessed Della to be nearly seventy. Her gray eyes were markedly lined with age and worries, and in them she wore only the expression of doubt and regret. Her once brilliantly red hair had dimmed many years ago and was all nearly gray by now. Della Nelson was only forty-three years old.

"But what about you guys? Have you heard anything?" Carrie whispered.

"I think we've lost him for now," Della answered. "Jack sent Tony to Chicago to follow up on a lead, but that's all we know."

Carrie looked at her pretty little sister, who was watching them with wide-open eyes. Never in her life had Carrie seen someone so beautiful. Her hair was soft, shiny black, and her skin was delicate olive. Her eyes were perfectly round, and the irises so black one couldn't make out where the pupil began and the color ended. The poor kid was only eleven years old and had been running her whole life.

"I'll miss you, Carrie," Charise said.

"We'll still see each other." Carrie put a gentle hand on her sister's shoulder.

"I know," Charise replied. "But it's so different now. You're all nice and pretty."

Carrie swallowed hard and fought the tears that burned in the back of her eyes. The enormous guilt she felt at having wasted so much of her family's life and her own on her drinking was a lot to bear at times. But maybe, with Noah's help, she could straighten herself out and have a brand new life.

Maggie May and Estelle entered the church, dressed in straight black dresses. Old-fashioned black net veils dropped from their old-fashioned hats, covering their eyes. They looked more like they were in attendance at a funeral than a wedding.

"Hello, Maggie," Mona greeted with a smile. She looked from sister to sister. "Estelle. You both look lovely this morning."

"Thanks, Mona," Maggie said with a frown. "I can't believe you're letting him go through with this. She's a terribly mean woman."

Mona sighed. "Well, Maggie, you know Noah. Nobody tells *him* what to do."

Maggie and Estelle scowled, nodded their heads, and went into the church to be seated.

Carrie's mother and sister came down the steps, and Mona smiled at them. "It's nearly time to seat the mother of the bride."

Della acknowledged Mona and waited patiently as they watched the very tall Alex Martin come down the steps with Joshua and Noah.

When Noah reached the bottom of the steps, he introduced, "Alex, this is Carrie's mother, Della Nelson. Della, this is my best man, Alex Martin."

Alex extended a friendly hand. "How do you do?"

"Fine, thank you," Della replied.

"And this is Carrie's sister, Charise Nelson," Noah introduced. "She's going to be Carrie's maid of honor."

Alex hid his surprise with a smile and bowed gracefully to shake the little girl's hand. "How do you do?"

"Fine, thank you," she politely repeated the response of her mother.

A very tall, dark gentleman approached them, dressed in an expensive navy-blue suit and tie. Noah smiled and said, "Alex, this is Jack Nelson, Carrie's stepfather."

Mr. Nelson looked into Alex's eyes and extended his hand in greeting. "Mr. Martin, how do you do?"

"Very well, thank you," Alex replied. He noticed Mr. Nelson's familiar accent because Tillie's family spoke with the same soft accent. *What a strange name for an Italian…Nelson?*

"Okay, we have to get going," Joshua said. "Let's go through this real quick. Noah and I will be waiting at the front of the church. Alex and Charise will come down the aisle when you hear the organist." He looked to Alex. "Do you have the ring?" Alex nodded, and Joshua continued, "Okay, Mr. Nelson and Carrie will come down the aisle. Mr. Nelson, you will lift Carrie's veil and then place her hand into Noah's, and then you take a seat beside your wife." Joshua looked at the small crowd around him and asked, "Any questions?"

Everyone shook their heads, and an usher came and offered his arm to Della. She nodded, tucked her arm into his, and was soon being escorted into the church.

Joshua looked at Mona. "Get Carrie."

She nodded and hurried up the steps.

Joshua looked at Noah. "Are you *sure* about this?"

Alex thought it was a strange question, but, considering Noah, he just smiled and waited with everyone else for Noah's response.

With a very serious expression and a nod of the head, Noah replied, "Positive."

"Alright then," Joshua sighed. "Let's go." And with that, Noah and Joshua disappeared into the church.

A young man with a camera approached. "I'm the photographer. Can I have some shots real quick."

"No!" Jack barked. "Do not take my photo, or I will destroy your camera."

The young man bowed away nervously and disappeared into the church.

Alex thought *that* was really strange. The whole wedding seemed to get stranger and stranger.

Mona and Carrie came down the steps, and Carrie smiled beneath her veil.

"Carrie, this is Alex Martin," Mona introduced. "He'll be Noah's best man."

Carrie looked embarrassed. "I guess you heard Theo's in the slammer?"

Alex swallowed to keep himself from laughing.

Organ music was heard, and Alex looked at Charise. "That's our cue." He gave her a wink and offered her his arm. "Are you ready?"

Charise giggled in response and reached up for Alex's arm. He led her slowly into the church.

"They look so cute," Mona commented with chuckle. Little Charise was barely five feet tall, and Alex was probably six and half, a good eighteen-inch difference, if not more. The scene of the two of them was a very precious moment. Too bad they wouldn't have a photo.

Jack turned to his stepdaughter and offered his arm. "I hope this works out for you, Carrie."

Carrie only nodded as they went into the church. It was then Mona finally noticed the very tall, red-headed man as he hid in the shadows in the back of the church. He took out a handkerchief, dried his eyes, and slipped out the door.

*****

After a small reception in the basement of the church, Noah and Carrie went over to his little cabin and packed up what he had. Noah's old boss, Pete Denis, had finished a split foyer in Chapel Valley, and Noah decided to buy it. The cabin was far too small for two people, plus they'd need extra room for the baby.

Pete's split foyer had four bedrooms, two upstairs and two down. Carrie and the baby could have the bedrooms upstairs and Noah the two downstairs—one for sleeping and the other for a home office. By early that evening, they'd moved what little they had between themselves into their new house and looked at their bare surroundings.

"I suppose we oughta buy some furniture for the place," Noah suggested as he looked around at the empty living room in the upstairs.

"A kitchen table would be nice," Carrie commented. "But where are we gonna get the money?"

Noah looked at Carrie with surprise and raised an eyebrow. "I have some money."

Carrie frowned skeptically. "You've *never* had money."

"Well I have money now."

Carrie's expression remained skeptical. "Well, do you have enough to buy some furniture and a table?"

"I think so. I'll call my accountant in the morning and find out."

Carrie rolled her eyes and shook her head. "You don't have an accountant."

"Yes, I do," Noah insisted. "He works over there in the First Federal Building. Alex got me set up with him."

Carrie looked doubtful. "Whatever, Noah."

*****

Noah was pleasantly surprised to find that he did, indeed, have enough money to shop for furniture. He was more shocked than anything and dismissed the large figures available to him as a mistake. He told himself he'd just spend a little of the money and ignore the rest so that, when the accountant realized his error, he wouldn't come up short.

Noah and Carrie shopped that entire Thursday and bought furniture at Fischer's. They selected a soft-blue couch with a matching love seat, a coffee table, two end tables, and two lamps for the living room. Noah found a wooden rocking chair for the baby's room, a decent table for the kitchen with some matching chairs, and a television set. Noah also thought it would be a good idea to pick up a washer and dryer so they wouldn't have to go to the laundromat when the baby came.

They stopped for lunch at Embers on Omaha and Jackson and finally finished their day at the grocery store. Carrie was quiet as she watched Noah fill the cart with what he thought to be staples. As they unloaded their groceries into their new kitchen, Carrie's face became worried and tense, and Noah noticed it right away.

"What's wrong?" he asked. "You look sick."

"I sorta am," she admitted as she looked at the groceries covering the countertops. She swallowed hard and took a breath. "I don't cook, Noah…Well, I can make sandwiches."

"Oh." Noah sighed as he looked at the fresh meat, vegetables, cans, and bottles before them. He'd *assumed,* since she was a woman, she'd be doing the cooking. He rubbed his chin. "Well, I can cook a *few* things."

"I *can* do laundry," she offered.

Noah smiled. "Okay then. You take care of the laundry, and I'll take care of the cooking. Sound like a fair deal?"

Carrie nodded. She could handle that.

*****

"The wedding was *really* weird." Alex raised his eyebrow and sent Sam a strange look. They were sitting in his office, preparing for trial, and Sam had asked how Noah's wedding had gone.

Alex chortled, "I knew it was going to be strange the moment I saw Noah. Apparently his best man was jailed the weekend before, and so I became the stand in."

Sam laughed out loud and shook his head.

"And then," Alex continued, "he's got this really creepy father-in-law who won't let anybody take his picture. He's got an Italian accent, but his last name is *Nelson.*" Alex frowned and wrinkled his nose. "Is that *weird,* or is it just me?"

Sam laughed again. "That's really *weird*, Alex."

Alex shook his head and smiled. "And they didn't even kiss. Well, it was sort of a kiss. When Joshua said, 'kiss the bride,' Noah just gives her this little peck on the cheek, and that was that." Alex sighed and shook his head again. "I'm kissing Tillie good at that wedding—"

Alex was interrupted by Sam's loud laughter. "Thank goodness you finally figured it out!" Alex laughed too, and Sam asked, "By the way, how's she doing on the house?"

"Oh, it's beautiful, Sam," Alex answered. "You should really try to get over there this weekend. It's like magic, and she makes it look so easy. You should see her pretty, little hands work with these chairs she's refinishing." He smiled contentedly. "I couldn't have made a better decision for a wife. Marrying Tillie Caselli is the best thing for me."

*****

As it neared Thanksgiving, Tillie's old house started to come together in a wonderful way. The old, rotten siding was replaced and painted crisp white. The broken shutters were taken down, and smart black louvered shutters where hung in their place.

Tillie salvaged as many light fixtures in the old house as she could. Others were replaced, but only with ornate Victorian pieces carefully matched to the existing fixtures. The leaky patio door in the dining room was taken out and a new French door with a storm and screen installed in its place.

Sam and Becky-Lynn had been by several times, amazed at the transformation. By this time, it was starting to look like an empty house instead of the broken-down nightmare Tillie had led them through six weeks before.

"And I already have a couple of place settings in the china hutch," she said with a soft smile as she led them into the dining room where the cabinetmaker had installed the built-in piece according to Tillie's specific sketch. "Some of Alex's friends in Boston have already sent gifts," she continued as she flipped on the hutch's light. "Inside illumination. What do you think?"

Sam and Becky-Lynn smiled with approval as they looked over the pretty Lenox pattern Tillie and Alex had chosen together. It was a lovely, cream-colored china with a delicate pink band around the outside and a shiny gold line that trimmed the edge. The salad plates were solid pink, and the tea cups had tiny gold loops for handles.

"But what I really noticed was the table," Becky-Lynn said as she admired the finished work in the middle of the dining room. She'd heard that Tillie had to reassemble the old table and chairs after having sanded each piece and then finishing it all in a light oak to match her hutch. Then she and Kate sewed cushions and skirts for the chairs. "How'd you do that?" Becky-Lynn asked with a curious smile.

"Oh," Tillie explained, "my brother put heat into the garage—"

"That took more than just a heated garage," Sam interrupted.

Tillie laughed. "Well, I just gave it some tender-loving care. The wood was in really good shape, and Kate helped me with the chairs."

"And what's in there?" Sam questioned as he pointed to the large box in the corner of the dining room.

"That will be the chandelier," Tillie answered as she went to the box, spinning it around so they could see the photo on the other side.

"Amazing," Becky-Lynn said with a quiet smile. "You are an amazing woman, Tillie Caselli. I would have never had the patience to work with all this."

Tillie shrugged with a smile. "It's just like a painting. First you start out with the image in your head, and then you find a way to get it onto the canvas."

*****

Guiseppi saw his pretty Rosa in her window seat. She was working on some kind of a list, occasionally glancing out the window. The boys and their wives would be arriving soon, and she was making plans. Guiseppi could tell. He stole up behind her as quietly as he could, placing a delicate kiss on the side of her neck. She didn't move.

"I heard you," she whispered.

Guiseppi sighed. She *always* heard him. He sat down beside her and peeked at the list. Groceries.

"Did you have time to look at Angel's house?" Rosa asked with a curious smile.

"Yes. I can hardly believe what she has already done."

Rosa smiled. "I was just thinking of that, and of all the other changes that have happened in just this one year. Remember last Thanksgiving?" She shook her head and laughed again as she looked down at her list and added biscotti. "Ellie is pregnant, *again*, this Thanksgiving."

Guiseppi smiled faintly. "And Alex was just starting to come around, and now look at where they are." He sighed and his eyes became thoughtful.

Rosa looked into his serious expression, and her smile faded. "What is it, Guiseppi?"

He shook his head as he looked out at the snow that was beginning to fall. "This wedding, my Rosa. Have I done right by our little Angel? Is she ready for this?"

Rosa put a loving hand on her husband's knee. "Why, Guiseppi, whatever would make you doubt?"

Guiseppi shrugged and turned his eyes back to Rosa. "Marquette. He is not happy at all with this."

"Marquette allows his passions to run away with him. He always has."

Guiseppi had to agree, but his eyes were still serious as he looked into Rosa's. She saw the lines of worry and regret.

"Guiseppi, what is troubling you so?"

Guiseppi reached for Rosa's hand. He looked into her eyes and whispered, "Has she spoke of him?"

Rosa swallowed away the sudden tears in her throat. "You mean Noah?" Guiseppi nodded. "No. Not a word. And you know, he has gotten married now."

Guiseppi took a breath. "And what of this friendship between he and Alex?"

Rosa forced away the emotions that had been upon her for the past year and a half. It was really too late to worry about any of that now. Whatever was to happen, would happen, and she decided to comfort her husband. "That is the least of our worries, Guiseppi. Angel is so in love with Alex and their new life to be. She thinks of nothing else anymore."

Guiseppi's black eyes shone with tears he couldn't explain. "But I worry, Rosa, there will come a time when she will discover—"

"She will not discover anything," Rosa interrupted. "And do not waste time fretting about it, Guiseppi. You made a decision based upon what God told you through prayer. We certainly cannot begin to second guess the will of God now."

"What if we have changed the will of God—"

"Guiseppi, we cannot even begin to change the will of God. *You know this.* We may choose another path, but all things will work out according to God's specific plan. God's plan will *not* be thwarted."

Chapter 20

Carrie Hansen heard the clock radio go off beside her bed, and she slapped the snooze button. She *hated* Christmas music. The holidays were quickly approaching again. It was a time of year Carrie had grown to despise since she was a child and her mother had taken up with Jack Nelson. Jack *never* celebrated Christmas, and he wouldn't even allow minimal decorations inside of the house, let alone a Christmas tree.

As she rolled over in her covers, she heard a strange scraping noise beneath her window. She crawled out of the bed, bundled herself into her robe, and looked outside. There stood her new husband, scraping the ice off of his old pickup truck's windshield. She felt a *slight* pang of guilt. The new car he'd purchased for her was in the garage, where it wouldn't collect frost and the windows wouldn't have to be scraped. She frowned as she watched him. *He's changed so much.*

She smelled the brewed coffee and shuffled away from the window, down the hall, and into the kitchen, where Noah had left half a pot on the warmer. She poured herself a cup and sat down at the new kitchen table and looked around the place. It wasn't anything like the way Jack lived, but it was nice, just the same.

Over the last six weeks of their "marriage," they'd become fairly comfortable living with each other. Noah always made them a modest supper, such as hamburgers, meat loaf, or macaroni and cheese. He was sure to serve some kind of a vegetable with the meal, because he thought the baby needed that. Occasionally, he'd be late and have a pizza delivered. *Those* were Carrie's favorite meals. Then they'd spend time playing cards or watching television before retiring to the separate bedrooms.

For Carrie's part, she kept all of their clothes washed, dried, and folded. The house didn't get that messy because they didn't have anything, and she spent the rest of her time trying to sleep away the melancholy that had absorbed her. Her doctor prescribed vitamins and plenty of rest. Carrie took the prescription at about ten o'clock in the morning and bedded down for a two- or three-hour nap. When she awakened, she fixed herself a sandwich and turned on the soap operas. It was amazing how parallel they were to what her life had become. For variety, she watched *Star Trek* reruns and imagined herself with someone alluring like Captain Kirk.

Her family didn't contact her at all, Roy didn't ride in on a white horse to rescue her, and she grew lonelier as the days passed. Noah was a nice guy to live with, but she didn't love him, and she certainly wasn't going to. He had a heartache of his own, and she felt sincere pity for what had happened to the man.

She heard footsteps on the back porch, and Noah came through the kitchen door.

She grimaced. "Mornin'."

Noah smiled in return. "I guess I need one more cup for the road." He pulled a mug out of the cupboard and filled it, blew carefully across the top, and took a hesitant sip. "So, what are you doing today?" He wondered if she was ever going to take an upturn on the whole depression routine.

"Same ol', same ol'," she said as she took a sip of her coffee. "How 'bout you?"

"Alex is in town. We're gonna take a look at LaCrosse, and then we're gonna rough out a deal with some guy at Baken Park. A little remodeling work, I think." Carrie nodded but didn't say anything, and Noah noticed her forlorn expression. "Are you feeling *any* better, Carrie?"

Carrie shrugged. "What's to feel better about?"

He tried not to smile. He remembered feeling like that, and so he said with deliberate excitement, "Hey, why don't you come to lunch with me and Alex?"

Carrie scowled. "What for? What if I spilled on myself or something?"

"We won't care."

Carrie took a sip of her coffee and replied snidely, "I ain't goin' anywhere with *that* smart aleck."

Noah almost laughed at her, but thought better of it. She'd allowed her depression to get so far out of control that she'd really become quite comical.

"Okay," he said with a soft smirk, "how 'bout if we go to church this weekend?"

She stared daggers at him for the very suggestion. "I don't go to church, Noah."

"Well, I think you should," he said smiling as he started for the back door, cup in hand. "Alex and Tillie sing in the choir together."

"Whoopty-doo," Carrie replied, taking another sip of her coffee.

Noah laughed. "See ya later, Carrie."

*****

"LaCrosse is coming along amazingly," Alex commented as he rode along in Noah's old pickup. He was used to the rusted-out vehicle with the dusty seats by now, but he was sure to never remove his trench coat while inside.

Noah agreed with a smile, "Inside work for the winter. That keeps me with a good, regular crew."

"Now how about this guy at Baken Park?" Alex asked curiously. "Are we talking *all inside* for the winter?"

"Yep. We're just gonna tear down some walls and do some carpentry work. Did you bring the bid?"

Alex patted his briefcase. "Got it right here."

It was quiet for a little while, and Noah's face grew thoughtful. "Say, what are you getting Tillie for Christmas?"

"Why?"

Noah shrugged. "I was just trying to come up with an idea for something to give Carrie, and I thought you'd probably have already thought of something really nice. What did you get her last year?"

"I got her an autographed copy of a play written by Robert Frost."

"Who's *that?*"

Alex sighed. "Just an old poet she was studying at the time."

Noah seemed to ponder Alex's answer for a moment, but then he began to shake his head. "I don't think Carrie likes poetry. What are you getting Tillie this year?"

Alex chuckled. He was so excited about the surprise, he was more than willing to share the details with Noah. "Well, I settled a fairly large case, and so I'm using the money to buy her her own car. She doesn't have one."

Noah shook his head. "I already bought Carrie a car. Got her a nice, little Chevy Malibu wagon."

Alex nodded. Noah didn't seem too impressed with *that* idea, and so he asked, "Well, what does she like? What are her interests?"

Noah looked surprised. "What do you mean?"

Alex laughed. "She's *your* wife. Come on, Noah, what does she like to do in her spare time?"

"Watch *Star Trek*," Noah answered, guessing that Carrie's interests were probably a far cry from "comparative literature," whatever *that* was.

"You just bought a new house and it probably needs a few things. How about really nice towels for the bathroom? Maybe to match the bedspread and the curtains in your bedroom. Dad did that once for Mom, and she really liked it.

Noah nodded, as if to consider the idea, and then he said, "You know, I should probably buy her some new clothes." Alex looked curious, so Noah explained, "Carrie's pregnant. She's gonna need some new things."

Alex's head whipped around for a surprised look at Noah. Another one of his bombshells. Alex *still* wasn't used to the way Noah just handed out fairly important information as if it were simply miscellaneous.

"Congratulations, Noah," he managed to croak out.

"Thanks," Noah replied. By then they'd reached Baken Park, and no more was said.

*****

Tara wiped the sweat from her forehead and neck, completely soaking the tissue, and reached for another. The humidity in Miami was even more unbearable than what they'd experienced in Oslo the previous year. Odd circumstances had brought them to Miami, as the owner of the motel where John Peters had stayed came across a file tucked between the box spring and mattress of a bed. On the front of the file was Marquette and Tara's personal D.C. telephone number. The owner's curiosity prompted him to make the call. After a brief conversation, Marquette and Tara were on their way.

"How do people live this way?" she questioned as she reached for another tissue.

"They are practicing for hell," Marquette mumbled. He didn't like Miami either. He looked up from the file he was reading and slid it closer to his wife. "This is a straight-up business. Apparently he genuinely owned a fishing company."

Tara leaned closer for a better look at the paperwork. "Is it incorporated or an LLC?"

"LLC…an apparent sole proprietor," Marquette answered. He leaned back in his chair and stretched his long legs out in front of him. "I do not understand this, Tara. Everything in John's file upholds that this man, Jack Nelson, was born and raised right here in Miami. There is not the tiniest speculation of why John went to New Castle, or why he was in Rapid City for that matter."

"But we do know that you do not have to prove United States citizenship to file papers for an LLC in the State of Florida," Tara commented as she slowly paged through the file.

Marquette scratched his chin. "Is it possible that Ponerello acquired his false citizenship and then came directly to Miami, where he started this little fishing company, sells it a few years after that, makes a bundle, and breezes into the great Midwest to hide forever?"

"Of course," Tara answered. "But why sell such a lucrative business? And why wait until 1972 to sell it? If Jack Nelson is Mario Ponerello, he was safe in Miami. The entire world has known we have been after the Ponerellos since 1968. Would it not make more sense for him to stay put?" She shook her head. "Perhaps he was running from something else."

Marquette shrugged. "Or *someone*."

Tara sighed and turned another page in the file. "Did John have anything else on Jack Nelson?"

Marquette shook his head. "No." He yawned and stretched. "We will think about Jack Nelson later. For now, let us go to dinner."

Tara agreed. Any place with air conditioning.

*****

Carrie heard some kind of a struggle at the back door and hurried from her bedroom into the kitchen. Noah was late, so maybe it was the pizza guy. She threw open the back door to see only a large, bushy evergreen tree as it teetered around at the top of the steps.

"Hello?" she asked cautiously as she watched the tree.

"It's me, Carrie," Noah's voice rang out from behind the tree, and Carrie *almost* smiled. She managed to fight away her delight before he got into the house and propped the tree up against the wall. She was determined not to let him think she enjoyed any part of this arrangement.

"Well?" he said with a smile. "What do you think?"

She frowned. "I *detest* Christmas."

"Oh, you do not," Noah teased with a chuckle. "I picked up some decorations too. They're still in the pickup. Now don't burn it down before I get back in!" He headed back down the steps, while she fought away yet another smile. She was profusely frowning at the tree when he returned with several sacks of decorations. "I thought it might be fun to put up a tree," he said as he closed the door behind him and then set his sacks on the kitchen table. "I haven't put one up since I moved out of Josh's house, and I thought, well—"

"What's for dinner?" Carrie interrupted.

"Frozen TV dinners," Noah answered. He pulled two boxes out of one of his sacks and let them drop onto the table with a loud clunk. "Do you think you could preheat the oven and pour yourself a glass of milk?"

Carrie looked horrified and turned to the stove. "What temperature?"

"Four hundred," Noah answered, not even giving her so much as a glance as he went through the rest of his sacks, placing his purchases on the table. "Look at these. I had forgotten how fun Christmas was."

Carrie rolled her eyes.

"Where should we put it?" he asked as he drew a plastic stand out of one of the larger sacks.

Carrie looked at him and wanted to throw something. Why on earth would he drag a Christmas tree into *this* nightmare? Did he forget they were just married because she was stupid and he was an idiot? Did Alex put up trees in Tillie's house? Was that what this was all about?

"I s'pose that dork, Alex, told you to do this," she grumbled.

Noah looked up with a surprised expression. "No. This was *totally* my idea. I told you, I haven't put one up since I moved out of Josh's place." He frowned and defended, "And don't call him a dork. He's a really nice guy. You'd like him if you ever gave him half a chance."

Carrie raised one eyebrow in an alluring way and smiled as she said, "Oh, I'd like to get to know him—"

"No talking trash. You're pregnant. Now let's figure out a good place to put the tree."

Carrie sighed and shook her head. It was almost exhausting trying to start a fight with Noah. His heart just wasn't in it. "How about over there," she relented, pointing to the window.

Noah looked to the place by the living room window and smiled. "I think that'll be just perfect."

A short time later, Noah had gotten the tree into the stand and had placed it in front of the living room window. While the TV dinners heated in the oven, he coaxed Carrie into hanging bulbs on the tree while he hung the lights. She hung a few bulbs and stepped back to look thoughtfully at the tree.

"You know," she began as she gazed into the tree, "Jack had this really screwed-up religion, and he would never let us celebrate

Christmas. He worshipped some Greek god. I don't know what he called it. Daedalus or something?"

Noah shook his head. "Never heard of it." He bent over and plugged in the colored lights. They sparkled off of the window.

Carrie smiled as she looked from the tree to Noah. "It looks nice. Thanks."

"You're welcome," Noah answered, surprised with her change in demeanor. The timer on the oven went off, and Noah hurried to get their dinners.

*****

The following Sunday, Noah talked Carrie into attending church services with him. Joshua was so surprised that he could hardly deliver the sermon. Carrie was the last person he ever thought he'd see sneaking into the back of his church. What surprised him even more was the relaxed expression on Noah's face and the calm resolve in his countenance. Just the year before, Noah was depressed and lonely about losing track of Angel, and now he was fairly happy. The sadness hadn't disappeared completely from his eyes, but it was markedly better, and Joshua was happy about that.

Mona tried to visit with Carrie a little after church, and it was uncomfortable and awkward. Carrie was hostile, especially when Mona offered to take her shopping for some maternity clothes.

"It's not like she's gonna need 'em or anything," Mona complained sarcastically to Joshua as they drove home from church. "I swear, that girl is positively wicked."

Joshua sighed and shook his head. "I can't believe Noah got himself into this."

Mona shook her head. "It's just plain loneliness and a broken heart that drove him to do it, and now he's stuck with the devil herself!"

*****

Marquette was wrapped in his bathrobe, sipping a cup of coffee by his parents' living room window and watching the snow fall. "More snow," he said with a smile. "That will please Angel and Vincenzo's babies."

Petrice laughed from his place in front of the fire, where he was giving Michael a bottle.

Tillie came down the steps, dressed in her favorite jeans and pink sweatshirt. "Merry Christmas, gentlemen," she said. "I hope you saved some coffee for me." She put a kiss first upon Marquette's cheek, leaned over Petrice and kissed his cheek, and then softly kissed Michael. "Hi, baby," she whispered with a smile. Little Michael let loose of the bottle just long enough to smile and send milk drizzling from the corners of his mouth.

"Oh, dear," Tillie laughed as she reached for the cloth that lay next to Petrice's chair.

"And why are you dressed so early on this Christmas Eve day?" Marquette asked with a smile.

"My *betrothed* will be stopping by," Tillie answered. She gave Marquette a mischievous look. "He said he's bringing my Christmas present."

Marquette looked at Petrice, rolled his eyes, and mumbled, "I can hardly wait to see him."

"I heard that Marquette," Tillie quipped with a smile.

Marquette sipped his coffee and snickered, "What? I love him *so much* I can hardly wait to see him. I thought you would be pleased." He laughed again and went back to watching the snow.

"Very funny," Tillie replied, and she looked at Petrice. "Can I hold him for just a minute? I haven't held him hardly at all."

"Of course, Angel." Petrice lifted Michael, along with the bottle, and handed him to Tillie.

"What is this?" Marquette mused from his place at the window. "I do not recognize *this* car."

Petrice had settled Tillie in his chair with Michael and joined his brother at the living room window where a blue 1977 Mustang Cobra II had just pulled in. They saw the red bow on the antenna and watched Alex Martin get out of the car.

"Well, well," Petrice said with a smile. "It seems Alex has purchased himself a new car. I wonder what he did with the Mercedes."

"I much preferred the Mercedes," Marquette commented. "It was far more sinister looking. More *his* type of vehicle."

"Marquette!" Tillie gasped in a whisper.

Petrice chuckled as he went to the door and let Alex step inside. Tillie looked up from her place in the chair and smiled at him. The white snow was sprinkled in his black hair and on the shoulders of his black leather jacket.

"Merry Christmas," she said with a smile.

"Merry Christmas, Tillie." He extended his hand, first to Marquette and then to Petrice. "Merry Christmas, gentlemen."

Guiseppi strode into the foyer and extended his hand to Alex. "Well, Merry Christmas, Alex. I thought I heard someone come in."

"Merry Christmas, Guiseppi," Alex greeted with a smile.

Tillie smiled at her father and then looked at Petrice. "We just have a short date, so if you wouldn't mind…"

"Of course." Petrice hurried to collect his baby. Tillie got out of her chair and went to the window for a look at Alex's new car. "The guys said you got a new car," she commented as she looked out the window. "Pretty nice."

"Well actually," Alex said with a nervous smile, "it's for you."

Tillie looked at him with surprise and back at the car parked in her driveway. "For me?"

Alex nodded his head.

Guiseppi laughed. "Well, Alex, *that* was so nice." He slapped his son-in-law-to-be on the back. "How thoughtful. She has about driven the tires off of that old Bel-Air."

Tillie skipped to Alex, put her arms around his neck, and kissed him. "I can't believe it!"

"Well, you're going to need something to get around in," Alex said as he put his arms around her waist and looked into her eyes.

"Why do you not try it out, Angel?" Petrice suggested.

Alex got her coat and helped her outside into the snowy driveway. He opened the door on the driver's side, and she slid in behind the wheel. Guiseppi and his sons watched from the living room window.

"What does a little babe need with a car so fast?" Marquette grumbled with a frown.

"He spoils her worse than you ever did," Guiseppi teased Petrice with an elbow and a smile.

Petrice caught his breath and faintly smiled…*She is not our little babe anymore*. "Do not be jealous, Marquette. It will make it so hard for the little Angel. She loves him, and we must love him as well."

Chapter 21
May 1977

Right on schedule, at the expiration of Vivian Olson's lease, she tracked down Noah at his office above Roger Frye's Paint & Supply. The bed and breakfast she'd named "Angel's Place" was doing very well, attracting people from as far away as Minnesota and Iowa.

They stood beside Melinda's desk in Noah's outer office area for their impromptu meeting.

"You sure have a nice place now. Business must be good," Vivian complimented, noticing the elegant and professional appearance of his outer office. She raised a black eyebrow as she looked at his dusty jeans and rumpled work shirt. "But you look a little out of place in here."

"Thanks, Viv," Noah replied with a dry expression.

Melinda almost laughed. The outer office had been decorated by Mona. If Vivian could have seen Noah's separate office with the old wooden schoolteacher's desk and a couple of old wooden chairs, she would have been surprised. He'd put a plastic eucalyptus tree in the corner, *for decoration*, and dirty venetian blinds hung askew on the windows.

"So, do you want to buy it?" Noah asked curiously. He hoped she'd at least give him an offer on the place instead of asking for another lease. *That* was the craziest thing he'd ever done, and he wished it would just go away.

Vivian opened her briefcase, pulled out a small file, and handed it to Noah. "I guess I'll take another lease."

"Why?" asked a surprised Noah. "I thought for sure you'd want to buy the place."

"I gotta tell you, Noah," she began. "I've gone over the figures a thousand times with my accountant, and it's a better move for me financially if I continue to lease and let you do the maintenance on the place."

Noah took a breath. "Well how long do you want it to run?"

"Three years," Vivian answered. "Renewable every three years, with plenty of option periods." She looked at Noah and raised one of her penciled black eyebrows. "I suppose that horrible Alex Martin will be calling me."

Noah replied, "I suppose he will."

"Well, whatever," she said as she closed her briefcase. "Thanks, Noah. It's a real pleasure doing business with you," and she extended her hand.

Noah shook her hand and smiled. "You too, Viv. Have a good day."

"Right," she muttered as she left his office.

Melinda handed Noah a small stack of papers. "She's such a *cranky* little thing."

Noah laughed and shook his head. "She really is. What's this?"

"These came from Mr. Martin this morning, and there was a note asking you to give him a call after you've read everything."

Noah rolled his eyes. "He *knows* I don't read that stuff. That's why I've got him."

Melinda shrugged. "You'd better at least take a look at it."

Noah groaned, "I s'pose." He handed Melinda Vivian's file. "Would you put this in the mail for Alex? He needs to take a look at it before I sign it."

"Did you read it?"

"Of course not," Noah answered. Melinda shook her head and laughed.

Noah had to laugh at himself, as well, because the paperwork his office generated had become so considerable that he'd hired two more people just to help Melinda. He didn't want to waste his time reading paperwork and redrafting documents. That's what Alex was for, and Noah sent everything to Sioux Falls for review so he could spend as much time as possible on the job sites.

"Mr. Martin will be in town at the end of the week," Melinda informed, and she searched Noah's expression for the faintest of a recollection.

"Oh, yeah. That's right," Noah remembered. He gave his chin a thoughtful scratch. "The McDarren deal."

"And the Costello deal. Noah, don't forget about Costello," Melinda chirped. "Do you want me to pull the file on that?"

"Please, no," Noah begged as he turned around and headed for his separate, tiny office. "I'm not gonna get outa here the way it is."

He hurried into his little office and closed the door behind him. This paperwork thing had turned into a nightmare, and he had other things planned for the day. It was Carrie's birthday, and Noah had found out almost by accident. She'd mentioned something to Mona about her mother always forgetting about her birthday, and so Mona made it a point to say something to Noah. Noah wasn't going to let Carrie's birthday go by unnoticed, and he, Mona, and Joshua made secret plans for a small celebration.

Carrie had changed gradually, and probably unconsciously, over the past five months—especially since her pregnancy had begun to blossom. Her little tummy was about the size of a balloon that just needed some more air, and she was startled to realize that very soon it would grow even more as the baby prepared for its arrival. The doctor said the baby seemed to be healthy, moved around as it should, and was growing on track with typical measurements.

Carrie's frown had softened, and her eyes began to shine with anticipation—and maybe even a little excitement. She kept her long hair brushed into a soft ponytail, and her cheeks glowed with the faintest of a soft-pink blush.

Other things, besides her appearance, had changed about Carrie as well. Mona brought over her old, portable Kenmore sewing machine and a few swatches of material to introduce Carrie to sewing. She hated it that Carrie sat alone day after day, watching *Star Trek* and sleeping her time away. *That's not healthy for the human mind*, Mona reasoned. *Everyone needs a little hobby of some sort.*

Carrie took to the sewing machine quickly, and Mona was surprised. Carrie was normally standoffish and short with Mona, but when Mona started to show her different patterns of easy sun dresses and pretty t-shirts, Carrie was engrossed.

" 'Cause you'll need somethin' pretty for summer," Mona coaxed sweetly as she patted Carrie's stomach. "Your little bundle will move out of here, and you'll have your body back!"

The most remarkable change in Carrie happened when, every Sunday, she started to attend church services with Noah. She sat beside him, and sometimes she reached for his hand while she listened intently to Joshua's sermon. On rare occasions, as Joshua looked out from behind the pulpit, he would observe Carrie and Noah as they smiled into each other's eyes, if only for the briefest of moments. This surprised Joshua and Mona, as they knew that was never intended to be a part of their "marital agreement." As the winter months faded and spring began to warm the Black Hills, the open hostility between the two dissipated little by little, giving way to the sweetest of friendships. *Something* had started between the two of them, and Joshua and Mona could only wonder what would become of it.

For Carrie's birthday, Mona was preparing a delicious meal of pork roast and baked apples that she and Joshua would bring to Noah and Carrie's house for dinner that evening. Noah ordered a cake from the Safeway bakery and told them to decorate it with white frosting and yellow roses. Yellow seemed springy and cheerful, and Mona prompted Noah to choose that particular color for almost everything they picked out for Carrie's special day. They'd taken an entire day to shop for something particular for Carrie's gift. They finally chose a sewing machine in a lovely oak cabinet and a yellow sewing box, filled with needles, threads, and other equipment. Mona picked out several patterns, a few dresses, and a pair of summer-weight overalls. She wrapped everything in white tissue, tied with yellow ribbons. Noah loaded the sewing machine into the back of Joshua and Mona's car, and they promised to deliver it when they came with the food. Noah was in charge of picking up the cake…*and the flowers*.

Carrie heard Noah's footsteps on the back porch and looked up from her place at the kitchen table. She was just finishing the hem, by hand, on a new dress she and Mona had started only a few days before. Noah came through the back door with the pretty cake and a bunch of yellow daffodils.

Carrie's expression was one of surprise, and she allowed a small smile. "What's goin' on?"

"Happy birthday, Carrie!" He set the cake down on the table in front of her but held onto the flowers. "Can I put these in some water for you?"

Carrie nodded with a surprised expression. She looked from the cake and then into Noah's eyes. "How did you know?"

"Mona told me." He went to the cupboard and located a glass tumbler. He filled it at the sink, put the fresh daffodils in the water, and set them down beside the cake.

Carrie couldn't stop smiling as she looked from Noah to the cake, to the flowers, and then back at Noah. "Thanks, Noah. I don't know what to say."

"Thanks is enough." He took a seat diagonal from her and smiled into her eyes. "You look like you're feeling better these days."

"A little," she answered. Her eyes grew wide with amazement as she felt her baby move. "Do you want to feel him? He's moving right now."

Noah looked a little hesitant. Carrie had never offered to allow him to feel the baby move, and he'd never dared ask.

"Don't be afraid," she said as she reached for his hand. She placed it gently on her warm stomach and smiled. "You'll like it."

Noah felt the tiny life move beneath his hand, and his eyes got big and round. There was a *real* baby in there, and it amazed him. He held his breath and waited for it to move again. Slowly, the little body began to shift inside of Carrie, and he gasped. He looked from his hand into her smiling eyes.

Carrie chuckled. "Isn't he something? Sometimes he gets the hiccups in the middle of the night and wakes me up."

"He gets the hiccups?"

Carrie nodded. "The doctor says he drinks the water he's floating in, and it gives him the hiccups."

"Why do you call it a 'him'? Do you know if it's a boy?"

Carrie shrugged. "I just think it's a boy. Don't you think he *feels* like a boy?"

Noah smiled and shook his head. He looked at his hand as Carrie's baby moved within her. "I don't know. Maybe. Have you thought about any names?"

"Maybe James Tiberius," she snickered. "No...I guess I'm just joking."

Noah caught himself laughing. *Carrie never makes jokes. What's gotten into her? And she's so peaceful lately. She put together a nice baby's room, and she reads books about breast feeding and diaper rash.*

Noah's thoughts were interrupted by footsteps on the back porch and then a knock. Whatever spell had come over them was suddenly broken, and Noah got to his feet to answer the door. Carrie was startled to see Mona walk in with a roaster and several helium balloons. Joshua followed with the sewing machine, wrapped in a bright, yellow ribbon. Carrie was without words as she got to her feet.

"Happy birthday!" Joshua said excitedly as he hauled the big cabinet through the back door.

"Oh, my goodness!" Carrie gasped in a whisper. She put both of her hands on her surprised face as she looked at the sewing machine. "Is that what I think it is?"

Mona laughed. "It is! Now you won't have to use my old clunker anymore."

"Oh, Mona, thank you!" Carrie exclaimed.

Mona laughed again. "Oh, no, Carrie darlin', this is from Noah. We just hid it out for a couple of days so you'd be surprised."

Carrie looked to Noah and felt the strangest sensation. Her eyes wanted to fill with tears, but she wasn't sad. She smiled and reached tenderly for his hand, gave it a gentle squeeze, and looked into his eyes. "Thanks, Noah. That was really nice."

*****

"Noah, are you *listening* to me?" Alex asked impatiently. They'd driven over to the LaCrosse site so Alex could see how close the project was to being finished, but Noah didn't seem like he was paying any attention to Alex. It was as if Noah kept losing focus on the duties at hand, daydreaming and lost in his own thoughts.

"What?" Noah glanced away from the road and looked at Alex.

"Noah," Alex said as he gave his shoulder a pat, "where are you today?"

Noah sighed. "I guess I was just thinking about Carrie." His expression was blissfully thoughtful. "Have you ever felt a baby move inside of someone?" Alex just smiled and shook his head, and Noah continued, "It's amazing, Alex. I could feel his little body when he moved. It was just really something."

Alex smiled as he watched the strange expression in Noah's eyes. "That sounds wonderful, Noah. When will the baby be here?"

"The doc says about the end of June."

"I bet you guys are getting excited."

Noah agreed with a smile, "I can't wait to see him."

"So you think it's a boy?" Alex asked with a curious expression.

"Yep. We think it's a boy." He took a breath. "By the way, we got your invitation for the wedding. Carrie really wants to try and make it."

"Are you sure she'll be up for the traveling?"

Noah replied, "She says she'll be fine."

*****

Tillie Caselli was twenty years old, and she and Alex had planned a small birthday party for her at their "new" home. By now, Tillie had finished the entire first floor. The Martins and the Casellis were stunned when she took them through the old house just a few weeks before the wedding. Meadowgreen Landscaping had cleared the yard and trimmed the bushes. The oak tree in the back was thick with leaves, and everyone was amazed. Tillie had been right about the old, dead-looking thing.

Victorian-style furniture was set perfectly into the formal living room, and cream satin drapes with gold rope tiebacks swooped gracefully over the windows. Matching drapes hung on the French doors in the dining room, and plush rugs covered the hardwood floor beneath the dining room table.

The king-sized, four-poster bed in their master suite was made up with a soft, periwinkle comforter and a white Battenberg lace bed skirt. Matching lace pillows were set perfectly at the head of the bed, and Battenberg lace curtains and white blinds hung from the window. More lace topped the dresser and chest of doors, and crystal lamps lighted the nightstands on either side of the bed. New white tile had been laid in the master bathroom, accompanied by soft rugs and towels. Fragrant soaps and bath beads waited in a basket beside Tillie's claw-foot tub.

The room adjacent to the master suite was set up to be Alex's at-home office, where Tillie had placed an old-fashioned, roll-top desk; a Victorian wing-backed chair; and simple venetian blinds.

Petrice had just called to announce the birth of his new baby girl. They'd named her Gabriella Elaine, and everyone cheered. Two babies for Petrice in less than a year!

Everyone else was at Tillie and Alex's house for the small birthday celebration, and they all marveled at the work she'd done over the winter months.

"This is incredible," James commented as he strode through the house with his young daughter-in-law-to-be. "You've got it about ready to move into."

"Just about," Tillie agreed.

James frowned and raised his eyebrow. "By the way, where's Alex?"

"He's in Rapid with Noah Hansen. Something got fouled up, and he missed his flight. He won't be able to make it back until tomorrow morning."

James nodded, forcing himself to pretend a smile of understanding… *So, it's already begun.*

Marquette scowled and whispered to his father, "I find it incredible he cannot be present for this event!"

"Please, Marquette!" Guiseppi admonished quietly. "This thing is *not* his fault!" He grabbed Marquette's shoulder roughly and shook him as if he were still a little boy. "Stop with this ridiculous jealousy for I have no more patience with you!" He released his grasp and abruptly stomped away.

As Marquette watched his father charge angrily into the backyard and pretend a friendly visit with Frances Martin, his heart sank. He had to swallow to force away the sudden sickness in his stomach... *Papa knows he has made a mistake.*

*****

Alex returned to the hard, wooden chair in front of Noah's desk and picked up the lease he'd been working on.

"So, can you stay long enough to finish up this lease for Viv?" Noah asked curiously.

Alex nodded and answered, "I switched my flight. I don't have to leave until tomorrow morning."

"I thought you had to be back tonight for something."

Alex shook his head as he focused on the lease. "It's just a birthday party. Nobody's going to miss me."

*****

Tillie had settled on a beautiful silk gown from Kopel's. It had a Queen Anne's neckline in lace that swooped from Tillie's nape, under her chin, and gracefully over her bodice. The sleeves were long and made of the same lace, and tiny pearls buttoned them to the elbows. The waist was high, and it was gathered with delicate silk pleats that dropped behind her in a long, elegant train. Her veil matched the lace on the sleeves and bodice, and it, too, had a long, beautiful train that rested on the back of the dress. It was a fantastic creation, and it fit Tillie's petite figure perfectly.

"I just cannot believe it," Rosa said. She began to cry as she watched Tillie with the seamstress during the final fitting. It was only a few days before the wedding.

"Don't cry, Ma'ma," Tillie said as she stood on the stool before the mirror while the seamstress made tiny adjustments to the hem of the dress.

"I cannot help myself." Rosa dabbed her handkerchief gently at the corners of her eyes. "You look so beautiful."

Tillie looked at herself in the mirror and smiled. Tears of joy and excitement began in her eyes.

"Now don't cry on the dress, young lady," the friendly seamstress said with a smile as she handed Tillie a tissue.

Rosa laughed through her tears. "We cannot help ourselves."

"No one can," the seamstress agreed as she stood back from the dress. "There. I'm finished. What do you think?"

"It is wonderful," Rosa whispered as she took Tillie's hand into her own and looked into her eyes. "You are beautiful, my Angel."

"Thank you, Ma`ma," Tillie replied as she dabbed her tears away before they fell on the dress. "Why do we cry when we're happy?"

Rosa smiled as she touched the corners of her eyes again. "My ma`ma used to tell me that it is God's love, and when there is so much of it, it leaks out in the drops of our tears so He may make room for more in our hearts."

*****

It was the Friday before the grand event, and everything was ready. Alex was in his office where he finished up last-minute details with Sam and Shondra concerning his clients and, of course, Hansen Development. He acquainted them with the necessary files and gave specific instructions on how to take care of each individual situation during his lengthy absence. He'd be out of the office for nearly a month, and he wanted to be sure his business was handled properly.

"Your airline tickets were delivered this morning," Shondra said as she handed Alex an envelope from the travel agency. "There's an itinerary inside, and I personally confirmed all of your hotel reservations. You'll have a limo drive you to the Ramada after the reception and then to the airport on Sunday morning." She paused and winked. "And Sam has arranged for a limo to pick you up at the airport in Paris."

Alex felt as if someone had knocked the wind out of him, and he leaned back in his chair with a heavy sigh. "Do you think we've forgotten anything?"

Sam and Shondra looked at each other and laughed.

"We'll be okay," she said as she smiled at Alex.

Sam smiled and put his hand on Shondra's shoulder. "The two of us can handle it. Now why don't you let me talk to my brother for a few minutes."

"Certainly," Shondra said as she rose from her chair. "I'm very happy for you, Alex. She's a wonderful girl."

"Thanks, Shondra."

"I'll see you guys tomorrow," she said as she left the office, closing the door behind her.

Alex sighed heavily and loosened his tie. "I'm incredibly nervous, Sam. I'm twenty-seven years old, and I feel like…I feel…" Alex was stammering, and Sam chuckled.

"What's on your mind, Alex?"

Alex sighed again. "Listen. Are you going to do the best man's toast? Because I don't want you joking around about, you know, personal stuff. You know, the kissing. I don't want the entire town to know you had to coach me on the kissing."

"I didn't coach you on the kissing," Sam said with a smile. "I just told you to let the Lord do the rest." He looked into his younger brother's troubled expression and smiled again. "Don't be afraid, Alex. It's gonna be great."

Alex turned his eyes away from Sam. "I'm so afraid I'll do everything wrong and wreck the entire honeymoon."

Sam nodded. "Just remember, she's going to be even more nervous than you are. *Know what I mean?*" Alex nodded, and Sam continued, "But you guys read those books I bought for ya…right?" Alex looked embarrassed but nodded in affirmation. Sam chuckled and went on, "I think it's God's greatest gift to two people when they choose to obey His Word and wait, like you and Tillie have. You've been praying about this, and He'll take care of things, Alex."

Alex took a breath and whispered, "Did you and Becky-Lynn wait?" Sam smiled and nodded. "Was everything okay?"

Sam smiled and nodded again. "It was wonderful, Alex. I remember waking up the next morning, and she was sleeping in my arms. I can't tell you the contentment and joy that comes from sharing yourself with only one person. It forges a bond between the two of you that nothing can break."

Alex smiled faintly and leaned back in his chair. "In less than twenty-four hours I'll be married to Tillie Caselli. Can you believe it?"

Sam shook his head. "I can't. I still remember the day Rosa and Guiseppi brought her home from the hospital."

"I remember that."

"Remember how Mom used to make us go to all of her little school plays and stuff?"

Alex nodded. "I remember teaching her how to ice skate." He laughed and shook his head. "She was sixteen years old, and I nearly left Harvard that winter. Thought maybe I'd finish up my degree at USD."

"No kiddin'?" Sam frowned.

"No kiddin'. I was completely smitten with her."

"You never told *me* about it."

"I was afraid you'd think I was sick or something. I mean, Sam, there I was, twenty-three years old, experiencing the first real crush of my entire life. She was *only* sixteen. Even *I* thought I was a little sick."

"Gads." Sam laughed and shook his head. "If she would have only known."

"Guiseppi would have had me arrested."

Their conversation was interrupted by the receptionist when she beeped in and said, "Noah Hansen on Line Two. Can you take it?"

Alex frowned and looked at Sam. "He's supposed to be on the road today. Wonder what the deal is." Sam shrugged as Alex picked up the phone. "Hey, Noah, what's up?"

"Well," Noah said with delight in his voice, "me and Carrie won't be making it to your wedding after all. Carrie had the baby this morning."

"Congratulations, Noah," Alex said with a smile. He looked at Sam and whispered, "The baby was born this morning."

"We got a boy," Noah announced, and Alex heard him sigh. "He's a feisty little thing!"

"He's a little early, isn't he?" Alex inquired.

"Just a couple of weeks."

"What did you name him?"

"His name is Tyrell Noah Hansen, but we're gonna call him Ty."

*****

Originally Carrie hadn't wanted Noah to be there, but, as the labor progressed, she sent a nurse to the waiting room to ask if he'd come in. The hospital staff assumed the baby belonged to Noah, and they put him into Noah's arms when it was time to move Carrie out of the delivery room.

Noah followed Carrie and an assortment of nurses down the hall to wherever they were taking her, while the little baby screamed for all he was worth. Noah looked into his red face and was amazed. Just a few weeks before, he'd felt the tiny life moving within Carrie, and now here he was, riding along in Noah's arms and crying like there was no tomorrow.

Joshua and Mona hurried to the hospital and were there when Noah came down the hall behind Carrie and the hospital staff. It was such an unusual sight to see—Noah dressed in surgical scrubs, holding a tiny blue bundle in his arms.

After the nurses had settled Carrie in her room and had taken the baby to the nursery for a newborn check, Noah went to tell her what a great job she'd done and how happy he was for her. She was lying very still in the hospital bed, covered with white blankets up to her chin, but her gray eyes shone with a smile when she saw Noah.

"Hey," he said as he took a very careful seat on the edge of the bed. "You did a really great job today."

Carrie smiled and looked into his handsome blue eyes. Were they dancing? "Thanks, Noah." She reached for his hand. "Thanks for being here for me."

"No problem, Carrie."

"Noah, can I put your name on the birth certificate?"

Noah's eyes opened wide with surprise. "Why?"

"Because I want *you* to be his father."

Noah hesitantly nodded his head. Carrie tried to nod in return, smiled sweetly, and closed her eyes. Noah felt the touch of her hand loosen from his own as she fell into a peaceful sleep.

He sat there in amazed silence as he recalled her request. *Father?* He looked into Carrie's sleeping face and felt the strangest compulsion to kiss her. He closed his hand around hers and placed a soft kiss upon her forehead…

Chapter 22

Ginger was the maid of honor, and Sam was best man. Alex and Tillie's mutual niece and nephew, Alyssa and Angelo, were flower girl and ring bearer, respectively, and there were no other attendants. Between family members and friends, the wedding party would have grown out of control had they done it any differently.

Christ the King was decorated in simple elegance. White roses and green ivy wound around brass candelabras on the alter, and tall candlesticks reaching far above the pews lined the marble aisle. They, too, were graced in the same white roses and ivy.

Ginger and Alyssa wore matching soft-pink formals styled with velvet, halter-style bodices and shiny taffeta ballroom skirts stiffened with full crinolines. Their hair had been done by Rosa. She'd tucked their locks upon their heads in a French twist and nestled sprigs of baby's breath within the tresses. They wore delicate white gloves on their hands. Ginger carried a bouquet of white roses, and Alyssa's basket was filled with rose petals which she was to scatter along the white runner on her way down the aisle.

"But I don't want to throw my petals away," Alyssa whined as they sat together in the dressing room at the church.

Tillie sat very still at the mirror while her mother put up her hair and fit the veil on top of her head. She was in agreement with the little girl. She remembered being the flower girl at Vincenzo and Kate's wedding, and *nothing* had to leave her basket.

"Ginger," Tillie said, trying not to move even in the slightest as she spoke, "is Marquette here yet?"

"He and Tara are lighting the candles," Ginger replied.

"There is a little flower shop just a few blocks from here." Tillie smiled into the mirror and caught Alyssa's eye. "Will you ask him, *for me*, if he will go there quickly and see what they have for a special bouquet for Alyssa?"

Ginger smiled. "I'll be right back," and then she hurried from the room.

Alyssa gave a little squeal and clapped her hands with delight. "Thank you, Auntie."

Rosa chortled, "Pray your brother returns *before* the wedding."

"We've got some time," Tillie replied, smiling at little Alyssa.

A soft knock was heard on the door, and Kate peeked inside. "Where is my little girl?"

"Here, Ma`ma," Alyssa answered.

"Can I take her for just a few minutes?" Kate asked with a smile. "I just want to make sure she gets to go to the bathroom before this whole thing starts."

Rosa agreed. "That is a good idea, Kate."

Kate looked at Tillie. "I'm going to see Alex in a few minutes. Do you have a message for him?"

Tillie sighed as her heart skipped a beat. "Tell him I love him with an everlasting love."

"Jeremiah 31:3. I'll tell him." She collected Alyssa, and they left Rosa and Tillie alone.

"There," Rosa whispered as she gave the top of the veil a tender pat. "I have finished. What do you think?"

Tillie looked at herself in the mirror. Most of her hair was pinned under the veil's cap, but Rosa had left a few, tiny curls along her neckline in the back. "I like it, Ma`ma," and she smiled at her mother in the mirror.

"Thank goodness," Rosa said, and she took a seat across from Tillie and reached for both of her hands. She looked into her daughter's eyes and tried to smile. "This day, you leave my home forever. How will your papa and I ever manage without you?"

"Ma`ma," Tillie whispered as she tried to fight away the tears, "it's not like I'm never going to see you again."

Rosa shrugged and squeezed Tillie's hands. "It is so very hard." Tears began to fall from her black eyes. "We will miss you so much."

"I'll miss you, too, Ma`ma," Tillie said as a tear escaped down her cheek.

Rosa chuckled through her tears, reached quickly to Tillie's face with her handkerchief, and dabbed away the tear. "Now, do not cry on the dress."

Tillie laughed quietly and looked into her mother's eyes. "I'm a little nervous, Ma`ma." She hesitated and rolled her eyes. *"You know..."*

Rosa nodded and smiled. "Of course, my Angel. But when a man loves a woman and is obedient to God, as Alex has been, Angel, there is nothing more wonderful in the world. In his arms you will find pleasure and contentment like you have never known."

Tillie nodded with a shy smile and whispered, "I'm…you know…excited too…" She swallowed hard and rolled her eyes again. "But…I've heard stories here and there. *Awful* stories."

Rosa laughed under her breath and squeezed her daughter's hands. "Those are probably stories you've heard from girls pushed into something by a blackguard who asked them to compromise their honor. Or perhaps you've heard the stories from girls who have married ungodly men." Rosa paused for a moment, and Tillie slowly nodded her head. Rosa continued, "Alex is your knight, my Angel. He is a man of God who cared enough to ask you to read a book on the subject." Rosa tittered and shook her head. "That took strength and character, and if I were a betting woman, I would bet he is in his dressing room at this very moment, praying with his father and his brother." She giggled and whispered, "Do not think for a moment he is at ease with what is to take place this night." Tillie looked into her mother's eyes and smiled so sweetly that it took Rosa's breath away. "Do not fret, my Angel," Rosa whispered with a smile. "Alex will be kind and gentle."

Tillie smiled and let out a soft sigh.

"Now," Rosa continued, "I have something I wish you to carry with your bouquet. Something *old*." She reached into her purse for a black, tattered leather book and put it into Tillie's hands. "Something old, something new, something borrowed, something blue." She chuckled. "We learned that little rhyme when Penny married Angelo. Anyway, my Angel, open the book."

Tillie looked down at the very old leather book and carefully opened it. On the inside cover, written in faded ink, was the name *Matilde Rosa Rochelle*. Tillie looked at her mother with surprise. "Was this your mother's?"

"It was my mother's Bible, and you must return it to me after the wedding. I carried it the day I married Papa." Rosa smiled as more tears shone in her eyes. "When the war came to Chianti all those years ago, we had to hide our Bibles from the Nazis because they would burn them if they found them. Before Ma`ma died, she told me to hide the Bible beneath Petrice's bed, and I did. Now you will carry it with you when you say your vows."

Tillie was without words as she looked at the name of her grandmother, which was the same as her own, and then into the eyes of her mother. "Thank you, Ma`ma."

Rosa dabbed gently at her tears and then at a few of Tillie's. "Your name came from my mother, who was named after her grand-mother, who was named after an Italian noblewoman, *la Gran Contessa, Matilde of Canossa.* She was a military giant for her time."

Tillie smiled. "I didn't know that."

Rosa nodded. "All of our names must have meaning, Angel. Now, what of something new? What will be on you that is new?"

Tillie held up her wrist to show off a delicate golden bracelet. "From Kate and Vincenzo, for my birthday."

"Lovely," Rosa approved. "Something borrowed?"

Tillie touched the diamond earrings dangling from her ears. "From Ellie."

"I wondered where they came from." Rosa smiled and asked, "Something blue?"

Tillie reached for a small box near the mirror and opened it up to reveal a dainty blue handkerchief. It was delicately trimmed in white lace and embroidered with her initials and the wedding date. She removed it and laid it in her lap. "From my brothers. They gave it to me this morning."

Rosa touched the elegant handkerchief. "It is beautiful. Angel, they have always loved you so much."

"I know," Tillie whispered as she smiled down at the handkerchief and then into her mother's eyes. "Nobody has brothers like mine."

Rosa slowly shook her head. There was a soft knock at the door, and Ginger came in. "Marquette is on his way," she said with a smile. "And your veil is perfect."

"Thanks, Ging," Tillie sighed. "How are things looking out there?"

"Pretty good," Ginger reported. She took a seat close to Rosa and Tillie and informed, "Most of the guests must be here by now. The choir was practicing earlier. They sound beautiful."

Another knock was heard on the door, and Tara and Ellie came in with smiles. They gave Tillie soft kisses on her cheek and kissed Rosa as they took hold of her hands.

Rosa smiled at Ellie. "Where are your babies?"

"Sleeping in the nursery," Ellie answered. "We were surprised. We didn't know there'd be nursery service today."

"I'm surprised to see you here," Ginger said to Ellie. "Didn't you just have that baby only a couple of weeks ago?"

Ellie answered, "I feel great. But I will have to stay close to the babe. She likes to nurse about every two hours."

"You look beautiful, Angel," Tara said, touching the soft curls around her veil.

Yet another knock was heard on the door, and Tara whispered with a smile, "Can we fit another person into this dressing room?"

The other ladies laughed, and Kate and Alyssa let themselves into the room. Alyssa swung her little basket into Tillie's lap, and Tillie smiled with surprise. "He's back already?" she asked as she looked at the tiny bouquet inside of Alyssa's basket.

Kate rolled her eyes and shook her head. "Don't even ask." She looked at Tillie and said, "I have a message for you from Alex…He thanks God every time he remembers you."

Tillie nodded with a smile. "Philippians 1:3."

Kate touched the corners of her eyes with a tissue and laughed at herself. "I will be crying all day. There is an usher in the hall waiting for you, Rosa. It's time to seat the mother of the bride."

Rosa gasped softly and reached for Tillie's hands one last time. As she looked into her eyes, she began to cry and whispered, "We love you so very much." Tillie's eyes filled immediately, and Rosa caught the tears with her handkerchief before they could drop onto the dress. "Do not cry on the dress," she said, laughing softly through her tears. Then she got up and looked at her daughter. "He loves you so much, Angel. We are so happy for you."

"Thanks, Ma`ma," Tillie whispered as she tried to control the tears that wanted to spill from her eyes.

"We should be seated as well," Kate said to her sisters-in-law. "At least before the mother of the bride." She looked at her little girl. "Alyssa, do you know what to do?"

Alyssa nodded. "Me and Angelo will go up together, after Uncle Sam and Ginger. I get to keep the flowers, but I have to sprinkle the petals."

"Perfect," Kate acknowledged. "And then come and sit by me and Papa."

Alyssa nodded, and Kate looked at Tillie. "Do you remember when you did this for me?" Tillie smiled and nodded at Kate.

Rosa let go of Tillie's hands reluctantly and backed slowly toward the door, smiling and crying at the same time. "I love you, Angel."

She opened the door, where Tillie's brothers were waiting to collect their wives. The three of them joined their husbands in the hall, but, to their surprise, their husbands dashed into Tillie's dressing room. She stood up to greet them, reaching out for their hands, but they all put their arms around her at once. They were openly weeping, and

Tillie couldn't help but smile as she wondered if they would get any of their tears on her dress.

"Oh, my Angel," Petrice cried, "how quickly you have grown."

"Angel, we love you so much," Vincenzo said as he gave her a soft kiss on her cheek. "I cannot believe this day has come so soon."

"Nor I," Marquette sighed as he forced a smile. His teary eyes suddenly held a mischievous look, and he whispered, "Quick! Let us run for the back door and escape!"

Tillie laughed at his horrible attempt at humor and put a soft kiss upon his cheek. "I love you, Marquette, and I always will."

Marquette kissed her forehead. "I know, my Angel. It is just so difficult."

"Do you have the hanky?" Vincenzo asked. In response, Tillie held up the handkerchief they'd given her that morning.

"Very good," Petrice approved.

"Gentlemen," a male voice from the hall said, and they turned to see the usher waiting patiently with Rosa. "Please be seated so I may seat your mother."

Petrice rolled his eyes and shook his head as he whispered, "Which one of those ladies set the poor boy up to hurry us along this way?"

"Probably Ma`ma," Marquette answered.

Vincenzo whispered, "And I see Papa is waiting now." He glanced into the hallway and saw his tuxedo-clad father standing near Rosa. His head was down, and his hands were folded. Vincenzo felt the strangest thing for his father as he said, "We must give him some time."

They all agreed, kissed her one last time, and left with their wives. The usher and Rosa followed, and Ginger took Alyssa by the hand. She led her into the hallway to wait for Sam and Angelo.

Tillie went to her father, whose head was still bent low and hands still folded. She put her hand softly on his arm, and he lifted his teary old, black eyes to hers, looking somewhat surprised as he reached for her hand.

"Angel, I was just praying for you."

"Thank you, Papa," she said as she reached to his eyes with the new handkerchief.

Guiseppi looked at his beautiful daughter, stepped back, and smiled with satisfaction. "It amazes me still."

"What Papa?"

"The miracle of you. Always only boys were born to the Casellis, and then Ma`ma starts to pray for a girl." Guiseppi chuckled. "And here you stand before me, my most precious gift."

"I love you, Papa."

Guiseppi's eyes filled with fresh tears that spilled onto his dark cheeks. "I hope I have shown you, with my actions and my words, how much I love you back."

Tillie whispered, "You have, Papa. More than you know."

Guiseppi smiled into his daughter's eyes as he reached for her left hand where she wore her engagement ring and her purity ring. He removed them both and placed them on her right hand. "To make room for Alex's ring," he explained as he smiled into her eyes. "God will bless you for your obedience."

Soft piano music was heard, and Sam and Angelo walked into the hall. What a comical duo *they* made. Sam, tall and broad shouldered, dressed in a striking black tuxedo, and little Angelo, who came barely above Sam's knee. He stood obediently next to his uncle in his own matching tuxedo. He held the frilly, white pillow that was supposed to have carried the rings. However, Kate had thought better of it and sewed two plastic gold bands to the pillow instead. Sam and Ginger were given the rings.

"It's time." Sam smiled at Ginger and then he looked down at his niece and nephew and asked, "Is everybody ready?"

Ginger took a soft breath and walked to where Tillie and Guiseppi stood. She placed the bouquet into Tillie's arms and helped her tuck the blue handkerchief and Rosa's old Bible into a safe place in the stems of the roses.

"Can you believe it?" Ginger breathed with a smile. She leaned close and whispered, "All those years we planned this day, and it wound up being Alex Martin after all!"

Tillie laughed and gave Ginger a kiss on her cheek. "Thanks, Ging."

Ginger smiled and returned to her place by Sam, who offered her his arm. They walked just to the entrance of the church and paused, and Sam glanced behind them.

"Okay, guys," he said as he looked down at his niece and nephew, "can you do this?"

Alyssa and Angelo gave polite nods, and Angelo offered his sister his arm. She hooked her arm clumsily into his, and they took their place behind Sam and Ginger.

"Now, you have to wait for Grandpa to tell you when to go," Sam instructed. He looked at Guiseppi and Tillie as they slowly made their way to the position behind Alyssa and Angelo. Guiseppi paused there, smiled into his daughter's eyes one last time, and gave her a soft kiss upon her cheek.

"How beautiful you are," he whispered as he lowered her veil.

Sam felt himself getting unexpectedly emotional when he saw Guiseppi and Tillie together. He swallowed as hard as he could, sternly nodding at Ginger. They walked through the entrance, stepping onto the white pathway in the aisle. They paused for just a moment, and then began a slow gate to the front of the church.

Guiseppi offered Tillie his arm and whispered, "It is almost time, Angel." Tillie nodded and took a deep breath. Her stomach felt like it was going over a hill really fast. "Go now, children," Guiseppi instructed his grandchildren, and they nodded in obedient response. They left the entrance and started down the aisle. Alyssa, thankfully, sprinkled her cherished rose petals along the way. "What a good babe," Guiseppi whispered as he watched her.

For what seemed like hours, they waited in the entrance for their cue to enter, which would be the piano music stopping and a long pause of quiet. Once they heard it, Guiseppi escorted Tillie to the back of the church. The loud organ was heard, the congregation got to their feet, and Tillie and Guiseppi started down the aisle.

Through her veil, Tillie saw Alex and Andy at the front of the church. Sam had taken his place beside Alex, and Ginger waited on the other side. By now, Alyssa and Angelo were with their parents. For a moment, Tillie thought she might faint, but she took a deep breath and continued to walk.

Alex's heart pounded so hard that he was afraid everyone would hear it when the organ stopped. It was finally happening. No more dates. No more dropping her off at her own house. Now she would come home with him.

The organ music suddenly stopped, and Guiseppi paused just shortly before they reached Alex. He lifted Tillie's veil, took her right hand into his own, bowed before her, and kissed it. He stood straight, smiled into her eyes, and placed her hand gently into Alex's. Then he took his place beside Rosa.

Alex and Tillie looked into each other's eyes and smiled. There were so many things they still wanted to say, but neither of them could hardly breathe, let alone speak.

"Who gives this woman to this marriage?" Andy asked with authority.

"We do," Rosa and Guiseppi answered in unison.

Andy nodded at the couple before him and smiled. "Then let us begin."

The wedding party was taken to Angelo's in a limousine. Georgie and old Doria had prepared the wedding feast and had set out the hundreds of traditional cookies Rosa and Kate, along with Barbara (the wife of Reata's foreman), had slaved over for weeks. It was an Italian tradition to serve cookies at the wedding and then give some to each guest as they left. They'd prepared cookies for Angelo and Penny's wedding in 1956, for Vincenzo and Kate in 1962, for Marquette and Tara in 1968, and now for Alex and Tillie in 1977. It was a delicious tradition, and their American friends always looked forward to it.

Two enormous beef roasts with baked vegetables and mashed potatoes had been prepared, along with plates of pastas and salads and loaves of crusty breads. A beautiful, four-layer cake decorated with pink rose buds sat in the center of the buffet table.

Angelo's was closed that day and decorated with the same white roses and ivy as at the church. The old wooden floors had been refinished for just this occasion. The booths and tables were scrubbed and shined, and the windows had been polished to sparkling perfection.

There was no formal seating arrangement, and the bride and groom moved around the room as they held tightly to each other's hands, trying to share conversation with everyone there. Neither of them could remember if they had gotten anything to eat, nor did they care. They laughed and talked as they enjoyed every moment of their time together.

When Guiseppi decided it was time to cut the cake, he hurried Tillie and Alex to the center of the buffet table and loudly clanged two knives together.

"Quiet, please!" he yelled in a happy voice, "for it is time to cut the cake!"

Silence fell over the guests as they positioned themselves where they could see. Guiseppi carefully placed the knife first in Tillie's hand, and then he covered her hand with Alex's.

"Okay, now," he instructed, and Tillie and Alex pressed the knife into the cake as the crowd applauded and cheered.

"And the best man shall make his toast now," Guiseppi said. He pointed his index finger toward Sam and picked up the special bottle of champagne near the cake.

Sam came to the table and took the open bottle from Guiseppi. He filled a glass for Tillie, Alex, and Ginger, who stood near the front of the crowd.

"Can't leave out the maid of honor," he said as he smiled at Ginger, and she giggled. He filled a glass for Guiseppi and finally one for himself.

Sam cleared his throat and smiled mischievously at Alex, who only frowned in return.

Sam laughed and lifted his glass as he spoke to the crowd. "Mere words can never express what I have watched happen between these two people over the last twenty years." He looked at Tillie and Alex. "I think we were all fairly amazed as we watched this tender courtship between my brother and this wonderful, lovely lady he is so obviously taken with. Things moved along a little more slowly than Alex would have liked. I think he would have preferred to marry Tillie about a year ago.

"Tillie, when he talks about you, his countenance absolutely glows. He talks about your pretty hands working on those old chairs you refinished, and he calls you his *dearest friend.*" Sam sighed. "Tillie, when you look at my brother, your radiance gives away the love you must feel for him, and my heart sings with delight. You are his perfect match, and may God always bless your marriage."

Sam gently clanged his glass first against Tillie's and then against Alex's, and the crowd applauded politely. Sam turned and politely clanged Guiseppi's glass and then stepped to Ginger.

"This is the shyest bridesmaid I've ever met," he said as he clanged his glass into hers, and the crowd laughed.

"And now we will dance!" Guiseppi announced with a smile, and the crowd applauded again.

While Tillie's brothers and the waiters moved the tables and chairs from the inside of the room, Guiseppi rushed off to the back room, where he stored his old Dean Martin records.

Petrice approached Tillie and Alex to give Alex's hand a hearty shake.

"Senator Caselli," Alex greeted. "Thank you for coming. We know how busy you've been this year."

"Congratulations, Alex." Petrice's black eyes sparkled. "You are my brother now." He turned to his sister and gave her a tender kiss. "Angel, I must go. My Ellie is very tired, and she needs to rest."

Tillie nodded. "I understand, but we'll see you and the babies when we stop in New York on our way back."

"Yes," Petrice remembered. "I will pray for your safe travels."

"Thanks, Patty," Tillie said with a smile. "And thanks for coming. I know how busy you've been."

Alex and Tillie watched him collect his family and, with the help of Marquette and Vincenzo, put them into the limousine waiting in front of the restaurant. Marquette smilingly waved away the few reporters, while Vincenzo held little Michael until his father was seated in the back of the car. He set the baby into Petrice's arms and closed the door.

"That'll make a great front page," Alex whispered into Tillie's ear as they watched the reporters snap photos of Petrice and his brothers.

"Did he even answer any questions?" Tillie asked with a curious smile. Alex shook his head. Petrice was already famous for avoiding questions when he was with his family, and it drove the press crazy.

Guiseppi had retrieved the old records, and the music began. Forgetting all protocol, Guiseppi led Rosa onto the floor and began to turn her about.

Alex smiled and bowed politely before Tillie as he took her hand into his own. "I don't believe we've danced since last summer."

Tillie smiled as he led her onto the floor, where other guests had begun to dance as well.

Marquette had taken a seat in a booth by himself. Tara was off visiting friends and relatives, and he decided he'd brood over a delicious bottle of champagne while he watched his baby sister dance across the floor with her new husband.

"You're not usually given to much drink, are you?"

Marquette looked up to see Sam Martin standing at his table.

"Can I join you?" Sam inquired politely.

Marquette shrugged and took a sip from his glass. Sam sat down across from him and helped himself to Marquette's bottle.

"That was a nice little speech you gave," Marquette grumbled.

Sam smiled into Marquette's sad eyes. "What can I say to help you Marquette. I know…We *all* know how you feel about Alex, but he's not the blackguard you assume him to be."

Marquette sipped a little more champagne and looked back at Sam. "I do not *assume* him to be a blackguard."

Sam smiled. "If you could only hear him talk about your sister." He looked at the newly married couple as they laughed and danced around the floor. "He has a profound respect for her. Did you know that he almost left Harvard for her?" Marquette's eyes were confused, and he slowly shook his head. Sam nodded with a smile. "He was afraid he was too old for her, and so he just fought the feelings for a long time. Marquette, my brother loves your sister with a depth and passion I've only seen between your own parents."

Marquette smiled curiously at Sam…*Then why could he not leave Harvard? Because, as always, he is more dedicated to himself than even the love of his life.*

Marquette raised his glass in a gesture of toast. "Well then, we must celebrate."

Sam clanged his glass against Marquette's, and it was then Vincenzo appeared with a pot of coffee and a cup. He set them down on the table and picked up the champagne bottle. He laughed and slapped his brother on the back. "Do not make this mistake. Believe me, I *know* of the pain that follows."

Sam laughed, and Marquette rolled his eyes.

As it became late in the afternoon, Georgie and Doria brought out trays of sandwiches made from the leftover roasted beef. The waiters made fresh coffee and set pots of it on the table beside what was left of the cake.

Tillie managed to break free from her latest dance partner and sneak into the kitchen for a drink of water. Shondra saw Tillie make her quick break and smiled. She couldn't have planned it better. She made a stealthy sideling approach toward Alex, who was saying good-bye to an old classmate, and touched his sleeve. Alex looked down at her and saw the mischief in her eyes.

"What are you up to, Shondra?"

Shondra crooked her index finger, indicating he should bend close enough to hear her whisper, and she said into his ear, "Tillie's in the kitchen, and there's a limo waiting in the alley. You can sneak out if you move quickly."

"Can we do that?" Alex whispered with a smile. "I mean sneak out? Don't we have to say good-bye to these people?"

Shondra rolled her eyes and shook her head. "How long do you want to be here? All night?" Alex laughed nervously and shook his head. "Then get outa here," she whispered with a smile. "Your luggage has already been delivered to the hotel, so don't wait around for anything. I'll cover for you."

Alex nodded his head and laughed. He gave Shondra a kiss on the cheek and patted her shoulder. "Thanks, Shondra. You're great."

"I know," she agreed with a smile. "Now get going."

Alex hurried into the kitchen and found his bride gulping down a glass of water. She saw him and smiled with surprise. "Do you want one? I was parched."

Alex shook his head and took her by the hand. "Do you want to sneak out of here?"

Tillie smiled and her stomach filled with butterflies. "Can we *do* that?"

Alex shrugged. "Shondra says she'll cover for us. She's got a limo waiting in the alley."

Tillie laughed out loud. A great escape! Just like in the movies!

"Come on," Alex whispered. He led her toward the back door where he paused, cracked open the old screen door, and stuck his head into the alley. He looked from side to side and saw only the driver of the limo leaning tiredly against the car. He drew his head back inside and smiled into his new bride's eyes.

"There's nobody out there except for the driver," he whispered. He couldn't help himself then. She had looked so lovely that day. He slowly lowered his lips to hers and gave her a tender kiss. "Did I even mention how beautiful you were today?" Tillie smiled and shook her head. "I'm sorry," he replied and gave her another gentle kiss. "I should have told you…When you came down that aisle this morning, it took my breath away."

Tillie smiled into his eyes and put a tender hand upon his cheek. "I love you, Alex."

Alex sighed with contentment. He opened the door, helped her gather her dress safely above the ground, and led her to the limousine. The driver opened the door and waited patiently. They all laughed as Alex helped her tuck the trailing gown into the car, and then he slid in beside her. The driver closed the door and hurried to the front of the car to make the planned escape.

Alex put his arm around her and pulled her close as they felt the limousine drive out of the alley and turn onto the road past the restaurant. From the light behind the windows, they saw people still dancing, and they laughed.

"They don't even know we're gone," Alex whispered, and Tillie sighed as she snuggled against him.

*****

Alex paced nervously around the bridal suite at the Ramada. Tillie had been in that bathroom forever. What was taking her so long? She said she was going to change into something else and be right back. Alex was still wearing the slacks from his tuxedo, but he'd removed his cummerbund, tie, and jacket and was in his stocking feet. He didn't have anything to "*change into*." Sam didn't say anything about *that*, nor had his books.

The bathroom door finally opened, and Tillie appeared. She wore a pale-pink satin gown with a scoop neck. Her veil was gone, and her soft curls rested upon her bare shoulders. The mellow light in the room glimmered on the pretty material of the gown and on her dark skin. She smiled shyly at Alex.

Alex could only stare at the lovely vision before him. He'd never expected her to look like *this*. "Wow," he whispered, embarrassing himself. "You look wonderful."

"Thanks, Alex."

He slowly walked to where she stood, put his arms around her, and looked into her eyes. He lowered his lips to hers and kissed her passionately. As he gathered her into his arms, he felt her soft, warm body through her gown. He carried her to the bed, laid her down, and looked into her eyes. He touched the soft curls framing her face and whispered with a smile, "I'm terribly nervous."

Tillie giggled. "Don't worry. It's gonna be great."

He softly kissed her lips, and she eased into his arms…

Chapter 23

The same limousine driver who helped them escape the wedding reception reloaded their luggage and took Tillie and Alex to the airport the next day, where they caught the early flight to Minneapolis. From there, they flew to Paris without stopping. It was a seven-hour flight across the ocean, and Tillie snuggled close to her new husband in the first class seat beside her. Alex put his arm around her, and she laid her head against him.

"Finally, a little vacation," he whispered and softly kissed the top of her head.

Tillie nodded. Between repairs on the old house, her second year of college, and a wedding, she'd been extremely busy. She was more than ready to slow down for a time. She sighed and closed her eyes as she felt the warm comfort of Alex's arm and heard the soft beating of his heart.

"You'll love Paris," Alex said. "I was there with my family years ago."

No response came from Tillie, and he looked down to see that she had fallen asleep! He smiled, tipped his head back, and closed his eyes as he remembered the wedding of the day before.

"Thank you, God," he whispered with a smile, and, somewhere over the Atlantic, Alex fell asleep and dreamed of nothing else but his beautiful new bride.

*****

The limousine Sam had arranged met them at the Charles de Gaulle Airport when they landed in Paris early Monday morning.

"So it's already Monday here?" Tillie asked as she watched the lights of the city go by.

"Let me think…If it's already six a.m. here, then it's still midnight on Sunday back in Sioux Falls," Alex answered.

The limousine came to a stop beneath the iron canopy of the Royal Monceau at 37, Avenue Hoche. Several young men rushed to open the door of the car for Tillie and Alex, while others collected the luggage from the trunk. Alex stepped from the back of the car and offered his hand to Tillie, helping her from the seat. Tillie stared in awe at the awesome white block building rising up in lights above them. Carved stone outlined the many windows graced in arched canopies. The French flag billowed from a mast just above the door.

"Wow," Tillie whispered as her eyes were riveted on the wonderful building.

Alex tugged her hand gently, and she went with him through the glass doors and into the marble lobby where a crystal chandelier sparkled in the high golden ceiling. A group of people had surrounded a certain man, and Alex paused and squeezed Tillie's hand.

"Do you know who that is?" he whispered in her ear.

Tillie followed Alex's curious gaze across the big room and shook her head.

"That's Jacques Chirac," Alex informed. "He's their former premier and was just elected mayor of Paris. Wonder what he's doing here."

Tillie giggled and whispered, "Maybe he's on his honeymoon."

Alex smiled at her, and they continued to the registration desk…or at least Tillie *thought* it was the registration desk. Everything was in French, and she didn't speak a single syllable of the foreign language.

The desk clerk greeted them with a friendly smile and spoke in her native tongue. Tillie's eyes opened wide with confusion. This would be difficult. She hadn't even *considered* the language barrier when Alex asked if she wanted to go to Paris for their honeymoon.

"*Bon jour,*" Alex responded in perfect French. "*Reservations pour Alex Martin.*"

Tillie's head snapped up, and she stared at her new husband in amazement. Had he just spoken French? Apparently the clerk had understood him, because she responded, *in French*, and opened a large, black book that lay upon the counter.

"*You speak French?*" Tillie whispered in an astonished tone.

Alex smiled curiously at her. He'd assumed she knew. "Did you come all the way to France with me, not knowing who would be communicating?"

Tillie almost laughed out loud. *Yes…That's what I did.* She began to nod and smiled into his dark eyes. "I didn't even think about it. I guess I forgot about…you know…"

Alex's eyes held the most curious expression. "Forgot about what?"

Tillie rolled her eyes and smiled. "You know, that they speak a different language here."

Alex laughed and put his arm around Tillie's waist as he whispered into her ear, "I speak Spanish too," and Tillie laughed out loud.

*****

Paris was bright and beautiful, and Alex took them everywhere. He began with the Champs-Elysees, which was two steps away from their hotel. They spent their first entire day there, shopped the fashion district, and checked out the stock market.

Other days were spent walking along the streets of the right bank of the Seine to visit the fashionable shops and enjoy the many artists scattered about. There were long, romantic walks in the French countryside where they visited wineries in Champagne and Burgundy. They held hands and looked into each other's eyes, not even paying attention to the information their tour guide gave them.

On the left bank of the Seine, they visited the Sorbonne, the Pantheon, Luxembourge Palace and Gardens, and a part of the Old Latin Quarter. They saw the Eiffel Tower on the Champ-de-Mars, and the small boat-shaped island of Ile de la Cite, where they toured the Cathedral of Notre Dame de Paris.

On their last night in the wonderful old hotel, Alex held Tillie in his arms and sighed with contentment.

"I can't believe we have to go back tomorrow," he moaned. He'd never taken a vacation in his adult life but was thoroughly enjoying it.

Tillie snuggled close to her new husband. "It feels like we just got here, but it's already been two weeks."

"Well, we get a couple of days in New York," Alex said.

"And we'll get to see the babies. I haven't even held Gabriella yet because they didn't get to town until after the prenuptial dinner, and we were so busy."

"I'm glad you're taking this year off from school," he said.

Tillie agreed, "Me too. I have so many things I want to get done at our house."

Alex propped himself up on his elbow so he could look into her eyes. "You've really done a great job on the house."

"Thanks."

He raised one eyebrow and admitted, "I was really terrified when you said you wanted to buy that thing."

Tillie giggled. "I know, but it's turning out so nice. I really love working on it."

"I can tell. You're very creative. Maybe you should think about changing your major back to art. I know you'd originally planned for that."

"I don't think so. I'm already halfway through, and besides, I've gotta finish my Russian." She looked into his handsome eyes. "You can't be the only one with a foreign language under your belt."

Alex nodded, looked into her sparkling black eyes, and sighed with contentment. "Tillie, I have loved you for such a long time. I'm so happy you're my wife."

She smiled into his eyes. "Me too." And then he gently kissed her lips, and she nestled into his arms...

*****

A few days later, Alex and Tillie Martin were back in Sioux Falls. They moved the last of their personal belongings into their house, along with a considerable number of wedding gifts. Rosa and Guiseppi had carefully packed each painting and sketch Tillie had ever made, separating out the ones of Noah. Tillie asked them to please "get rid of" those particular pieces, but the others were brought over to Tillie's house.

As they unpacked and organized, Alex came across Tillie's blue ribbon paintings, *Obedience* and *Refugees*, and was impressed with her work. He even went so far as to ask her if he could hang one in his office downtown.

"*No way!*" Tillie laughed. "I don't paint any more, and I don't want anybody looking at that old stuff."

"But it's really *good*," Alex tried to coax. "Maybe you should think about starting back up again. You could still switch your major."

Tillie just rolled her eyes and laughed. Her painting days were over. Besides, she wouldn't be going back to school until September of 1978, and her class schedule was the furthest thing from her mind.

"How about my office here at home?" Alex suggested as he held *Obedience* into the light. "I think it would look really nice in there."

Tillie relented. If he wanted the old thing, what could it hurt?

******

Carrie Hansen came through the back door of their Chapel Valley home. She carried a bag of groceries and the six-pack of root beer Noah had asked for. She set everything on the kitchen table and listened. Where were they? She'd left the baby home with Noah to run a few errands but returned as quickly as possible.

She crept down the hall and peeked into the baby's room. Nobody was in there. She listened again and thought she heard the television going in the family room downstairs. With a curious expression, she went down the steps. She heard the television as she got closer, but still no sound from either Noah or Ty.

As she came into the family room, she saw them and had to smile. There was Noah, lying on his back on the couch, sleeping, while the little baby slept on his chest. An empty baby bottle lay on the floor beside them, and Carrie almost laughed. What a precious sight.

By now, Ty was six weeks old. Noah had nicknamed him "Tiger," because of the insistence the baby had when it was time to eat in the middle of the night. Noah could hear him wailing all the way from his room in the downstairs. He'd come running up the steps, at all hours of the night, and offer to give him a bottle so Carrie could get some sleep.

Carrie looked into Noah's handsome sleeping face and smiled. He'd been so kind to her. He'd stayed with her through the whole birth, when not even her own family had been by to visit. Not only that, but he'd taken a real interest in helping her care for the child. Never once had he complained about the fussy baby or the lack of sleep he suffered on the nights he was awakened. Nor did he complain when the bills from the hospital and the doctor arrived. He simply paid them, without comment.

It was these kind actions of Noah that had completed the softening of her heart to the Lord. And, known only to Noah, Joshua, and Mona, was the precious fact that Carrie had accepted Jesus as her Savior. In a few months, the whole congregation would find out when Carrie was baptized.

She crept closer to the sleeping duo and knelt down beside them. Noah must have heard her, because he opened his eyes and smiled.

"Hey," he whispered, "you're back already?" Carrie nodded in answer. "Did you remember the root beer?"

She nodded again and whispered with a smile, "Can I put Tiger into his crib? I think he sleeps longer there."

"Sure. We were just so beat we fell asleep in front of the game."

Carrie tried not to laugh as she picked up the sleeping baby and snuggled his warm little body close to her own. She smiled at Noah and asked, "Is this what you call 'training him up in the way he should go'?"

Noah nodded with a smile, and Carrie got to her feet. She took Ty to his bed upstairs, tucked him into his covers, and closed his door. She headed for the kitchen to put her groceries away. To her surprise, Noah had already opened a bottle of the root beer and was searching through the sack for some kind of a snack.

"I'm starved," he said. "What did you get?"

"There's some chips and a couple more bags in the car," she answered. "But I really want one of your famous hamburgers. Would you mind?"

"Sure," Noah answered with a smile. "I'll start the grill." He smiled into Carrie's eyes and said, "By the way…" He hesitated, and Carrie thought maybe he'd blushed. "…Is that one of those dresses you and Mona made?" Carrie nodded, and Noah continued, "Well, you look really nice. You're totally back to normal."

Carrie smiled and looked down at the pretty yellow sun dress she was wearing, and then back at Noah. She raised one eyebrow, "*Normal?*"

Noah replied, "Yeah, you know. The baby, chubby part is gone."

Carrie gave him a curious smile. "Thanks, Noah. I think."

Noah sighed with frustration. He had wanted to compliment her, but it came out awkward. He reached for her hand and looked into her eyes. "What I meant to say is that you look really pretty."

Carrie felt that strange flutter in her heart she'd started to feel every time Noah looked at her. She wanted to fight the unfamiliar feelings, but lately it was easier to let them be. "Thanks."

Noah smiled, and then he did something so unexpected. He lowered his lips to hers and gave her a tender kiss.

Carrie nearly fainted. This had never been part of their agreement. They were just going to live together and take care of the baby. What was happening?

"Noah," she whispered as she put her hand on his chest and looked up into his eyes, "what are you doing?"

"I'm kissing my wife," he answered with a smile, and then he did it again. This time he took her into his arms and held her close. "Carrie, I love you."

*****

Maggie May was cleaning behind some old jars beneath the counter when she felt her hand brush against something. Curious, she bent over and took a peek under the counter for a better look. *An old envelope? What's that doing under there?* She pulled it out and began to open it up when she suddenly remembered. The snapshots Noah had given her when he was building Angel's Place. First the undeveloped land, then the hole, the foundation, frame, walls…Angel's Place.

Maggie spread the photos out on the counter before her and shook her head. *How was I duped into such idiocy?* She sighed. *At least no one else knew what I was thinking.*

Maggie May looked at the photos and swallowed as hard as she could. The *second* dream she'd ever allowed of herself...*Why didn't it come true? Why couldn't they get it together? How did it get so out of hand? I gotta be tough! Don't think about nonsense like that. This is the real world. Not some happily-ever-after garbage.*

She glanced at the haunting painting that still hung by the bar and shook her head...*I wanted him to bring you back where you belong...You belonged with us.*

She looked back to the photos on her counter and noticed that a tear had dropped onto one of them.

"Old fool!" she admonished herself out loud. After hastily wiping her eyes on her apron, she stuffed the photographs back into their envelope and under the counter they went.

*****

In Tillie's old developing lab in the basement, Guiseppi's shaky hands tenderly went through the stack of photographs he'd been instructed to "get rid of." Beside him were the two paintings he couldn't bring himself to part with. Instead, he'd lovingly wrapped them in paper and stowed them away in a place he knew his daughter would never find them.

Tears fell from his black eyes as he looked at the photographs of a man he had assumed to be a blackguard. He paused when he came to the photo of Angel in Noah's arms as they sat upon a rock at Roubaix Lake...She looked lovingly up into his eyes, and Noah's gaze upon her was one of absolute endearment...*Alex has never looked upon you in such a way.*

Guiseppi was suddenly shaken by the sobs in his heart, and he bowed his head in shame as he whispered, "Oh, Father, what have I done?"

To be continued...

A Special Message for the Reader

Carrie Hansen was the proverbial "wanton woman." She'd been with many men, drank excessively, and wasn't sorry for a thing she'd done—until she became pregnant.

Carrie had lived a hard life; and, in that hardness of life, she hadn't been shown the grace of Jesus. She did what she wanted, when she wanted, and how she wanted! She didn't know about God's love and acceptance and the special rules He'd written to govern her life.

Through the honesty of Mona Hansen came the message: "Carrie, darlin', you gotta pray. You're in some sin here…"

Carrie had done horrific things, but she'd never had a label for it until then. She was in sin, and it was separating her from the love and forgiveness of a Savior.

Mona was honest with Carrie when she explained, "Jesus is God's Son, and He knows what it's like to be human, what it's like to suffer, what it's like to cry. He died for us, Carrie. He put His own life aside so we could have salvation."

Carrie asked, "What's salvation?"

Mona answered, "It's when you believe your sins are completely forgiven because you asked the Lord Jesus for forgiveness…"

Beloved, if you are reading this and don't know Jesus Christ as your Savior and Lord, don't be afraid to ask Him for forgiveness of your sin. We ALL sin, and we must all turn from it. "If we say we have no sin, we deceive ourselves, and the truth is not in us. If we confess our sins, He is faithful and just to forgive us our sins, and to cleanse us from all unrighteousness." I John 1:8-9

Like Carrie Hansen, we have all sinned. Whether we have mistreated someone in the slightest of ways, drank to excess, or even broken a commandment, we have all sinned. Carrie turned from her sin and confessed that Jesus Christ was her Savior. She didn't ask for special favor or fanfare, and she didn't make excuses for what she'd done. She took responsibility for her sins and began to set them aright through the grace of her new Lord, Jesus Christ. Through Jesus, Carrie's sins were forgiven and she was cleansed from all unrighteousness.

Just as Noah took Carrie for his bride and made her an "honest woman," cleansing her from the unrighteous choice of abortion or being stigmatized as a single mother, so Jesus desires to take you for His bride, make you His own, and cleanse you from all unrighteousness!

He stands at the door of your heart and knocks. He's waiting out there, beloved. Won't you let Him come in?

For future release date information, check out
www.TaMaraHanscom.com

Book II
Pit of Ambition

Tara raised one brow. "What are you up to, Angel?"

Tillie rose from her place on the couch. "Wait here a second. I wanna show you something." She hurried off to her bedroom, and Tara heard the closet door open and then the soft rustle of a box. Soon Tillie appeared again, holding a small, red book with tattered corners, and she took her seat on the couch.

"This is from my first semester at Augie," she said with a smile. She shook her head as she nervously continued. "I found this at the college bookstore. It has an old poem in it…*Annie Laurie*." She opened the worn pages to reveal a photograph tucked into the text of that particular poem. She took the photograph of her and Noah at Roubaix Lake and handed it to Tara. "I found this at Ma`ma's the day the babies came."

As Tara took the photograph, she felt the tremendous weight of her secret press upon her heart and briefly considered telling Tillie all she knew about Noah.

"Alex's friend, Noah," Tillie whispered, for she could barely say the name without a soft smile.

Tara nearly fell from her place on the couch. *Does she know? Has she known all along?* She struggled to control every expression and reaction as Tillie continued.

"I've never met the man or spoken with him, but..." Tillie hesitated and sighed, "...and I don't know how it could be..." She looked into Tara's eyes as she bit her lip. Of everyone in her family, Tillie trusted Tara the most. She was solid and secure and would never betray a confidence. "Everyone saw him at the hospital that night, including you."

Tara dropped her focus away from Tillie and pretended to study the photo in her hands. She floundered with what was the truth and what had actually come to be. She wanted Tillie to know, and wanted it desperately.

Tara slowly began to shake her head as she decided to lie. "He is not the same man, Angel."